Colorado
Dawn

Colorado
Dawn

Love Lights the Way for Three Historical Brides

ERICA VETSCH

BARBOUR BOOKS
An Imprint of Barbour Publishing, Inc.

Before the Dawn © 2011 by Erica Vetsch
Light to My Path © 2011 by Erica Vetsch
Stars in Her Eyes © 2012 by Erica Vetsch

Print ISBN 978-1-63058-452-8

eBook Editions:
Adobe Digital Edition (.epub) 978-1-63058-979-0
Kindle and MobiPocket Edition (.prc) 978-1-63058-980-6

All scripture quotations are taken from the King James Version of the Bible.

This book is a work of fiction. Names, characters, places, and incidents are either products of the author's imagination or used fictitiously. Any similarity to actual people, organizations, and/or events is purely coincidental.

Published by Barbour Books, an imprint of Barbour Publishing, Inc., P.O. Box 719, Uhrichsville, Ohio 44683, www.barbourbooks.com

Our mission is to publish and distribute inspirational products offering exceptional value and biblical encouragement to the masses.

 Member of the
Evangelical Christian
Publishers Association

Printed in the United States of America.

Dear Readers,

As a born and raised Kansan now living in Minnesota, every time I visit the Rocky Mountains, I am awed by their sheer size and ruggedness. My eyes are drawn to the summits with their up-thrusting peaks and sharp tree lines. How big must our God be to create something so immense and imposing? And how small our problems become when we realize how capable God is.

The characters in these three stories—*Before the Dawn*, *Light to My Path*, and *Stars in Her Eyes*—all face what seem to be insurmountable, impassable mountain ranges between themselves and their goals. But though their problems seem impossible, they learn that when they are obedient to God, when they place their trust in Him, He lights their way, making the path before them clear, no matter how steep the trail.

Thank you for choosing *Colorado Dawn*, and I hope you will enjoy the stories of David and Karen, Sam and Ellie, and Silas and Willow as they journey from darkness to light, from despair to joy.

I love to hear from readers, and you can reach me on Facebook at www.facebook.com/ericavetsch or via e-mail at ericavetsch@gmail.com

Erica Vetsch
Psalm 119:105

BEFORE THE DAWN

Dedication

For my parents, Jim and Esther Bonam.

Chapter 1

Karen Worth's mild impatience gave way to moderate annoyance and finally to outright anxiety as she paced the depot. David Mackenzie was never late.

She checked the timepiece hanging on her lapel, comparing it to the solemn face of the Seth Thomas clock on the depot wall beside the ticket window. Her handbag toppled off the valise beside her, and she bent to pick it up. For three quarters of an hour she'd waited here like unclaimed baggage.

Behind his barred cage, the clerk shuffled papers and flicked inquiring glances from under his visor. His pinched mouth twitched, making his mustache stick out like a fussy mouse sniffing a trap.

Where could David be? Karen's visions of a tender, warm reunion with her fiancé evaporated. She crossed her arms and stilled her tapping foot for the tenth time. The unease she'd been trying to ignore over his lack of communication during her absence renewed its assault. The two notes he'd sent the first week of her trip were everything a girl could desire in the way of love letters. Then nothing from him for three weeks.

She'd told herself no end of stories to explain things, but with each passing day, the doubts had grown.

Flap, slap, flap, slap. The clerk worked a rubber stamp as if the papers might somehow escape his inky wrath.

Karen gathered her gloves, her bag, and her courage. She'd simply have to ask him to find her some conveyance after all.

The door crashed open. Whirling, she pressed her hand to her chest then let it drop to her side as she relaxed her tense muscles. Jesse Mackenzie filled the doorway, blocking out the weak sunlight. She offered her hands in greeting, though a tickle of unease scampered through her chest.

The large, gray-haired man strode across the station. "Karen, sorry I'm late." He kissed her offered cheek, brushing her skin with his bushy whiskers.

"Mr. Mackenzie, what a surprise. I expected David."

The older man rubbed his beard and didn't meet her eyes. "Lots going on at the mine and at the house."

The tickle of unease became a tremor. "Where *is* David?"

The clerk cleared his throat, and Jesse glared at him. "We'll sort it out at the house." He whisked up her bags as if they weighed nothing and headed toward the door. She followed in his wake, stopping to tug on her gloves and anchor her hat against the fitful, wind-tossed snowflakes gusting about.

The Mackenzie buggy stood at the hitching rail. Jesse stowed the luggage. Then he helped Karen aboard and let her get settled before spreading the lap robe over her skirts. Cold dampness flowed over Karen when he urged the horses into a brisk trot, and she pulled her cloak tighter. He lifted the reins. "Be time for the bobsled if this snow keeps up."

The horses' hooves made splashing plops in the muddy road of the main thoroughfare. Buggies, wagons, and saddle horses lined the streets. This late in the fall, the trees lifted bare limbs to the sky and the clouds bespoke more snow. Jesse's coat collar stood up around his cheeks, meeting his hat brim at the nape. His gloves creaked on the reins as he slapped them against the horses' rumps.

Karen wrinkled her nose at the familiar tang in the air. Black clouds billowed from the smelter smokestacks night and day. The streets teemed with men of varied nationalities, all drawn to this cleft in the high Rockies by the lure of silver.

When the buggy passed the county registrar's, her heart squeezed a little. She missed the bustle of the office, the desk she had called her own, the neat columns and ledgers. Her boss had relied on her to know where every piece of paper in the office could be located. She had enjoyed the work, but she'd given it up for a very good reason.

Though that reason had failed to meet her train.

Her companion's unusual silence forced the questions out of her. "What's wrong, Jesse? Why didn't David come? Is it something at the mine? Have you found a new ore deposit?" If another rich stope had been located, David, as the mine engineer, would have to be on hand.

Jesse shifted on the seat and urged the horses on, though they were already trotting briskly. Bits of slush and dirt flipped backward, spattering the lap robe. "Sure is getting cold out."

Fingers of dread formed a fist in her middle. She clasped her hand over one of his. "Please, just tell me what you're trying so hard not to say."

"I knew I should have sent someone else to pick you up." He scowled as he muttered. "Or brought Matilda along."

Karen gripped his hand tighter. "Please."

"There was an accident—" His shoulders hunched, and he shook the lines again. "Get up there." His words came out in a frosty plume. "At the mine."

Her chest turned frosty, too. An accident. She tried to swallow, but her mouth was slag-heap dry. "Was anyone hurt? Is that where David is? Helping with the rescue and clearing up?"

"The rescuing's been done, and the clearing up, too, mostly."

"Then, what? Jesse, you're scaring me."

He hesitated, dropping his gaze to his hands. "Karen, I hate to be the one to tell you. . . . David was hurt. He's—"

"Is he alive?" Air crowded into the tops of her lungs, and she couldn't draw a deep breath.

"He's alive." Jesse cleared his throat. "But he's blind."

Icy shock gripped the back of her neck. She shook her head, and blackness crept in around the edges of her vision. Gradually the mists in her head cleared. "What happened?"

"There was a cave-in the week after you left for your aunt's. We had just deepened the shaft and started putting in the bracings and square sets when the whole support system gave way. We lost eight men, and another five, including David, were injured. David broke an arm and got hit on the head by a beam. He was senseless for three days. When he came to, he couldn't see a thing. Sam was the one who pulled him from the wreckage. A terrible thing for one brother to have to do for another. Doc says the damage is permanent."

Numbness settled on her, making her lips stiff and her limbs heavy. All the time she nursed her Aunt Hattie in Kansas City, David had been hurt, blinded. Her peeve at his lack of correspondence and his failure to meet her train melted away. What he must've suffered, and she hadn't been there. "We should hurry home, then," she said at last. "He'll be worried if we don't show up soon."

Jesse winced. "Well, Karen, there's one other thing I have to tell you. You see, David isn't expecting you."

"But I sent a telegram with my arrival date and time."

"David hasn't been himself since the cave-in. He dictated a telegram to release you from the engagement." He shook his head, his shoulders bowed, his brow creased in morose lines. "David doesn't want to get married anymore."

The words hit like a physical blow. "I never received a telegram."

Jesse shot her a glance, half-sheepish, half-defiant. "Truth is I didn't send it, though I let him think I had."

"Why not? Why didn't someone tell me what happened?" Heat bloomed in her chest.

"Matilda can explain it all." He shrugged, not looking at her. "I didn't send the telegram because my son isn't thinking clear. He seems to think— I don't know, that somehow you won't love him anymore now that he's blind. I told him you weren't like that, that he was selling you short, but he won't listen. I figure you showing up might bring him to his senses."

Karen's imagination stirred up scenes in her head of the cave-in, of the dead and dying miners, of her fiancé, broken, wounded, imprisoned in blackness within and without.

Jesse remained silent and frowning until they pulled up in front of the Mackenzie house. Three stories of gleaming windows and gingerbread trim, balconies, turrets, and fish-scale siding rose from the hillside.

Karen leaned forward to glimpse the mansard roof with its widow's walk, the very place David had taken her to propose. They had looked up to the rugged peaks rising all around them and planned out their future together that happy summer evening.

Jesse helped her alight. "You go on in by the fire. Buckford will see to the bags."

She nodded to the faithful houseman who held the door for her. A welcoming blaze crackled in the front parlor fireplace. David's mother, Matilda, rose from her chair and glided across the foyer, as graceful and regal as always. "Karen, my dear." Lamplight raced along her dark blond hair shot through with silvery strands. "I trust your aunt is on the mend?"

"Aunt Hattie is fine. She sends her regards, and she will see you in two months for the wedding. . . ." Karen's voice trailed off as she looked to Jesse. He shifted from boot to boot and shrugged out of his coat.

"Jesse, you *did* tell her?"

He nodded, his shoulders slumped and his face more lined than Karen remembered.

Matilda gripped Karen's hand. "At first we didn't write because of the ongoing rescue attempts, and then nursing David. . .and the doctor held out some hope initially that the blindness would be temporary. But as more days went by, we had to resign ourselves to the bitter truth." Matilda sighed. "I am sorry now I didn't write to you immediately. I had hoped to spare you and be able to greet your train with the news that David would fully recover. Can you forgive me?"

Karen nodded. What else was there to do? Nothing could be changed now, and David was foremost on her mind. "Is he upstairs?"

Matilda shook her head. "He's all but barricaded himself in the study, and no matter what we try, he won't come out." The starch and drive Karen always associated with Matilda Mackenzie had been replaced with uncertainty and despair. "We had hoped this anger and lethargy would fade, but he sinks deeper each day. I don't know what to do anymore. I've never prayed so much in my life."

"Maybe I'd better see him first." Jesse tossed his coat at the hall tree. It missed the brass hook and slid to the bench below. "I'll have to fess up to not sending the telegram."

"No, Jesse." Karen stopped him. "I'll go in. I would have come even if you had cabled me David's wishes. Perhaps you're worrying about nothing. Our love is strong enough to survive this." Karen loosened the cape from around her shoulders. She lifted her chin and squared her shoulders, giving Matilda a smile. "I'm sure he'll be glad to see me, especially once I assure him his blindness makes no difference to how I feel about him." She crossed the foyer and eased aside the heavy pocket door to slip inside.

He sat behind the desk in the large red leather chair, his beautiful brown eyes focused on nothing. "Is that you, Buckford?" Dark circles smudged the skin under his eyes, and a greenish-blue bruise painted his right temple. Whiskers dusted his cheeks and chin, and his dark brown hair stood up, as if he'd run his fingers through it many times. He rubbed under the edge of the white sling encasing his arm. "Who's there?"

Karen stirred herself and walked toward him.

He must've heard her skirts rustling, for he asked, "Mother? I don't wish to be disturbed now." He pushed his chair back and braced his good hand on the desk to rise.

Before he could stand, she found her voice. "David?"

He flinched and leaned back in his chair. The skin tightened over his cheekbones, and the bruise stood out as the blood left his face.

"David, it's Karen."

He drew a long breath. "You were told not to come." His flat, emotionless tone chilled her. So far removed from his usual affectionate, charming self, she blinked and searched for a reply. This man before her was a burned-out lamp. Only the charred wick and the smoked glass remained. "Why did you come when I told you not to?"

"David, I. . ." She didn't want to bring his father and the unsent message into this. "I had to come. I had to see you."

"Well, you've seen. You've done your duty, and you can rest your conscience." He rose and faced her.

"My duty? What are you talking about, David?"

"You can go back to your life knowing you made your noble gesture and I refused. I've released you from the engagement, and you won't be tied to a cripple for the rest of your life."

A chill slid down her spine. This wasn't her strong, brave, confident fiancé. This man was broken, his words jagged glass cutting her from his life. She touched his arm.

He jerked away and crashed against the chair, sending it bumping into the wall. She grabbed his wrist to steady him, and he flung her grasp away.

"Don't touch me. Don't you understand? Everything has changed now. I don't want you here."

"But, David, I love you." She lifted her chin and straightened her spine. "I can't believe you think I would desert you. Nothing has to change."

"Everything *has* changed. It's over. Just go."

"David, this is far from over. I'll leave you now, but know this: I love you, no matter what has happened to your eyes." Karen fought down the lump in her throat. "I can appreciate the turmoil you must feel right now, but that's no reason to throw away our marriage plans."

He flinched then felt behind him for the chair. He eased down and covered his sightless eyes. "Just go away and leave me alone."

She stood still, not wanting to give up the fight but not knowing what to say or how to get him to change his mind. On the ride from town, she'd been sure that once they were together David's insecurity would vanish. It never once entered her head that he wouldn't change his mind about calling off the wedding.

When she turned to leave the study, her legs seemed to belong to someone else. The hollow ring of her heels on the hardwood floor echoed as if from far away, and her hands were so cold the brass latch on the study door felt warm to the touch.

Jesse and Matilda waited in the foyer. Matilda raised her eyebrows. "What happened?"

Karen shook her head. "He's adamant. The wedding is off." A dozen questions and thoughts clattered in her head, but she couldn't grasp any beyond wondering what she would do now.

Jesse's mouth tightened. "This has gone far enough."

Matilda turned to her husband. "What can we do? I thought things would get better, but they're getting worse and worse. I hoped having Karen here would jolt him out of his misery and remind him that he was still loved, but. . ." She twisted the handkerchief in her hands.

Jesse scowled. "I think it's time I had a talk with my son." He marched to the door and slid it open.

Karen raised her trembling hand to her temple and closed her eyes. She drew a breath, hoping to shake off the feeling of being caught in a bad dream. But when she opened her eyes, the nightmare remained and her dreams fled.

Chapter 2

Regret swamped David, pushing against his chest until he found it hard to breathe. It took everything he had not to call out for her, to cling to her and let loose the pent-up grief and fear that had stalked him since the moment he knew he would never see again. He choked back the rock-hard lump in his throat and forced himself to concentrate on holding fast to his decision not to marry Karen.

Heavy footsteps sounded in the hall and then the quick sliding of the door open and shut. Only one man in the house moved like that. David braced himself for parental wrath.

"Well, what do you have to say for yourself?"

Keeping the high back of the office chair between himself and the door, David didn't answer. Karen's perfume lingered in the air, reminding him of all he had lost. She deserved better than half a man, a shell, an object of pity. Any moment now she'd realize he was doing her a favor. And himself. Putting her aside before she had a chance to reject him.

"Well?"

"Leave me alone." David's throat tightened until it ached.

"Not till you face what you've done."

"What I've done?" The chair swiveled toward his father's voice. "You've got nerve coming in here to accuse me. I made my wishes regarding Karen clear."

"You aren't thinking straight right now. You don't mean what you say. We all know you're hurting, but taking it out on those you love isn't going to get your sight back."

"Don't pretend to know how I feel." David got to his feet, his fists clenched. Impotent humiliation sloshed inside him like kerosene in a can. "It's your fault she's here. You can deal with it." Heat rose up his throat and raced to his hairline at the thought of Karen seeing him like this.

"Why are you acting this way? I raised you better than to be rude to a woman, much less a woman who loves you like Karen does, a woman you promised to marry."

"How can you ask me that? I'm in no condition to take on a wife. What kind of husband would I be? How could I be the leader of my household? Karen might think she still wants to get married, but once she realized I'd forever be dependent on her, she'd regret her decision. Are you forgetting what happened with Uncle Frank and Aunt Bernice?"

Father sucked in a breath as if he'd been gut punched. "I told you never to mention their names in this house again." His words hissed, and David pictured his father's narrowed eyes and clenched teeth. "They're dead. It's finished. Karen would never do something like that to you."

"Circumstances change people."

"What happened fifteen years ago has nothing to do with right now. That's over and done with, and we've all moved on."

"If it's over and done with, why don't you ever talk about it? You want to act like it never happened, which is ridiculous considering Marcus is here as a reminder. You may want to think the situations are different, but I'm not willing to risk it. I'm not dragging this family down that road again."

David followed his father's movements, envisioning his scowling face and restless pacing. Then the movements stopped, and Father turned toward him again. "So, what am I supposed to tell Karen?"

The pain in David's head intensified, and his gut twisted. "If you'd have sent the telegram like I told you to, she would've stayed in Kansas City with her aunt." He brushed his fingers against his temple, gauging the soreness that lingered there. "I'm tired. Please close the door on your way out."

"You can't hide from life forever, David. And I'm not doing your dirty work for you. You and Karen need to sit down and talk about this rationally. She deserves better than you're giving her." Boots clomped on the floor, and the door opened and shut with force.

David massaged his injured wrist in the confining bandages, resigned now to the persistent ache. A wave of panicked remembrance swept over him. *The earth trembled, timbers snapped, rocks thundered and cascaded as the mine caved. Thick dust choked him. He coughed and staggered, bracing himself against the unstable walls, dropping his blueprints. A shattered brace hurled downward, landing on his wrist with a sick crunch and bouncing away. All around him men's cries of pain and terror ricocheted off the rock walls. Despite the agony screaming through his arm, he staggered upright, trying to reach the injured. A blinding flash burst through his head when something crashed into his temple and everything went black.*

He gulped, trying to force air into his lungs, to remind himself he wasn't trapped in the mine, that he was alive in the study. For the past three weeks, everyone had been telling him he was one of the lucky ones. But the blackness still surrounded him. And it would forever.

There's no reason why that shaft should have collapsed. He bounced his good fist off the desktop. He had gone over the calculations again and again, and each time he concluded the structure should've been stable. As the mine's engineer, it was his duty to see that things proceeded as safely as possible while finding the richest deposits of ore. The deaths and injuries from this disaster rested on his shoulders alone. His father hadn't said so, and neither had anyone else, at least not in his hearing, but he knew the truth. Where had he gone wrong?

All his supports had been kicked right out from under him. Like the mine, his life had caved in, filling his interior with rubble where there had once been a strong support system. Where was his faith? Where was the surety he'd always had that God loved him and heard his prayers? He'd never been so alone and frightened.

God, You've got to help me. You've taken my sight. You've taken my future. The least You can do is help me solve this problem. Show me where I went wrong.

He rose and inched across the room until his hand hit the carved back of the settee. Rounding the rolled arm and claw-and-ball foot, he eased onto the upholstery. A sigh pushed out of his lungs as he slid to his side and put his head on the pillow.

Someone knocked and entered without waiting to be invited.

David stiffened. Did no one in this house know what *alone* meant?

"It's me, David, Sam."

"What do you want?" David clenched his teeth, in no mood to be berated by his younger brother.

"Just talk." The chair at the end of the settee creaked, and something thunked the low table beside him.

He almost smiled. Mother forbade boots on the table, but she had yet to break either of her sons of the habit. Then he stilled. He would never see his mother's disapproving stare again. "Have you come for your pound of flesh?"

"Nope, I just figured you could explain a couple things for me."

The scent of fresh air and the outdoors filtered toward David off Sam's clothes, something he hadn't smelled in weeks. But then, Sam was free to come and go as he pleased, not imprisoned in darkness in this house. David pictured his brother, as unlike David as could be with his blondish hair and blue eyes, and his easygoing manner and take-life-as-it-comes outlook. Easy enough for Sam to take life as it came. Life had never pummeled Sam as hard as it had David.

"I'll stoke the fire for you. It's almost as cold in here as outside, and that's saying something. The temperature is dropping like an anvil down an air shaft. Snowing, too."

David fumed. He couldn't even do something as simple as lighting the fire. He sat up, scowling. "Leave it."

"Dave, you have to let some of this stuff go. Exploding like a pint of nitro every time someone tries to be nice to you is no way to live." Logs clacked together, paper crumpled, and a match scritched on the hearth. Faint crackles and pops filled the air, along with the smell of burning resin. "There," Sam said, satisfaction in his voice. "Now things'll warm up in here. It'll be more comfortable while we talk."

"There's nothing to talk about."

Sam went on as if he hadn't heard. "I had some time today, while I installed that new pump in shaft two, to do some thinking. I was thinking about that party we had here a couple of months ago."

David gritted his teeth. His insides writhed, and his muscles tensed.

"Engagement parties are always the best kind, don't you think? I tried to get a dance with the prettiest gal at the shindig, but she didn't even notice me. She only had eyes for one fellow that night and saved every dance for him. And that fellow, well, the stars could have fallen from the sky and he wouldn't have known."

"What is your point, Sam?" David tried to ignore the broken glass tearing his heart.

"My point is, that much happiness and caring and loving shouldn't be thrown away. I can see what you're doing, and you think you're doing it for Karen, but you aren't. You're doing it for you. You're too proud for your own good. You want folks to think you're making a noble sacrifice by not tying Karen to a blind man, but the real truth is you are just plain scared. You're scared she won't love you anymore. You're pushing her away before she has a chance to hurt you. You're trying to act like you've stopped loving her." He paused. "Have you? Stopped loving her, I mean?"

Trust Sam to ferret out David's deepest fears and pull them out for casual inspection. "You know I still love her. I've loved her since the moment I first saw her. I will always love her. That's why I have to break the engagement. I love her too much to tie her to a cripple." A giant fist grabbed his heart and squeezed until he couldn't breathe, trapping him as effectively as the cave-in.

"Don't you think Karen should be the one to decide what she wants? I'm not saying it would be easy, and I'm not saying things won't be different than you've planned, but you're not even going to try? I want to know why."

"I won't be the object of her pity. One would think, after all we've been through, that my own family would support me in this decision. I was foolish enough to mention Frank and Bernice to Father, and he still can't bring himself to talk about them. He shut me down."

Sam emitted a low whistle. "That was either brave or stupid, or both. You're lucky he didn't punch you. Anyway, you're not comparing Karen to Bernice, are you? That'd be plain foolish."

David rose on stiff legs. "You're meddling in something that is none of your business. I've made my choice. I'd like you to leave now."

"Running me off won't change anything. You're scared, and you're shoving people aside before they have a chance to reject you or make you feel less of a man." Sam's words hammered like a rock drill, hitting places so raw and fragile it took David's breath away. "You're afraid you're not man enough to marry Karen and let her love you." The chair creaked, and Sam's voice came from higher up. "Don't throw away everything you have with Karen. She still loves you. She can help you through this. We'd all like to help."

"I don't want to *need* your help. Can't you understand that?" David flung wide his arm, lost his balance, and toppled. He crashed into a marble-topped table, hit the glass lamp standing on it, and sent it to the floor. The smell of kerosene enveloped him just before his head hit the rug, exploding bright, white stars in his brain.

"David?" Sam's hands reached for him. "Are you all right?"

David shoved aside his brother's help. Sharp pain stabbed up his broken arm. Gasping for breath, he held his good hand to his head. "Just leave me alone. Why don't you just get out of here?"

❧

Karen jumped when the lamp broke, covering her mouth and gripping the edge of the study door.

Sam motioned her to be quiet. "At least let me help you get up. You don't want to cut yourself on this glass."

When David stood upright, cradling his injured arm to his middle, Karen exhaled and bit her lip.

Sam brushed at David's clothes, until David shoved his hand away. "Go away, Sam."

Someone touched her arm. Buckford stood at her elbow. She drew him away from the door to whisper, "A lamp got broken."

"I'll see to it."

Sam edged through the doorway, glanced at Buckford's retreating back, and then met Karen's eyes. Everything she'd overheard watered her parched heart. Tears blurred her vision, and pain, sweet and sharp, flowed through her chest.

David still loved her.

She swung from hope to despair. What good did his still loving her do if he remained adamant about not marrying her? And who were Frank and Bernice, and why hadn't she heard of them before?

All through dinner—at which David did not make an appearance—she played the what-if game. What if Aunt Hattie hadn't gotten ill? What if

Karen had been here when the accident occurred? Would it have made any difference? What if David didn't change his mind? What would she do? Without David, Aunt Hattie was the only family she had left. Her thoughts scampered like squirrels in an oak tree while everyone transferred to the parlor.

Sam dropped onto the settee and plunked his boots onto the table. At his mother's frown, he eased his feet back, a sheepish grin twisting his mouth.

Jesse took up his post by the mantel, hands behind his back, staring into the flames.

Buckford carried in a silver tray of coffee cups and poured the fragrant drink.

"Did you get the lamp cleaned up?" Sam took a cup. "I'm sorry about the mess. I got Dave riled up."

The houseman nodded. "Everything is tidy now. He's resting, though he didn't eat much of the meal I took to him." Buckford's brows descended and he shook his graying head.

Matilda cleared her throat and smoothed her skirts. "We've accommodated David, hoping the bitterness would pass, and now that we can see it's lingering, we haven't changed our ways."

"What do you plan to do?" Karen pressed her lips together to stop their trembling.

Matilda's chin came up. For the first time that day, Karen felt like smiling. The fighting glint had returned to the older woman's eyes. If anyone could right this ship, it was Matilda Mackenzie. "The first thing we have to do is stop showing pity. Feel sorry for him, cry for him if you must, but never in his presence. David must learn to live with his blindness, and so must we. We'll find ways to help him be more independent, and we won't take no for an answer."

At her words, Jesse came to stand behind her, his hands blanketing her shoulders and squeezing.

She looked up at him, the affection between them evident even after all their years of marriage. "This will be difficult and, knowing David, will take more than enough patience from all of us, but I refuse to let him shut himself away from the rest of the world forever."

Karen cradled her coffee, trying to warm her fingers. Sleet pinged against the windowpanes, and the wind whistled under the eaves. "Do you think he'll change his mind about the wedding?"

No one spoke for a moment. Then Matilda leaned forward. "Karen, you must make very sure that David is still what you want. You do realize the blindness won't go away? You can't marry him and then decide in a few months or even years that you don't want all that goes along with being married to a blind man."

Jesse frowned and harrumphed.

Matilda tucked her lower lip in for a moment, her eyes tensing. "Well, she has to be sure."

Karen glanced from Jesse to Matilda, then at Sam, who put his cup down and contemplated the crown molding. A strange undercurrent flowed through the room and around Karen. She frowned and set her cup down to clench her hands in her lap. "I'm sure. I love David, and I know he loves me." Her glance flicked back to Sam whose mouth quirked. He nodded encouragement to Karen. "David, blind or not, is what I want, and I'm willing to fight for him. I'm willing to do whatever I can to assure him of my love."

Matilda leaned forward and patted Karen's arm. "Good. Then the changes for David will begin in the morning. It will take all of us together to bring this about. He's gotten a fair dose of stubbornness from each of his parents. If you are certain, then I think I have a plan that will at least wake him out of his malaise." She glanced over her shoulder at her husband. "Jesse and I have discussed this, and we're in complete agreement." Jesse returned his hand to her shoulder. "Sam, you will need to ride to town early with a message for Josiah Fuller." She outlined the bare bones, and Karen could hardly believe what she'd come up with.

When she finished, Sam picked up one of the chess pieces from the table beside him and tossed it lightly into the air. "This could prove to be mighty interesting. Dave won't know what hit him. I hope you know what you're doing."

Matilda sighed and closed her eyes, leaning her head to the side to rest on Jesse's arm. "I have no confidence that I know what I'm doing, but we can't keep on as we are."

After chasing ideas and posing possible scenarios for another hour, Jesse finally sent everyone to bed.

Karen went through her nightly ablutions, her head and heart heavy, but once under the coverlet, sleep eluded her. Everything they'd talked about tumbled around in her head, and she sifted through what David's blindness would mean to her.

She searched her soul long and hard. Though she had given Matilda her assurance that David's condition made no difference in her love for him, she examined her heart to make absolutely certain. Could she spend her life happily married to a blind man? Would he give her the chance?

Flipping back the covers, she prowled the confines of her room, crossing and re-crossing the moonlit carpet, praying, wrestling, arguing, and praying some more. The limitless questions came from every corner of her mind, until at last she hit on the one question that answered the rest. It wasn't a matter of would she be able to live happily with David, but rather would she be able to live happily anywhere without him.

Chapter 3

In his dreams David could still see. Colors so vibrant and motion so vivid and beautiful it almost hurt. Sunshine bathed every flower and mountain peak in golden light. Every leaf and blade of grass stood out in crisp, glorious detail. He felt strong and steady, grounded and yet ready to soar like a bird. Karen stood before him in a flowing golden gown. She held an armful of pink roses, and her face glowed with love. She held out her hand to him, beckoning him to take it and walk with her along a creek bank where diamonds of light shattered off the water. His fingers touched hers, and warm, white brightness surrounded them.

Then he opened his eyes.

Dreams and sight vanished, swallowed by perpetual dark. Reality sat on his chest like a grinning stone gargoyle.

He ignored the door opening and the light footsteps tapping on the study floor, burrowing his head into the pillow and resigning himself to another dark day. His ankle knocked the end of the settee. He probably should sleep in his own bed instead of this narrow sofa, but that would mean navigating the house, and he preferred the safety and familiarity of the study.

"David, get up. It is after ten." His mother's voice cracked like a twig breaking.

He groaned and flexed the fingers of his mending arm.

She prodded his bare shoulder. "Get dressed. You have ten minutes. Your presence is required in the parlor. A family meeting."

David grimaced at her brisk tone. "Have it without me. You don't need me there."

"Nonsense. You're the guest of honor. I suppose, if you force us, we could hold the meeting in here with you in your current state of dishevelment." She marched across the room and closed the door before he could muster another protest.

Stung, David moaned and tried to untangle his legs from the blanket. The clock ticked as he cradled his forehead in his good hand. He had no doubt Mother would make good her threat to hold a family meeting here with him in his nightwear should he fail to appear in the parlor.

He groped for his clothing, his head pounding so hard he could almost hear it. Biting down the bile rising in his throat, he castigated himself for being too proud to ask for assistance in taking his pain medications the night before. Though he would have welcomed the relief from the head-ache, he couldn't bring himself to ask for help after throwing everyone out of the study. His conscience pricked at behaving so poorly, but he quashed it.

David managed to dress, and after a fumbling search, found his boots. Unshaven and in yesterday's clothes, he must look like a saddle tramp. Served them right for rousting him out when he felt so poorly. If the family wanted a meeting, they'd take him like this or not at all. He dragged across the study and groped for the door.

Their voices traveled across the foyer from the parlor—his father's loud, Sam's softer but just as insistent. Sam started again, but Mother interrupted him.

He couldn't hear Karen. She must've gone, then. Her absence made him ache, but a small part of him felt vindicated. She'd left him. That proved he'd done the right thing.

He inched his way to the parlor doorway, noting that all the voices had stopped. They were watching him. Keeping an arm straight out in front of him, he groped for the doorjamb. Fabric swished, telling him his mother's location at the same time his hand hit the fringe decorating the doorway. A boot scuffed and coins jingled in a pocket. Father, by the fireplace.

"Good morning, David." Mother's voice was as bland as cream. "Please, sit down." She must be in her favorite chair near the hearth. "There is an empty chair just a few steps in front of you." Her voice reminded him of a crisp winter morning. He grasped the back of the chair and directed himself into it, determined to hear what they had to say then retreat back to the study.

Father said nothing, but the poker clattered against the grate. The mine collapse, their argument of yesterday, his refusal to marry Karen—these things stood between him and his father, and the gap appeared to be widening.

"Morning, Dave." Sam, off to the left by the bay window.

His mother cleared her throat. "We have much to discuss, and I don't want to get sidetracked. David, I feel that we owe you an apology."

He lifted his head and raised his brows.

She continued. "We've done you a grave disservice. As a family, we have coddled you, catered to you, and cloistered you. That was an error on our part. We've allowed you to become so self-centered as to be harmful to yourself. For that I apologize, and believe me, we will rectify this situation."

He gripped the arms of the chair, and his back straightened. Every muscle in his face tensed as he bit back a hot protest. If they'd dragged him in here just to chastise him, then he was leaving. He braced his hands on the arms of the chair to rise.

"Sit still. I'm not finished." His mother's dagger-like tone froze him. "No longer will you shut yourself away in the study like a coward. I have always enjoyed that room and see no reason why I should be deprived of its use so you can flee from your problems. You will sleep in your bedroom from now on. You will also eat your meals with us in the dining room. I know it makes you uncomfortable, but if you can't feel safe learning and making mistakes here with the people who love you, you'll never go out that front door again."

David flinched at her tone. He had no desire to go out the front door. He only desired to be left alone. Cotton dryness spread through his mouth, and his arm ached anew.

Mother continued, and his stomach clenched. "You will learn to dress yourself properly, to care for your personal hygiene, and to be responsible for yourself. You will learn to face your life as it is now and show some courage. We will procure whatever outside help we need to assist you. Rest assured, we will not leave you alone in this."

The words David forced out through tight lips tasted like ashes. "You ask too much."

"You are still a very valued member of this family, and the problem has been we've not asked enough of you," Mother shot back, her words peppering him like buckshot. "We are all agreed on this. Buckford will spend the morning cleaning the study so we may have use of it again. You will stay here and keep Karen company for the time being. Her guest should arrive before too long."

His face heated, and his teeth ground together. Karen was here? And she'd heard every word of his humiliation at the hands of his family. He swallowed hard and fumed at the high-handed way his family insisted upon running his life. Further proof of his helplessness.

His father and brother stalked out, their footsteps receding and the front door slamming. Mother pressed her hand on his shoulder as she passed. He refused to acknowledge her, and with a sigh, her touch dropped away. Her light footsteps crossed the parlor and receded. Then he was alone with Karen.

"I thought you'd left," he said, keeping his voice expressionless.

"Your mother invited me to stay as her guest. I accepted." Her voice cut through him.

He closed his eyes against a wave of love for her, but he forced himself to harden his heart against it. Though he longed for the comfort and assurance of her arms, to hear her say once again that his blindness didn't matter, he refused to give in to the need. Whatever declarations she might make now would only make her leaving that much more difficult. "You're expecting a guest? It seems a bit soon to be entertaining, having just broken off our engagement."

She was quiet for a moment then spoke slowly, as if measuring her words. "If you will recall, I am not responsible for our broken engagement." Her voice turned away from him.

His nails indented his palms. How he wished he could see her, to look into her eyes once more, to ascertain if she was hurting or if she was relieved the wedding had been cancelled.

A teacup rattled in a saucer. "David, I wish you'd reconsider your decision."

"No. There will be no reconsidering. Who are you expecting?" He could've bitten his tongue for asking.

"Actually, I had need of a lawyer. Sam took a message to town early this morning and brought back word that Mr. Fuller would see me today."

"A lawyer? What for?"

"I don't think it would be prudent to discuss this subject with you before speaking to my lawyer."

The knocker banged on the front door. Deliberate, slow footsteps—Buckford's—crossed the foyer. The door swung open.

"I have an appointment with Miss Worth, Buckford. Something about filing a lawsuit?" Fuller's voice boomed, as big and rotund as he.

"This way, sir."

A gust of chilly air swirled into the room.

"Hello, David. Ah, Karen, my dear."

David staggered to his feet. "What's this about a lawsuit?" He turned back toward Karen. "Who's getting sued?"

"Why, *you*, David. I'm suing you for breach of promise for breaking our engagement." Her voice hitched, then steadied. "If you will excuse me, I have things to discuss with my lawyer in private." Her gardenia perfume wafted toward him, contrasted by the steel in her voice.

David stood rooted to the spot as their footsteps faded down the hall. Suing him? Breach of promise? The hammer and anvil in his head pounded out a beat in time with his heart, and weakness crept over him. He groped behind himself to find the chair once more and sank into it.

She wasn't serious, was she?

Chapter 4

Karen bit her lip and led Mr. Fuller to the dining room. David's vulnerability made her want to give in, to assure him she didn't mean it, that it was all a hoax. He must've felt as if everyone had turned their backs on him, but what else could she do? David's parents thought it would shake him up, and they knew him well. She would go along with it for a while, and they had assured her she could back down any time.

Karen seated herself at the dining room table and poured Mr. Fuller a cup of coffee. She'd always liked him from her days as a clerk in the land office. Those halcyon days when she had been new in town and on the cusp of falling in love with the handsomest man she'd ever met.

"A terrible thing." The lawyer bent his round frame and hung over the chair for a moment before he dropped onto the needlepoint seat covering with a sigh. "I wish there was something I could do for him." He opened his case, took out a thick law book, paper and pencil, and tapped the pages into a neat pile. His fussing continued until the papers and the pencil were perfectly aligned and squared up before him. "Let me make sure I have this clear." He rubbed his side-whiskers and consulted her note. "David has called off the engagement and you'd like to sue him for breach of promise?"

"Actually, I don't really want to sue him. I just want to get him to change his mind, but I have to look like I am suing him."

"This isn't a joke, right?" He regarded her soberly, his small eyes boring into hers. For all his jocularity and bonhomie, Josiah Fuller had a reputation as a shrewd lawyer. "From the moment I file the lawsuit, it will become public record. David will be served with papers and the waiting period will begin. He will have thirty days to reach a settlement out of court or the case will go on the docket to be heard."

"If he hasn't changed his mind within thirty days, I will have failed anyway. I'll withdraw the lawsuit."

"So you don't intend to take this to court?"

"No. I just want him to think I will. I'm trying to snap him out of this malaise and get him to realize we belong together. I love him too much to walk away from him, especially now." She ran the tip of her finger over her lower lip. "Mrs. Mackenzie said if I love David then I should fight for him and let nothing, not even David, deter me. I intend to do just that."

Warmth flooded Mr. Fuller's eyes, and his cheeks jiggled as he laughed. "I don't think David knows what a gem he has in you, Karen." His whiskers twitched as he cleared his throat and squared up the already square papers before him. He poised the pencil over the pages. "I haven't handled a breach of promise suit before, so I bent the ear of a colleague of mine who has experience in these matters." He paused to write a line in precise all-uppercase letters, then withdrew another sheaf of papers from his bag. "This is a copy of his latest breach of promise lawsuit, which should give us a framework to pattern our document after. Let's go through this step by step and see what we have."

For the next hour, Karen answered his questions. He consulted his casebook and papers frequently, pausing to think between questions, probing methodically through her courtship and engagement, filling out page after page with her answers.

At last he sat back and laced his fingers over his vest. "My dear, you have the most compelling case I've heard. Much better than any in here." He nodded toward the casebook. "If David doesn't change his mind, you would be sure to win in court. Perhaps you can explain to me why you wouldn't go through with the lawsuit when you're sure of winning?"

"It's wrong for one Christian to take another to court."

"It's wrong for a young man to promise to marry a girl and then yank all that away, leaving her with nothing." Fuller closed the papers into a file folder and shut the book. "As for one Christian suing another. . .if they didn't, I would be out of business. You'd be surprised at how many 'Christians' I have for clients."

"Just because a behavior is prevalent doesn't make it right." One of Aunt Hattie's maxims came out before Karen knew it. What would she tell her aunt about the wedding? A sigh forced itself past the lump in her throat.

"He's done you a grievous wrong, and you deserve something besides his broken promises. The court will take into account his accident and his blindness, but they'll also take into account that he's a member of one of the wealthiest families in Colorado. He promised you that you would be a part of that family, and now he's withdrawn that promise. No one would blame you for suing."

Karen shook her head. "That wouldn't be right. This isn't about the money. It never has been. I'd marry David if he didn't have a penny. The lawsuit is just to jar him, to make him realize he's hurting other people— besides himself—with his actions."

Josiah stood and patted her shoulder. "I'll be back this afternoon with the papers. Until then, it would probably be best if you didn't discuss anything with David."

"I don't think that will be a problem."

◈

David stayed in the parlor until he heard Fuller leave.

Suing him. He never would've believed it of his gentle Karen. It just proved he was right to call off the wedding. If she could turn on him so quickly, how long would it have taken her to despise him after they said their vows?

Sinking lower into the chair, he tried to block out Mother's voice demanding he show some courage, face his life, and stop moping for how it used to be. He'd never considered himself a particularly brave man, but neither did he consider himself a coward. Until now. He'd add it to his list of shortcomings.

He pushed himself upright and probed his way out to the staircase. Holding the banister, he kicked his toe out to measure the steps. Why hadn't he ever counted them before?

Turning to the left at the top, he brushed the wall, inching forward. His parents' door first, then the guestroom Karen used, Sam's door, turn to the right at the end of the hall, straight ahead five steps, his own bedroom door. Relief that he'd made it this far alone trickled through him.

He opened the door and stepped in. Freshness, as if the window had been left open recently, greeted him. The bed sat before him and a little to the left. His hand glided over the smooth comforter. Though no longer able to see the rich dark blue, it surprised him that he could enjoy the texture of the fabric so much. His hand wrapped around the newel post at the foot of the bed, feeling the ridges of the carved walnut, smelling the lemony, beeswax aroma of the polish Sally Ann used.

The light scent made him aware of his own smell. With a wry twist of his lips he turned to find the dresser. With tentative fingers, he searched the drawers, feeling the fabrics, trying to identify what shirt he held. At last his fingers brushed pin-tucked linen. His favorite white shirt. Laying it across the foot of the bed, he turned to select a pair of pants and some socks. Blue, brown, black? He slammed the drawer shut.

Removing his rumpled shirt, he groped his way to the washstand. To his surprise he found the water in the pitcher warmed. Buckford must have known about the family meeting and put his money on Mother to have her way. A wry smile twisted his lips once again.

Through all his ablutions, his mind mulled the pending lawsuit. He'd underestimated Karen's resolve. But, then again, she had underestimated his.

He managed to cut himself at least twice, but he did get shaved and dressed. Now for some coffee and pain medicine.

He made it to the bottom of the stairs again without mishap. His legs shook, reminding him of all the time he'd spent bedridden over the past month. A yeasty, warm fragrance came from the back of the house, drawing him down the hall to the kitchen. He pressed his hand against the swinging door and eased it aside.

"Mr. Mackenzie."

"Mrs. Morgan." David acknowledged the woman who had cooked for the family for several years. "Could I have some coffee, please?" He concentrated so hard on remembering the layout of the kitchen that he made it halfway across the room before he realized he had closed his eyes. A rueful chuckle rose to his throat. He found a chair and sat down at the table.

"I must say, sir, you are looking much better. You've taken your sling off. Is your arm healing, then?" She set the coffee down in front of him.

"It's fine." He groped for the cup. "You wouldn't happen to have the laudanum, would you? For my headache?"

"I do, and I'll add it to your coffee directly. I've been baking today. Would you like a muffin or some fresh bread?" Cupboards opened and cutlery clanked.

"No, thank you, Mrs. Morgan, just the coffee. Has Mother been in to talk to the staff?"

She hesitated. "Yes. She came in and had a few words with Buckford and myself and Sally Ann."

"And what did my formidable mother say?"

"Well, now. . ."

"It's all right, Mrs. Morgan. Just tell it straight."

He pictured the comfortably upholstered Mrs. Morgan crossing her short arms under her considerable bosom and tilting her head before speaking. "She said no more trays in the study and no more coddling. She said you wouldn't learn to live in this house without your sight unless we made you, and no matter how hard it seemed, or how you might fight us, we weren't to give in."

He pursed his lips. "No quarter given, eh?"

"That's right, sir. Buckford said we had to be obeying the missus, and he told Sally Ann he'd take care of your room from now on himself. Here's your coffee. You sure you won't have a bite to eat?"

"No, thank you. I couldn't eat a thing right now. Maybe later."

She harrumphed.

He couldn't seem to please anyone in this house today.

&

"The lawyer has returned, and David is waiting with him in the dining room." Buckford's eyes held a note of laughter. Not much escaped his knowledge in the Mackenzie abode. Karen had no doubt he was fully aware of the pending lawsuit.

She nodded and braced her shoulders for the coming battle. Her resolve must not waver.

"Gentlemen." She lifted her eyebrows in a silent question to her lawyer as she entered.

Both men rose and David cleared his throat. "Karen, we need to talk." He had shaved and dressed in clean clothes, as if preparing to do battle. At least she'd gotten him to do that much.

"Of course."

Mr. Fuller held a chair for her and then seated himself at the end of the table.

Karen smoothed her skirts and forced her hands to relax in her lap. "Please, sit down, David."

Tiredness etched his pale face. The lingering signs of pain and illness clung to him, but he held himself erect, as if he had no intention of giving in to weakness.

Forcing himself to be strong all alone broke her heart while at the same time brought out her fighting side. He had made the choice to separate himself, pushing everyone away. And why?

David released a slow breath. "I'm sure you'll agree it would be in everyone's best interest to reach a settlement outside the courts."

Karen kept her voice even. "It would be in everyone's best interest if the wedding went ahead as planned."

"No."

Fuller smoothed his whiskers and laced his fingers together, bracing his weight on his forearms. "We would be interested in hearing your proposed settlement, but rest assured, David, we will not be easily satisfied. You've done grievous harm to my client, and we are seeking due compensation."

"Your client? Use her name, Josiah. We're all friends here. Or at least we used to be." A whisper of regret clung to his words. He pressed his lips together and placed his hands flat on the table. "I am a fair man. I realize Karen's life has been disrupted by all of this. I'm not averse to compensating her for her troubles."

Compensate her for her troubles? He made her sound like one of his employees. "Just how much would you deem suitable?" Karen leaned forward, ignoring the damping motions from her lawyer. "I don't want your money, David. I want your heart." She twisted the garnet on her finger, the ring she hadn't removed since the night he placed it there. "You said I would always have your heart, but you've taken it back and pushed me aside. I put my future in your hands, and you've dropped it like an old teacup. I'm trying to pick up the broken pieces. I've got no job, no home, and no future." She rose and put both palms on the table, leaning forward. "Open the door on that self-imposed prison of pride you're locked in and think of someone besides yourself for a moment."

David flinched but rallied. "And whom are *you* thinking of in this lawsuit? Yourself, right?"

"Would you believe me, David, if I said I was thinking of you?" She straightened. "Of course you wouldn't. You've wrapped yourself so deep in your hurt there's no room for anything or anyone else. You act as if our love meant nothing to you."

He sucked in a breath, and for a moment she thought she had gone too far. How had they so quickly descended into name-calling and accusations? "I'm sorry, David. I apologize for my bad manners. Mr. Fuller, if you could leave the papers you've drawn up, I'll go over them and get them back to you."

"Of course, my dear. Why don't you show me out?" He gathered himself and heaved to his feet. "David, I am sorry about all of this, but Karen is my client, and I must do my best to guard her interests."

She walked Fuller to the door and took the papers he offered her.

"Read them carefully, and if they meet with your approval, sign them and return them to me. And think about what I said. You have a very strong case."

When he'd gone, she leaned against the door and swiped at the tears on her cheeks. Was this doing any good at all? She and David were further apart than ever.

&

Buckford entered the dining room, his soft tread as recognizable to David as his lined face. "Mr. Quint is here to see you."

"Marcus?" David's cousin hadn't visited once since the cave-in. Not that David really blamed him. No doubt he'd been busy with the cleanup at the mine and running the office in David's absence. Sick calls probably weren't high on his to-do list. "Is he in the parlor?"

"Yes sir."

"I know Mother instructed you not to lead me around, Buckford, but for the sake of greeting my guest in a timely manner and without benefit of a black eye from walking into a door, could you escort me?" He gripped Buckford's arm, grateful for the support.

Gathering his courage and his wits—both scattered from his encounter with Karen and Fuller—he greeted his cousin. "It's good of you to come, Marcus."

Buckford placed David's hand on the back of a chair.

Hoping Marcus wouldn't comment on how he inched around, David eased onto the seat.

"David, I feel terrible I haven't been to visit you before now. Things have just been so busy."

David formed Marcus's image in his mind, tall and slender, sandy-brown hair just beginning to thin. A capable assistant.

"Have you made much progress? Are things getting back to normal?" It hurt to even ask. Not only had David caused the deaths and injuries of several good men, he had crippled himself to the point where he was helpless to make any sort of amends. He couldn't even assist with righting the damage at the mine and getting production under way once more.

Marcus sighed, and David could only imagine the horror of pulling the broken bodies of friends and co-workers out of the depths of the mine. "All the bodies have been recovered. The shaft is a shambles, though. It has taken all this time just to clear it out."

"What are the workers saying?"

"Accidents are a part of mining, David. You can't blame yourself. Sometimes things happen that we don't intend. You can't plan for every contingency."

The sadness in Marcus's voice prodded all the sore places in David's heart. "How could I have miscalculated so much? The square sets were in place and should have been more than adequate for the load. I can't think of a single reason why that part of the shaft should have collapsed. Be honest with me, Marcus. I know I can trust you. Tell me, what did I do wrong?"

"You can't beat yourself up over this. Things happen and sometimes we never know the cause. You can't know how sorry I am about your. . .injury. That's what I really wanted to say. I didn't come to talk about the mine. I came to say how sorry I am that all this happened, and now I hear your marriage is off, too."

"You heard? How?"

"Sam told me. Is she really suing you?"

"Word gets around quick. Yes, the engagement is off, and yes, Karen is suing me. It seems God is not on my side at the moment. Nothing but lightning bolts from the blue."

"Was Karen horrified that you are. . . ?"

"You can say the word, Marcus. I'm blind." David gritted his teeth. When would people stop dancing around the fact? He didn't want people to talk about his blindness, but neither did he want them to skirt around the fact. "Karen seems to think my circumstances should have no bearing upon our wedding plans, but that's naive. I broke the engagement for her." Though he'd had no idea she would resort to legal action. "I'm trying to spare us both a lot of heartache. If anyone could understand my motives, it's you."

Marcus shifted. "You're right. Nobody would understand like me." He leaned forward and gripped David's shoulder. "It would take a brave man to face the fact that things won't be the same from now on. Releasing Karen is the only logical thing to do."

"I wish other people would realize that it's for the best." David clenched his fists, forcing himself to believe his own words. "I have a favor to ask of you."

"Anything. You know that."

"Help me. Help me find out why the mine collapsed. Help me keep it from happening again. I need you to be my eyes at the mine. I need you to go over those blueprints, the load figures, rock samples. . .everything."

"Are you sure you should be worrying about that sort of thing now? You need to heal. It hasn't been all that long since the accident. Give yourself some time. You have this situation with Karen to deal with. I can handle things at the mine."

"I know you can. It's just. . .I need to know what happened."

"I'll do what I can, but I doubt we will ever know what really happened."

"Thank you, Marcus. I knew I could count on you."

Chapter 5

Karen waited on David's next move. He followed the letter of the new law of the house, showing up for dinner and spending the evenings with the family in the parlor or study, but the spirit of the law he ignored completely, picking at his food and sitting in stony silence.

Three tense days passed in which she got little sleep and prayed for a breakthrough. On the evening of that third day, she joined the Mackenzies in the parlor.

Sam and Jesse began a game of chess while Matilda dug yarn from her workbasket. Her brows lowered as her knitting needles clicked.

Karen couldn't take her eyes from David who sat by the fireplace, his profile outlined by the reflection of the flames. He held a pencil between his palms, rolling it back and forth, his sightless brown eyes focused on nothing.

If only he would let her past the wall he'd erected between them. She longed to soothe his hurt, to hold him and have him hold her. Why couldn't he realize she needed him, not for his eyes but for his strength of spirit, his integrity, the caring heart she knew still lived somewhere inside him? Why couldn't he realize the more-than-awkward position he'd put her in by breaking the engagement? She picked up her book, and though she turned the pages, she comprehended nothing of the story. When Matilda sighed and frowned at the yarn in her hands, Karen lowered her book and asked, "Is that a difficult pattern?"

"No, it's just that my state of mind is evident in whatever I'm knitting. If I'm tense, the stitches get tighter. These last two rows are so tight the yarn is squeaking on the needles." She thrust the points into the ball and stuffed the entire project back into her workbasket. "Let's talk of something else."

Sam looked up from his game. "How's the arm feeling, David? You've quit wearing the sling."

"It's fine."

Matilda lowered her chin and folded her hands in her lap. "Karen, I understand you met with Josiah Fuller again today. How did that go?"

David's head snapped around to face their voices.

Matilda had dropped the cat among the pigeons, and her pale blue eyes gleamed with satisfaction.

"As well as could be expected." Karen unfolded the document Matilda had requested she bring along after supper. "He brought me my own copy of the lawsuit. Would you like to read it?"

"It might be best if you read it out loud, since it concerns all of us." The older woman's voice was as bland as rice pudding, but she had David in her sights.

David scowled, and Karen's hands trembled as she smoothed the papers on her lap. Her heart thrummed in her ears. So much hinged on David's reaction. Her voice shook a bit as she read through the opening paragraphs but steadied as she got to the heart of the matter.

"...did freely and publicly announce their betrothal and intention of joining together in marriage. Such being the case, the private setting aside of the betrothal will substantially damage the plaintiff's ability to obtain a suitable marriage in the future, as well as severely affect her good reputation. The circumstances of the breach of promise defame the plaintiff's good name and standing in the community. The plaintiff cites the economic hardship that has befallen her as a result of the breach of promise on the part of the defendant. She gave up her employment situation at the urging of her betrothed, and the position has been filled by another."

Jesse grinned like a well-fed cat, his arms banded across his broad chest, his booted ankles crossed toward the hearth. Sam tipped a pawn on edge and rolled it in a circle, not looking up, though an arrow of concern formed between his brows.

When Karen got to the monetary compensation clause, the pencil David had been toying with snapped. "That's outrageous." The words burst from him like bullets from a gun. "That sum is preposterous. This entire situation is preposterous."

Karen lowered the papers, not trusting herself to speak. She wanted to tell him this was a farce, that she had no intention of going through with it, that she loved him and wanted him to *want* to be married to her.

Matilda nodded, a smile playing around her lips. She must think her plans were working at least in part. David was talking to them.

"Whew, Karen, that's a sight of money." Jesse whistled. "Fuller thinks he can get you that much?"

David shot to his feet, sending his chair crashing into the wall. "Over my dead body. And, Father, I can't believe you aren't livid about—"

Matilda cut him off. "There is a simple solution to this problem, David. I believe Karen is entitled to something out of this whole affair. If you aren't prepared to do the right thing by her, then she deserves compensation. Of course, you could end this entire business by marrying her. The family is agreed in this, and it is what you want, isn't it, Karen?"

"With all my heart," Karen whispered, choking back the tears.

David snorted. "That is not going to happen. Karen, you've lost your senses. You will not coerce me this way. Neither will you rob my family in this manner. Mother, I've abided by your new rules, but as of now, my evening is finished. Good night."

David skirted the settee and ran straight into the potted palm on the table by the door. The pot teetered for a moment, then crashed to the floor, shattering and sending dirt and palm fronds across the rug. Redness barged up David's neck and across his high cheekbones. He stumbled through the wreckage and groped for the door handle before anyone could move.

Karen's mouth hung open. She was the one who had lost her senses? She rose to go after him.

Matilda tried to restrain her. "No, Karen, don't back down now."

"Don't worry." She gently removed Matilda's hand from her arm. "I have no intention of backing down." Her footsteps rang on the foyer floor. "David Mackenzie, stop this instant."

He stopped, his hand gripping the rail, halfway up the staircase.

She lifted her hem and marched up the steps. "How dare you! How dare you claim I am out of my mind or somehow out of order in seeking recompense. I didn't break this engagement. You did. You called the tune, now you can pay the piper. You've been nothing but rude and cold since I returned, and your treatment of your mother was atrocious. You owe her an apology for your unkind words, and you broke her vase and didn't even have the decency to say you were sorry."

"My mother's vase?" His head tilted and his eyebrows rose. Then his face hardened once more. "When you receive your payout from the lawsuit, you can buy her a new one."

His voice flicked at her, and she burned to grab his shoulders and shake some sense into him, to make him realize how much he was hurting all of them, how much he was hurting himself. "Stop being so difficult. I don't want the money. I only want to marry you. I love you, David, and I know you love me. Why must you be so blind?"

He froze, his face going white at her words.

She wanted to call them back, but it was too late.

A ripple went through his body, as if she had struck him.

Her apology was halfway up her throat when she touched his arm.

But he stiffened and thrust her hand aside. "*My dear. . .*"

She winced at the endearment he used to say with such tenderness.

"You claim you still want to marry me? You say you'll sue me if I don't capitulate? Well, if nothing else will please you, and since you have the support of my entire family, then I will marry you and leave you to suffer the consequences brought about by your rash actions."

The fight rushed back into Karen, and she stepped up onto the riser beside him. "Don't toy with me, David. If this is some kind of joke to get me to withdraw the lawsuit, I'm warning you, I won't be trifled with."

"You are warning me?" His hand gripped the banister so hard his arm shook. "You are the one who is in trouble, lady." He grabbed her by the shoulders, shifting one hand to her chin. He kissed her, fierce and quick. It was over before she could react. "You have your wish, *my dear*. We'll be wed tomorrow afternoon, and I expect this lawsuit to be dropped by the following day." He turned and walked up the stairs every bit as if he saw each one, seemingly in too much of a temper to be tentative.

Karen sank down onto the steps and stared after him, incredulous, her trembling fingers raised to touch her lips, still tingling from his kiss. She remained staring up toward the landing until a door slammed on the second floor. Her bludgeoned mind could hardly take in what had happened. At a noise below her, she turned.

Sam, Jesse, and Matilda crowded in the parlor doorway. Sam rubbed his cheek. "At least Dave's out of his doldrums now."

❧

"What made you change your mind?" Sam plopped into the chair beside the bed and propped his boots on the comforter, making the mattress lurch.

David tucked the fingers of his good hand behind his head and pressed back into the pillow. "General idiocy? Or maybe I thought it would be less expensive to marry her than to go through with that lawsuit."

"Or maybe it's what you want deep down in your heart? You said you still love her."

The memory of Karen's lips under his, even though he'd kissed her in anger, seared David through. He loved her and he wanted her. His abdomen trembled. He knew he was using the lawsuit as an excuse to push past his fears and marry her. But what about later? What about when everything fell apart? "Why did you come up here, Sam?"

"I guess I wanted to make sure...I don't know. You know I wouldn't have pushed going through with this wedding if I wasn't one hundred percent sure you two still loved each other, right? If I didn't think it was the best thing for both of you, I never would've gone along with this breach of promise idea."

"How can you say it's for the best? I'm getting railroaded every which way from Sunday. I never would've thought Karen capable of coming up with an idea like this. It's so unlike her. More something Mother would do if she got the bit between her teeth."

Clearing his throat, Sam shifted his weight. "Well, truth be told, the idea did originate with Mother— Now, don't explode. She had the full backing of Father, and Karen just went along with it. You hit it square when you said Mother had the bit between her teeth. And her plan worked, too. You're out of the study, dressed, and things are moving forward for the wedding."

David fisted his hands and pounded his thighs. "You're joking, right? This was all Mother's idea?" And he'd fallen right into it. "I'm such an idiot."

"You aren't going to back out now, are you? Mother will kill me for opening my big mouth. Things are so close to working out between you and Karen. You won't let this upset the ore cart, will you?"

Impotent anger washed over David. He was no more than a rag doll. Without his sight, he couldn't even fight back, falling into the trap Mother had laid for him. And Karen, dancing to Mother's tune, though she didn't bear as much blame since she hadn't known his mother as long as he had. "I won't back out now. I'll give Karen the protection of my name, and she'll be provided for, but don't be fooled into thinking this is some sort of happily-ever-after. Eventually, she'll regret marrying me and she'll leave, or she'll stay and be miserable. And you and Mother and Father will have to live with knowing you pushed us both into this."

Sam tapped him on the leg. "You know, time's going to prove you wrong. When you've been happily married for ten years and have half a dozen kids, I'm going to remind you of this little discussion."

"Stop kidding around. Time isn't going to change the fact that I'm helplessly blind and no fit husband for any woman. This is a legal move, nothing more."

His brother moved to the door. "I'll expect you to name at least one of those kids Sam. See you in the morning, bridegroom."

Chapter 6

I don't think I can do this." Karen drew a deep breath, then several more. The bouquet of flowers from the conservatory trembled in her hands. Jesse leaned down to whisper in her ear. "Don't let my son's sour face fool you. Deep down, he's getting what he wants. Believe it. David loves you and needs you. This is for the best."

She pressed her free hand against the hummingbirds bombarding her stomach.

With little ceremony, Jesse led her into the parlor. Sam stood beside David and ran his finger around his collar as if he was the one getting married. Dear Pastor Van Dyke, his suit rumpled and his white hair running amok, held his Bible before him like a shield. Matilda smiled and nodded encouragement, and beside her, David's cousin Marcus stood. He didn't meet her gaze, and he checked his watch as if he'd rather be anywhere else.

Marcus. He had been one of the first people she'd met when she first got her job at the registry office. She lost count of the times he'd asked her permission to call. Though he was nice enough, she just wasn't interested, especially after meeting David.

She glanced at her soon-to-be husband. He looked like he might try to beat Marcus to the door in a footrace. She blinked back tears. *You're doing the right thing, even if he doesn't realize it right now. Once he learns that your love for him hasn't changed, he'll feel safe showing his love to you. Rome wasn't built in a day, and neither will his confidence return overnight.*

Jesse put her hand into David's, and the ceremony began.

David didn't falter in his vows, though his voice lacked enthusiasm. She repeated her promises, squeezing his hand when she vowed to love, honor, and obey him until death parted them. He gave no indication he felt it.

Pastor Van Dyke pronounced them man and wife. "You may kiss your bride."

Air crowded into her throat. David fumbled for a moment, placed his hand on the side of her face, then kissed her cheek as if she was his mother. She blinked, and the chill that blew through her lingered.

He signed the marriage certificate, his name scrawling off to the side like a primer student's. Karen wrote her name beneath his, swamped with misgivings and doubt one moment, sure she was doing the right thing the next.

Marcus shook David's hand and patted Karen on the shoulder then scooted out the door like his tail was on fire. Karen couldn't blame him, what with David acting like he was taking part in his own execution.

Only once during the wedding breakfast did she catch a glimpse of the David she knew hidden beneath the wounded exterior. Buckford set David's plate before him and leaned down to whisper something Karen didn't catch.

The grim expression cemented on David's face all morning softened, and a smile relaxed his lips. He blew out an easy sigh. "Thank you, Buckford. Thank you for understanding and not judging."

The older man patted David on the shoulder and cast a glance at Karen. If she didn't know better, she'd think Buckford was pleading for understanding himself. She lifted her brows, but he shook his head and returned to the kitchen.

Jesse rose when it came time to serve the wedding cake. "A toast to Karen and David."

Karen lifted her glass of punch. Would David take part? A trapped breath escaped her chest when he felt for his glass and held it before himself.

"Karen, you are a gracious and lovely addition, and Matilda and I welcome you as the daughter we never had. We know that things don't always work out according to our plans, but they always work out according to God's plan and for our good." He smiled and nodded several times, his eyes suspiciously bright. "David, you've had a bumpy road this past little while, but with Karen by your side, I foresee things smoothing out for you. If I didn't know how much you love each other, I would've suggested waiting for this union, but if ever two people were meant to be together, it's you. I wish you all the happiness you deserve." He raised his glass. "To Karen and David."

Matilda and Sam echoed his words. "Karen and David."

Karen pressed her glass to her lips and took a deep drink, all the while watching David over the rim. He lifted his punch and took a sip, his face thoughtful. Was he softening?

The family scattered as soon as they could decently do so, leaving Karen and David alone together for the first time all day.

She folded her napkin into a square and laid it beside her plate.

"So, what's your next move, Mrs. Mackenzie?"

"I was just going to ask you the same thing. Where do we go from here?"

"You're not already regretting your decision, are you?"

"Of course not. It would be natural for me to ask what your plans are for the near future."

"How appropriate, because I do have plans. Buckford is upstairs packing my things. I'm headed to Denver to take up residence in the town house. Certain information has come to my knowledge that makes it prudent I separate myself from my family for the time being, my mother in particular. The train departs in two hours."

"You're leaving?" She gripped the napkin, crumpling the precise folds she'd just created. "What about me?"

He rubbed his hand down his face and tested his temple with his fingertips. The bruise had faded to a pale yellowish green, and he didn't wince as he probed. "I can't very well travel alone, now can I?" His lips twisted. "I can't do much of anything alone anymore. You can come along and get a taste of what it means to be married to someone in my condition."

"Why leave your family? And why your mother in particular? I would think you'd prefer to stay here where everything is familiar."

"Suffice it to say, I've had enough of my family pushing me around. Mother can't help herself, and I'd rather you were away from her influence as well. At least if we're in Denver, she won't be dreaming up any wild notions like having her own son sued."

Karen stared at her plate. "You know about that?"

"I know about a lot of things. You've gotten your way about the wedding, you and my mother, but that's as far as I'm willing to go. We're leaving in two hours, so if you're coming, you'd best gather your things."

She swallowed and took a staggering breath. Denver. Perhaps it wasn't such a bad idea. They could be alone, just the two of them in the family's town house. Maybe then some of the barriers to their happiness could begin to come down.

ə

Karen boarded the railcar first, with David following, his hand on her shoulder.

Jesse helped the porter with their bags and hovered in the doorway. "Wallace said to congratulate you on the wedding, and that he's happy he could provide the private railcar for you, especially on such short notice."

Karen stood on tiptoe and kissed her father-in-law's cheek. "Thank him for us. I've never traveled in such luxury before. And thank you for all you and Matilda have done. I'll wire you when we reach Denver, and I'll write every chance I get."

"Be sure you do." Jesse hugged her, his voice gruff. The door slammed in his wake, and Karen stooped to look out the window at his tall frame striding across the platform.

"Alone at last." She unpinned her hat and set it on the table. "It will be nice not to be interrupted for a while. Here, there's a chair just to your right."

David shrugged off her hand and found the back of the chair himself. He removed his overcoat and hat, and once seated, leaned his head back. "We won't be in to Denver until well after dark. I didn't sleep well last night. I'm going to nap." With that he closed his eyes, shutting her out.

She contemplated the transom windows in the high point of the roof. Every time she thought she might have found a way past the armor and walls he'd erected, he cut her off. She dropped onto a velvet upholstered davenport, and her hand fell on the *Godey's Lady's Book* Matilda had given her. Her mother-in-law had written a letter of introduction to her dressmaker in Denver and instructed Karen to purchase a trousseau and spare no expense. Karen leafed through the pages, but her mind hopped from one thought to another so she couldn't concentrate. Finally she put the book aside to contemplate her husband.

She studied his features, loving each plane and angle of his face. In sleep, his face looked younger, less careworn, relaxed. He had loosened his collar and tie. His watch and fob glinted in the lamplight from the wall sconce.

Jesse had taken the crystal from the watch so David could feel the hands and know the time. His entire family had worked hard to show him they cared, that they loved him and wanted to help him, and yet he'd repelled them at every turn.

"Oh, David," she whispered, "where do we go from here? The more I try to fix what's between us, the more snarled things become."

Conviction whispered through her soul, forcing her to own up to what she hadn't wanted to face. She'd rushed into this marriage, scheming and plotting instead of praying and waiting. Now they were married, and there could be no turning back.

Lord, please forgive me. I have been selfish and willful. Instead of asking for Your will and direction, I rushed ahead, grasping for what I wanted, taking it without waiting for You to give it to me. I'm like Jacob in the Old Testament, conniving to get the blessing rather than waiting for You to give it to me. How can a marriage based upon a scheming plot ever be happy? How can love grow, or how can we glorify You? I am broken, Lord. I beg Your forgiveness and ask You to show me Your will. Help me to love David. Help me to show him Your love.

She wiped at the tears on her cheeks and moved to the desk in the corner. A quick check of the drawer revealed stationery and pen and ink.

Dearest Aunt Hattie,
There is so much I need to tell you, that I feel a letter can hardly hold it. The first thing you must know is that I am now married.

Karen tried to explain about the accident and David's blindness and thus the quick and quiet wedding. As she wrote, she could almost feel her aunt's arms encircling her. What wouldn't she give to be able to see her aunt now, to petition her for advice?

Hattie had been Karen's lifeline, her only family after her father passed away. Hattie, who had accompanied her brother to the mountains to help him raise his daughter, who had waited until Karen was grown before moving back to Kansas City, her much-loved and much-missed hometown. Perhaps, if Hattie was fully recovered from her illness and back to full strength, she could come to visit them. Maybe for the Christmas holiday.

When David awakened some time later, Karen knew a measure of peace, though she was no closer to knowing how to reach her husband. "Did you have a good nap?"

He rubbed his hands over his face and rolled his shoulders. "Have I slept long?" He reached into his vest pocket and retrieved his watch, his fingers whispering across the face.

"Almost two hours. Are you hungry? A porter brought a tray, but you were sleeping so soundly I didn't wake you."

"I'm not hungry."

"You hardly ate anything at the wedding breakfast. You need something. There's chicken and biscuits and some apple pie." She lifted the cover on a plate. "I had some. It's really good."

"I told you I'm not hungry. Stop hovering."

She replaced the lid and tugged at her lower lip, considering him. "I believe I'll excuse myself for a while. If you change your mind, the tray is on the table beside you. I'll just be down the hall, so if you need me, call out."

"I'm quite capable of sitting here alone without your help, Karen."

Her steps swayed with the movement of the train, and she kept her hand on the wainscoting as she edged down the narrow passageway. She passed a bedroom where a double bed took up almost all the space then another small compartment with two chairs facing one another and a bed folded up into the curve of the ceiling. Beyond that a tiny galley and a washroom.

She splashed water on her face and patted it dry, then took pains to re-pin her hair. When she'd wasted nearly ten minutes, she made her way back to the salon.

He'd eaten at least a little, confirming her suspicion that his proposed lack of hunger was a ruse to avoid eating in front of her. A few biscuit crumbs dotted his vest, but his face was clean.

"This is the most beautiful railcar I've ever been in. There are green velvet drapes and stained-glass transoms overhead. The woodwork—I'm not sure what kind—is stained a honey gold. And the chairs and davenport are a deep blue. There's a patterned carpet on the floor in greens and blues and golds that harmonizes everything. There's the most cunning little bathroom about four doors along the passage. Though the tub is so small I imagine you'd have to step outside to change your mind."

His hand caressed the armrest of his chair, and his shoe moved slightly, as if picturing in his mind all she said and testing it for himself.

Because he remained silent, she found the courage to continue describing things. "I'm wearing a dark burgundy dress. It has a high-standing lace collar and white cuffs. The skirt is full, probably too full for traveling, but I wore it because you once told me you liked it." She picked up the catalog. "Your mother told me to order some new clothes for the winter season while we're in Denver."

"I'd rather not talk about my mother right now." He stretched his legs out and laced his fingers across his vest. His brows puckered and he brushed the fabric, scattering the few crumbs onto the floor. "I have no idea what I'm wearing. I merely put on what Buckford laid out."

This glimpse into his new dark world set up an ache in her heart. She tried to keep her voice matter-of-fact. "You are wearing gray trousers, a white shirt, and a black silk vest." Her gaze traveled over him, assessing and describing. "Your face is thinner now, and your hair is a bit longer. Only a trace of bruising remains on your temple."

"No one has bothered to describe things for me as you have just done."

Fearful of saying the wrong thing, she tried to put into words what he needed to hear. "Perhaps they didn't know how best to help you. Your family loves you, David. They would do anything for you. They just need to know what." She held her breath for his reaction.

Before he could answer, the train began to slow. A shutter fell over his face, cutting off whatever he had been going to say. His lips formed into a taut line.

She began gathering things and placed David's hat and coat in his hands. "I'll see to a cab and getting our luggage aboard," she said. "Do you want to wait here or in the station?"

"I'll wait here."

A heavy weight sat on her shoulders. He'd been relaxed, almost as if he enjoyed her company, and then he'd reverted to the hurting man hunkering in his shell.

She stepped from the train and scanned the platform. A row of cabs stood lined up at the end of the depot in spite of the late hour. She hailed a driver, and when he'd trotted over to her, beckoned him to retrieve the bags. The conductor walked by, and she gave him the directions Jesse had given her about seeing to parking the private railcar in a siding. Then she turned to get David.

He stood on the railcar platform, hat on his head just so, his coat buttoned. He held the handrail and eased his way down the steps.

She walked over to him and, instead of taking his arm, slipped her hand into the crook of his elbow as she would have if he could see. "This way," she whispered, guiding without being too obvious, she hoped.

≈

David mocked himself for his uselessness when the cabbie asked Karen for the destination. Shame licked at him that Karen had to see to everything—the cab, the luggage, and the instructions for siding the private car.

Her hand came to rest on his arm, and her body moved against him as she turned in her seat. "David, I don't know the house address."

Realizing now just how much he had disrupted her life, yanking her out of all that was familiar, marrying her in haste, tying her to a blind man who couldn't even walk from the train to a cab alone, he hated himself. He gave the address and sank back into the corner of the cab, inching away from her to cocoon himself in solitude.

The horse's hooves clopped on the hard-packed dirt street. A hurdy-gurdy's tinny melody washed over them as they passed a dance hall, and a tinge of smoke hung in the air. Somewhere someone was cooking cabbage. He tried to envision just where in the city they were and surprised himself when the cab turned when he thought it should. The hooves plopping changed to a clatter as they crossed a wooden bridge. Then the cab rocked to a stop.

"There's a light burning in one of the lower floor windows."

He noticed the relief in her voice. "Father said he sent a telegram to Mrs. Webber to inform her of our arrival."

"Mrs. Webber?"

"The housekeeper." He realized anew how little he'd prepared her for this abrupt uprooting. The house they had planned to build in Martin City this spring would forever stay unbuilt. How could he orchestrate the building when he couldn't see? Yet another piece of his future to throw into the bottom drawer of his mind to molder and decay.

The doorknob rattled. "Is that you, Mr. Mackenzie? Bless me, but come away in. The night's too damp to be standing on the doorstep. And this must be your lovely bride. You could've knocked me down with a gesture when I got your father's telegram."

He pictured the housekeeper as he'd last seen her, gray haired, deep bosomed, motherly, and chatty. "Good evening, Mrs. Webber." His hand hit the iron railing, and he made his way up the steps.

She latched on to his arm and tugged him into the house.

The sounds of footsteps on the walk and the thunk of bags hitting the parquet floor informed him that the baggage had been deposited. Coins clinked, and the cabbie muttered, "Thank ya, ma'am."

Once more his wife had to do tasks that should be his, leaving him sidelined like a toddler in a world of adults.

Karen sighed, as if grateful to have arrived, and the fabric of her dress rustled. He pictured her removing her hat and gloves.

Mrs. Webber's familiar lemon verbena scent surrounded him as she bustled past. "I'll take the bags upstairs." The housekeeper patted his arm again, and he just refrained from brushing her away. "Here you go, missus. You take the lamp and I'll follow you up."

Karen linked her arm through David's. The faint odor of burning kerosene reached him. She stopped him when they reached the upstairs hall and directed him aside.

Mrs. Webber lumbered by with the baggage and deposited it on the carpet.

"Thank you, Mrs. Webber. That's all for tonight."

"Very good, sir. I'll see you in the morning. Sleep well." The housekeeper chortled and coughed, then padded down the stairs humming Mendelssohn's "Wedding March."

Karen's heart lodged somewhere in her throat and beat painfully, making it hard to draw a controlled breath. Her wedding night. She set the lamp on the bureau beside the door and stooped to move the bags so David wouldn't trip on them. "What a lovely room." Did her voice sound as nervous as she felt? "I suppose we can leave most of the unpacking for the morning, don't you?" She crossed to close the navy velvet drapes.

David stood in the doorway. "You can leave my things." He leaned his shoulder on the doorjamb. "Your room is next door. The water closet and bath are across the hall."

She looked at him over her shoulder, her hands gripping the fabric. "My room? But, I thought I would sleep in here. After all, we did get married today."

"That's right. I married you. But this will be a marriage in name only. I have no intention of consummating our union. When the time comes that you realize your mistake in marrying me, you can apply for an annulment."

The air rushed out of her lungs and her head spun. An annulment? "When are you going to understand that I have no intention of leaving you? Did you not hear me today? I promised to love, honor, and obey you until death parted us."

"I heard your promise. Now obey me and take your things to the next room. I'm tired and I'd like to go to bed. It's been a long day." He stepped farther into the room and waited.

Numb at this turn of events, Karen gathered her valise and straightened. "David, can't we talk about this?"

"This is not a matter for discussion. Go to bed."

She gathered the lamp and stepped into the hall. He closed the door behind her, shutting her out as effectively as putting out a cat for the night. The final humiliation came when he turned the key in the lock.

Tears blurred the flame in the lamp she held and smudged the shadowy outline of the carpet runner and the doorways that gaped open like eyeless sockets along the hallway. She went into the bedroom David said was hers and placed the lamp on the dressing table. With chilly fingers she turned up the wick. The furnishings and décor matched the master bedroom exactly.

Her feet sank into the carpet when she crossed to the bed. Cold satin pillowed her body as she lay back across the coverlet. Rejected and humiliated, she tried to make sense of why he would do this to her. Was he punishing her for pushing him into this marriage? And why mention an annulment?

The sobs burning in her throat clamored for release and she gave in, rolling to her side, curling into a ball, and letting go. Nothing had been right between them in such a long time, and now everything was very, very wrong. She had won a victory in forcing him to go through with the wedding, but it was a Pyrrhic victory, indeed.

❧

David rolled over and shucked the blankets twisted about his legs. Karen's sobs had quieted, but that didn't make him feel less a heel. In a moment of weakness he'd let himself be goaded into this marriage against his better judgment. Now he was stuck.

He couldn't, *wouldn't* be her husband in every sense of the word. The possible consequences were too great. Not only might he father a child who might grow to despise his crippled parent, but David knew he would not be able to get that close to Karen, to love her in that way, and then survive when she left him. Better not to give her the chance to hurt him that utterly. Better to keep her at arm's length.

His face flamed at the thought of how inept his attempts at loving would be. He couldn't have borne it if she'd laughed at him or, even worse, pitied his attempts. He would not take that chance, no matter how much he loved her.

She said she loved him right now, but what about later? What about when reality didn't meet up with her fairy-tale expectations and she realized she'd made a mistake? What about when she realized how hard life would be with a cripple who couldn't do the simplest tasks for himself anymore?

His profession was lost to him. Every last shred of who he was and why he existed had vanished. He was dead weight, contributing nothing to the marriage but his name and family fortune. How could he be a husband to her? How could he be the leader in his home, the head of his household?

Chapter 7

Light footsteps sounded on the stairs.

The fist of anxiety resting under David's breastbone since Karen left the house early that morning loosened a bit. He hated the idea of his wife roaming the streets of Denver alone, but what could he have done? He was in no position to stop her, nor did he relish the idea of trailing after her through the city as if she were the governess and he the charge to be watched over. At least she'd had the sense to take the carriage.

Fingers tapped on the door.

"Come in." He straightened in his chair and crossed his legs, lacing his fingers in his lap.

When she entered, he schooled his features to appear disinterested and calm. Then her perfume assailed him—light, sweet, beautiful. Just like Karen.

He swallowed. "You were gone a long time."

"Yes, I had lots to do."

"Shopping, I suppose."

"No, actually, I didn't do a bit of shopping, though that's on the list for tomorrow." The fabric of her dress whispered, and her footsteps sounded on the rug.

"What are you doing? Are you pacing?"

"I'm making the bed and tidying your clothes. You didn't go downstairs today, and you didn't let Mrs. Webber in, so the room could use a little looking after." The bedcovers rustled and pillows thumped. The armoire door opened, and the latches on his cases jingled. "You didn't unpack last night, so I'll help you while we talk."

"You sound cheerful." He fisted his hands. Why did it bother him that she did these simple things for him, things the housekeeper would've done?

A drawer slid open. "I am, though I'm tired clear through. I didn't sleep well last night, and I had to go clear across town today."

"What for?" He turned his face toward the sounds of her movement. "And will you stop fussing with my belongings?"

She laughed, and a shaft of pain sliced through him at the musical sound. "Actually, I'm nervous, and I hoped by straightening the room I could buy myself some time to gather my courage before the vials of your wrath fell upon me again."

Though she kept her tone light, he sensed her worry. He timed the sound of her movement, and when she passed close, he reached for her, grasping her wrist. Though a sense of dread at her words formed in his chest, guilt pushed to the forefront of his mind. He didn't want Karen afraid of him, no matter what had happened. "What did you do?"

Her arm twitched, and he realized she had taken a deep breath. "First, I had a chat with Mrs. Webber, and she mentioned the new school for the blind they've just built across town. That's when it hit me. They would be a wealth of information for us. I went straight to the school to find a tutor. A tutor can help us in so many ways. We can make the house easier to navigate and devise some organizational tactics for your wardrobe and office. So many things to make all of this better." Her words rushed out, as if once she started, she wanted to finish without giving him a chance to interrupt.

A protest made it as far as his teeth. He didn't need a tutor. Accepting a tutor meant accepting his blindness. Though the rational part of him knew his blindness was permanent, an unreasoning, fearful part of his heart held on to a shred of hope that this hadn't really happened, that he would wake up one morning and it would all be a bad night that evaporated into a glorious dawn. He would see colors and movement, light and life, and not be shackled in darkness.

"David? Did you hear me?" She knelt before him and placed her hands on his knees.

The warmth of her palms through his pants legs seared him, reminding him of the closeness they had once shared. He shifted and shook his head. "You had no right to interfere this way. A tutor won't change anything. I refuse to have a stranger in the house staring at me and pitying me."

A giggle escaped her lips, making her sound very young. "David, I can guarantee Rex Collison will not stare. He's blind, too."

His thoughts tumbled like water through a sluice. Accepting yet more help, acknowledging again his need for aid, his inability to do the things he used to do. Every moment since he realized he was blind seemed to be proving he was no longer a man.

After an eternity of silence she ventured, "Will you meet Mr. Collison? He's waiting in the parlor. I know he can make things better for you."

"Do you think this will change anything? There is no way you can make this 'all better.' A sightless tutor. A true case of the blind leading the blind. Why can't you leave it alone?" Why couldn't she grasp the fact that his blindness meant the death of her hopes for their future as well? The man she thought to marry, the strong, protecting, professional man she'd fallen in love with didn't exist anymore. That man had died in the bottom of a mine.

She removed her hands, and he derided himself for the feeling of loss her action brought. "David, you have nothing to lose. Just as being blind won't go away, neither will I go away. I won't stop trying to help you. Where is your faith? Where is your courage?"

"When you've walked a mile in my darkness, Karen, perhaps you will have the right to speak to me in such a manner. You know nothing of what it is like to be blind."

"No, I don't know, but Rex does. I should think you'd be willing to at least speak with him."

He could picture her, crossing her arms, her blue eyes, fringed with dark lashes, studying him. The late afternoon sun would caress her hair and a light flush would ride her cheekbones. His feelings for her, carefully leashed, prodded him to acquiesce. "Very well, I will meet him, since nothing else will please you. But remember this. . .I never asked for a tutor. If I so choose, I'll have him out of here before dinner."

She took his arm. "I think you'll like him. He's nearly your age, I would think, and very smart."

"You don't have to sell him to me. I reserve the right to make my own judgment." They navigated the staircase, and David took pains to count the number of steps. Would the shame and regret of his limitations ever dull? His heart rate picked up when they entered the parlor. Hard enough to greet friends and family. Strangers were another ordeal altogether.

"David, this is Rex Collison. Rex, I'm sorry we kept you waiting. I hope Mrs. Webber made you comfortable."

She led David across the room in the area of the fireplace. He could detect the smell of the fire and, when he moved his face to the left, the smell of coffee. "Pleased to meet you."

Something bumped his arm, and he instinctively grasped Collison's hand and shook it.

"I'll leave you to your discussion." Karen squeezed his elbow. "If you'll take a seat, I'll pour some coffee for you and go consult Mrs. Webber about dinner. I hope you'll stay, Rex."

"Thank you. I'd like that."

Her footsteps retreated, leaving them alone.

"Your wife tells me your blindness is recent."

David lifted his cup to his lips and breathed in the warm aroma. "That's right. About five weeks now."

"I hope you took the news better than I did when it happened to me." Rueful amusement tinged Collison's voice. "I was a trial to my family for half a year or more."

David said nothing. Trial he might've been the last month or so, but he wouldn't discuss it with a stranger.

Rex tried again. "I understand you're an engineer."

"Was. I *was*. I'm nothing now."

"On the contrary. You're still an engineer with several years of experience to call upon. There is no reason, with some adaptation to your routine and with a little help from an assistant, why you should cease your work. Your wife told me you have a very capable assistant to call upon."

David set his cup down with more force than he intended, splashing hot liquid onto his hand. "Excuse me, Mr. Collison, but do you have any experience working in a mine? An engineer has to be able to read, to write, to calculate loads, design square sets, gauge the quality of the stope. I cannot work without my eyes."

"In time, you will be able to read Braille and to write in Braille and in script. Your brain wasn't affected by the explosion, only your eyesight. With a competent assistant, your career need not be halted."

For one moment he allowed himself to hope, to believe things might return to the way they had been, but the foolishness of those thoughts crashed down on him. Reality was darkness. Reality was the need to rely on others to help him because he couldn't help himself. Reality was that even before the accident he'd been a bad engineer. Otherwise, the mine never would've caved in. Shame licked through him like greedy tongues of fire, incinerating hope and devouring possibilities.

"My career is dead, and there's nothing I can do about it." He rested against the antimacassar, wishing he could stop the jangling in his head. Everything he had once identified himself as had been stripped from him, leaving him nothing to hold on to. Had he somehow angered God and earned this judgment? Did God even know or care?

"You won't know what you can do until you try. Think of how the children at the school will admire you and seek to be like you when you prove that even without your sight you are a successful engineer. This will show them there is nothing they might not accomplish if they just try." Collison's chair creaked, as if leaning forward in his zeal to convince David. "You have advantages that many sightless persons do not have. You have the love and support of your family, especially your wife, and you have ample resources at your command. You have a career waiting for you if you have the courage to pick it up again."

David gripped the arms of his chair so hard his hands shook. "I never asked to be a role model."

"You may think I don't understand what you're going through, but I do.

Before I became a teacher for the blind, I had just graduated from college. The ink wasn't even dry on my diploma when I fell ill. When the doctors told me I would never see again, I thought it meant saying good-bye to my dreams of teaching." He chuckled. "I never did become the college history professor I wanted to be, but now, looking back, I wouldn't exchange my students at the academy for any cap and gown. God took my dreams and, through a refining fire, made them into something that would glorify Him."

Hot bile rose in David's throat. How much better would it have been if God had seen fit to merely take his life instead of taking his sight? Refining fire. He swallowed, hard. "I think we're finished here for the day." He stalked out of the room and up the stairs, and only when he reached his room and closed the door did he realize he hadn't counted the steps across the foyer or up the staircase.

&

Karen tipped her head back and blinked to stem the tears blurring her vision. She'd been silly to hang so much hope on the meeting between David and Rex. They had so much in common, and yet David hadn't let Rex past the walls.

She took a firm grip on her emotions and entered the parlor. "Rex"—she sat opposite him—"I'm sorry the interview didn't go well."

He placed his cup on the table at his elbow. A patient smile played around his lips. "I thought it went very well."

"He stormed out like his coattails were on fire. Didn't you hear his door slam?" She smoothed her skirts, then crumpled them again by crunching her hands into the fabric.

"He's dealing with a lot of emotions right now. Anger, bitterness, fear. Overwhelming fear." Rex steepled his fingers under his chin.

"That breaks my heart. David has always been so confident, so sure of himself and his abilities. He had his life planned out, and up until now, his life has gone as he planned."

"That probably makes the situation harder for him to swallow. He's afraid he won't be man enough to face his new circumstances."

"He won't even try, and I can't seem to make him."

Rex inclined his head. "My dear, I hope you'll forgive the familiarity, but I fear you are as much the problem as the solution here."

"What?"

"If I were in David's shoes, I'd be scared stiff myself. According to your housekeeper, you are a strikingly beautiful woman. I'd venture to say you didn't lack for suitors before David claimed you as his fiancée."

Heat tingled in Karen's cheeks, but she didn't interrupt. She would need to speak to Mrs. Webber about chattering too much while serving guests their coffee.

"I can imagine David feels in his heart that he is no longer worthy of such a bride. You told me he tried to break the engagement and that only under pretext of a lawsuit did he go through with the ceremony. I suspect it was less the lawsuit than the fact that he couldn't bear the thought of your walking out of his life that made him marry you. I would suspect he is terrified you will wake up one day and realize you've made a mistake, that you regret marrying him."

"I would never." She spoke through stiff lips and clenched teeth, her hands fisted in her lap. "I love David, blind or not, though he's testing my patience to the limit."

Rex laughed, putting his hands up in surrender. "I believe you. I'm just trying to help you understand things from David's perspective. I think, in time, he'll come to trust that your love for him hasn't changed. It's the time before that will be difficult. You're going to need all your patience and wisdom to withstand the coming storm. I speak from experience, both as a man who was blinded as an adult and as a teacher who has encountered many a troubled student. Things are likely to get worse before they get better."

Karen rubbed her temples. "I can't imagine their getting worse. I barely know myself anymore. My feelings are all jumbled up. On the one hand I want to cry and comfort him and help him heal, and on the other I want to throw something and stomp my foot and scream at him for ruining what is supposed to be one of the best times of our lives. We've had no honeymoon, and the newlywed phase of our marriage has been less than cordial." Her voice cracked. A tear trickled down her cheek, and she scrubbed it away, mortified to have broken down in front of a guest, a man she barely knew.

Rex reached out a searching hand and awkwardly patted her arm. "I'm sorry. I will do all I can to help both of you, but you'll have to be patient. Nothing will change overnight. Much like he's done with me, David hasn't sent you away, so he must want you here. Cling to that hope and try not to brood. You'll feel better if you stay busy."

"What can I do?"

"There are several practical things we prescribe for all our students, and you can get started on those now—things like labeling his clothing and organizing his possessions. When I get back to the school, I'll talk things over with our headmaster, Mr. Standish, and together we'll come up with a plan."

He rose and his ever-ready smile encouraged her. "Don't worry. I've handled tough cases before. David didn't expressly forbid me to return tomorrow, so I'll be here in the morning. We'll continue his first lessons here at the house, but eventually, I'd like him to come to the school. The students would benefit from meeting him when he's gotten over the worst of things, and there are some resources there that would be helpful."

Chapter 8

Karen snipped her thread and ran her thumb over the bumps. She rechecked the notes Rex had given her, making sure the small French knots were in the right positions to represent the colors. Something else to cross off her list.

Along with reorganizing his wardrobe and toiletries, she and Mrs. Webber had removed nearly half the furnishings from the parlor. Though current fashion leaned toward dozens of occasional tables, tightly packed chairs and settees, and bric-a-brac on every surface, Karen had to admit she liked the sparse look to the room now. David had said nothing of the changes, but he moved with more confidence now that he didn't have to circumnavigate so many obstacles.

A Braille book sat on the desk across the parlor. David had yet to pick it up on his own, though he had allowed Rex to return every day this week for lessons. Karen rejoiced in this small success, but Rex's prediction that changes would come slowly was proving all too depressingly true. At the moment the pair was in the dining room, where they had spent the majority of the last two days.

Mrs. Webber appeared in the doorway. "Ma'am, there's a fellow here to see you, says he's the butler." A scowl marred the housekeeper's normally sunny face. She stepped back and revealed Buckford standing in the foyer. "I didn't know you'd hired a butler."

"Buckford." Karen rose, letting the shirt drop onto her sewing basket. "What are you doing here?" The sight of his familiar face, so comforting and bracing, caused tears to prick Karen's eyes. The older man had a box under one arm and a valise under the other. "Did you walk from the station?" Red suffused his nose and cheeks, and a wintry air perfumed his coat. "Did Mr. and Mrs. Mackenzie come with you?"

"Yes ma'am, I did walk, and no ma'am, the family is not with me. Mrs. Mackenzie thought I might be of some help to you. She sends her regards and this letter." He set his bag down and fished in his coat pocket.

"I can't wait to read it. You don't mind if I take a peek now, do you?" Karen tore the envelope open with eager fingers. She scanned the page, letting the comforting words seep into the lonely places in her heart.

Dear Karen,

I've had to resist boarding the train to Denver every day since you left, so great is my desire to come to you and to ascertain how you are coping. Since I know this wouldn't be prudent, I've done the next best thing and sent Buckford. He and David have always shared a close bond, and perhaps Buckford will be a comfort to you and a help.

I hope you've taken me at my word to acquire a new wardrobe for the winter. Bill everything to the Mackenzie accounts and spare no expense. There was no time to assemble a trousseau for you, so consider this a wedding gift.

I know you weren't keen on the idea of the lawsuit, and in retrospect perhaps it wasn't the best idea, but the truth is, I was at the end of my rope. I love my son, but he has inherited all my stubbornness and a fair dose of his father's as well. He had bested all my efforts, and I was not of a mind to let him continue in his current path of action. Though the end result, the wedding, was what I was after, having talked things over with Reverend Van Dyke, he has reminded me that the ends don't justify the means. If I pushed you beyond what you were comfortable with, I apologize. I can be quite headstrong, as you know. David gets that from me.

All I can advise with David is that you keep your generously loving heart open to him. With you working on the outside and God's Spirit working on the inside, his heart will heal. I knew such joy when you two first began courting because you loved David so much. That love and God's strength will bring you through.

Know that I am lifting you both up daily, even hourly, in prayer, and know that you can call upon us for anything you need.

Love,
Matilda

Warmth at her mother-in-law's thoughtfulness bathed Karen, and she looked up through watery eyes at Buckford. "I don't know how they'll get along without you in Martin City, but I can't tell you how glad I am that you're here." There were so many things that David wouldn't allow Karen to help him with but that Buckford could do without undue embarrassment to his employer.

"Mr. Sam sent this box of papers and ore samples and a letter for Mr. David." He picked up his satchel.

She nibbled her lower lip. "Mrs. Webber, show Buckford to the room at the end of the hall."

"Yes ma'am." The housekeeper's narrowed eyes continued to travel up and down Buckford's frame, sizing him up.

Buckford rejoined Karen in the parlor a few moments later. "How may I best assist you, ma'am?"

"David is in the dining room with his tutor, Rex Collison. The box you brought can go in the upstairs office. I don't think David should be bothered with anything from the mine right now. He's concentrating on his new studies."

"Very good, ma'am. Then perhaps it would be politic to go smooth Mrs. Webber's ruffled feathers. I'll reassure her that I have no intention of usurping her place here."

"Thank you, Buckford. You're very astute."

Karen packed her sewing basket, then took a moment to read again her mother-in-law's letter. *Love David generously.* If only he would let her. She took the precious pages upstairs, along with an armful of David's clothes.

When she came downstairs a short time later, David and Rex stood in the foyer.

Buckford appeared from the back of the house. "Good afternoon, sir."

"Buckford?" David's voice went high. His eyebrows arched, then tumbled. "What are you doing here?" He stuck his hand out, and Buckford clasped it.

"Your mother thought I might be of use to you."

"I'm glad you're here." The warmth in his tone reminded Karen of how much regard David had for Buckford. She quashed a bit of jealousy that her husband was more comfortable with his hired man than with his wife.

"Gentlemen"—she walked down the last few stairs—"I hope your lessons went well today." She slipped her hand into the crook of David's elbow.

A smile crossed Rex's face, but David stiffened as if she'd jabbed him in the ribs. When he didn't say anything, Rex offered, "Very well, thank you."

"Can you stay to dinner, Rex? We'd love to have you. Mrs. Webber's making her specialty, beef Wellington. It should be ready soon."

"I wish I could, but I'm expected back at the school. David, I'll be back tomorrow morning. I'll also expect a report of how tonight goes."

Her hand must've tightened, because David shifted. "Rex expects me to dine at the table tonight. I hope that meets with your approval."

"Really? That's wonderful." She shared a smile with Buckford. "I shall enjoy your company." She prayed that perhaps he might enjoy hers as well.

❧

Mrs. Webber announced dinner just as David closed the door on Rex's departure.

Karen tucked her hand into his arm once more, sending a jolt through him and making his heart hammer. As loath as he was to admit it, the idea of dinner with Karen brought a curious lightness to his chest, a faint echo of the way he'd felt when he first began courting her.

She waited beside him, her light perfume drifting around him. Her skirts rustled in a purely feminine sound. How he wished he could see her face, her hair in the candlelight, her graceful walk.

He took a deep breath. "Shall we go in?" He called down thankfulness upon Rex's head for making him practice seating a lady at the table, though he was sure Mrs. Webber had grown weary of the exercise before he'd finally mastered it. When Rex suggested Karen take part in the practice, David's reply had been curt and decisive. He might bumble in front of the housekeeper, but he would not appear a clumsy oaf in front of his wife.

"Thank you, David."

A thrust of pride shot through him at the surprise in her voice, and he exhaled a tight breath when he managed to push her chair in without mishap. He sat at her left hand and lightly fingered the silverware and goblet placement, trying to force his muscles to relax.

Mrs. Webber placed his plate in front of him. The china clinked as she rotated it to the correct position. "There you are. Ring when you want dessert."

He spread his napkin in his lap and picked up his knife and fork. *Small bites, slowly, main course at twelve, sides at four and eight. Let your fork hang over the plate for a count of three. Lean over.* Rex's instructions cycled through his head in a continuous loop. He held the fork lightly, focusing on the sensations coming from the tines to his fingers.

"I was so surprised when Buckford showed up." Karen's utensils clinked against her plate, and her sleeve whispered on the tablecloth.

David moved his fork to his mouth, pleased when nothing dripped down his chin. The flavor of beef and gravy burst on his tongue. "Good of Mother to send him."

Silence fell. When first courting, they had spent hours talking. Time had flown when they were together, and it had seemed they would never run out of things to say to one another. He'd wanted to know everything about her and tell her everything about himself. Now they sat like strangers. No. Worse than strangers. Strangers would at least make small talk.

His skin prickled and tightened. She watched him—he could feel her appraisal. How clumsy he must look to her, like a tentative toddler. His fork clattered to his plate, sending droplets of warm gravy across his face. When he scrambled to retrieve the fork, the heel of his hand hit his plate and dumped the contents into his lap.

"Oh no." Her chair shot back, and before he could move, wet cloth dabbed his face. "Hold still."

He writhed away from her, shoving the napkin aside. "Don't." In his effort to get away, he knocked her arm.

She gasped an instant before cold liquid bathed his chest. Something thumped on the carpet. "I'm so sorry." She mopped at his shirtfront. "I had my water glass in my hand to dampen my napkin and I dropped it."

He gritted his teeth, grabbed her wrists, and shoved his chair back. "Stop, Karen. I should've known better than to try this. I'm a clumsy fool and always will be." The warmth of her skin in his grasp, the heady aroma of her perfume swirling around him, the soft sound of her breathing all taunted him. "Why did you ever marry me? Can't you see this was all a mistake? I'm inept at even the simplest task. I'm not a man. I'm a liability." He stumbled against the table, rattling the china, and made his way out of the room.

ﻩ

Karen sank into her chair and put her elbows on the table. She rested her face in her hands, utter weariness cloaking her, pressing her shoulders down and squeezing her heart. Why did it seem that for every inch of hard-won progress David made, a stumbling block tripped him up and yanked him back toward a yawning chasm of despondence?

"Lord," she whispered, "I don't know what to do. I can't get close to him. He won't let me help him. The more I press, the faster he retreats." She swallowed against the spiky lump in her throat and took a staggering breath. She needed to find something positive, something to be thankful for, to gain some equilibrium. "Thank You for Rex. Thank You that David is at least willing to listen to him."

She sat quiet for a while, calming her heart, letting God's peace return. "Please, Lord, help me to be patient. Help me not to be jealous that David is turning to Rex or Buckford for help when he won't turn to me. Help me to rely on You for direction, and please, break down the barriers around his heart. Help him to forgive himself and to accept his blindness. Please help him to accept his marriage as well." Karen leaned back and put her hands in her lap. She blinked rapidly, bringing the plaster medallion on the ceiling into focus.

"Missus?" Mrs. Webber hovered in the doorway. "Should I bring in dessert?"

Karen pushed her plate back and rose. "I'm sorry, Mrs. Webber. The dinner was delicious, but I think we'll save dessert for tomorrow. If you could just clear away. David has retired for the night, and I think I will, too."

The housekeeper's eyes shone with sympathy as she took in the splattered tablecloth and the water glass on the floor. "The poor creature." She clucked, shook her head, and began stacking plates and cutlery.

Karen didn't know if "poor creature" meant her or David.

Chapter 9

"This is ludicrous." David slammed the book closed and tilted his head back against his chair. Nothing had gone right the entire week, not since his disastrous dinner with Karen.

"David, you just have to be patient." Rex's soothing tone rasped on David's nerves. "It will take time, but you're making progress."

"Don't patronize me. Braille is beyond me. I can't do this."

"I think what you really mean to say is you don't want to *have* to do this." Rex slapped the desk. "I think it's time someone told you a few home truths. You say to stop treating you like a child, but your actions are childish. You haven't accepted your blindness. You will never be free to learn until you accept the fact you are blind and destined to stay that way."

Rex rose, and the direction of his voice told David he was leaning over the desk. "Do you think you are the only one to ever go through something like this? Do you think you are the only one in this house who is suffering? Stop for just a moment and think how this is affecting someone else. I may not be able to see, but I'm not stupid. I haven't heard you say one kind or affectionate thing to your wife since I arrived in this house. You speak better to your servant or to me, a virtual stranger, than you do to the woman you married. You are so swamped with fear, you aren't just blind. You're emotionally paralyzed."

He wanted to squirm. Rex had no business hitting so close to the truth. "You know nothing of the situation, and I'll thank you to keep your nose out of it."

Rex gave a short bark of laughter, all traces of patience and understanding gone. "You think I don't know what you are going through? I wasn't born blind, David. I was a college graduate with dreams of becoming a teacher and eventually a professor of history. I had prospects in the academic field, a fiancée, a future all mapped out. Then, in the space of a few weeks' illness, I had nothing. My fiancée couldn't face marrying a blind man and fled. My teaching job ended before it got started, and for a while, I thought even God had abandoned me. I now know He was there all the time, watching over me, guiding me, healing my hurts. Though I couldn't see with my physical eyes, God brought new sight to my spiritual eyes. He had better things in store for me, and I would have missed them if not for the blindness."

"Better things?" Bitterness coated David's tongue. "How can blindness be better than sight? You lost your job, your girl, and your independence."

Rex's chair creaked and his voice moderated. "While I was busy making plans for my life, I never once considered if those plans were God's will or if I would be serving Him by being a college professor. I wanted the recognition and the status of teaching at a university someday. I was so full of my own plans and desires I left God completely out of the equation. God had a better plan for me. I lost a girl who wouldn't stick by me when I became blind. I'm just thankful I found it out before we were actually married. I'm now engaged to a wonderful, godly young woman I met at the academy. And before you say, 'Of course, one blind person marrying another. What else can you expect?' I'll tell you she's not blind. Her father, Mr. Standish, runs the school, and my Aimee loves God and loves me enough that my blindness doesn't matter to her a bit. As for losing my independence, isn't that what God wants most for us as His children? God doesn't want us to be independent. He wants us to be totally dependent on Him. Without Him, even men with perfect vision are blind."

David snorted his disbelief. "I prefer to think that God helps those who help themselves, and I can't very well help myself now, can I?"

"You realize that little homily isn't even in the Bible? When I met with your wife about taking this job, she said you were a Christian struggling with God over your blindness. It was one of the reasons I was willing to take this job. I thought I could help you, because I struggled, too."

David put his elbows on the desk and slid his fingers into his hair. "I don't want to talk about this anymore."

"I know you don't, but you can't continue as you are. I know how exhausting it can be running from God. You won't have any peace until you realize there is nowhere you can go to get away from Him. He will pursue you with His love to the ends of the earth or the depths of your despair. Give up on the bitterness and the running away, David, or it will consume you. It will ruin your relationship with God, your marriage, and your career."

"All of that is ruined already." His chest ached. "I have nothing left."

"I'll be the first to admit things won't ever be as they once were for you, but you're selling yourself short if you think you have nothing left to offer anyone."

David's heart smoldered. It was galling for a man of his education and accomplishments to be forced to begin his schooling over again like the smallest primary student. To learn his letters at his age. No matter how proficient he became at reading those exasperating bumps on the page, he would never be able to work in the mine office again. It was like a death to him, the loss of his career. He *was* an engineer. All his adult life he'd been identified by that term. He sought elusive ore, directing an army of miners to find hidden treasure. David Mackenzie was an engineer. Was... Was... Was...

Rex opened the book before him. "Shall we begin again?"

He sighed, placed his fingertips on the paper, and settled them along the top row. Before he could once again begin sounding out the words, the door opened.

She was home. He knew it was her before she even spoke. Every day this week his wife had gone shopping, leaving the house early, lunching uptown, and coming home in the late afternoon. A swirl of chilly air accompanied her entrance into the parlor, and the smell of snow vied with her perfume. He envisioned her shrugging out of her coat and tugging off her gloves.

David pushed back his chair and rose a fraction of a second after Rex's chair scraped the floor.

"Good afternoon, gentlemen. How are the lessons going?"

"I think we've done enough for the day. I'll be taking my leave." Rex closed his book. "David, we'll meet again tonight? I hope you'll consider carefully what we discussed this afternoon."

"Tonight?" Karen asked. "What's happening tonight, David?"

"There's a program at the school tonight, recitations and such. To raise funds, I gather. Rex could explain it better. In a weak moment I promised we'd attend."

"You're leaving the house? That's wonderful. We haven't had a night out in ages."

The excitement in her voice made David purse his lips. When they were courting, they'd attended every production at the Martin City opera house. Several times over the past few weeks, she'd asked him if he would like to go to the symphony or to a play. Each time he had declined, a fine sweat breaking on his skin at the thought of going out in public, having to meet new people he couldn't see. He could barely navigate his own house. How could he escort his wife to a public function? The only saving grace about tonight's affair was that it would take place at the blind school where most of the people wouldn't be gawking.

⁂

Karen gave her reflection a cheeky wink and scooped up her new cloak. For the first time in her month-old marriage, she and her husband would be doing something normal—going out for the evening.

Her heart tripped as lightly as her feet on the way down the stairs. She'd mulled over everything Rex had said about David's fears and why he was having such a difficult time adjusting to his blindness, putting it together with David's own comment about being a liability. She'd have to prove to him over time that she had no intention of leaving him and pray that as he studied and worked with Rex his confidence in his abilities would return. Until that day, she would take each hurdle as it came. As for tonight, she planned to enjoy herself.

David waited in the foyer. The sight of him in evening dress made her breath hitch. So handsome with his broad shoulders, fine features, and strong personality, no man had ever come close to him in her estimation. She bit her lip and steadied herself.

Be yourself. Act as you would if the accident had never happened.

"Good evening, David." Before she could talk herself out of it, she walked to his side, put her hand on his arm for balance, and rose on tiptoe to place a kiss on his cheek. "You look so handsome tonight. Would you help me with my cloak?" She handed it to him before he could refuse and turned her back.

He was still for a moment. Finally, he placed his hand on her shoulder, sending warm, golden arrows through her, and, only fumbling a little, settled the garment about her.

She tugged on her gloves and threaded her arm through his. "It's a beautiful night, and the stars are out." She waited for him to close the front door and escort her down the steps.

He kept one hand on the rail and hesitated with each step, but he got her to the curb without mishap.

She smiled. Much better than when they'd first arrived in Denver when he'd stood to the side and waited on her to guide him everywhere.

He handed her up into the carriage and settled in beside her. With a lurch, they were off.

"It's been so long since we had an outing. It feels nice to dress up and go somewhere together."

"It must be a bit boring for you, staying in every night." He ran his fingertips along the windowsill and down the side of the carriage.

"I miss my friends in Martin City, though your mother is so good about writing to me. I'm sure once word gets out that we've gone to one event, there will be invitations to parties and gatherings. We've already received one for a Christmas dinner and dance at the Windsor in a few weeks." The invitation sat on the mantel. She hadn't told him about it until now, hoping for some indication that he might be adjusting to his new circumstances before asking him if they could go.

"A trip to the blind school is one thing, a party at the Windsor something else altogether. I'm not going to mingle with Denver society to be stared at and gossiped about."

"Even if they did, wouldn't it be just a nine days' wonder? When they saw how you haven't really changed, that you're still the same handsome, intelligent man you always were, wouldn't they find something else to talk about?"

A chuckle escaped him, and for a moment she thought he might relent. "Flattery won't change my mind, Karen. I'm not opening myself up to their speculation. No parties."

She blew out a breath and tried not to be disappointed. "Then I'll have to make the most of tonight, then. I'm glad the dressmaker had my things finished so I could wear a new gown. A new dress always makes an evening special."

"I suspect my bank account will feel the weight of today's plunder."

The coach lamp hanging just outside the door outlined his profile in soft, gold light. A smile played around his lips, as if he didn't particularly mind the expense.

"Actually, my trousseau is a wedding gift from your parents. Wasn't that nice of them?" She took his hand and placed it on her sleeve. "Feel. It's indigo silk with beaded trim, and the cloak is black velvet." She picked up the edge of her cloak and brushed it across the backs of his fingers.

A curious softness came over his expression, and his eyes narrowed ever so slightly, as if concentrating. "I told the dressmaker that each dress needed to be of a different fabric. Moiré taffeta, linen, wool, brocade satin. . ."

"Why such variety?"

She swallowed, hoping he would understand. "If each dress has a different feel, then you'll know what I'm wearing without having to ask. I wanted each outfit to have a unique texture for you." A laugh at herself bubbled up. "I know men don't think about such things as what their wives wear, but it was something small I could do for you." She tucked her hand inside his.

As if he couldn't help it, his fingers closed around hers, nestling her hand in his like a bird.

Tears pricked her eyes as she studied his face, waiting, praying for some response.

He pressed his lips together and his throat lurched. "That was very thoughtful of you." The low, husky quality of his voice sent shivers up her spine. "Thank you."

The coach swung into the semicircular drive in front of the school. Karen couldn't help but hope that perhaps they'd turned a corner in their journey together.

Chapter 10

Different fabric for each dress? David marveled at her ingenuity, and her generosity humbled and shamed him. Would he, in her place, have been as thoughtful?

Her hand in his felt right, and he hadn't missed her subtle demands on him to behave as a gentleman regarding opening doors and helping with wraps. And he'd surprised himself by accomplishing those tasks without mishap.

He touched his cheek where he could still feel the brush of her lips and the whisper of her breath against his skin. The delicate scent of her perfume wrapped around him.

When the coach lurched to a halt, he almost bolted out the door. Remembering his manners, he stopped and held out his hand to help her.

When she stood beside him on the sidewalk, she tucked her hand into his elbow and gave him a squeeze. "I'm so glad Rex talked you into coming tonight."

Guilt pricked him. Karen was young and beautiful, full of life. She deserved to go to parties and plays, the opera or the symphony. He blew out a breath. Would her departure take place in stages? Would she start going to those places without him? Would he try to stop her?

"There are six stairs up to a stoop." Karen waited for him to take the first step. "The building is brick, three stories, and every window is lit. Very welcoming."

Piano music provided background to what sounded like a hundred different conversations. "How many people are here?" Apprehension feathered across his chest. He shrugged out of his coat when someone asked for it, then turned to help Karen with her wrap.

"Rex, good evening." Her voice held genuine warmth.

Rex introduced his fiancée. Aimee had a pleasant contralto voice that took on a special quality when she spoke to Rex. David recognized the proud and proprietary tone of Rex's voice.

Karen took David's arm. "We're in the foyer, and there are paper chains everywhere for decorations. The party is being held in a room to our left. It looks like it might be the school dining room. Chairs have been arranged in rows, and there must be about sixty adults here."

With subtle pressure, Karen directed him through the room. "We're following Rex and Aimee to where the headmaster and his wife are greeting guests."

Rex introduced everyone and directed them to the seats he'd reserved.

Mr. Standish had a firm handshake. "Good to meet you, David. Rex is treating you well, I hope?"

David forced himself to smile. "Better than I deserve, most likely. During this afternoon's lesson, I was prepared to hurl a book across the room, but he talked me out of it."

Standish steered him to a chair, talking all the while. "Ha, I can imagine. Do you know how many books I had to dodge when teaching Rex?"

David took the chair and eased himself into it. With half an ear he listened to Karen and Aimee chattering about dresses and the decorations. He tried to get a sense of the room, of the space, by listening. The ceiling must be high overhead, and he had a sense of space before him. Karen sat on one side, with Mr. Standish on the other.

"You're in the front row, David." Mr. Standish leaned in. "This room doubles as both dining room and assembly hall. With only two dozen students at the moment, there's plenty of room to grow."

With the way Standish could read people, he must be a good headmaster. David settled back and categorized the sounds and smells around him. Furniture polish, books, boiled potatoes, chalk, and soap. Laughter, conversation, the squeak of a chair as someone shifted his weight, a nervous giggle from a young person.

Rex's voice came from in front and above him, on the stage. "Good evening and welcome. Thank you all for coming to our evening of recitation."

The crowd stilled.

"Our first student tonight is Charles Barrow who will be reciting Psalm 139."

Polite applause rippled through the crowd, and Karen tucked her hand into his.

She'd done that several times this evening, and he had to admit he liked it, even while he reproached himself for those feelings. Each crack he allowed in his armor would only mean more pain when she left him.

"'O Lord, thou hast searched me, and known me.'"

The student must be about ten or so, his voice still pitched high. Had he been blind since birth? Would that be better or worse?

"'I will praise thee; for I am fearfully and wonderfully made: marvellous are thy works; and that my soul knoweth right well. My substance was not hid from thee, when I was made in secret, and curiously wrought in the lowest parts of the earth. Thine eyes did see my substance, yet being unperfect; and in thy book all my members were written, which in continuance were fashioned, when as yet there was none of them.'"

Fearfully and wonderfully made? Maybe once upon a time, but now, ruined as he was, David couldn't imagine those words pertaining to himself.

"'Whither shall I go from thy spirit? or whither shall I flee from thy presence? If I ascend up into heaven, thou art there: if I make my bed in hell, behold, thou art there. If I take the wings of the morning, and dwell in the uttermost parts of the sea; even there shall thy hand lead me, and thy right hand shall hold me.'"

David's neck muscles tightened and his throat constricted. How long had it been since he felt God's presence?

"'If I say, Surely the darkness shall cover me; even the night shall be light about me. Yea, the darkness hideth not from thee; but the night shineth as the day: the darkness and the light are both alike to thee.'"

The night shining as day? Dark and light might be the same to God, but everything was darkness to David now, as if he were imprisoned in the deepest mine shaft. God had stolen everything David treasured, then left him alone in the dark.

Karen's hand moved in his. He loosened his grip, only now aware of how hard he'd been squeezing her fingers. She rubbed small circles on the back of his hand.

"'Search me, O God, and know my heart: try me, and know my thoughts: And see if there be any wicked way in me, and lead me in the way everlasting.'"

David heard little of the rest of the recitations. His thoughts behaved like ball bearings dropped on a hard floor. He chased first one, then another, never able to line them up squarely.

What had gone wrong at the mine? What should he have done differently? Why had Karen married him when he was so obviously flawed? Would he ever master Braille, and what difference would it make if he did? Why was God so far away? Was his blindness a punishment from God for being so careless at the mine?

Not until Karen stirred beside him did he realize the program had ended. They filed out, her hand under his arm. He forced his face into a pleasant expression and let her steer him toward the side of the immense room.

She stood on tiptoe and whispered into his ear, "There's a donation table by the door." A tinge of doubt flavored her tone.

He pressed his lips together. Before leaving the town house he'd tucked his wallet into his inner coat pocket. Though it seemed strange, for now he couldn't tell a five-dollar bill from a fifty. He withdrew the leather wallet and handed it to her. "There are blank checks in there. Write one out for a hundred dollars."

"Thank you, David."

He could hear the smile in her voice and warmth spread through him. "They deserve it. Rex has been very patient with me."

The only awkward moment before their departure came when he had to sign the check. "They have a fountain pen. You'll do fine." She spread the slip for him and positioned his hand. "You've signed your name a thousand times."

The pen scratched on the paper.

She picked the check up, and it rustled as she waved it to dry the ink. "Perfect."

He declined the finger sandwiches and asked only for a half cup of punch to minimize what he could spill.

Karen stayed by his side, but he didn't sense she was hovering or afraid to leave him alone. It seemed she took every opportunity to touch him, smoothing his lapel, taking his arm, letting her fingers brush his.

Almost before he was ready, they were back in the carriage headed home.

Karen yawned and laid her head on his shoulder. "Thank you for taking me out tonight. I had a wonderful time. You seemed to enjoy yourself. Did you have a good time?"

"I did."

She laughed. "Don't sound so surprised. I can't believe how much scripture those children had memorized. Did you have a favorite?"

"The first one, I suppose."

"That was my favorite, too. Can you imagine? God knew everything about us before we were even born. There's nowhere we can hide from Him and nowhere that His love can't reach us." She sighed and rubbed her cheek against his topcoat. "I find that very comforting, don't you?"

What he found comforting was having her so close to him. In the close confines of the carriage, with the success of the evening behind them and with her head on his shoulder, he almost felt as if he were a whole man. The longings her touch had fired repeatedly throughout the evening overwhelmed him once more. He turned to her, took her face between his palms, and ran his thumb across her lips. Gardenias perfumed her hair, and the smooth, satin lining of her hood tickled the backs of his hands, reminding him of her thoughtful choice of wardrobe.

Her pulse thrummed along her neck, and her breath caught in a soft pant that made his heart thunder. Before he could stop himself, he lowered his lips to hers.

The kiss went straight to his head, familiar and unknown all at the same time. Softer than her velvet cloak, warmer than a fireside in winter, more comforting than an embrace, and more exciting than a runaway train. He was transported, carried out of his misery into a peaceful place where only they existed. He freed her lips and trailed feathery kisses along her jaw and temple, trying to catch his breath.

Then he opened his eyes, fully expecting to see her face, to see the love shining there.

Darkness.

Reality doused him like ice water. He eased back, swallowing, trying to moisten his suddenly dry mouth. His defenses had lowered for only a moment, and he'd been swept away. Doubts swamped him, and all the reasons he needed to keep her at arm's length surged back.

"David?" She leaned into him again and cupped his cheek.

He captured her hand and set it in her lap. "No. No more. You don't know what you're doing."

"I know that I love you. I know that we're married." She cupped his cheek again.

He reached up and took her hand, placing it in her lap once more. "No, Karen." He turned away from her and tried to gather his scattered wits. How would he survive when she left him? One kiss and he was undone.

Chapter 11

The carriage lurched to a halt, and Karen wiped her damp cheeks, gathering her cloak around her.

David helped her descend from the carriage but released her hand quickly.

The clock in the parlor chimed as they entered.

Buckford held the door, taking their outer wraps as they shed them. His keen eyes searched her face, and she gave him a rather watery smile and a small shrug. He pursed his mouth and leveled a stare at David, shaking his head.

"Sir, you have a visitor in the parlor. She insisted on waiting, though I told her you'd be quite late."

"A visitor? At this hour?" David stopped on the bottom stair, one hand on the newel post.

"A Mrs. Patrick Doolin. She said she'd come all the way from Martin City and had to see you tonight."

David flinched. His shoulders slumped, and he rubbed the back of his neck.

"David? Who is Mrs. Doolin? Do you know her?"

"We've met. Her husband used to work for Mackenzie Mining. He died in the cave-in."

The breath Karen took skidded in her throat. Still rocking from his kiss and being pushed away, she had no strength left for a visitor, especially one with a grievance against the Mackenzies. But what else could they do? "Thank you, Buckford. David, let's get this over with."

Buckford had stirred up the fire, and a tea tray sat on a low table beside the woman. Dressed in black from head to foot, her brown hair streaked with gray, she had a careworn and lined face.

"Mrs. Doolin? I'm Karen Mackenzie. I'm sorry you had to wait so long." Karen held out her hand.

Like a bird, the woman hopped out of the chair and bobbed her head. "I'm the one who should be apologizing, barging in on you. I'll be real quick-like and leave you in peace." Her brogue was as thick as Irish stew. The woman's black, lively eyes darted a look over Karen's shoulder to David. "Mr. Mackenzie, 'tis me, Maggie Doolin."

"Mrs. Doolin." David inched forward until his hand brushed the edge of the desk. Deep lines formed on his forehead, the flickering firelight accenting the creases.

"Please, Mrs. Doolin, do sit down. What is it you've come to talk to my husband about?" Karen took the chair next to their visitor's.

David leaned against the edge of the desk and crossed his arms as if bracing himself for a barrage.

The lines on Mrs. Doolin's face spoke of years of hardship, but peace shone from her dark eyes. Her fingers kept up constant motion, picking at a thread, tapping her lap, never still. "I'm on me way back East, and I had something to say to my late husband's boss. I should have come before, but I was making ready to return to me family. Me oldest boy lives in Boston. He's asked me to come to him now that I'm alone."

Karen leaned forward. "We're so sorry for your loss."

"Aye, lass, I know you are. 'Tis a terrible thing for the women, isn't it, waiting to see if our men will come back out of the earth when they search for buried treasures? You haven't escaped the sorrow yourself. I'm that sorry about Mr. Mackenzie's eyes. My Paddy thought the world of Mr. Mackenzie, he did. And he was that proud of his dynamiting. An artist he was. The best powder monkey in the silver fields." She dug a handkerchief out of her sleeve, using it to wipe the corners of her eyes. After a moment, she gathered herself. " 'Twas about Paddy I've come, Mr. Mackenzie."

David grimaced. "I'm so sorry, Mrs. Doolin. I hope you can believe that. I have no excuses to offer. The structure I designed failed in some way. I know there's no recompense I can make that will replace what you've lost, but I do hope you understand that you will be provided for. You've spoken to my father or brother?"

"Oh, now, don'tcha be worried, sir. I didn't come to bother you. Paddy wouldn't have blamed you, and neither do I. Your family's been very generous. Your lady-mother herself came to see me. I've no quarrel with Mackenzie Mining. I came to tell you what Paddy said to me afore he died. He lingered two days after they dug him out of the rubble. The doc couldn't do anything for his broken back, though 'twas God's mercy my Paddy could feel no pain. When he knew he was dying, he held my hand that hard and made me promise on me mother's grave I'd tell you his last words."

David's knuckles showed white.

Karen wanted to go to him, to put her arms around him and offer some comfort, but she couldn't bear to be rebuffed in front of a guest.

"What is it your husband wanted to tell me?"

"Paddy was pretty far gone, so I don't know if I heard him right, but he said, 'Tell David about the coyotes. He'll know what to do.' I think he was out of his head." She shrugged. "It didn't seem important at the time, what with you being taken down in the same cave-in. I couldn't be bothering you about wild beasts with you hurt in bed at the time."

David rubbed his palms down his cheeks. "Were you having trouble with coyotes in the mining camp?"

"We had some trouble awhile back with a pack digging through the rubbish heap and killing some chickens, but Paddy took his rifle and cleared them out."

"Has anyone else reported trouble?"

"Nay. Paddy said to tell you and no other. The poor man was agitated about it, mixing things up in his mind. No doubt he was thinking back to the bit o' trouble with the pesky creatures and worried they might return. I don't know why he wanted me to tell you, but he did, and I have." She levered her hands on her knees and rose. "Me duty's done with the telling. I'll be heading to the rooming house. It's getting terrible late, and me train leaves at seven."

Karen walked the older woman to the door. "You're sure you don't need anything? You have enough money?"

" 'Tis a good lady you are, Mrs. Mackenzie. I have more than enough. Your husband's family has seen to that. I've plenty to get home on. I'll be praying for you and the mister. Such a sorrow about his eyes, and him such a fine gentleman."

"Thank you. You will be careful getting to your rooming house, won't you?"

Buckford cleared his throat behind them. "Perhaps I could escort your guest to her rooming house?"

"That's very thoughtful of you. Thank you."

Karen closed the door behind them. Had the visit done more harm than good? Mrs. Doolin's words made no sense, and yet, Paddy Doolin had used practically his dying breath to implore her to get his message to David. What could varmints possibly have to do with the accident? Nothing, that's what. As she said, the man was out of his head.

A pile of letters on the hall table caught her eye. She sorted through them, bills and accounts, the newspaper, circulars, and personal correspondence. Perhaps David would like her to read the newspaper to him before bedtime.

Aunt Hattie would be scandalized if she knew Karen read the newspaper. Speaking of Aunt Hattie, a fat letter from her lay at the bottom of the stack. Karen scooped up the paper and the letter and returned to the parlor.

David sat before the fireplace, his face in his hands. When she took the chair across from him, he sat up and sighed. "She's gone then?"

"Yes, Buckford is seeing her to the rooming house. Did you know her husband well?"

"Paddy Doolin was the best dynamiter in Martin City. Every mining engineer in the Rockies tried to pinch him from us. A giant of a man and as capable as they come, always smiling and laughing. I can't think why he'd want to tell me about a problem he'd taken care of himself."

"More likely he wasn't in his right senses."

David thought on this. "That could explain it. Or maybe she misunderstood." He smacked his thigh with his fist. "I thought maybe she had a clue for me, something that Paddy knew that would tell me why the shaft collapsed— Something to tell me what I did wrong."

"Isn't it possible that it isn't anyone's fault?"

He shook his head. "Something caused that cave-in. Marcus is supposed to be looking into it, but I haven't heard anything from him." His feet shifted, and he pounded his leg again. "Though if he finds something that shows I was at fault, I don't know if he would tell me."

She needed to change the subject, give David something else to think about before bedtime. "I sorted the mail." She tugged at her bottom lip. "The evening paper arrived while we were out. Would you like me to read to you?"

"No, thank you."

She swallowed her disappointment. "There's a letter from Aunt Hattie, too." Slipping a hairpin from her coiled hair, Karen slit the envelope and withdrew the closely written pages. She tilted the paper toward the fireplace and scanned the first page. A wave of homesickness sloshed over her, and a lump formed in her throat.

"David, she's invited us for Christmas." A smile stretched her lips. "Wouldn't that be wonderful? I miss her so much. When she got sick, I was so afraid. She's the only one I have left from my family. I don't know what I'd do without her." She turned the page. "Listen to this:

You and David could make a visit here part of your honeymoon trip. We could spend the holidays together. It would be like old times to have you with me. I get so lonely for you at Christmas. I remember how you love everything about this time of year. Even if you could only come for a week or two, it would make me so happy. I'd travel to see you, but the doctor is advising against it at the moment, the old fusspot. I think he's planning to send his children to college on the fees he collects from me. Anyway, do say you'll come."

Karen lowered the letter. "David, Christmas in Kansas City, won't that be fun? I'm not sure where the time has gotten to. It's only two weeks until the twenty-fifth. I'll have to do some shopping and see about tickets."

"Karen, stop."

"But there's so much to see to. I should start making a list, so I don't forget anything." She bounded out of the chair and headed for the desk to find a pencil. What a blessing it would be to talk face-to-face with her aunt. Christmas with family. Her eyes grew misty at the thought.

"Karen."

His voice was so sharp, she stopped with the drawer only half open. "What?"

"I'm not going to Kansas City."

Her mouth fell open. "But. . ." She blinked, her heart tumbling into her shoes. "It's Aunt Hattie."

"I'm not going to Kansas City for Christmas. I'm not going to Martin City for Christmas. I'm not going anywhere for Christmas."

"But you went out tonight and everything went fine." Except for the way their kiss ended. She touched her lips, remembering the bliss of being in his arms. "And Aunt Hattie won't judge or make you uncomfortable. You've never met a kinder soul. She'll love you. I wanted you to meet her at the wedding." Her voice hitched. "The doctor told her she'd be well enough to travel by early summer when we originally planned to marry. Since we moved up the wedding date and she wasn't able to come, this will be the perfect solution. It shouldn't interrupt your studies too much. We'll be back in less than a month. Two weeks if that is all you can spare."

"You're not listening to me." His hands fisted and relaxed, only to fist again. "I am not traveling. There's a big difference between a few hours' visit to the school and traipsing across the plains to stay in the house of a complete stranger."

"But she's not a stranger. She's family."

"No, Karen. This is not open for discussion."

Karen took in his impassive face, as stubborn and set as ever, and clenched her teeth. Tears gathered in her eyes and spilled over. One fat drop plopped onto Aunt Hattie's invitation. Karen folded the pages and stuffed them into the envelope to read later. "Very well." She couldn't keep the sound of tears out of her voice and didn't care. She wanted him to know how much he'd hurt her. Why must she be the one to always sacrifice? "I'm going to bed." Before she gave vent to the harsh words she wanted to hurl at him, she escaped.

❧

David pushed his forehead against the heels of his hands. He'd made her cry. Again. But couldn't she see she asked more than he could give? A train trip? To a strange city, to a strange house? To be presented to her sole remaining family member as the cripple she'd married?

No. He couldn't do it. They would spend the holidays here. But maybe he could make it up to her—extend the peace of the season and make some smaller concessions. He'd grown weary of his own recalcitrance. Perhaps it was possible for them to achieve some measure of happiness together. Tomorrow he'd talk to Buckford about sending a message home. Karen's Christmas gift lay in his bureau drawer at the house. Mother could send it in plenty of time.

Straightening, he leaned back in the chair and rested his head, pushing his guilt over Karen to the back of his mind. For now, he would examine everything Mrs. Doolin had said about her husband's last words. Perhaps, if he thought on it enough, he could make some sense of the cryptic message.

Chapter 12

The letter to Aunt Hattie needed two stamps, but it weighed much less than Karen's spirit. She battled down resentment and tried to understand things from David's perspective, but it took much prayer and soul-searching, and nothing she did seemed to alleviate the heaviness. In the same mail, she sent a letter to David's parents, declining both their invitation for Karen and David to come to Martin City and their offer to journey to Denver so they could all be together for the holidays. She shopped for gifts and contemplated the idea of going by herself, but the thought of spending their first married Christmas apart didn't sit well with her, and she discarded the idea. Perhaps he'd feel more confident by springtime and they could travel to see Aunt Hattie together. Or Hattie could come to them as soon as the doctor gave her leave.

The closer they drew to Christmas Day, the more homesick and lonely Karen became. The package from Aunt Hattie nearly broke her heart. Buckford brought her the crate and helped her open it. Beneath layers of excelsior, she unearthed the hand-carved crèche and figures of her aunt's beloved nativity set. Brought from Europe by Karen's great-grandmother, it had held a place of honor in the Worth household. The card expressed Hattie's disappointment at not being together for the holidays, but now that Karen had her own home, the nativity should be hers. Karen didn't try to stop the tears as she lifted the wooden animals and shepherds and wise men from the crate and set them on the mantel. Each dear, loved figurine only made her miss her aunt more. By the time she lifted the natal family into place, she was sobbing.

Voices in the hall had her scrambling to mop the tears and present at least a facade of calm. Lessons must be over for the day. She straightened her hair and tucked her handkerchief away and went to say good-bye to Rex until the new year. When she reached the doorway, she stopped, not wanting to interrupt.

"You'll never have any measure of independence until you're willing to leave the safety of this house. Why won't you even take a walk down the street with me? You have to be weary of being cooped up here day after day. The only place you've gone in almost two months is a single reception at the school, and I had to strong-arm you into going then." Rex placed his hat on his head and his hand on the doorknob. His walking stick, twin to one he'd brought for David that stood unused in the umbrella stand, jutted from under his arm. "Your training won't be complete until you can go where you want, when you want."

"I don't need that. I wish you'd stop pushing me."

"It's my job to push you."

"Then it's my job to push back. I appreciate what you've done for me—teaching me to read again, to eat and dress and organize. I don't want anything beyond that."

"But there's so much more that you're capable of. So much more you could do."

"Good-bye, Rex. Until the new year."

Rex left unsatisfied, and Karen sympathized with him. She was unsatisfied, too.

♠

Early on Christmas morning, Karen donned a russet wool dress and wrapped her cape about her shoulders. As she passed David's door, she had to blink back tears. In spite of her best efforts, she had gotten no further than Rex had, and David refused to accompany her to church, not even on Christmas.

Though he must have felt some remorse for denying her request that they go to her aunt's. Or maybe it was the holiday that brought about the subtle changes. He had seemed softer these past few days.

She slipped into the back pew and surveyed the congregation. How she missed the fellowship of the little whitewashed church in Martin City and dear old Pastor Van Dyke's sermons. Though the soaring spaces and stained glass of this large church in Denver inspired awe and she was surrounded by many times the number of worshippers in Martin City, the experience left her remote and cold. The droning, vibrating tones from the pipe organ sent chills across her flesh, and she shivered as she opened her Bible for the reading.

If she and David had gone to Kansas City for Christmas, she would be sitting with Aunt Hattie in the nice church Karen had visited when she went there to take care of her aunt. Was it really less than three months since she'd been there, listening to the young preacher, Silas Hamilton, deliver a poignant and stirring message? If she was with Hattie in that church, Christmas and Christ would seem very near.

As it was, she sat through the formal service, detached and unable to focus. Her thoughts bounced from missing her aunt, who was distant from her by days and miles, to frustration with her husband, who was distant from her by pride and fear.

When she got home, she draped her cloak over the banister to carry to her room later and wandered into the parlor. Off-key humming accompanied the clank of cookware from the back of the house and made her smile. Taking a long match from the holder on the wall, she touched it to the coal fire then went around the room lighting the candles among the pine and holly. Not even the spicy, resinous scents that mingled with the smell of roasting goose lifted her spirits.

"God Rest Ye Merry, Gentlemen" boomed from the kitchen. Mrs. Webber, a choir of one.

Karen stopped before the nativity scene, touching the pieces lightly, her heart sending Christmas wishes to her aunt and to David's family. Karen fingered the cameo at her throat, a gift from the Mackenzies.

She turned when footsteps sounded in the hall. "Hello, David. Merry Christmas." She forced the words out. So far the day had been anything but merry.

"You're back. How was church?" He crossed the room easily and reached for his chair.

"Fine. It's a beautiful building, lots of brick and stained glass. Their organist is very. . .enthusiastic."

The corner of his mouth quirked. "So is Mrs. Webber. She's been singing carols all morning. I think it's her not-so-subtle way of bringing Christmas cheer into the house." He breathed deeply. "Though I have to admit, the place sure smells like Christmas. Would you like your gift now?"

Her head came up. "I didn't know if we would be exchanging gifts. I got you something, too." Weeks ago.

"I know you've been upset with me about staying here alone for the holidays, and I'm sorry you were disappointed. Maybe we can declare a truce from hurt feelings for today?" He spread his hands, palms up. "After all, it is Christmas."

She tugged on her lower lip then dropped her hand to her lap with a sigh. "Very well. You're right." A wry smile touched her lips. "Peace on earth, goodwill toward men."

"That's the spirit." He pulled open his jacket and dug into the inner pocket. "Now I can return your greeting. Merry Christmas, Karen." He withdrew a velvet pouch and held it out to her. When she hesitated, he swung it toward her a bit. "Go on. It's for you."

She took the bag and loosened the drawstring. Running her fingers over the gold-embossed jeweler's name on the bottom of the pouch, she tipped it upside down. A glittering ribbon of white and red stones slid into her hand. She gasped then breathed, "David."

He smiled. "I bought that when I bought your engagement ring. The garnets match the setting in your ring. Do you like it?"

The jewels captured and shot back the lights from the candles, winking warmly as she turned them. "They're beautiful." She rose and went to the mirror over the mantel where she draped the necklace at her throat. "Thank you." A lump formed in her throat.

He came to stand behind her. She stood stock-still when he cupped her shoulders. "Their beauty must pale beside your own. You always were the most beautiful woman in any company." Then, as if he thought he had gone too far, he stepped back and shoved his hands into his pockets. "Now, what's this about a gift you have for me?"

Karen turned from the mirror and laid the necklace on the table beside her chair. "It's in my room. I'll get it." A truce, for today. Their marriage so far had been one long, pitched battle interrupted by small truces. When would they reach an accord they could both be happy with? She retrieved the package from her bottom bureau drawer and returned to the parlor.

David stood at the mantel, his fingers trailing over the nativity figurines. When she entered, he turned toward her. "That's a really fine set. The carving seems so detailed, and there are so many pieces. It was nice of your aunt to gift it to you."

She exhaled slowly. "I think it would be in the best interest of our truce if we don't talk about Aunt Hattie. Please, sit down and I'll hand you your present."

When he had resumed his seat, she placed the squareish object into his hands and stepped back. The qualms she had when she first bought it came galloping back. Would he think the present emphasized his blindness? Or would he realize she only wanted to help him? She laced her fingers under her chin and waited.

Slowly, he pulled the end of the store twine and pushed back the brown paper. His fingertips grazed the fine wood. "An abacus." The beads whispered on the rods and clacked together when he tilted the frame.

"I found it in a shop downtown. The owner is Chinese, and the place was stuffed with herbs and tea and artwork. I saw this in the window, and it was so pretty, much better than the one Rex loaned you from the school." She knelt beside his chair and spun one of the wooden beads. "The frame is cherry, the rods white hard maple, and the beads are polished walnut." She searched his face for a reaction. "I thought it might be useful."

He flattened his palm and ran it across the face of the abacus, rotating the walnut disks. "This is really fine. Thank you."

"You like it? It's all right?"

"Very much. You're very thoughtful." He reached out and touched her hair, letting his fingers trail down her cheek. Then his hand dropped away. "How about if we go in search of our Christmas dinner. It must be nearly time to eat."

"You're eating with me?" She tipped back on her heels and gripped the arm of his chair to steady herself.

He rose and the paper and string in his lap drifted to the floor. "Would you mind?"

She gathered the paper and tossed it on the fire, trying not to read too much into his offer. "I'd like that." Smiling for the first time in days, she tucked her hand into his arm.

He set the abacus on the table beside his chair and walked with her to the back of the house.

❧

Late that night, David sat in his bedroom with the abacus in his lap. Idly, his fingers did calculations while his mind drifted. Dinner together had been a success from where he sat. He'd managed not to spill anything on himself or her, and the conversation had flowed passably well.

In keeping with both their families' traditions, once they'd returned to the parlor, Karen had read aloud the Christmas story from Luke chapter two. They'd passed the rest of the evening with Karen reading aloud from a new book Sam had given her for Christmas, *Life on the Mississippi* by Mark Twain. David had relaxed in his chair and let her voice take him through a history of the mighty river and Twain's exploits as a riverboat pilot. Altogether the best evening they'd spent together in months.

He ran his hand along the abacus frame. A beautiful and thoughtful gift. Useful, too. He wished he'd known how to use one before the cave-in. It would've lessened his workload considerably not having to work everything out on paper.

His mind turned back to his work. The images of his maps and drawings remained firm in his head, the calculations and projections. He still hadn't been able to find the weakness. Where had he gone wrong? If he was starting from scratch on the project, what would he change? And where did Paddy Doolin's message come in? Was it just the raving of a dying man or did it have some bearing on the cave-in?

David rubbed his forehead and got up to prepare for bed. The more he worried the problem like a terrier with a rat, the more muddled he became. Perhaps he'd have to accept the fact that he would never know where he'd gone wrong. Marcus had remained silent, which meant either he hadn't found anything or he'd found something he didn't think David should know. Relief mingled with defeat as he thought about letting go of the past.

He set the abacus on the desk in the corner. A smile pulled at the corner of his mouth. He wished he could've seen Karen's face to determine if she really liked the necklace and if she recognized it for what it was: a peace offering. Just like the cave-in, perhaps it was time he accepted things the way they were and get on with living, an action that included letting go of his fears and having a normal marriage—or as normal as he could manage—with his beautiful wife.

Worms of doubt wriggled through him, whispering that he was a fool to consider it, that he wasn't man enough, that he would only get his heart broken.

Stop it. You tried to hold Karen at arm's length, but it didn't work, did it? She's in your heart, and you need her. Not having Karen in your life would be worse than being blind. You should be doing everything in your power to make her happy. You heard it in her voice when you did something as simple as eating dinner with her tonight.

One successful dinner didn't mean he was ready to conquer the world, but perhaps it wasn't too early to begin planning a trip to Kansas City in the spring. He wouldn't tell Karen right away, but when Rex came back after the first of the year, David would take him up on his offer to learn to navigate the streets of Denver by himself.

Chapter 13

Karen looked up from her correspondence when Buckford entered the room. "Ah, thank you for the interruption. I think my writing hand is about to fall off. I could use a cup of tea."

"A telegram arrived for you, ma'am." He held out an envelope. "I'll see to your tea right away."

"Thank you. Would you see if David would like some tea or coffee? I think he's still upstairs reading."

Buckford nodded and left.

Karen leaned back in her chair and rubbed her wrist. She'd long grown weary of sending out her regrets for one party after another. She hadn't known the Mackenzies knew so many people in Denver, nor that their friends were so social. Each invitation to a ball, soiree, or fete must be answered, and the deluge of envelopes for tonight's New Year's Eve festivities had taken most of the morning to respond to. A yawn tugged at her jaw, and she turned her attention to the telegram.

MRS. DAVID MACKENZIE

REGRET TO INFORM YOU MISS H. WORTH PASSED AWAY LAST EVENING, DEC. 30. FUNERAL SCHEDULED JAN. 4. CHURCH SENDS CONDOLENCES AND LAWYER AWAITS INSTRUCTIONS.

REV. S. HAMILTON.

Karen read the words, each one slicing like jagged glass. Tears blurred the type, and the paper fell from her nerveless fingers. A deep trembling started in her middle and radiated outward, chilling as it went. A fist of pain lodged in her throat.

Sobbing reached her ears, a mournful cry torn from an anguished soul. She tried to shut it out until she realized it came from her. Loss crept around her like a black mist, and the room began to whirl.

Buckford rattled the teacups when he plunked the tray down and hurried to her side.

Karen put out her hand to grip the edge of the desk.

"Ma'am? Are you all right? Should I call someone?" In an unprecedented move, he took her arm. "Perhaps you'll feel better if you lie on the couch." He didn't wait for her assent but helped her to her feet and put his arm around her waist, assisting her to the settee.

A small, detached part of her mind reasoned that she must look very shocked and shaky indeed for Buckford to break protocol like this. She lay back against the cushions and stared at the ceiling.

Tears leaked from the corners of her eyes, wetting her temples and trailing into her ears, but she didn't care. Aunt Hattie was dead. Her heart throbbed as if a giant heel had ground on it. She would never see her beloved aunt again on this earth.

"Lie still. I'll get some help." Buckford patted her shoulder then disappeared into the foyer.

Karen couldn't have moved if she wanted to. Boulders of grief tumbled over her, swallowing her in an avalanche.

Footsteps clattered on the stairs, and David knelt beside her. "What is it, Karen? Are you ill?" He felt over her arms and legs. Then his fingers touched her tear-soaked face. "Are you hurt?"

His caress burned her skin. Anger such as she'd never felt before welled up inside her, and energy returned like a lightning flash. She shoved his hands away. "Don't touch me." Grabbing the back of the settee, she struggled upright, banging into David in the process.

He rocked and tumbled onto his backside. "Karen, what's the matter with you?" He leaned back on his palms, his eyebrows climbing toward his hairline.

She got up and brushed past him toward the desk. The telegram lay on the floor by the chair, and when she reached down for it, the blood rushed to her head, renewing her dizziness. She snatched up the paper and crumpled it to her chest. Her control cracked, and she spewed out hurt-laden words. "My aunt passed away last night, and thanks to you and your colossal selfishness, I wasn't there." A spike-laden sob clawed its way out of her throat, choking her.

David clambered to his feet and approached her with his hand outstretched.

She shrank from him, pushing into the corner. If he touched her, she would be sick. "Stay away from me."

His hand dropped to his side. "Karen, I'm so sorry about your aunt."

She shook her head. Tears dripped from her chin onto the telegram. "No, you're not. You didn't even know her. You didn't want to visit her. She was the only person I had who really loved me. And now she's gone."

"That's not true. Karen, I love you. Let me help you through this." He reached for her again, but she evaded his grasp.

"You don't love me. I thought you did once, but I was wrong. If you loved me, you would've married me without being coerced. You would've let me help you, and you would've treated me like your bride. I'm a secretary not a wife, taking care of household accounts, overseeing the help, writing your correspondence. No matter what I do, you still aren't ready to love me more than you love yourself. You keep me at a distance. You never share your thoughts and feelings unless you're angry or bitter, and then you deny me the chance to see Aunt Hattie one last time. Does that sound like love to you?" She choked on a sob and pressed her knuckles to her mouth, not wanting to look at him anymore. She only wanted to get out of the room, to find somewhere she could breathe and think and grieve. Knocking his outstretched hand away, Karen hurried to escape.

"Where are you going?"

She paused at the doorway. "I'm going to pack. I have a funeral to attend." She brushed past Buckford at the bottom of the stairs. "And don't even think about offering to come with me. It's too late for that."

𐫱

Her door slammed at the top of the stairs as effectively as she'd slammed the door on his efforts to comfort her.

David groped for the edge of the settee and sank onto it. He put his face into his hands, trying to make sense of what had just happened, but only one thing stood out in his mind.

She was leaving him.

Packing her bags and boarding a train.

The truth hit like a blow from an ax handle. Though he had tried to prepare himself for it from the moment he married her, the reality halved his heart. He had let his guard down, had actually started imagining she might stay with him, that together they could find happiness in spite of his infirmity. What if he had gone with her to her aunt's? Would she have come back to him if he had sent her alone?

She thinks I don't love her.

Shoving his fingers into his hair, he squeezed his hands into fists. Her accusations zipped through his head, and he was guilty of every one of them. He *had* held her away from him and kept his most intimate and personal thoughts to himself. Because he had been afraid and ashamed, he had refused to accompany her on a family visit. But that didn't mean he didn't love her.

He had been trying for days now to think of a way to swallow his pride and tell her he wanted to be a real husband to her, to share their lives together the way they had planned when he first asked her to marry him. He'd even had Buckford send a note to Rex about learning to get around outside the house starting as soon as the winter break ended in order to be ready to take Karen on a trip in the spring.

But it was too late now. She was leaving him. She didn't want him to go with her, and he had no right to ask her to stay.

He pushed himself up from the settee and shuffled across the room to the doorway. "Buckford?"

David jumped when a voice came from quite close by. "Yes?"

"My wife"—the words jabbed—"is going on a trip. I would appreciate it if you would go to the depot and procure her ticket in a private compartment with a sleeper. Spare no expense. I want the best you can get. Then go find a shop and procure a traveling blanket and pillow and some reading matter. Anything you can think of to make the trip easier." He swallowed against the ache growing in his middle. "When you get back, be ready to take her to the station."

"Very good, sir." Buckford's voice held not a note of censure. "One ticket?"

"One ticket, Buckford. There's money in the cash box upstairs." He hadn't been in the office since they'd moved into the town house. He'd shut the door on that part of his life. After handing Buckford the key to the cash box, David resumed his seat in the study, helpless to do anything else.

What seemed like hours later, Buckford returned to the town house. The smell of smoke and sunshine lingered on his clothes. "Sir, I've been to the depot." He pressed a pasteboard rectangle into David's hand. "Here is the ticket. I did as you asked and reserved a private compartment in a Pullman car. The train leaves in two hours." He paused. "There is still room on the train if you should choose to accompany her. I can pack for you very quickly."

David shook his head. "No, she has enough details to see to without having to look out for me, too. Though I'd like to be there to support her during the funeral, she'll have an easier time without me." Just as he'd thought. Life would be easier for her without his clogging things up and needing to be looked after. "Check with her to see if she needs any telegrams sent ahead to anyone and be sure to cable the depot in Kansas City and have a carriage waiting for her and someone to handle the baggage."

"Very well."

Before Buckford could leave, David rose and touched his arm. "Thank you, Buckford, for taking care of all these details I can't do myself."

"My pleasure, sir."

A giant fist crushed David's chest. Mackenzie history was repeating itself, and he was helpless to stop it.

He accompanied her to the depot. She didn't speak to him on the journey, and she didn't cry.

He recalled the last time he had seen Karen before the accident, the last time he'd put her on a train. Bags at her feet, checking her pocketbook for her ticket, torn with excitement at seeing her aunt again, worried about Hattie's ill health, and saddened to be parted from him, even for a little while. She had chattered all the way to the train that day. He hadn't been conflicted in the least. He had known without a doubt he would miss her every day they were apart, and his world wouldn't be right until she returned. With no regard for the fact that they were standing on the platform at the depot with anyone and everyone looking on, he had swept her into his arms and kissed her. His embrace had knocked her hat askew, but she hadn't seemed to mind, returning his kiss with passion. He had looked into her beautiful blue eyes and brushed her lips with his once more before putting her on the train.

This time, he might've been a stranger to her. She took the ticket he presented her while Buckford instructed a porter to label her trunk and wheel it to the baggage car.

David stood helplessly by, listening to the sounds the train made, hissing and clicking in preparation for its trip across the plains. "You've got money for your meals and anything you might need?"

"Yes, David."

"You'll cable when you arrive?"

"Yes."

"If you need more money, the First Union Bank in Kansas City will honor your personal check. Or I can wire you funds."

"Yes."

The train whistle shattered the air, startling him. Someone—the conductor?—shouted, "All aboard!"

All he wanted to say jammed in his throat. He settled for touching her arm, her shoulder, then her face before lowering his lips to her cool cheek. "Good-bye, Karen."

She moved away, and Buckford guided him back from the train. With a growl, tons of metal began to move. Steamy mist drifted across his skin and the smell of cinders and ash filled the air.

Chapter 14

Dear Karen,

Buckford is writing this for me, as my own handwriting is still deplorable, and in any case, I don't like using the metal frame to write for myself.

Thank you for sending the wire confirming your safe arrival. Buckford tells me the funeral is today, and I hope you will accept my condolences.

Things are much the same here. Rex is coming to resume our lessons on Monday.

I am sure you are busy settling your aunt's estate, so I won't take any more of your time. It's awkward dictating to Buckford. I never realized before how easy it was to speak my mind when it was you taking down my correspondence. I guess we never realize what we have until it is gone.

Do you know when you will be coming home?

Sincerely,
David

Karen spread the page out on her black skirt and read the scant lines for the tenth time. How different from the love letters he had mailed to her the last time she stayed in this house. Though with all that had happened to them and between them, it wasn't surprising.

"We never realize what we have until it is gone."

How many times had that truth been brought home to her over the past week? She glanced at the calendar on Aunt Hattie's kitchen wall. Monday, the seventh. Rex would be there now. Would he be making David use the despised handwriting frame and practice his letters?

The funeral had been the loneliest day of her life. Her heart ached for Aunt Hattie, and every time Karen turned around, she expected to see her aunt's dear face. Pastor Hamilton delivered a beautiful service, touching and full of remembrances and words of comfort. Later, Karen knew she would draw on those words, once she could think about them without breaking down. She withdrew a black handkerchief from her sleeve and dabbed her eyes before folding David's letter and putting it back in the envelope.

David.

Under the layers of grief for her aunt, Karen had piled up a store of guilt for the way she'd treated her husband, for the harsh words she'd spewed at him. That guilt was in no way assuaged by the knowledge that she had been in shock, overwhelmed with loss and sorrow.

Tiredness washed over her, a lethargy that had dogged her on the endless train trip and continued through the funeral. Her thoughts were wooly and chased each other like fat, stumbling sheep. She didn't know which one to follow, so she followed none. For now, Aunt Hattie's house was a safe, soothing refuge where she didn't have to think too much and didn't have to battle her stubborn husband. She could just drift.

Pushing back the teacup, she rose and went to the bedroom to lie down. She'd think about her husband later.

☙

February 1, 1884

Dear David,

Thank you for your note of January 4. I apologize that it has taken me so long to send a letter in return. I've been so tired and absorbed with a thousand details. Settling an estate, even one in such good order as my aunt's, takes time. I've been going through her things, trying to decide what to keep and what to give away. Everything holds memories for me. The sorting is going slowly.

Pastor Hamilton has been very good, stopping by to visit at least once a week with some of the ladies from the church. The church here reminds me of the congregation in Martin City. Many of Hattie's friends have come by as well, and they have welcomed me into their church family. It feels good to be a part of their congregation, to be accepted and cared for. I've never really felt at home in the church in Denver, though that is probably because I always attended alone.

Hattie's friends are a delight and have banded together in a matchmaking scheme that occupies them constantly. Pastor Hamilton is a handsome, single man, and they would like nothing more than to see him properly and happily wed. He is, however, quite adept at outmaneuvering them. I am surprised at his dexterity in avoiding their traps.

The lawyer seeing to probating Aunt Hattie's will, a Mr. Drury, is currently unavailable. He's gone to Springfield on family business. It appears his daughter has made an unadvisable match, and he's gone to see about helping her obtain an annulment. I hope he is successful in extricating her from this trouble. He seems a dear man, and he's very upset about the situation, as I'm sure you can understand.

As to your question about when I will return, I'm afraid I don't have an answer. Things have been so strained between us. Perhaps this time apart will benefit us both. You can concentrate on nothing but your work with Rex, and I can think things through. In any case, there is still much to be done here, and I cannot come home until it is completed.

Sincerely,
Karen

"Read it again, Buckford." David folded his hands in his lap then remembered to add, "Please."

The houseman read the letter once more, slowly. "Would you like to dictate a reply, sir?"

He stirred. "Later." At the moment, he could think of no way to frame a reply that wouldn't either sound dictatorial or pleading. "Could I have the letter, please?" He took the paper and tucked it into his jacket over his heart. "That will be all, Buckford. Thank you."

When the houseman's footsteps receded, David was left with nothing but his thoughts chasing one another like ravenous wolves. His insides writhed as he lined up the facts. A month had passed before she could bother to send a letter. The handsome, single pastor was coming to call, and the ladies of the church were matchmaking. Karen mentioned an annulment case, and she didn't know when she would be coming home. Even a blind man could put those pieces together. All the excitement surging through him when Buckford brought a letter from her had dried to a trickle of guilt-ridden malaise for having driven her to these circumstances.

Would she come home at all? Had he lost her for good? Was this how Uncle Frank had felt, as if everything truly precious in his life was slipping away and there was nothing he could do to change it?

❧

February 11, 1884

Dear Karen,

As you can see, i'm writing this letter myself, and of necessity will be brief. the situation being what it is, please take all the time you need. i am fine here. buckford is taking very good care of me. and mrs. webber too.

David

Karen stared at the letter, a total of a quarter of a page, and her heart

92

wept. Not because he had written it himself, though that fact was poignant enough, but because of his words.

"Take all the time you need. I am fine."

What had she expected? A stern, laying-down-of-the-law order to wrap things up here quickly and get herself home? What had she hoped for? Declarations of love and longing and a plea for her to return to him as soon as she could? The paper blurred.

She had gotten neither. He didn't need her, and he didn't want her back. He couldn't have put it more plainly. Buckford and Mrs. Webber were seeing to all his needs, and she was to take her sweet time.

Her throat closed, and she put her head down on her arms on the kitchen table.

❧

March 31, 1884

Dear David,

I have finally completed the task of winding up Aunt Hattie's estate. The house has been sold and the new occupants will take up residence tomorrow. The possessions dearest to my heart have been crated and will reside in storage under the care of Mr. Drury until I can direct him to the best place to forward them. Those items I did not wish to keep I have sold and donated the proceeds to the church here.

I will miss this church family. They have included me in every way and made my stay here so much easier than it could have been. I'm sorry to be leaving them, though I know I will see them all again someday.

I received another letter from your mother this week. She tells me that Pastor Van Dyke is ready to retire and that the denomination has sent them the name of his successor. Imagine my happy surprise to know that the man who will take up the pastorate in Martin City is none other than Silas Hamilton, who has been such a good friend to me here. He has often mentioned his desire to move farther west, and he is eager, after hearing my stories of the beauties of life in the Rocky Mountains, to relocate to Martin City. He expects to preach his first sermon there by Independence Day at the latest. I am sure the parishioners, including your parents, will make him most welcome.

As I had hoped when I left Denver three months ago, this time apart has given me room to consider our marriage, the unorthodox way it came about, the barely civil way it has been conducted, and where it should go from here. I am hopeful that we can discuss our future rationally and without recriminations. It should be obvious to both of us that we cannot continue this way. I know we can sort things out to both our satisfactions

93

if we just try. To that end, as soon as I turn the house keys over to the new occupants, I will board a train for Denver. I expect to arrive early on the morning of April 4.

Sincerely,
Karen

"She'll arrive the day after tomorrow." David tilted his abacus slowly forward and back, listening to the slide and click of the beads. Would she stay? For how long? Would she come seeking an annulment? Would she listen if he tried to apologize?

Buckford slid the letter across the desktop. "It will be very nice for the church in Martin City to have a new pastor so quickly."

With a stab, David remembered that Buckford was a member of the church in Martin City. Uprooting and moving to Denver to get away from his family and the scene of his accident had caused turmoil in not only his life and Karen's but Buckford's as well.

The front bell shrilled, and a fist pounded on the door. Buckford's hasty steps on the hardwood weren't in time to open the door before it crashed wide. "Dave, where are you?"

"Sam? What are you doing here?" David pushed himself up from his chair and braced himself for Sam's familiar crushing handshake and hearty backslap.

"I figured you'd stewed down here in Denver long enough. You've ignored all my letters." Cloth moved and damp air swirled. "Thank you, Buckford. I needed that coat when I left home, but it looks like spring has come around here. Oh, and I left my bag and a box on the front stoop. Could you slide them inside for me?"

David resumed his seat. Sam sagged into the chair opposite, and David could feel his brother's appraisal on his skin.

"We need to talk." Sam's boots scraped on the floor and the springs in his chair creaked.

"What about?" David tensed.

"Quite a few things, actually, but a couple items are vying for the top of the list. We need to talk about the mine, and after that, we need to talk about Karen."

"I have no desire to talk about the mine, and Karen is none of your business." The familiar shell of defensiveness, the walls he'd been working so hard to lower, flew up again, full strength. He took a grip on himself and battled down the old feelings.

The sigh Sam emitted seemed to come from his toes. "Dave, I don't want to fight with you. I strongly disagree that Karen is none of my business since she's my sister-in-law and I care about her. I'll leave off talking about her for now, but we have to talk about the mine. I need help, and you're the only one I trust. I can't go to anyone else with this. Not yet."

The earnest edge to Sam's voice sent uneasiness skittering across David's skin. He sat forward and put his elbows on his knees. "What's wrong at the mine, and why can't you talk about it to anyone else?"

"When Mother sent Buckford to you before Christmas, I gave him a box of papers and samples. Where is that?"

"I'm not sure. I think it's in my office upstairs. My papers have been the last thing on my mind in recent months."

"Well, you'd best stoke up that brain of yours for some hard slogging. I'll ask Buckford to bring some sandwiches and coffee to the office. What I have to say is going to take awhile."

Chapter 15

David took the chair behind the desk in his office upstairs and placed his hands on the carved, wooden arms.

Sam entered and something weighty hit the desktop. "Now, where's that other box? Ah, here it is." Papers rustled, and David recognized the clack and grit of rocks scraping against each other. "Let me move this inkwell and spread out some of these pages." Thumps and bumps as Sam got things settled.

David couldn't ignore the dueling excitement and fear in his middle. Excitement at delving, even in a small way, into his former occupation and fear that he wouldn't be up to the task. What if Sam had come all this way, putting his faith in his older brother, and David let him down? David couldn't help but feel he faced a test tonight, one he desperately wanted to pass.

"What are you looking for, and what help do you think I can give?"

Sam dragged a chair close. "First, you can tell me I'm not going crazy or missing something and jumping to the wrong conclusion. Then I want to compare some of the paperwork I sent with Buckford with what I brought today. Something isn't right, and I have a feeling it hasn't been right for longer than any of us would like to think."

Buckford arrived with a tray, and the aroma of hot coffee filled the room. Matches scritched and glass tinked as he moved around the room lighting the wall sconces.

David sipped his coffee while Sam rummaged through the boxes again.

"Buckford, why don't you stay?" Sam asked. "You know a lot more than you ever let on, and you've been in the mines. You might see something I missed. What's that contraption?"

Bumpy wood touched David's hand. "I thought you could use this, sir."

David closed his fingers on his abacus. "Thank you, Buckford. Sam's right. Stay and listen. Sam, stop fidgeting with that stuff and cut through the chaff."

Sam sighed and stilled. "All right. At first, I thought the trouble at the mine started with the cave-in, but looking back on things, I can see indications that something was going on even before then."

David's chin came up. "What?"

"Well, think about it, Dave. Remember that axle on the ore wagon that broke? The team had to be shot, broken legs on both. Then there was all the trouble at the company store. First, somebody makes a big error on ordering and supplies run short. Then, the day after the new inventory comes in, the store is robbed and ransacked. We thought these were just coincidences, but what if they weren't?"

"That's reaching a bit, Sam. There were a few petty thefts in town around the time the store was robbed, and wagon axles have been known to break before."

"True, but what about the four braces of mules that were stolen? Then we get a bad batch of blasting caps. And in September, I spent nearly the whole month working on one pump or another. Parts that shouldn't have failed did. Fluids 'accidentally' drained away. Debris 'somehow' got into the motor. I couldn't keep more than two pumps going at a time, and we were running in circles to keep the mine dry. Then there was the cave-in."

"That was my fault." David's shoulders slumped, and he rubbed his temple.

Sam gripped David's shoulder. "I know you think that, but why? You've never come up with a definitive reason why the supports should have failed and neither has anyone else. I think we need to comb through all the paperwork again—the plans, the surveys, and the ore samples—and figure this out."

"How can I? I can't see." David straightened and gripped the arms of his chair. The familiar helplessness rolled over him.

"I'll help you. I think the answer is here, but I can't find it on my own. Last week, the mine office was ransacked twice. I think whoever it was that did it was looking for the papers that have been in your house the past few months. Nothing else was missing. Marcus and I checked."

David frowned. "Why didn't you have Marcus look these things over? He's the better engineer. If he'd been in charge of the mine, the cave-in wouldn't have happened."

Sam rose and paced the area in front of the desk. "Dave, I'll match my time on a rock drill or pickax against any man in the mine. I can about sharpen a pencil with a stick of dynamite, but I can't decipher these charts and papers by myself. I need you. Not Marcus, not Father, you. I'll read aloud anything you want me to. I'll help you do the figures, but I know, if you'll just work with me, you'll be able to see what I can't." David snorted at his word choice, but Sam went right on. "You'll come at this from your logical, intense, black-and-white view of the world, and you'll put the pieces together."

David swiveled his chair, listening to the creak of leather and the doubts in his head. He wanted to pray, to ask for guidance, but he was afraid.

Afraid God wouldn't hear him. Even more afraid the answer would be no. He swallowed, clenching and unclenching his hands.

"Well, Dave? How about it?"

"I don't know how much help I'll be, but I'll give it a go."

Sam pounced on the box, as if he wanted to get started before David changed his mind. "Let me read to you a list of things that have gone on at the mine over the last ten months or so. Where'd I put my notebook?"

"Is this it, sir?"

"Thanks, Buckford." Pages scraped and shuffled. "Here it is. Any one of these alone wouldn't draw too much attention, but when you list them, it becomes more than a coincidence."

Sam read and David tried to organize the items into a mental list, visualizing them in his head the way Rex had taught him:

1. *Axle broken on new wagon. Team put down. Reason for failure unknown.*
2. *Ordering mistake leaves company store short on inventory.*
3. *Store robbed and ransacked. Four teams of mules stolen.*
4. *Shipment of faulty blasting caps. Work halted for two days till replacements are found.*
5. *Pumps falter. Time lost repairing and replacing parts. Reason for failure unknown.*
6. *Square sets fail, mine collapses. Eight dead, five wounded. Reason for failure unknown.*
7. *Transport bucket winch system fails, bucket falls to bottom of mine. One man injured, leg amputated. Winch and motor in good repair. Reason for failure unknown.*
8. *Pump fails entirely in No. 3 shaft, shaft flooded. Reason for failure unknown.*
9. *Ghost story begins to circulate. Men restless. Some walk off the job and hire on at competing mines.*
10. *Stope output in No. 3 well below predictions. New tunnel produces nothing.*
11. *Office ransacked.*

David's brows came down. "What? Predictions showed shaft three should have the richest ore."

"We were delayed having to clear the debris from the cave-in. Then the shaft flooded when the pump failed, so we had to install another pump. When we could finally send in the crews, we found nothing but rock. Then the standby pump failed. No sense throwing hard effort down a wet hole with no silver in it." Sam resumed his chair beside David. "None of us wanted to quit on it, not with all we'd lost trying to bring it in, but in the end we just had to abandon the shaft. Marcus urged us to keep trying, said we were losing faith with you if we stopped, but with no results. Father finally called a halt to digging in that tunnel."

Heat tracked across David's chest and up his neck. How could he have been so wrong? All the indications had pointed to a rich vein and stable rock to dig through. "I was so sure." He took a deep breath, then set his abacus flat on the desk. "I want to go over every page. Start with the earliest ones you've got, and we'll work our way forward."

Sam riffled the papers. "Buckford, can you sort through this box and put it all in chronological order? I'll start reading these. Dave, you stop me when you need to."

Sam read slowly, and David sat very still, absorbing, visualizing the charts and reports in his old handwriting, remembering and immersing himself in the work he had loved so much. He asked Sam to repeat some things and asked for clarification and expansion on others. Several times he did calculations on his abacus, but mostly he listened and collated the information to get an overall understanding of the data at hand. "You didn't read the initial survey and sample sheet I did on shaft three. I need to hear that."

"I don't have those. Not ones you did, at any rate. I have the ones Marcus did."

"No, I need the ones I did last June. My name should be at the top of every page. When I told Father I suspected there might be a rich vein there, he told me to handle all the preliminary work myself and not to bring anyone else in on it. There should've been no reason for Marcus to have filled out survey or sample sheets."

"I'll look again." Sam shuffled papers, rolled and unrolled charts, and shifted chunks of rock around. "I can't find any survey for shaft three other than this one Marcus did."

David shook his head. "Read out Marcus's report then." As Sam read, David tried not to give in to the growing doubts. "Those don't match at all."

"The question is why not?"

"You sound like you have an idea."

"You won't like it, but. . .think about it, Dave. Besides you and me, who has had access to everywhere in the mine *and* the store *and* the offices? Whose name is on this report? Who would know enough about mining to make sabotage look like random accidents?"

David shook his head, not wanting to believe it, though the doubts had been growing with every new report. "No, I can't believe that. Marcus? That's impossible. Our own cousin? He wouldn't do such a thing, not after all we've done for him."

Buckford spoke up. "That's quite an accusation. If you voice it outside this house, you will have to substantiate it. A very serious business."

Sam rapped his knuckles on the desk. "Men have died. Whoever did this is responsible not only for the loss of revenue and the loss of equipment, but also for the lives of eight men, plus the wounded, including David."

"But Marcus?" David asked again. "Why? Why would he do such a thing?"

"I don't know. I don't know what his motive could be. The only hard evidence we have is this report. We know the figures here don't match what you originally surveyed. We know you found a rich strike in shaft three, but according to this"—the paper popped, and David envisioned Sam holding it up and jabbing it with his finger—"shaft three is a played-out dead end. And we can expect that if Marcus is the guilty party, then when he finds out I'm here in Denver talking to you, he's going to be on his guard."

David put his elbows on the desk and his forehead on his fists. "If it turns out that Marcus is behind this, Father is going to be devastated. We can't do anything more here. The answers we need are in Martin City." They would have to go. He would have to return to the scene of his accident. Clammy sweat broke out on his skin. He would never enter a mine again. He couldn't. Too many nightmares, too many shattered hopes, too many dangers, physical and mental, lurked in mines.

Sam put his hand on David's shoulder. "The minute we show up at the mine, Marcus will have to be suspicious. I would be. When we get there, we won't have much time. He'll either run or he'll try to destroy whatever evidence remains that could tie him to the sabotage." His hand dropped away. "Buckford, throw some things in a bag. We can leave on the morning train."

David slipped his watch from his pocket and touched the hands. "It's late. If we're leaving early, we'll need to get to bed."

Buckford cleared his throat. "Excuse me, sir, but Mrs. Mackenzie is due to arrive this week."

David jerked. He'd been so absorbed in the discussion and so focused on the task he'd completely forgotten Karen's return.

"David, just what's going on with you and Karen?" Sam put the question to him gently.

David rubbed his palm down his face and turned toward Buckford. "Sam and I will take the morning train. You'll stay here and await Karen's arrival. After the situation with Marcus is settled, I'll come back here and hear what she has to say."

"Very good, sir." Though Buckford would never contradict his employer, David got the feeling Buckford thought the plan of action anything but "very good."

When David and Sam were alone, Sam asked, "What's going on with you and Karen? Why didn't you go with her to her aunt's funeral? I hate to think of her dealing with all of that by herself."

David shook his head. "She preferred to go alone, so I gave her the space and distance she wanted." He gave a brief outline of events leading up to her departure, not sparing himself in the telling. "When she gets back, she might very well ask for an annulment." The idea lanced his heart, and he chastised himself. He had no one to blame but himself. She'd tried every way she knew to love him, and he'd pushed her away. He'd brought about the very thing he feared. She no longer loved him, and he'd lost her for good.

Sam sighed. "I'd like to lock you both in a room until you straighten things out. You've been going about this all wrong. Instead of giving her space, you should've held her and kissed her and groveled. She was looking for comfort and strength from you. At the very least, you should've written and told her how much you missed her and how you needed her and wanted her to come home."

"Since when did you become an expert on women?"

"I never claimed to be an expert, but even a blind man can see that a wife needs her husband to want her in his life. And eventually, everyone has a breaking point. You've pushed and tested and tried Karen to the limit, and she broke. It's up to you whether you want to attempt to put the pieces back together."

"What if I can't? What if it's too late?"

"What do you have to lose by trying?"

Chapter 16

With every mile of prairie she passed, Karen tried not to hope David would meet her train but failed miserably. Checking her watch didn't make the time go faster, but she couldn't stop. She had so much to tell David, so much forgiveness she needed from him. In the back of her mind, a niggling doubt taunted her. What if David couldn't forgive her? What if they really couldn't find happiness together?

Passengers sidled down the aisle, their canes, umbrellas, and valises jostling and vying for space. Though she wanted so badly to hurry them up, Karen forced herself to sit still until the majority of the occupants cleared the car.

She scanned the faces through the window searching for David's. Weak morning sunshine trickled through thin, high clouds, promising warmth.

Karen made her way outside. Baggage carts lined up beside the train. She picked her way over three sets of tracks to the platform and joined the stream of people heading up the stairs to street level. As she emerged into the terminal waiting room, she caught sight of Buckford standing by the ticket windows.

He waved and nodded to her, then crossed the tile, weaving around people to get to her side. "Welcome home."

His familiar face gladdened her heart, but she couldn't stop herself from looking behind him for David. "Thank you, Buckford." She adjusted her coat collar and checked her hat, trying not to be disappointed. There were so many people and so much noise and confusion she didn't blame David for not coming. "I can't wait to get to the house. Tell me, how is David?" The question uppermost in her mind came tumbling out. "Is he anxious for me to get to the house?"

Buckford cleared his throat and took her valise. "I'm sorry, ma'am, but he's gone to Martin City. Sam came to Denver and enlisted his help with some trouble at the mine. They've gone up there to rectify the situation."

"He's gone?" Her heart lurched. "When?"

"They left yesterday morning. The situation at the mine is most urgent."

She reached out and grabbed the valise from Buckford and started toward the ticket windows.

"Ma'am, where are you going?"

"Martin City."

"I'm supposed to take you to the town house to wait for him to return."

Karen stopped and looked up at him. "I am tired, Buckford. I'm tired of being apart from David. We've been apart in one way or another since last fall. This is going to end now. You are welcome to come with me, but I'm going."

He took the valise once more, a resigned cast coming over his features. "Very well, ma'am. If you'd like to go to the ladies' waiting room, I will procure the tickets. The westbound train won't leave for an hour yet. There will be time to get some coffee and send word to Mrs. Webber at the house. Would you like me to telegraph ahead to Martin City to let them know we're coming?"

"No. I believe we'll just surprise them."

"Of that I have no doubt, ma'am."

Arriving that evening in Martin City brought Karen a feeling of having come full circle. Was it only five months ago she and David had left for Denver, he wounded and embittered, she uncertain and wary? They had both changed and grown in those months, but was it enough to move forward to have something better than they possessed right now?

She swallowed and twisted her fingers while Buckford lifted her bags from the back of the surrey he'd rented at the livery. Lights shone through all the ground-floor rooms of the Mackenzie home, beckoning. Piles of dirty, slushy snow lay along the foundation and mingled with the smell of smoke and hot metal from the smelters, the damp promise of spring settled over her. She knocked on the door.

"Why, Karen! Buckford!" Matilda enveloped her in a hug, pressing her cheek to Karen's in a gesture so reminiscent of Aunt Hattie's that Karen had to blink back tears. "What a surprise. Come in, come in. Jesse will be thrilled to see you. David didn't mention you were coming. I thought you were still in Kansas City. Please, dear"—Matilda drew Karen along into the house—"do accept our condolences on your aunt's passing. I know you must miss her terribly. Buckford," she tossed over her shoulder, "it's so good to see you again. As well meaning as the new man is, he's not you. Leave the bags. I'm sure Mrs. Morgan will want to sit you down in the kitchen for some coffee and a good talk."

Before Karen could get a word into the conversation, she was seated in the parlor sans cloak and gloves and accepting a cup of hot, sweet-smelling tea.

"Now, I expect you're very anxious to see David, but I'm afraid he isn't here." Matilda picked up her knitting and settled into her chair.

"Isn't here?" Dismay trickled through Karen. "Buckford said he set out on yesterday's train."

Matilda laughed and touched her temple. "I didn't mean he isn't in Martin City. I meant he isn't in the house. I don't know what kind of miracle worker that tutor you hired is, but David is a changed man. So confident, so focused and sharp. He was almost like his old self. This morning they had hardly finished breakfast before they were off and out of the house. Sam said not to wait up for them, because they would most likely be gone late into the night."

Karen could hardly fathom her mother-in-law's descriptions. A confident David, like his old self? He ate breakfast with his family, and he'd left the house voluntarily? Had being separated from her been that beneficial to him? Her sense of loss grew. How was she to reconcile with a man who thrived without her?

Matilda went on. "I'm so glad to know you've met the new pastor who's coming later this summer. Pastor Hamilton? You'll have to tell me all about him. I was so sad when Pastor Van Dyke said he was retiring, but I suppose it comes to all of us in time. Though I don't know that Jesse can retire. I think he'd dry up and blow away if he had to stop working."

Karen put her cup down and asked the question foremost on her mind. "Matilda, do you know why David came back home? I wrote him when my train would arrive, and when I got to Denver, he was gone."

The knitting needles stopped clicking, and Matilda's brows formed straight lines over her eyes. "None of the Mackenzie men would tell me anything. When Sam and David arrived last night, they took Jesse into the study and closed the doors. Whatever it is must be serious. David wouldn't have come otherwise, not with you expected back."

Karen wasn't sure about that. Her return to Colorado might have been the thing that sparked his flight to Martin City. "And you have no idea what it might be about?"

"No, just that it was mine business. It is good to have David involved again. I know you must've been disappointed that he wasn't there to meet your train, but it has to feel good to know he's here and working again." Matilda smiled. "I know you only went along with the lawsuit idea to please me and because we were out of options at that point, but you have to admit, it's all turned out beautifully."

❧

The next morning, Karen paced the flagstones of the conservatory behind the house. She should start gathering the flowers Matilda had sent her to get, but her thoughts tumbled and roiled like a snow-freshened creek in the spring.

David and Sam had not returned last night. Jesse came in near midnight, grave lines etching his face and his hair seemingly whiter than she remembered. He shrugged out of his coat, sagged into a chair, and put his face in his hands. "I don't know if the boys will be home tonight. They've been up at the mine office all day, and they're still working." He dragged his fingertips down his cheeks. "Matilda, I can hardly believe it, but Marcus is guilty. He's been systematically sabotaging the mine. They've tied him to nearly every disaster we've had over the last year. My own nephew."

Karen's jaw dropped. "Marcus? But why?"

Matilda rose and went to her husband, squeezing his shoulder and touching his hair. Jesse sighed. "We don't know yet. Nobody's been able to find him."

"Was he responsible for the cave-in?" Karen's mouth went dry. Marcus was David's cousin. His friend and coworker. Marcus Quint had asked several times for permission to come courting, though by that time she'd met David and wanted no other.

"They're still working on that one. They know he's guilty but not how he did it. The sheriff has a warrant for Marcus's arrest, and they're looking for him now. He wasn't on the night train to Denver. Beyond that, we don't know where he's gotten to."

As of this morning, there was no further news. Jesse had gone to the Mackenzie Mine to insist Sam and David come home for some rest. David should be here any time now. He'd be exhausted and in no shape for a discussion of his marriage. With everything going on with Marcus and the mine, it might be some time before they could talk things out.

She stopped pacing and picked up the clippers on the potting bench. She'd take some of the irises and some of the forsythia branches for a table arrangement. Calming herself, she breathed deeply of the warm, peaty smell of the hothouse.

Though Jesse teasingly grumbled about the cost of heating the greenhouse all winter, Matilda loved her flowers and Jesse loved her. He paid the bills and enjoyed the pleasure his wife took in the plants.

Gathering her armful of blossoms, Karen replaced the clippers and latched the door securely behind her. She could only see the chimneys of the Mackenzie house over the tops of the trees on the slope above her. Wending her way up the zigzagging path, she tried to avoid the dirty scarves of snow melting along the path. This early in April, further snowstorms were almost a certainty in Martin City, but for now a definite tang of spring flavored the air. She put her head down and hurried to get back to the house before the chilly air damaged the flowers.

Her heart jerked when someone stepped out of the trees onto the path, blocking her way. She had an instant to realize it was Marcus before he grabbed her and slapped a cloth over her mouth. Though she screamed, the cloth muffled the sound. Cold, hard fear throttled her senses. The flowers fell from her hands as she grappled with him, struggling for breath. Sickeningly sweet fumes invaded her lungs and blackness crept into the edges of her vision. Weakness suffused her limbs and everything disappeared.

&

David awoke to a rock drill battering inside his skull. Stones jabbed his cheek, and when he tried to move, he thought his head might explode. Fizzing sparks snapped in his brain, but none stayed lit for long.

Footsteps scraped nearby and earth scritched as if something were being dragged across it. The sound echoed, and he became aware of. . .panting? The unmistakable smell of being underground enveloped him—dank, musty, earthy. "Who's there?"

A thump and quick rustle. "You should've stayed out cold."

Dread shot through David. "Marcus." His dry throat made his voice sound like paper crumpling. He coughed and wished he hadn't. "What are you doing?"

"This is your fault. If you'd have just stayed in Denver, everything would've been fine. You two made me do this."

"Two of us? Is Sam here? Sam? Where are you? Are you hurt?"

"Sam's not here, though I wish he was. His snooping brought you back here. If he'd have left well enough alone, I wouldn't have had to get rid of you."

Something soft subsided onto the floor. Satin brushed David's cheek and wisps of long hair feathered across his face. He tried to brace his hands against the ground to rise, but he couldn't seem to get his limbs to cooperate. A familiar perfume drifted to him.

Karen!

He tried to pull his thoughts together. How did she get here? Where *was* here?

"Why kidnap Karen? She has nothing to do with the mine. I still can't believe you'd do any of this to us. Why, Marcus?" He tried to keep Marcus talking, to stall the moment when he'd kill them both.

Marcus snorted. "Do you have any idea what it's like to always come in second place to the Mackenzies? Just because your name is Mackenzie, you think you're so much better than I." His voice echoed off the rock. "You should've been working for me. I had seniority. I had the experience."

Hard hands shoved David, and his cheek impacted a rock wall. Pain spun like a pinwheel in his head, making Marcus's voice sound far away. He gathered himself, gasping, trying to control the vertigo washing over him. "But we were kind to you. Took you in. My father paid for your schooling. Marcus, you're family."

"Your father crammed his charity down my throat until I choked on it. He was ashamed of me, of my parents—his own sister. He couldn't even bear to speak her name!" A clanking sound, like glass on stone. "Another dose with the last of this chloroform should ensure she stays out for a while longer."

A cloying aroma assailed David. "Stop it! Leave her alone!"

"Shut up."

An explosion of glass hit the wall over David's head and rained down on his hair and shoulders. His nostrils stung and his head whirled. David groped for Karen, his heart in his throat. The venom in Marcus's words made him sound on the verge of madness.

Her breath fanned his temple, and his heart started again. She was still alive.

Something clanked and squeaked. David, groggy from the knock on the head and the anesthesia permeating the air, inched his hand from beneath himself and felt around. His knuckles grazed wood then a metal wheel. A cart? He'd seen a hundred of them before, flat, with a metal pole on one corner to hang a lantern. Used to haul equipment from one tunnel to another. An icy finger traced up his spine. That must've been how Marcus got them underground by himself.

"Marcus." David clutched the edge of the cart. "What are you going to do? Don't leave us down here."

"Someone has to pay for what your family has done to me. Once I've blown the entrance to this mine, nobody will ever find you."

"Don't you think I've paid enough? I'm blind, Marcus."

"You've always been blind. You, the favored one. The one Jesse always bragged on. Your whole family is blind. There I was, right under their noses, and they never saw me."

A violent tremor started in David's core and radiated outward. He sucked in a staggering breath. "I can understand your anger at me, but why Karen? She has nothing to do with this."

"She has everything to do with this. Do you think you were the only one who loved her? She wouldn't even look at me after she met you. You took everything from me. I offered her all I had, but it wasn't good enough. She wanted you." He spat the words like vinegar. "You've no one to blame but yourselves. I want your last thoughts to be of how you wronged me." He grabbed David's shirtfront and shoved once more, cracking David's head against the wall.

Stars burst behind David's eyeballs, and a groan shot from his lips. He slid to the ground, gasping, trying to hold on to consciousness. Marcus's footsteps and the creak of the cart faded away, and David was helpless to stop him.

Time passed, though he had no way of knowing how much. He drifted in a murky half consciousness. Clammy sweat trickled down his temple and into a cut on his cheek, but the stinging was mild in comparison to the evil pain in his head and his inability to make it recede through sheer force of will. Far away a muffled blast sounded and a faint tremor rippled through the floor on which he lay. He finally gave in to the fog enveloping him.

Chapter 17

Hearing returned first. His own breathing and heartbeat. He became aware of time having passed and of being able to marshal his thoughts again, a little at a time.

Karen.

Had Marcus hit her on the head, too? He inched forward until his fingers brushed her dress. Satin, with velvet trim. The one she had told him was pale green.

He started with her head, touching her, searching for wounds, swelling, bruises. She made no sound, nor did she move again. He turned her from her side to her back, arranging her arms at a more comfortable angle, then felt along her ribs and down her legs. No blood or broken bones that he could find. He gathered her to himself, sliding back until he rested against the rock wall. Her hands were icy so he chafed them. Her head lay on his shoulder, and she fit perfectly in his arms. Gently, he kissed her brow.

When Father had come to drag him and Sam home this morning, he'd informed David that Karen had arrived. Sam had gone to the sheriff's office, and David had been waiting for him to return so they could go home. He'd assumed it was Sam's boots on the porch that he'd heard, but it must've been Marcus coming to get his revenge. Revenge that meant he and Karen were in the bottom of a mine shaft, shut in by an avalanche of rock and debris.

What if she didn't wake up? What if he'd lost her before he could tell her how much he loved her and needed her? What if he had to go through life alone?

His conscience kicked him and long-ago memorized scripture filtered through his head.

'Whither shall I go from thy spirit? or whither shall I flee from thy presence? If I ascend up into heaven, thou art there: if I make my bed in hell, behold, thou art there. If I take the wings of the morning, and dwell in the uttermost parts of the sea; even there shall thy hand lead me, and thy right hand shall hold me. If I say, Surely the darkness shall cover me; even the night shall be light about me. Yea, the darkness hideth not from thee; but the night shineth as the day: the darkness and the light are both alike to thee.'

He wasn't alone. He was never truly alone. Though he had spent the past several months trying to push God away, considering himself unloved and unlovable because he had nothing to bring to any relationship, God hadn't abandoned him. Now that David had nothing left, he knew he had to turn back to God, acknowledge his sin and his need, and ask for forgiveness. He must make things right with God if he ever hoped to make things right with Karen.

David swallowed and flexed his rusty prayer muscles. "Father, I know I've been doing everything in my power to blame You for my blindness, for ruining my plans, or for just not caring. And all along I've known that wasn't true. I thought I was strong. Strong in body. Strong in mind. Strong in my faith. And in one blow, all that disappeared. But You've been there every step of the way. Watching over me, waiting for me to realize that I can't run away from You. Since the night of the recitations at the blind school, Your Spirit has gently reminded me of the truth."

His voice, though a whisper, seemed loud. Nothing he had done or felt or thought had escaped God's notice. Not his blindness, not his treatment of Karen, not his own pride in his engineering, and not his tantrums when his world blew apart and he couldn't put it together again. Remorse coursed through him.

"God, I'm so sorry. I've been such a fool, trying to blame You and fix everything on my own. I've made a colossal mess of things. I need Your forgiveness, and I need Your strength to show us a way out of here. I've so much to make up to Karen. I pray it isn't too late for us. I want to spend every day for the rest of my life proving to Karen I can be a good husband. Help me kill my pride over needing help."

He continued to pray as he waited for Karen to awaken.

❧

Karen fought her way upward through clouds of fog, forcing her mind to push through layers of cotton batting. A dull ache pressed against the backs of her eyes. She opened her eyelids a crack. Or at least she thought she did.

Nothing.

She lifted her sluggish hand up to make sure her eyes were open. They were.

But where had the light gone? Where was she?

Her breath came faster as she struggled to see even the tiniest spark of light. Before she could stop it, a scream rose in her throat.

Someone clamped a hand over her mouth.

She flailed, fighting to break free of the iron-hard arms that imprisoned her.

"Karen! Stop it! Karen, it's me, David!"

She stilled, her muscles stiff.

His hand eased away, and she tried to suck in a breath, but it snagged somewhere in the top of her lungs. She tried again, blinking and turning her head. She raised her hand in front of her nose but couldn't bring an image into focus. "David, help me! I. . .I. . .I can't see!" Her voice echoed, and she scrabbled against his shirtfront, seeking an anchor in the blackness. "I can't see." This time her words came out a whispered plea.

He clasped her to his chest, forcing her head onto his shoulder and stroking her hair. "Shhh. I've got you." He rubbed his chin against her hair. "You're not blind. We're in a mine. There's no light down here. He must've taken the lantern with him."

Karen clung to him, trying to make sense of his words. She squeezed her eyes shut then opened them wide, straining every muscle for the faintest glimmer of an outline, a form, anything in the dark. Her heart thundered in her ears. The blackness was a malignant thing, pressing against her. Her only point of reference was the security of her husband's arms. A mine? Why?

Memory came roaring back. "David, it was Marcus! He found me walking back from the greenhouse. He grabbed me." She grimaced. "He pressed a wadded cloth over my face, and there was a strange odor. I tried not to breathe it, but I must have. I don't remember anything after that." She pushed herself upright. "Did he do the same to you?" If only she could see his face. If only she could see anything.

"I'm afraid Marcus chose a more violent method to render me unconscious. He bashed me in the head."

"Are you hurt?" Her fingers flew, touching him, trying to find signs of injury.

His hands captured hers. "I'm fine, dearest. A little headache and some sore ribs, but nothing terrible." He pressed his lips to her fingers. "Are you hurt anywhere?" He brushed a kiss on her temple, and she pushed against his chest.

"How hard did Marcus hit you?" Her fingers moved upward, feeling the strong line of his jaw and the swelling and dried blood on his temple.

"Are you thinking I've lost my senses, darling?"

A lump formed in her throat. How she wished she could see his face, to judge for herself.

A chuckle—a chuckle!—leaked from him.

"You don't seem entirely yourself." What would she do if he truly was addlepated?

He hugged her close, rubbing his chin across the top of her head. "I certainly hope not. Karen, there's so much I need to say to you, so much to apologize for, but there isn't time. Suffice it to say, Marcus bashing me on the brainpan has finally brought me to my senses." He took her face between his palms and kissed her forehead. "I've made my peace with God, and the instant we're out of this mine shaft, I intend to begin to make amends to you. I've been a complete and utter fool where you are concerned, and I only hope you can find it in your heart to forgive me and start over. Oh, Karen, we have so much to talk through, but for now, we need to see about trying to get out of here."

Her breath hitched and the hollow, fluttery feeling behind her breastbone grew. "Do you think we can find our way out? Even in all this blackness?"

"The darkness won't matter to me. And remember, it doesn't matter to God. He sees us, He knows right where we are, and He can help us get out of here."

He brushed a kiss across her hair, and she wanted to weep at the miraculous change in him.

"Ready?"

"I think so, but which way?"

"Marcus's footsteps faded out to our right. If we go that way, we can be reasonably sure we're at least heading topside and not farther into the mine." He helped her to her feet. "I'll need both my hands free, but we don't want to get separated. Keep hold of my belt, and keep one hand on the side of the tunnel. If you stay right behind me, I can warn you about any low-hanging rocks or crossbeams."

Karen stumbled. "I can't seem to maintain my balance. I've never been in such utter darkness."

"That's how I felt at first, too, right after the accident. Maintaining your balance does get easier after a while. Brace your feet wide apart and put one hand on the wall. Now, grab my belt, and we'll walk a few paces."

୬ଈ

David kept one hand above and in front of his head, and with the other, he maintained contact with the wall. The last thing he needed was to bash his already aching noggin on a crossbeam. Their footsteps echoed off the solid rock all around them, distorting distances and filling their ears. Every twenty or so paces, he stopped to listen, but only the sounds of their own breathing filled his ears.

David vaguely recalled the tremor and impact of what had to be Marcus blowing the entrance to the mine, but surely that would've drawn some attention. The family had to know he and Karen were missing by now, and they would be out searching. If David could find the mouth of the mine, would it be choked with rock and debris too thick for them to dig out? Perhaps the mine had more than one entrance or ventilation shafts. He knew he was grasping at thin straws, but what choice did they have? If they waited for rescue, they would die. If they wandered this rocky maze until exhaustion overtook them, they would die.

God, help us. You know where we are, and You know how to get us out of here. Guide our steps and lead us. Prayer was the only thing that kept despair at bay.

"How are you doing?" David stopped once more and reached behind him for her hand. She'd not uttered a single complaint as they inched along.

She gripped his hand and moved until his arm encircled her. Her head burrowed into his neck. "How far do you think we've come?" Her voice sounded small and weary.

"I wish I knew." They had to go so slowly, for fear of stepping off into space and plummeting down a vertical shaft. If only the mine would've had a narrow-gauge track, they could've followed it easily. He racked his brain for any clue as to where Marcus might've dumped them, but the slopes around Martin City were riddled and honeycombed with burned-out mining holes, and most had been plundered for any equipment and gear to aid in the next quest for treasure. He gave her what he hoped was a reassuring squeeze, then directed her hand to his belt in the back and started off again.

Karen stumbled. "Whatever Marcus drugged me with seems to be lingering. I can't think clearly."

"It might be the darkness." He talked to keep her spirits up. "Right after the accident I had a terrible time just organizing my thoughts. You'll be fine once we get you out into the light." He injected his voice with confidence, though his mind cringed at the reality of their situation. He couldn't tell if they were still heading the same way Marcus had gone. If they missed one side tunnel, they could wander down here until they dropped.

A faint, low rumble tickled his ears. He halted, straining to fix the origin of the sound, his heart in his throat as memories of the cave-in bombarded him. The tremor, the groan of rock, the cascading boulders and splintering wood—he stopped his stampeding thoughts and concentrated on the sound.

Water.

They edged along until the low rumble became a louder roar, the unmistakable sound of water falling into a pool. David turned and put his hands on Karen's shoulders. "Wait here. Sit down and don't move.

I'll be right back."

"Can't I go with you?" She latched on to his hand.

"I'll only go a few paces. I need to check things out. I don't want to risk your tumbling into an underground river. Wait here and don't move." He squeezed her fingers and brought them to his lips. "I'll be right back, Karen. I promise."

Feeling with a probing toe and keeping one hand on the roughhewn rock wall, he crept toward the sound of the rushing water. The overhead lowered, and he had to hunch down, holding his bent arm over his forehead. Spray misted his skin, and the sound of the rushing water filled the rock-crevice and ricocheted. His foot swung over nothing, and he stopped and knelt.

Easing onto his stomach, he stretched his arm over the edge. The icy current caught his hand, dragging it from left to right. He could put his arm in up past the elbow, yet he couldn't touch the bottom. It was impossible to judge how deep it was. Sitting up, he grabbed a handful of pebbles and one by one he threw them in an arc around himself. Stone pinged on stone each time and plopped into the water. He retraced his steps.

"Karen," he called to her before he reached her. "Karen."

"I'm here." Her hands scrabbled for him, grasping on to his sleeve as if to a lifeline.

He put his arms around her. "We can't go that way. There's an underground waterfall and stream. I threw some rocks to see if the tunnel continued on the other side of the water, and there's nothing there but solid rock. I couldn't feel the bottom of the stream with my arm. The miners must've quit this tunnel when they hit the stream. We can drink here, but we'll have to go back and see where we missed a side tunnel. This is a dead end."

"A dead end." She spoke woodenly, as if her lips were stiff.

"Come on, Karen. We'll look on it as a blessing. We needed water, and we found it." He took her hand. "The overhead is low, so watch your head. And drink plenty. It might be awhile before the next water."

❧

The jagged rock wall scraped Karen's fingertips, and her back ached. She tried to wet her lips, but her mouth was so dry. How long had it been since the stream? How many tunnels branched off this one? Were they in the main tunnel, or were they once again nearing another dead end?

When the third tunnel they'd tried ended in a solid rock wall, she wanted to sag to the ground and admit defeat. "Can we stop for a while?" She hated to ask. Stopping meant delaying their escape, but her legs wobbled and she knew she needed to rest.

"Are you all right?"

"Yes, just tired. I'm sure if I rest for a minute, I'll be fine."

"Come here." He took her elbow and eased to the floor, scooting until his back rested against the wall. He eased her down between his outstretched legs and pulled her back against his chest. His arms came around her shoulders and crossed under her chin.

Warmth and comfort enveloped her, and she leaned her head back. "How far do you think we've come?" Sleep tugged at her eyes, tired from straining to see in the darkness. She closed them, relaxing, her limbs growing leaden.

"I wish I knew. I wish I knew how far we had to go." He yawned and apologized.

"I'm sleepy, too. It feels like the middle of the night. What time do you think it is?"

"I had the same feeling, of it being night, I mean. When I tried to check the hands on my watch, they hadn't moved, so I think it's broken. I must've landed on it when Marcus dumped me on the floor. If our senses are telling us it's night, it probably is." He yawned again, this time not bothering with an apology. "Rest, Karen. You'll need your strength. I'll wake you in an hour or so."

Chapter 18

"We need to get moving again, Karen."

Reluctant to wake, she snuggled closer into his embrace and wrapped her arms about his waist.

"Karen?" He stroked her cheek. "Wake up."

She eased upright, still caught in the gossamer wisps of a delightful dream—a dream where sunlight shattered in rainbows over everything in brilliant, vivid colors. David laughed and teased as he walked beside her under a never-ending sky, his hands in his pockets and his hat pushed back at a jaunty angle.

Then she opened her eyes. Total darkness. Persistent damp and grit. A cold wind blew through her chest, and the blackness pressed around her like an inky shroud. She knelt, hunching her shoulders and wrapping her arms at her waist with her head bowed. Reality obliterated the last shreds of her dream.

David groaned. "I got stiff sitting there so long." His hand grasped her elbow.

She gripped his arm to help her rise. "Ow!" Staggering, she hit the rock wall with her shoulder.

"Karen, are you all right?"

She pushed herself up, her lips tight against the pain. "Pins and needles." A million tiny stabs trickled through her legs. When the pain lessened, she took a few wincing steps. "There. That's better."

"Are you ready to keep going?"

She closed her eyes and gave her head a little shake. Panic fluttered through her chest and parched her mouth. "I can't remember which way we were heading before we stopped." If they chose wrong, they'd wind up right back where Marcus left them.

"Don't worry. Before we fell asleep, I slipped my watch out and put it on the ground. I laid out the chain in the direction we're supposed to head."

She sniffed back a few hot tears and swallowed the scream. "I never would have thought of that. You're so capable."

His hand trailed down her arm until he found her fingers. Lacing their hands, he squeezed. "You can't possibly know how much that means to me. I haven't felt capable for a very long time. Just knowing you need me gives me courage."

Grasping his belt once more, she braced herself to go on. If he could be courageous, after all he'd been through, she would be, too. They hadn't gone far when the hand she dragged along the rock wall brushed something metal. "Wait."

David stopped. "What is it?"

Karen swiped gingerly until she made contact with the metal once more. Thin, cold, driven into the rock. The jutting end coiled upward. "Just another candle holder." But no candle. Couldn't the miners have left *one* behind? When they got out of here, she planned to light every lamp and candle she owned, just for the joy of seeing them glow.

They continued on. Since turning back from the waterfall so long ago, David had suggested they walk almost side by side so he could keep one hand on one wall and she could keep one hand on the opposite wall, thereby hoping not to miss further branches that might prove to be the way out. But each tunnel they tried dead-ended.

David talked, and Karen was sure it was to encourage her. She tried to respond, but weariness, thirst, and an ever-increasing sense of despair made it difficult. How long since they'd had any water? She forced her mind back to what David was saying.

"I'm beginning to think we must be in the old Wildcat Mine. I could be wrong, but there are so many tunnels, branches, and offshoots. I can't think of another mine within a day's ride of Martin City with such a labyrinthine layout."

"Will that help us, knowing which mine it is?"

"If I knew for sure it was the Wildcat, and if I could remember the details of the plan I saw one time, and if I knew exactly where in the mine we were. . ." He chuckled. "No, I guess it doesn't make any differ—" An odd *thunk* stopped him, and he plummeted to his knees, tearing her grip from his waistband.

"David?" Karen went down beside him. His hands pressed against his head, and he moaned. "What happened?" Her fingers flew over his face, taking in the tense jaw and the rigid muscles in his neck.

Through gritted teeth, he whispered, "Got distracted and hit my head on something."

"Is there anything I can do?"

"Just wait."

She scooted around to pillow his head on her lap and gently stroked his shoulder and upper arm. Eventually he began to relax.

"Does it hurt very much now?"

He sat up, and his arm came around her shoulders. "It's better. What a stupid thing to do, getting distracted and walking into a brace. I might have knocked myself out completely, and then where would you have been? Dead stupid."

"You're not stupid. You're the most brilliant, caring, wonderful man I've ever met."

David sat silent for a minute. Then he said, his voice rueful, "I'm surprised you would say that, Karen. Brilliance, caring, and wonder have all been sadly lacking in my treatment of you."

The soft caress in his voice broke her heart. "David, I. . .I. . ."

"I love you, Karen," he whispered against her cheek. "I know I haven't acted like it, but I've never stopped loving you." His hands came up to frame her face, and he brought his mouth down to hers.

With a grateful heart, she accepted his kiss.

Breaking apart, he rested his forehead against hers.

"David, I don't want to accuse you, but I need to know. . .why? Why did you put us through so much agony over the past few months?"

"I'm so sorry, my love. You can't know how I regret it. After Marcus left us here, I had a long time to think while I waited for you to wake up. I finally had to acknowledge the reasons behind my actions."

Karen held very still, not wanting to distract him from the words she needed to hear and the words she knew he needed to say.

❧

David breathed a quick prayer that God would slay his pride and help him conquer his fears, and he gathered his wife close. "The morning of the cave-in, I sent Sam and Marcus to the surface to go over some new figures. I was standing at the edge of the square-set framework I'd designed. Several miners worked the stope above and to my right removing ore we'd blasted a couple days before. A row of candles in their little holders flickered along the tunnel, each tiny flame giving enough light for the miner to see to dig. Paddy Doolin came toward me, pointing to the floor and yelling. I couldn't hear what he said over the sound of the drills and sledgehammers, but as he came closer, a shower of dust and pebbles fell from somewhere overhead. Then the framework groaned and cracked, and I knew it was all coming down. I think I yelled to Paddy to run, but it was too late."

His arms tightened around her, and his heart beat thick in his ears, reliving those moments when he thought he'd died. "I thought of you in that instant, Karen. While the rocks tumbled down around me, while the dust choked me, filling my eyes and nose and lungs, I thought of you and how sorry I was to be leaving you."

She stroked his upper back, clinging to him. When he could relax, she asked, "Then what happened?"

"I remember being trapped, pinned to the floor by rock and timber up to my waist. At first I thought I might suffocate, the dust was so thick. I managed to pull the collar of my coat up over my head as best I could and tried to breathe the air in that little tent. Rubble kept raining down on me. One good-sized rock or piece of timber must've come loose overhead and crashed into my temple. I blacked out."

Karen gripped his hand as if to give him strength and sympathy all at once.

"I don't remember Sam pulling me out. Father said Sam wouldn't leave the mine until he found me. I didn't wake up for two days." He swallowed and rubbed his thumbs on the backs of her hands. "When I did, I wished I had died in the mine. Karen, there's something in our family, something we don't talk about. In fact, once things were settled, Father forbade us to ever mention it. Most of it happened when I was just a boy, but the aftereffects have lingered on. So much so that you were caught up in them without knowing."

"What happened?"

"I told you once about my father's younger sister, Bernice?"

"Only that you said she was Marcus's mother and never to mention her because it was a sore spot with your father."

"That's right. Bernice was beautiful and vivacious and smart, and she married a man named Frank Quint. This was when we still lived in Ohio. When the Union called for soldiers, Frank went off to war, and when he arrived home a year later, he'd lost both his legs and his right eye. His face had been badly burned, and he couldn't do much for himself. Marcus was about fifteen at the time, and I was around twelve. I remember being horrified at the sight of Frank's injuries. Every time I looked at him, a shiver would race up my back. I wanted to help him, but I was repulsed."

He swallowed and laced his fingers through hers, pressing his palm to hers. "Bernice took one look at him and was sick. She refused to be near him, and at the first opportunity she left. His condition so disgusted her that she ran out on him. Father went after her and tried to drag her back, but she wouldn't come. Said she wouldn't be tied to a freak for the rest of her life, and that Frank would've been better off dead."

"What happened to her?"

"For a while she kept in contact with Marcus. She would send him letters from time to time all about her glamorous life. She spent some time on the riverboats, then went to New Orleans. Then one day a trunk arrived along with a letter. The steamer held all her belongings, and the letter was from a doctor in a sanitarium. She'd died of consumption after working in a brothel for a few years."

"That's terrible. What happened to your uncle Frank?"

"He went mad when she left him. Started drinking and talking to himself. He refused to bathe or eat, and he started hurting himself on purpose. Father tried to help him and was in the process of getting him committed to a hospital when Frank snapped. He drank a whole bottle of laudanum. He just couldn't face life without her."

"That poor man." Tears thickened her voice, and when he touched her cheek, his finger came away damp.

"I always wondered how he got the laudanum. Mother kept it locked in a cabinet in the kitchen. I guess a part of me always wondered if Marcus had given it to him." He took a deep breath. "So when I woke up unable to see, I guess I thought history was repeating itself. There I was, engaged to the most beautiful woman in town, and I was a cripple, like Frank. I did you a grave injustice fearing you would be like Bernice, but I was so afraid. I'd lost my sight, and at the time, I was sure I had killed several good men through my negligence. I hated myself and thought you would, too. Even if you didn't loathe me right away, eventually you would. Then you would leave me."

"So you tried to leave me first."

"I didn't want to be tossed aside as damaged goods." He stroked her hair. "Then my mother devised that entire lawsuit scheme, and I found myself married. I've never been more scared in my life."

She hiccupped on a sob. "I shouldn't have done it, but I was so desperate. Then you wouldn't take me as your wife, and I wondered if I'd made a terrible mistake. You threw the word *annulment* in my face."

"What I said to you on our wedding night was unforgivable, and yet, I do beg your forgiveness. It took everything I had in me not to open that door when I heard you crying, and yet, fear held me back. I thought you would be repulsed or I would be inept as a husband, and that fear kept me from you that night. And I feared fathering a child. Someone who would despise me like Marcus did his father. Someone who would be ashamed of his crippled dad."

She ducked her chin, and her breath came quickly. "I wish you would've told me."

"As I said, it was something our family was in the habit of not talking about."

They were quiet for a while. Then she stirred in his arms. "David, I'm so sorry for the way I acted when Aunt Hattie died. I shouldn't have blamed you."

"Ah Karen, you shame me with your apology. I was the one who refused to go visit her. I was so wrapped up in my hurt and pride, afraid of being a burden to you, afraid of being the object of curiosity or worse, pity, that I kept you from being able to see her one last time. Then you went away and took my heart with you. I was afraid you wouldn't come back, or that if you did, you'd announce you wanted an annulment."

"I was so hurt and grieved I barely knew what I was doing. I just knew I couldn't fight you anymore. I needed to get away to think, but I always knew I would come back. I'll admit your letter scared me, telling me to take all the time I needed. I thought you didn't need me at all."

He groaned. "I was trying to be supportive. If you only knew how I labored over that letter. I just wanted to ease your mind that Buckford and Mrs. Webber were taking care of me. You were the one who kept writing about how wonderful Pastor Hamilton was and about the matchmaking ladies of his church. You even mentioned that your aunt's lawyer was working on some annulment proceedings." He gave her a little shake.

"Oh David, we've been rather foolish, haven't we? Is it too late to start over?"

His hand found her chin and lifted her face to his. Gently at first, but with the growing hunger of knowing they were at last free to love each other without misunderstandings, fear, or guilt, he took her lips with his own.

When he broke the kiss, she wiped at his cheeks, wet from her tears, and brushed her lips across his chin. "When you kiss me, when you hold me, I don't think of you as being blind. I just know I love you."

"As much as I'd love to stay here kissing you, I think we'd better get moving. But trust me, when we do escape this infernal mine, you're going to get a thousand more kisses, and you're never going to have to wonder if I love you."

She laughed and scrambled to her feet. "Is your head still paining you?"

Bracing himself against the wall, he pushed himself upright. "I'm a bit light-headed, but that might be relief and your kisses more than any crack on the skull."

"Then lead on. I want to get out of here and make you fulfill some of the promises you've just made to me."

Chapter 19

Rocks and ruts filled the floor of the shaft. Their progress had been slowed to a crawl by the jagged terrain. A dogged certainty that they were going the wrong way clung to Karen, making her sluggish.

"Careful, darling. There's a big rock to step over." David put his arm around her waist to help her over.

"The way is getting so rough."

"If things don't improve soon, we'll have to go back and try the other tunnel." He sighed, stopping for a moment. "I can't think that Marcus brought us this way. The going is too uneven for the cart he had with him." He started moving again, and Karen had to follow.

When the walls narrowed and the tunnel ended in yet another unyielding rock wall, Karen sank to the ground and let sobs overtake her. "I can't go on anymore."

David knelt at her side, lifting her to her feet, gripping her shoulders. "You can. You have to. Karen, you're the bravest woman I know. You won't let this defeat you. We *have* to believe we will get out of here. Don't give up now. You're brave, remember?"

"I don't feel brave, David. I feel tired and scared and small and lost. This darkness is pressing in on me. There's nothing here but rocks and timbers and blackness."

"I know how you feel, darling. I do. But you mustn't give in to the fear. Remember what it did to me? I let it paralyze me, but I refuse to be afraid any longer, and I refuse to let you be afraid. We're together. We have each other, and God hasn't abandoned us."

Karen licked her dry, cracked lips. "I thought I knew what you were going through with the blindness, but I didn't. I didn't know how horrifying it could be not to be able to see. I'm so sorry, David."

He laid his cheek against her hair, his hand rubbing her shoulder. "Shhh. None of that. We'll get through this together, right? There has to be an end to this tangled burrow, and we'll find it if we just keep going. We'll meet each obstacle as it comes, and if we have to dig our way out, we'll do that. By now, I imagine Sam and Father are moving mountains to get to us, literally. So we are not going to abandon hope, right?"

"Yes, David."

"I love you, Karen. Don't forget that."

They retraced their steps, and Karen tried to be brave, to pray, to think of anything that might get her mind off the despair that threatened to overwhelm her. Thoughts echoed and ricocheted in her head. She shook it to clear her mind. *Think! What's nagging at you? It's something David said.* "David?"

"Yes?"

"You said that just before the cave-in Paddy Doolin was coming toward you."

"Yes." They stumbled along a few more paces, and when she didn't continue, he asked, "Why?"

"Paddy Doolin's widow came to see us in Denver, right? I've been trying to think why he thought it so important for his wife to tell you about the wild animals. He must've been going to tell you just before the accident. You said he was coming toward you, pointing to the floor."

"That's right," David said, the doubt clear in his voice as he inched forward, keeping a tight grip on her hand.

"So what was under him? And what did it have to do with coyotes?"

"The floor was under him." He inched along a little faster, as if trying to escape her questions. "A few million tons of rock were under him. If he went far enough, China was under him."

"I'm sorry, David. I won't pester you anymore."

He stopped. "No, darling, I'm the one who is sorry. It's just so hard to think about. I feel so guilty. I should've been able to forestall the cave-in. I should've cottoned on sooner to what Marcus was up to, and for the life of me, I can't understand how he did it. It might very well have been a design flaw of mine that caused the failure." He stumbled, his grasp tearing away from hers as he fell.

"David!"

"I'm all right. The wall disappeared. I think I found another side tunnel."

She edged forward as his boots scraped on the rock. Groping for him in the blackness, she found the wall first.

He muttered and stretched away from her, reaching for something. "What on earth?"

"What is it, David?" Fear rose in her throat. If only she could see.

"It's a tunnel of sorts, but the opening is small. The base of this side tunnel must be three or four feet above the floor of the tunnel we are standing in."

"Why would they do that? Is it a ventilation shaft?"

"No, it's—" He stopped.

"What?"

"It's a thieves' tunnel." The wonder of discovery filled his voice and sent chills up her arms.

"What?"

"Why didn't I think of this? Of course. All the pieces fit." He gripped her shoulders. "Paddy Doolin was right! When he said coyotes, he didn't mean the ones he shot for raiding the henhouse."

"David, tell me what you mean."

"When word gets out of a possibly rich lode at a mine, there are always men who want to get to it before you do. That's why we keep things quiet when we think we're getting close to a big strike, right?"

"Right."

"We were very close to what I had a hunch might be the biggest strike we'd ever hit. My early boring samples indicated an extremely rich stope, more silver and lead per ton than we've ever pulled in before. And the only ones who knew about it were Father, Sam, me—and Marcus. It's possible that Marcus told someone or was working with someone to get to the stope first. When thieves want to get to the treasure, they don't file a claim, they don't start operating high, wide, and handsome. They dig narrow, tight, quick tunnels, looking to get to the strike first and take what they can before anyone is the wiser. Sometimes this is referred to as a coyote. Paddy Doolin must've seen signs of coyote digging and been coming to warn me. And if he was pointing to the floor, they must've been digging beneath the shaft." He gave her a little shake. "Don't you see it? The shaft didn't collapse from above. It collapsed from below."

"Then that means. . ."

"That means the cave-in *was* sabotage. I *didn't* do anything wrong." Relief radiated from his words. "Karen, I think this coyote tunnel may be the answer to our prayers." He sucked in a harsh breath. "I didn't want to tell you, because I hoped it wasn't true, but before he left us, Marcus said he was going to blow up the entrance to the mine. I've been praying for another way out, just in case, and here it is."

Blow up the entrance to the mine. She pressed her hand to her middle, as if she could stay the feeling of her insides turning to sand and trickling away. "You mean. . ." She swallowed, praying her knees would hold her up. "I'm glad you didn't tell me before now. I'm not sure what I would've done."

"I know it won't be pleasant, since it is so cramped, but this tunnel should lead us to the surface. Are you willing to try?"

"How cramped?"

"It will be big enough for us to get through, but not tall enough for us to stand up straight. And it might angle up pretty sharply, depending on how deep we are, but it probably doesn't have any offshoot tunnels. Thieves don't waste time. It's dig straight for the treasure and get out quick."

"If you think it is best, then, yes, let's go."

"I'll go first to make sure it's clear." He climbed into the hole, sending a cascade of pebbles bouncing to the floor. His hands reached back for her. "Here, I'll help you up. We'll have to crouch and go carefully. If I say stop, you stop right away."

After eons of climbing in the narrow shaft, her knees hurt and her palms burned from contact with the rough rocks. A hundred knives pierced her hunched back. "Can we rest for a minute?" Ever since David had realized he wasn't responsible for the deaths of his friends and employees, he'd been rejuvenated, picking up their pace, hopeful of reaching the surface soon. Karen had been so happy for him and so thankful for a way of escape from the mine, she had done her best to keep pace, but the long hours in the dark had taken their toll. She couldn't go on without a break.

David must've sensed her despair. "Yes, let's rest. Come, let me hold you for a minute."

She sidled near him and eased down. Feeling his arm, she reached for his hand, content to sit side by side with her head on his shoulder for a while.

He yawned and drew his knees up as far as the cramped shaft would let him. "Strange as it seems, and as long as we get out mostly unscathed, I can't say I'm sorry for this experience."

She choked on a breath. "You're not?"

"I know. It's odd. But would we have been as open with each other? We had so many misunderstandings and things to hash out. I thought you were leaving me for good; you thought I wanted you out of my life. When you left, I was still fighting with God about being blind, and I was afraid to leave the house. Our marriage was dying under the weight of my pride. If God hadn't stripped me of everything and allowed Marcus to kidnap us, I don't know when I would've broken down and asked for forgiveness. I was pretty useless to myself and everyone around me."

"How could you think that? My life is nothing without you."

"Do you know how long it has been since I thought you really needed me? Do you know what it's been like to have you be the one to arrange our transportation, hail cabs, see to the mail, pay the bills? I know you're more than capable, but I wanted to be the one to do those things for you. I was used to being in charge."

She tried to imagine what it had been like for him, and her fingers curled around his. "David, I need you for so much more than you can even imagine. I've never felt put upon taking care of mundane tasks like paying bills. I do those things because I love you, not because I'm trying to take control. You're the head of our home."

He kissed her temple. "Are you rested enough? Think you can go on?"

Chapter 20

"Did you feel that?" David stopped, and Karen bumped into his back.

"What?"

"I thought I felt. . .fresh air?" He sniffed.

Karen pushed her hair off her face and tried to swallow. The universe consisted of nothing beyond plodding in the dark, the scrape of their shoes on the rocks, and the persistent ache in every muscle and joint. The dank, dusty, earthy smell of the mine had clogged her nostrils for such a long time, she didn't know if she would recognize fresh air.

"There, there it is again." David's voice lifted. "We're almost there." His hand reached back for her and took her hand to help her along once more. "Can you see daylight?"

She forced her eyes open wider and strained to focus on anything. Disappointment washed over her. "No, I'm sorry. I don't see anything."

"Maybe we're around a bend." They stumbled on.

Gradually, Karen became aware that the darkness wasn't as black. Her heart lifted. "David, I see—"

"What? Sunlight?"

"No, I think it's. . .starlight?"

"That makes sense. We must've been walking all night. Can you see the opening?"

"Not yet."

With each step, objects and shapes began to emerge from the gloom. She discerned David's outline, hunched shoulders, torn shirt, and tattered pants. Dried blood and dirt caked his hands in dark streaks as he sought handholds to help them up the slope. "David, I can see it. About ten yards ahead maybe? I can see stars through branches."

"Do you want to go first, since you can see it?" He stopped and spoke over his shoulder.

Tears pricked her eyes and altered her voice. "No, David. You've led us this far. You go first." A cool breeze that smelled of night dew brushed her cheeks.

David reached the opening and swiped his hand across the bramble stretching across it. Twigs snapped, and the opening widened. "We made it." David shouldered his way through the limbs of tiny new spring leaves, and once free, turned back and held out his hand. "We made it, Karen."

She struggled the last few steps up the rocky slope and all but fell into his arms. Tears wet her cheeks, and she clung to him. "Thank You, Lord. Thank You, Lord." Her light-starved eyes took in every contour of the hills, every tree and shrubby shape. Pale stars winked overhead in an indigo sky. Fresh, sweet, cold air swept over them and murmured in the sparse pines, and somewhere a cricket chirped.

"Can you tell where we are?" David lifted his face to the wind and breathed deeply.

Karen loosened her grip on him and turned to survey the valley below and the hill behind them. "We're about halfway up a fairly steep hill, and there's a creek in the ravine below. You can just hear the water."

"That's our first priority, then. I don't know about you, but I could use a drink of water about now."

They skidded and slid down the slope. Loose stones and tufts of grass made the going difficult, but eventually they reached the water. David moved with more confidence than she would've thought possible just a few months ago, keeping hold of her hand until they knelt beside the creek.

Water had never tasted so good. She cupped her hands again and again, wetting her neck and splashing the front of her dress in her haste. When she couldn't hold another drop, she sighed. "Which way do we head now?" Weariness crept over her again, and her limbs turned to lead. If only she could curl up and take a nap. She chafed her hands, icy after plunging them into the stream.

"Downstream."

She didn't question him. "The creek curves to the left around this hill."

"I know you're tired, but the sooner we get back to town, the quicker someone can get after Marcus."

Rocks littered the streambed and made for slow going. Tailing piles from played-out mines lay like giant tongues on the hillside. They picked their way around the base of the hill, and Karen kept a watch out for a lamp or sign of habitation.

She found none until they rounded the brow of the hill, and she stopped to get her bearings. Above them, she thought she caught the glow of firelight. The skeletal frame of an abandoned derrick lay twisted, hanging down the slope as if pushed over by a giant's hand. A sharp, new scar marred the earth, darker than the surrounding dirt and rocks. "David, there are people up there. Can you hear them?"

"Where?" His face turned to the sound of rocks and men's voices.

She hugged him. "We're rescued. I think there's a road here. . .or at least a path. It zigzags up the grade."

Halfway up, the muffled noises clarified into the sounds of digging and men shouting. A mule brayed, and metal implements struck rock again and again.

"Hello?" David shouted, but the work above didn't stop. He tried again. "Hello!"

"What can they be doing in the middle of the night?" Karen stubbed her toe on something. Her skirt caught and she had to stop and free it. "David, you said you thought you knew which mine we might've been in. What was it called?"

"The Wildcat?"

Karen lifted the board she'd stepped on and angled it to get a better look. "I think you were right. I've got a piece of a sign here. It says Wildcat Mining."

The sound of timber splintering cracked through the air, and cheers went up. "We're making good progress now. You men with the pickaxes, get started on those boulders."

"That's Sam!" David's face brightened. "They must be digging for us."

With the last of her energy, Karen climbed the hill. David kept his hand on her shoulder, and at last they topped out on a little plateau. Bonfires roared in a semicircle around a pile of boulders and shattered wood. A dozen men crawled over the rocks, lifting them down and carting them away. Dust sifted through the air and swirled in the breeze.

"Sam!"

She sank to the ground, exhausted. Sam broke from a group of men and charged toward them, grabbing David by the arm then pulling him into a hug.

"You're alive! How did you get here? We've been digging for hours."

Karen could barely see through her tears as David tried, between backslaps and handshakes, to explain how they got out of the mine. Someone pressed a warm cup into her hands and dropped a blanket around her shoulders.

Sam knelt before her. "Are you all right? We've been worried to death."

She sipped the coffee, letting the hot liquid warm her from the inside out. "I'm fine. We're both fine. Just so very tired."

"Right. Explanations can wait. Let's get you two home."

❧

Nothing had ever felt as good as the hot bath and clean nightclothes Matilda prepared for Karen. She fussed and mothered, supervising the bath and washing Karen's hair for her. All the while she marveled at their escape and at the changes in David. "David seems so much like his old self. I don't know what happened down there, but I'm thanking God for it."

Karen eased her feet into the lamb's wool slippers Matilda had warming by the fire and stuck her arms into the sleeves of a thick wrapper. "I am, too. We got off to a rocky start, but everything is wonderful now."

"Praise the Lord." Tears glistened in Matilda's eyes, and she turned away, swiping at her cheeks. "Now, drink this tea. Then it's bed for you."

The clock struck six times. "No, there's something I want to see first." She padded downstairs to the study, following the sound of male voices. She stopped in the doorway, still holding her tea.

David, freshly tubbed and in a dressing gown, stood by the fire, leaning his forearm against the mantel.

Sam sat on the corner of the desk, one booted leg swinging. Dust and dirt streaked his face and clothes, and sweat plastered his hair to his head. "Marcus had a snitch in the sheriff's office. The minute we left there after getting the warrant, one of the deputies ducked out and ran right to Marcus."

"How did you know we were in the Wildcat?"

"When Karen didn't come back from the greenhouse, Mother got worried and went down there. She found flowers all over the path and sent Buckford for us. We were climbing the walls because you were missing."

Jesse rocked in the chair behind the desk. "I knew in my gut that he'd come for you both, but we had no idea where he would take you or what he'd do to you."

Sam turned his hat in his hands. "Then a couple of men came belting into town yelling that there had been an explosion on Wildcat Hill. Father remembered that Marcus had done some work for Wildcat Mining just after he finished his schooling."

Turning his back to the flames, David tucked his hands into the pockets of his robe. "Where's Marcus now?"

Sam swallowed and darted a look at Jesse. Jesse's brows lowered and the lines beside his mouth deepened. "Marcus must've misjudged the explosives. We found him in the rubble. He's dead, David."

Karen's hands shook, sloshing her tea.

Matilda appeared at her shoulder and took it before it spilled. "Come away, Karen," she whispered. "You need your rest."

Karen shook her head.

David shoved away from the mantel. The blood had drained from his face. "Do you think it was an accident, or did he take his own life, like his father did?"

Jesse flinched. "He was under a lot of pressure. We don't know what was going on in his head. Accident or not, it cost him his life."

Sam stood. "You girls can quit hovering in the hall. We're done talking. I'm going to get cleaned up. Mother, don't you think Karen should be in bed?"

Karen inched into the room and stood on tiptoe to place a kiss on Jesse's cheek first then Sam's. "I won't be long out of bed."

Jesse hugged her as if she were spun glass. "Drag David upstairs with you. He looks terrible."

The family filed out, leaving David and Karen alone.

"It's not true, you know." She crossed the room and wrapped her arms around his waist, leaning her head against his chest. He smelled of soap and clean linen. She breathed deeply, her eyelids heavy.

"What's not true?"

"You don't look terrible. You've never looked better to me."

His heart thudded steadily under her ear.

"I'm sorry about Marcus."

He nodded. "Why aren't you in bed? You're practically falling asleep in my arms."

"I can't think of a better place." She smiled. "I wanted to wait for you, and I knew if I got into bed, I'd fall asleep before you got there."

They walked out of the study arm in arm and up the stairs.

At the landing, she stopped. "David, the sun is up." Faint warmth came with the light, and she squinted against the brilliance. "Can you feel it? The dawn of a brand-new day."

LIGHT TO MY PATH

Dedication

To Mr. David Heter, teacher and friend, who nutured my love of words and books and who encouraged me to write. Thank you for your guidance and all the prayers you prayed for me.

Chapter 1

He should've known she was hiding something. From the moment Sam Mackenzie had asked Yvette Adelman to marry him, something had been wrong. Only he'd been too besotted by her beauty to want to dig any deeper, which compounded his foolishness.

Sam tilted his head toward the conversation in the next room and considered the old adage about eavesdroppers never hearing any good about themselves. If that wasn't the plain truth. He blew out a breath and wondered at which point he should push the door open and confront his fiancée and her mother. Maybe he'd best listen a little more and make sure he had heard right.

"I won't have any trouble. Sam Mackenzie is an absolute sheep and too dumb to realize it." Yvette's lyrical tones belied the insulting words.

Sam's mouth twisted, and his chest felt hollow.

"He's loaded. That's all that matters." Hortense Adelman's voice carried across the drawing room and through the inch-wide gap in the pocket doors. For a tiny woman, she sure had a powerful speaking voice. He hadn't been at all sorry at the thought of leaving his soon-to-be mother-in-law behind in a few days.

"He adores me." Yvette laughed. "I've only to mention that I want something, and he's around here with it in a trice. And he's eager. I barely had to suggest moving the wedding date up, and he pounced on the idea. In two days I'll be Mrs. Sam Mackenzie, we'll be on a train for Colorado, and I'll be rich. A few weeks in the Mackenzie mansion in Martin City—doesn't that sound like a dreadful frontier hamlet?—then I'll tell him how homesick I am for St. Louis, how much I need my mother. I'll be back here by Easter. Once I'm in the city, I can put off returning to Colorado indefinitely. I'll have money to burn. By next fall, things will be settled, and I'm sure I can be back in St. Louis society with no one the wiser."

"What about Anthony? You won't see him anymore, will you? That would ruin everything. If Sam caught you two together, everything would explode."

"Oh pooh, I could explain Anthony to Sam. Sam would believe whatever I told him."

Sam's neck muscles knotted, and his throat tightened. The bouquet he held shook, and his thumb made a crease in the foil cover of the chocolate box. He eased them onto the table beside the door.

"I'm still amazed at him appearing in our hour of need, Yvette."

"I told you things would work out fine. I just needed to find the right man to come along. And soon."

Her laugh, one of the things that had first drawn Sam's attention, lilted like music. How could something that looked and sounded so good be such a sham? He squared his shoulders and pushed open the pocket doors. "Good afternoon, Yvette, Hortense."

The way they both jumped would've been comical if he hadn't known what they were up to. Yvette got to her feet, graceful and fluid as always. Sunshine from the bank of windows shone and raced along the fiery ringlets on her cheeks. Her skin, usually white and cool as marble, now showed a hint of color. She widened her sapphire eyes and flicked her lashes. "Why, Sam, I didn't expect you so early." She crossed the room and held out her hands, raising her face for his customary kiss. When he failed to oblige, she pulled back and ducked her chin. "What's this? You're not getting shy practically on the eve of our wedding?" She batted his arm.

"Shy?" He shook his head. "A sheep like me?" Turning from her, he took the chair beside the fireplace. "That is what you called me, isn't it?"

Yvette shot a glance at her mother and then shrugged. "You've been eavesdropping. Darling, you misunderstood. Whatever you thought you heard has been misconstrued." She pursed her lips into a bow and blinked at him, the picture of innocence. From her auburn curls to her kid slippers, everything about her was perfect. The white, frothy dress with blue flowers just the color of her eyes, the cameo threaded on a ribbon around her slender neck, her long, delicate fingers ending in perfectly rounded nails—everything calculated to please a man's eye. She put her hands behind her back in an appealing gesture, one he'd fallen for too many times.

"I don't believe I misunderstood. I believe I understand for the first time." He shook his head. "You've been deceiving me from the minute I met you."

She spread her hands, palms up. "Sam, I can explain."

He looked at Hortense, who sat frozen in her chair, her skin mottled and her mouth slack. "I don't need to hear any more of your lies. This farce of an engagement is over. You'll have to find yourself some other idiot."

Yvette's mouth opened, and a little squeak came out. She shook her lovely head. "No, Sam, you don't mean that. You love me."

A rueful chuckle escaped him. "I sure thought I did. I feel almost as much of a fool as you made me out to be. Suckered by your looks and your pretty talk. I think I was in love with the idea of you, flattered that someone so beautiful would fall for the likes of me. I let you manipulate me, talk me into a short engagement." He shook his head. "I should've known. Something's been off about our relationship from the start. You had me measured up for a matrimonial noose the minute we were introduced."

Hortense gave a strangled cry. "Don't do this to my girl. You'll ruin everything."

"Mother, please leave us alone. I know we can sort this out if we can just be alone for a little while."

Hortense scuttled out of the room as if her hem was on fire. She threw one last desperate glance over her shoulder before closing the doors behind her.

Two perfect tears squeezed out of Yvette's eyes. "Sam, please, I beg you not to do this. Let me explain." She stepped toward him, but he rose and rounded the chair, putting it between him and his ex-fiancée.

"No, it wouldn't be the truth. I think being truthful is beyond your capabilities. You've traded on your looks and gotten favors from men for so long, it's become a habit. You say whatever you think they want to hear. You lie when it suits you, and you deny the truth when confronted." He sighed, giving free rein to all the doubts that had been building over the past month. "This isn't the first time I've caught you lying, but I believed your explanations because I wanted to believe."

Yvette's face crumpled. "Please, Sam, say you don't mean the engagement is off. I'll apologize if something I said hurt your feelings. I don't really think you're a sheep. I love you, and I know you love me." She edged around the chair and stroked his arm.

His guts roiled. Where once he had eagerly anticipated her touch, now it felt akin to a snake slithering across his skin. He jerked back. "No. It's over. They say there's a sucker born every minute. Well, I'm all done being your sucker. I used to believe in love. I think that's why I fell for you so quickly in the first place. I *wanted* to fall in love. But being with you has cured me of that notion for good."

Yvette dissolved into sobs, though he noted how controlled and perfect her crying appeared and how every few seconds she glanced reproachfully at him, as if she were gauging his response for signs of capitulation. More games, more lies.

Sam brushed past her and shoved the doors open.

Hortense jumped aside and pressed against the wall opposite the doors, her hand on her chest.

He grabbed his hat and the flowers and chocolates. Jamming his hat on his head, he couldn't resist one last jab. "Baa!"

Eldora Carter kept her chin up and refused to cry, though the tears burning the backs of her eyes demanded release. Staring straight ahead, hands clasped in front of her, she tried to be brave in the face of the tirade coming from her employer.

"I will not stand for this impertinence." Mrs. Gamble's bulk nearly overwhelmed the chair. She placed her pen into its holder and leaned back. "You will apologize to my son, and you will remember your place in this household." She crossed her arms under her broad bosom and contemplated the pelmet. "This is what I get for my charity. I told Mr. Korbin I wanted someone who would know her place, do her work, and not cause me any trouble. And he sends me you." Her hand waved in a dismissive gesture. "Dressed like a scarecrow, eyes like saucers, and no sense of what being a domestic requires."

Eldora adjusted her shawl, crossing it over her chest like armor. Her hands stung from the hours of scrubbing she'd already put in today, and her lower back ached from her time over the washtubs.

"You've been here three weeks, and this is the third time I've had to reprimand you." Mrs. Gamble's eyes looked small in her puffy face. Like a colt, she had fine whiskers around her lips that quivered when she was angry. They quivered now. "I don't know what they taught you at that orphanage, and I suppose I should've expected no better, but for you to try to entice my son is beyond the scope of common decency."

Beau Gamble hadn't even had the courage to own up to what he had done. Was the red mark of her hand still evident on his cheek? She hoped so. The lout. She swallowed against the lump in her throat and returned her attention to Mrs. Gamble.

"I will not tolerate such behavior under my roof. If you want to comport yourself as a common trollop, you will do so elsewhere. You will apologize to my son and give me your promise you will behave yourself, or I'll send you straight back to the orphanage, and Conrad can deal with you."

Eldora said nothing. She shifted her weight, trying to ease the discomfort on the bottom of her right foot where the sole of her boot had worn through. She'd stepped on a sharp stone on her way to the grocery for the cook this morning, and the resulting bruise throbbed.

"Well, are you going to apologize?"

She finally looked her employer in the eye. Though her mouth was dry, she refused to back down. "No ma'am, I am not. I have nothing to apologize for."

Mrs. Gamble blinked and gasped. Her mouth slacked, and for a moment the whiskers stopped trembling. "What do you call throwing yourself at my son like a tart?"

"I did no such thing. Your son is the one to blame." Even as she said it, Eldora knew it was useless to protest her innocence. Mrs. Gamble would never believe her precious son could be lascivious. Any trouble would always be the fault of the girl. But she refused to be accused any longer without standing up for herself.

"Your son is the most disgusting man I've ever met. I couldn't walk from my room to the basement laundry without him accosting me. His suggestions and comments were filthy. Why do you think you have such trouble keeping help in this house? It's your awful son. He tried several times to kiss me, but I managed to evade him. Today, I'd finally had enough. He deserves worse than a slap across his horrible face, and if you don't put a stop to his actions he'll go on until he finally ruins some poor girl. Well, I refuse to be that girl."

Mrs. Gamble's eyes glittered like a snake's. "You lie. All you servant girls are alike. You try to capture a man, and when he rebuffs you, you make wild accusations." She levered herself up and stood toe-to-toe with Eldora.

Though Eldora's insides quaked, she refused to show fear. She might be about to be turned out into the cold, but she would not cower before this tyrant. "It is you who is lying to yourself, Mrs. Gamble. I may only be an orphan, and not very pretty. And I have nothing of my own but my dignity and my virtue. But I will give neither to you or your son. I quit."

Mrs. Gamble looked like she might strangle on all she wanted to say.

Before the woman unscrambled her thoughts, Eldora walked out of the sumptuous room. She marched up three flights to her attic bedroom, stuffed her nightgown and comb into her small bag, and headed downstairs. Since she didn't own a coat, her shawl would have to suffice on the long walk.

Beau waited on the landing, his handsome face sneering. She stopped, instantly wary, though taking small satisfaction that the outline of her fingers still showed on his cheekbone. "Leaving? Too bad. I would've liked the chance to tame that feisty temper."

"Let me pass."

"Not without a kiss good-bye."

"You're a rogue and a rake, Beau Gamble. If you touch me I'll scream this house right down."

"Can I carry your bag for you, miss?" The houseman stood at the foot of the steps. His face seemed carved from granite. Relief washed through Eldora even as disappointment flashed in Beau's eyes.

"Yes, please." She edged by Beau and hurried to the first floor.

Jimson took her bag and her elbow. "I'm sorry you're leaving us, miss." The older man tugged her arm when she would've turned to go to the back door. "You'll go out the front, like a lady." He kept looking straight ahead, but his expression softened somewhat from its usual sternness. Bowing slightly, he held the door for her and handed her the parcel she'd given him. "Godspeed, miss."

"Thank you, Jimson." She smiled and squeezed his arm. It was the first time in her three weeks in the Gamble house that she'd called the man by his name. When he closed the door, she headed down the gravel horseshoe drive toward the street to begin the long walk back to the orphanage.

She stopped when she got to the street and looked back at the mansion. How could something so beautiful on the outside be so rotten on the inside?

Chapter 2

Eldora trudged up the snow-covered steps to the orphanage, weary, wet, and wishing she could be anywhere else. Entering the front hall, she stomped her numb feet to rid them of their icy encasement. The familiar smells of cooked cabbage, lye soap, and damp wool wrapped around her.

Behind the classroom door on her left muffled recitations emitted, and from the back hall pots clanked and water poured. She turned to her right, determined to get the lecture over with. Her chest tightened. What if he wouldn't take her back? She was of age and had no real right to be at the orphanage any longer. If Mr. Korbin refused her refuge. . .

Please, God, let him take me back. I don't have anywhere else to go.

Placing her bundle on the bench beside the door—a bench where children in need of discipline often sat awaiting Mr. Korbin's ire—she tapped. Her knees trembled as the door swung open.

Mrs. Scrabeck wore a smile until she recognized Eldora. Her nostrils flared, and her lips pinched like she'd just kissed a dill pickle. "Eldora Carter, what are you doing here?" She poked her head around the doorjamb and spied the bundle of Eldora's belongings. Her sigh nearly parted Eldora's hair. "Again? Mr. Korbin is not going to like this." She glared, appraising Eldora from her not-quite-blond-not-quite-brown hair to her wet hem and water-spotted shoes. "I suppose you'd better come in, but keep in mind, Mr. Korbin has a board meeting in a few minutes."

Eldora swallowed hard and resisted ducking her head to scuttle in like a mouse. Her cheeks burned, and she pressed her lips together.

Mrs. Scrabeck pointed to a chair before slipping into Mr. Korbin's office. A frosted pane bore his name in black-and-gold letters, and through its semiopaque glass, dark shapes moved.

Eldora clasped her hands in her lap and shut her eyes. Mr. Korbin's voice, deeper and louder than Mrs. Scrabeck's, rose high. Footsteps, and the door crashed open.

"Miss Carter, why are you here? Have you been dismissed again?" He loomed over her, solid and stern, the ultimate authority in her life for the past nine years. "I told you not to return. You had a perfectly good placement with the Gambles."

She cringed and then forced herself to straighten. "Mr. Korbin, I couldn't stay there."

His sigh was even bigger than Mrs. Scrabeck's. "I suppose you had better come into the office." He held the door, and her shoes squished as she dragged into the room. Mr. Korbin took his time rounding the desk and easing down into the plush chair.

Eldora stared at the blotter, heartily sick of being called to account for her shortcomings.

"Go ahead. What was it this time? Impertinence?"

She lifted her chin. "Mrs. Gamble said I was impertinent, but I had to be." The memory of Beau Gamble's hard hands on her, his squishy lips on her neck and cheek, and his pushing her up against the wall made her skin crawl.

"What did you do?"

She loathed the patient forbearance in his voice that said she was nothing more than a nuisance he'd like to scrape off the bottom of his shoe. Heat bloomed in her chest. "What did *I* do? I refused to let Mrs. Gamble's grown son take advantage of me. He tried to compromise my virtue, and I slapped his face for it. I knew it would cost me my position, and I knew there was every chance you wouldn't take me back here, but I couldn't stand that arrogant man. He deserved worse than a smack. I wish now I'd hit him harder." She trembled, remembering his leers and disgusting suggestions.

Mr. Korbin pressed his lips in a hard line, and his neck went rigid. "You slapped Beau Gamble?" A cough stuck in his throat, and he leaned forward to take a sip from the glass of water on his desk. "Do you realize that Olivia Gamble is one of the most generous patrons this orphanage has? Do you know how many of our orphans she has taken into her home and given jobs?"

"How many of those were girls? How many of them do you think Beau Gamble has ruined? I'm not the first girl he tried his tricks on." Libby and April, the upstairs maids, were afraid of Beau and whispered of another girl who had gotten in the family way as a result of his attentions and was dismissed for low morals. "I would think you'd be more concerned about the welfare of the girls you place out."

Mr. Korbin leaned forward, his eyes like ice. "That's enough. I won't have you spreading vile gossip about the son of one of our patrons. This is the third time you've lost a perfectly good job that would get you out of my hair once and for all, and this is the third time you've come crawling back here. Might I remind you that you are no longer of an age to live at this orphanage? We've done the best we can for you, and it is time you made your own way in this world."

A feeling like sand trickling through fingers started in her chest. How would she make her own way? She had no skills beyond being a domestic, and she had no references without the orphanage's backing. "Are there any other positions available? I assure you, Mr. Korbin, I don't try to get fired. The first one wasn't my fault. The family moved out of the state and didn't wish to take the servants with them. The second time, well, I couldn't stand by and let the housekeeper beat that poor boot boy to death. His transgression didn't warrant getting caned senseless. As for Beau Gamble, you can't tell me you think I should've accepted his advances just to keep the position of laundress?" She shook her head hard enough that a hank of hair came out of its pin and slid over her right eye. With a shove, she tucked it behind her ear. "Not even if I had to sleep on the street in the teeth of a blizzard."

Hands flat on the desktop, Mr. Korbin levered himself up and leaned over the blotter. "Don't take that tone with me, missy. Sleeping on the street isn't outside the realm of possibility for you tonight." He shook his finger, his face a dull red. "You're too old to live here anymore. We've done the best we can for you, placed you with three good employers, and you've managed to lose every position. As of this minute—"

Mrs. Scrabeck knocked on the door and stuck her head inside. "Mr. Korbin, there's a policeman here to see you, and you have a board meeting upstairs in three minutes."

At the mention of a policeman, Eldora's insides sloshed. Surely slapping a lout wasn't a criminal matter. Had Mrs. Gamble set the police after her? She tried to moisten her dry lips, but her mouth was parched.

"Show him in."

When Eldora edged to the door, Mr. Korbin held up his hand. "Wait. I'm not through with you."

A burly police officer entered, pushing the door aside and dragging someone after himself. "Korbin, I thought you were going to keep this one under close watch." He heaved, and Phin Bartholomew skidded into view. His black forelock hung in his eyes, and those eyes glowed like coals through the strands. A dirty smear decorated his swarthy, thin cheek.

Mr. Korbin braced himself on the desk, dropping his head momentarily as if his burdens were too great for one man to bear. "What did he do this time?"

"Caught him down at the grocer's helping himself to the food and folks' wallets."

Phin glared, unrepentant. He kept trying to worm out of the policeman's grasp, but the beefy officer appeared not to notice the attempts, nor did he loosen his ham-fisted grip on Phin's collar.

Eldora's heart went out to the boy. They were both caught in untenable situations with no hope of escaping their fates.

Mr. Korbin walked to the door and summoned Mrs. Scrabeck. "Please take Phin to the matron. She's to see to it he doesn't leave the premises again, and she has free rein to discipline him as she sees fit."

"That old cow can't keep me here, and you can't either." Phin swung out, trying to land a blow with his skinny arms, but the policeman dangled him until he stood on tiptoe. "She can beat me with that radiator brush all she likes, but I'll get away. See if I don't. . ." Phin protested all the way out of the room.

Eldora closed her eyes, fisting her hands, impotent to change anything for the boy or for herself. The matron, a sour woman who had no fondness for children, would no doubt do as Phin predicted. The radiator brush was a favorite method of discipline in the orphanage.

Mrs. Scrabeck showed the policeman and Phin out and then poked her sour face around the edge of the door. "Sir, your meeting?"

Mr. Korbin turned back to Eldora. "Wait on the bench in the hall until my meeting is over. Then I'll see what's to be done with you."

❧

Sam wanted to shake the dust off his feet when he stepped out of the Adelman house. How could he have been so blind? A sheep, was he? He chuckled. Baaing at Hortense had been childish, but it sure had felt good.

He checked his timepiece and waited for a wagon loaded down with barrels to roll by before crossing the street. Plenty of time until he had to meet Great-aunt Tabitha at the orphanage.

Thoughts of his father's aunt brought a smile to his face. No-nonsense, wise, and funny, he had no doubt she would have plenty to say about his broken engagement.

Barges and riverboats lined the shores of the muddy Mississippi, and Illinois lay wreathed in low clouds on the far side of the water. He strolled down Lucas Place toward Missouri Park. As he passed the art museum, he considered stopping in to kill some time, but as stirred up as he was after his confrontation with Yvette, he had no desire to stare at paintings and sculptures. Better to walk off his mood.

Turning up his collar against the brisk wind, he tucked the candy box and flowers under his arm and ambled through the park. Black branches outlined in snow stood starkly against the sky. With less than two weeks until Christmas, bells rang out merrily on passing sleighs, and wreaths hung on many of the front doors of the town houses that bordered the park.

When he'd gone as far toward the river as he could go without wading, he turned south toward downtown and the orphanage. In just a few days, he'd be back in Colorado, out of this bustling city where he'd spent the last three months and breathing the cold, crisp air of the Rockies. Thoughts of home carried him to the doorstep of the orphanage about ten minutes before Aunt Tabitha's meeting was scheduled to break up.

He entered, noting that the cold had browned the edges of some of the flowers he carried. Fitting, he supposed. He was certainly browned off with Yvette. The hothouse Christmas roses had cost him plenty. How much money had he squandered keeping the acquisitive Yvette happy?

He twisted his mouth and, once inside, glanced around to get his bearings. Humiliation pricked his skin. How was he going to tell his family, who would be expecting him to arrive in a few days as a newlywed, that he'd been suckered by a gold digger with a pretty face?

A girl sat on a bench in the front hall with her feet primly together and her arms anchoring a dun-colored shawl around her thin shoulders. The shawl matched her hair, some of which had slipped from the pleat at the back of her head and lay on her cheek. One of the orphans, no doubt. Maybe fourteen? He scrubbed his feet on the mat, and at the noise, she looked up.

The biggest, light brown eyes he'd ever seen. He sucked in a breath and nodded to her, touching his hat brim. She was older than he'd thought, though not by a lot. Eighteen or nineteen maybe? Her lashes were gathered into damp points, and when she looked at her lap again, she dabbed at them with the corner of her shawl. More than a few inches of her hem bore water stains and damp spots

He cleared his throat and knocked on the door marked OFFICE. Somewhere upstairs a thumping, pounding ruckus started up with muffled yells. He frowned. Sounded like a stampede.

The girl darted a look up the stairs and twisted her hands in her lap. Her bottom lip disappeared behind her teeth.

A door opened above, and several whacks rocketed down the steps. "Stop that yelling. You've no one to blame but yourself. If you want more of this brush, then you just keep up your caterwauling. I'll give you something to yell about." The door slammed, making the young woman on the bench flinch.

Sam was of a mind to go upstairs and investigate when the office door opened, and a pinch-nosed woman stuck her face out. "Yes, can I help you?"

"Sam Mackenzie. I'm meeting my aunt here in a few minutes. Miss Tabitha Mackenzie? She's in a board meeting, I believe?"

Her sour expression softened into more pleasant lines. "Of course. Please, come in. Can I get you some coffee?"

Another loud thump upstairs made the gaslight rattle. "What's going on up there? A wrestling match?"

The woman made damping motions with her hands. "I'm sorry. One of the boys is in a bit of trouble, and matron has had her hands full with him for the past hour. Don't worry. She has a way with boys. They need a firm hand, you know."

It sounded as if the matron would make a good prison guard. Whoever the kid was, he felt sorry for the boy.

Sam placed the candy and flowers on the table, wishing he'd disposed of them on the walk over. Still, the inmates at this charming establishment might like a few caramel drops to brighten their existence. Aunt Tabitha could have the flowers. He consulted his watch, comparing it to the clock on the wall.

The secretary went back to her desk, but she darted looks at Sam, making him shift in his seat and rotate his hat in his hands.

When he thought he couldn't stand her furtive glances any longer, the hall door opened and Aunt Tabitha entered, followed by a tall, spare man with iron-gray hair and black bushy eyebrows that dominated his hatchet face.

The man closed the door to the hall. "It's the perfect solution, and the rest of the directors agree with me. We'll be solving several problems at once."

"I prefer to think of them as children, not problems, Conrad." Aunt Tabitha leaned on her cane. Her voice, though soft, carried a note of steel. " 'Out of sight, out of mind' isn't a solution; it's dereliction of duty." Sam rose, and Tabitha nodded to him but continued to address the hawk-faced man. "I realize I'm new around here and I'm not familiar with all the procedures, but I do know those children deserve better than being shunted off in the middle of the night."

The man—Sam assumed he must be Conrad Korbin as the name on the interior office proclaimed—clenched his jaw as if holding on to the last thread of his patience. "The matter has been decided. You might be grateful the little girl isn't being sent to an asylum. That would be far more in keeping with her condition. They will depart on tomorrow night's train. I'll pen a letter to be delivered upon their arrival in Denver."

Tabitha turned to him. "Sam, I'm sorry to have kept you waiting. What should've been a routine business meeting turned into something else altogether." She lowered her brows at Mr. Korbin. "I've sent for my carriage."

"Hello, Aunt Tabitha." He kissed her offered cheek, breathing in the scent of licorice and lavender, a combination he always associated with her. The tissue paper around the flowers rustled when he picked them up.

"These are for you."

She took the roses and buried her nose in the dark red buds for a moment before tilting her head back to peer at him through her pince-nez. "Not that these aren't delightful, but I have a feeling there's something you need to tell me."

"There is, but we can talk about it on the way to your house." The chocolates remained on the table, and he considered telling the secretary to pass them out to the children, but something about the woman didn't sit well with him. Her pinched mouth and the way she looked down her nose made him think she might be as mean as second-skimmings. He scooped up the candy box and took Tabitha's arm. Escorting her to the hall, he nodded to Korbin and opened the door.

The girl still sat on the bench. Her shoulders sloped as if the entire world bore down on them and a slight hiccup hitched her frame. Poor kid. The atmosphere in this place was more like that of a prison than a home for children. Enough to make anyone cry.

He stopped Tabitha when she moved toward the front door. "Just a minute." Squatting beside the girl, he placed the box of chocolates on her lap.

She looked up, surprising him again with her enormous gingerbread-colored eyes. In a flash, her lashes darted downward as she ducked her chin. Her long, thin fingers traced the Currier and Ives snowscape on the top of the gilt cardboard, and her pink lips parted with a short, sharp intake of breath.

"This is for you. Share it with some of your friends here." He almost chucked her under the chin, but something stayed his hand.

She held herself rigid, as if expecting him to grab her.

Shrugging, he stood and turned to his aunt. As he held the door for her, he glanced over his shoulder.

The girl watched him, her eyes filled with gratitude out of proportion for such a small gift. Her lips moved slightly, enough for him to make out what she said. "Thank you."

He nodded, wishing he could do more for her than a box of candy, and chided himself. He didn't know her situation or anything about her. He had enough women troubles without inviting more.

Chapter 3

I'm not asking you to adopt these children. Just ease their way a bit on their journey. They won't be any trouble." Tabitha adjusted the sable stole around her throat and glanced up the depot platform toward the engine. "It's providential, I tell you. You've made a good escape from the clutches of Yvette, and you're traveling on the same train as Miss Carter and the children. You can look in on them from time to time and make sure they all arrive safely in Denver."

Providential didn't exactly fit Sam's description of the situation. "You're taking my broken engagement awfully well." He guided Tabitha to a less-busy corner. "Though I have to admit, the celebratory dinner last night was nice."

Tabitha chuckled. "I never liked Yvette, but you were so taken with her I didn't like to say so. The entire relationship felt so hurried. You barely knew the girl before you got engaged, and the rushed wedding plans didn't sit well. Having Hortense Adelman for a mother-in-law wouldn't have been pleasant either. Hortense is not well received in St. Louis society, and she was using the engagement to get invitations into the best parlors and salons of the city. She'll no doubt have her petticoats in an uproar over the broken engagement."

"Yvette didn't want to wait to be married, and fool that I am, I was flattered by her...zeal?" He rubbed his chin and grimaced.

A baggage handler approached them and touched the peak on his cap. "I've placed your bags in your private car at the rear of the train, sir. Is there anything else I can do for you before departure?"

Sam opened his wallet and pulled out a bill. "No, that will be all. Thank you."

The porter eyed the paper and blinked. "Thank *you*, sir." He hastily tucked the money out of sight and backed away with a bow.

"Where is that girl? If they don't get here soon, they'll miss the train." Tabitha leaned on her cane and looked up and down the platform.

The locomotive hissed and clanked, smelling of grease and coal smoke and spewing clouds of steam that hung in the frosty air. Gaslights illuminated the platform, and the milling passengers cast shadows. A baggage cart squeaked by laden with trunks.

"I have grave reservations about what Mr. Korbin is doing with these children, but it's out of my hands. I was outvoted. There are things going on at that orphanage that need looking into. That's why I got myself appointed as a board member last month—though it took a hefty donation to get the matter accomplished. If yesterday's meeting is any indication of how things are run, I shall have to take things in hand and make some changes."

Sam had no doubt she would be running the place inside of three months. Old Korbin wouldn't know what hit him.

"You will keep an eye on the children, won't you?" The lines in her face deepened.

"I'll do my best." He caught the flash of lamplight off russet hair, and his heart jolted. At the same instant, someone bumped his shoulder. He did a nifty two-step to avoid tottering into Aunt Tabitha, all the while keeping his head on a swivel for another glimpse of who he thought he'd seen.

It was her.

And she'd spotted him.

Men stopped to stare after Yvette, but for the first time in his recollection she gave no heed to the admiring glances. Her blue eyes burned like holes in her white face.

Uncertainty swamped him. Was she really taking the breakup so hard? He hadn't thought her emotionally involved at all, or he might not have been so abrupt—not that he regretted his decision. Breaking the engagement had been the right thing to do.

Aunt Tabitha harrumphed and hobbled a few steps away but not before elbowing him and giving him a don't-make-a-fool-of-yourself-again glare. Not that he was of a mind to stick his head back into the bear trap of romance ever again.

"Sam, thank goodness you haven't left yet." Tears hovered on Yvette's coppery lashes. "I need to speak with you."

"I can't see what we have to talk about."

"Please, won't you let me apologize?" A man jostled her on his way by and muttered an apology.

Sparse snowflakes hovered in the air, and Sam realized she wore no hat. "You look cold. Let's go into the waiting room."

He turned to Aunt Tabitha, but she looked past him. "I see Mr. Korbin with the children." She leveled a hard stare at Yvette. "You deal with Miss Adelman, and then come and find me before departure."

Sam took Yvette's elbow and led her into the building. The smell of damp wool and wood smoke curled around him. He spotted a place beside a mountain of luggage where traffic seemed to eddy and flow by. When they reached it, he dropped her arm and crossed his.

She laced her fingers and held them to her chest, her eyes turned upward to him. "Please, Sam, won't you reconsider? I'm so sorry for what you heard. I let myself get carried away talking to mother. I don't really think you're a sheep. I don't know why I said that." She reached out to touch his forearm and flicked her lashes. "Don't you remember all we meant to each other? You feel something for me. I know you do. Please, tell me you'll still marry me." She leaned close, eyes full of appeal.

Another pair of eyes interposed itself in his memory. Big, brown eyes, as honest as the day was long. Brown eyes so grateful for a simple box of chocolates that he'd felt warmed through. Yvette's appeal only left him cold and ashamed that he'd ever been duped by her facade.

He leaned back. "It's over, Yvette. I accept your apology, for what it's worth, but I have no intention of marrying you. You'll have to look elsewhere for your sacrificial lamb."

"I can't accept that." The tears spilled over, and her hand gripped his arm. "You have to marry me. I'll be. . .I'll be ruined if you don't."

"Your social set won't bat an eye at the broken engagement. You'll soon land a new victim to work your wiles on. What about that Anthony character your mother mentioned? Why not track him down?"

She swiped at her tears, and her shoulders shook. "I. . .I. . .did. I tried. He just laughed and said I wouldn't trap him into marriage. Sam, I have to get married. . .and soon. Please," she pleaded again. "You've always been so gallant, won't you be gallant now? Save me, save my reputation, please?"

Her desperation suddenly made sense. The whirlwind courtship, the rush to the altar. . . She'd lined him up from the minute he'd said hello. "Who's the father?" Like it mattered.

A sob choked her, but she managed to whisper, "Anthony."

"And the bounder has no intention of marrying you? He knows about the child?" Outrage, not so much for Yvette as for the child, boiled through him. What kind of man walked away from a woman when she was carrying his child?

"He knows. He ran away even faster than you. On the morning train to Chicago."

Sam jammed his hands into his pockets and gritted his teeth. What a mess. He shook his head, rocking on his heels. "You know, I didn't think my pride could be beaten down any further after overhearing you call me a sheep, but I hadn't reckoned on this. Worse than just marrying me for my money, you planned to rush me to the altar so you could pass off your child as mine? We've known each other for almost six weeks. Have you known the whole time that you were carrying? Did you think I wouldn't know? Or that I was so besotted with you that once I found out I wouldn't care?

You must think I'm as dumb as a sack of hammers."

Her legs seemed to give way beneath her, and she wobbled. He had to grab her to keep her from collapsing on the floor. Lifting her into his arms, he made for an empty bench.

She wrapped her arms around his neck—a motion that had once sent his heart into orbit—and whispered against his neck, "Please, Sam, won't you help me?"

Kneeling, he placed her onto the bench and disengaged her arms. "Yvette, I'm truly sorry for your situation, but I won't marry you." She sobbed into his handkerchief, and he motioned for one of the porters hovering nearby. "Will you get one of the lady porters from the ladies' waiting room?"

Several people stopped and whispered among themselves.

Sam's collar tightened, and he glanced at the wall clock. Less than a quarter of an hour until the train pulled out.

Yvette swung her legs over the edge of the bench. Her shoulders hunched, and she looked small and defenseless, not much like the vivacious, confident woman he'd thought he'd known. "What will I do now? Everything's ruined."

He sighed. "You'll go home to your family and sort this out. Your mother can have the authorities track this Anthony joker down and make him do right by you. At the very least, you won't be out on the street. You've got money."

Another wail burst through the handkerchief. "But we don't. It's all a sham, don't you see? The house and furniture are rented. At that, we only kept the salon nicely furnished. The rest of the house is bare bones. Mother overdrew her account to see me clothed for the season. If you don't marry me, we'll be out on the street in less than a month."

He hung his head. Christian charity demanded he do something, but what? Not marriage, that was for sure. At the least, he could see she had some money to tide her over. He reached into his inside pocket for his wallet. He frowned. It wasn't there. Then, shaking his head, he remembered tipping the porter outside. He'd slipped his wallet into his coat pocket afterward. But when he checked his coat pocket, he found only lint.

Tracking quickly back through his mind, he remembered the dark-haired urchin who'd bumped into him on the platform. The little rat had stolen his wallet!

❧

"You have your tickets, dear?"

Eldora nodded at the elderly Miss Mackenzie and patted her pocket. "Yes ma'am." She returned her hand to Tick's, whose little face looked pinched. On her other side, Celeste sat primly, her glossy black braids lying just so on her shoulders and her hands folded in her lap. She kept her scarf pulled high, and her beautiful blue eyes missed nothing of the bustle around them. Eldora couldn't help but compare her to an exquisite china doll she'd once seen in a shop window. White skin, thick black lashes, sweet disposition, delicate nose, serene brow. She sighed. Nearly flawless.

"I hope you know I had nothing to do with this. My strenuous veto was overridden in the board meeting." Miss Mackenzie fussed with her stole. "Those men can be so thickheaded. Mr. Korbin can be particularly trying." Her mouth pinched. "What we need is a few more women on the board of directors. Then we'd see some progress. That's one of the first things I intend to change."

Miss Mackenzie sniffed and dabbed her nose with a lace handkerchief. "I can't believe he just dumped you here. The least Mr. Korbin could've done was to see you onto the train and wait for your departure before running away." She shifted, and the scent of lavender sachets drifted from her beaded dress.

Eldora breathed in. Her mother had used lavender, and the smell took Eldora right back to the time when she had been the doted-on daughter of two happy parents. She shrugged away the memory. "It's all right. I do thank you for waiting with us though. I confess I'm rather nervous being in charge of three children all the way to Denver." Eldora made another conscious effort to loosen her stomach muscles. Every time she stopped thinking about relaxing, the tension returned until her muscles trembled. "I've never done anything like this."

Miss Mackenzie patted Eldora's knee. "You'll do just fine. And I told you, my nephew will be on the train, too. If you run into any trouble, or if you need anything, send for him."

Her nephew, Sam Mackenzie. The nice young man who had given her the box of chocolates. Her imagination brought him instantly to view. His broad shoulders, his trim waist. Sandy-blond hair and tanned skin. And the kindest blue eyes she'd ever seen.

She could almost taste the chocolate caramel on her tongue and hear the excited squeals of the children when she'd shared the bounty. Each piece had been cut in two so there would be enough. For some, it was the first time they'd tasted such a treat, and for others, it brought back memories of better times, before the orphanage. Before oatmeal twice a day and cabbage and salt pork every evening.

"You have the letter to the Denver orphanage?"

Eldora suppressed a smile, knowing all this checking and rechecking was Miss Mackenzie's way of assuring herself they would be fine. "Yes ma'am. Mr. Korbin gave it to me before he left, along with enough money to feed us on the trip." The director had given her multiple warnings not to lose or squander the money. His voice held no confidence she could accomplish the task, something she feared he was correct in. She glanced once more at Celeste and then at Tick. She'd have to be a fool not to know Mr. Korbin was merely ridding himself of four problems, shunting them off to another orphanage because he didn't want to deal with them anymore.

"When are we leaving?" Tick coughed and squirmed. "Will we really sleep on the train?" He coughed again and swiped at his nose with the heel of his hand.

"Sit still, young man." Miss Mackenzie subdued him with a glance. "Children should be seen and not heard."

Tick set his mouth in a mutinous line and stopped his squirming. Eldora patted his bony knee. She'd never subscribed to that old adage, since children often had excellent observations and thoughts to express. Though she believed in kind, respectful speech, she thought it wrong to stifle children in the presence of adults.

She glanced over her shoulder to where Phin was supposed to be watching over their single valise until the call to board. The valise sat alone, unguarded. Eldora drew her hands into fists. "Miss Mackenzie, will you wait here with the children? Phin seems to have wandered off." She rose, not waiting for an answer, and hurried to their bag. Snatching it up, she spun and surveyed the room, looking for his lithe figure and dark hair. The little monster. He'd promised.

She took two steps toward the door marked To Trains when a commotion caught her eye. Several people surrounded a redheaded woman on a bench who appeared to be crying. Was she ill? A large woman wearing a porteress's uniform parted the crowd. The waiting passengers seemed to draw a collective sigh at the sight of authority, and they began to disperse.

That's when she spied Phin. He dangled from the grasp of a very angry Sam Mackenzie.

Chapter 4

Eldora ran across the waiting room, bumping into people and not stopping to apologize. The valise banged against her leg and collided with people in her haste, and she swept it up into her arms to keep from losing it altogether. "Sir, what are you doing?" The words burst from her as she skidded to a stop beside Mr. Mackenzie. "Put that child down."

"Child? Hardly that. He stole my wallet." The man lowered Phin until his feet touched the ground and shifted his grip from the boy's arms to his collar. The man's irate expression softened to surprised recognition. "Say, you're the girl from the orphanage."

While it was pleasant to be remembered, they had more important things to deal with. She turned her attention away from him to confront the boy. "Phin, you promised."

The boy didn't even have the grace to look abashed. He set his jaw and crossed his arms, glaring through his coltish forelock and leaning away from Mr. Mackenzie. "Turkeyhead, picking on a little kid. You gonna beat me, mister? A poor orphan?"

With a shake that made Phin's forelock bounce, Mr. Mackenzie dragged them back toward one of the walls. "Little kid? You've got to be what, thirteen? Beyond old enough to know better. You're fortunate I don't call the authorities to deal with you."

"I ain't scared of you. Call them. I'd rather stay here in jail than get on the train anyway."

Keeping an unrelenting grip on Phin's collar, Mr. Mackenzie went through the boy's pockets. In the last one, he found his own wallet. The lines alongside his mouth deepened. "I'm of a mind to turn you over and shake you just to make sure that's all you've got on you."

"You don't scare me. I bet the matron could take you out with one whack of her brush." Phin puffed up and took a swing at Mr. Mackenzie, but his arms were too short, and he flailed the air.

"Phin, enough." Eldora wanted to shake the boy herself, though she'd breathed a sigh of relief that the wallet was all Phin had apparently stolen this time. "Please, Mr. Mackenzie, don't call the authorities. I'm so sorry. Phin, apologize to Mr. Mackenzie so we can get on the train."

"Forget it." Phin glared at her. "I'm not going. I can't leave the city.

My uncle's coming back for me. He won't be able to find me if I'm in Denver. I'm better off here in jail than hundreds of miles away in another orphanage."

Familiar pain sliced through Eldora. Phin boasted often of his uncle, the one who was coming back any day now to get him. The one who had dropped him off at the orphanage five years before with a promise to return. She turned to Mr. Mackenzie. "Are you going to bring in the police, Mr. Mackenzie?"

His grip eased. "No, there's no time for that. They'll be calling us to the train any minute."

"Hey." Phin stuck out his bottom lip and lowered his brows at Eldora. "How is it you know this big skite?"

The call to trains saved her from having to answer. "We've got to go." She grabbed Phin's hand, though he tried to tug out of her grip.

Mr. Mackenzie released his hold on the boy's collar with a scowl. "I'll be right back. Go over to my aunt, and I'll meet you there and see you on the train." He turned and marched over to the bench where the redheaded woman still sat.

No wonder she'd been crying. Perhaps they were in love and going to be parted for a while. Eldora sighed and shook her head, hearing the matron's admonition to stop her woolgathering daydreams and be practical.

She turned to go back to Tick and Celeste, but Phin dug in his heels. "I told you I'm not going on the train. I'm staying here where Uncle Myatt can find me."

Though slight, Phin was wiry-strong, and Eldora knew she couldn't physically force him to go. But if he didn't go, she couldn't deliver him to the orphanage in Denver. If she failed to deliver all three children to the orphanage, Mr. Korbin would not wire her the money for her return ticket. Desperation thickened her voice. "Phin, please. We left word with Mrs. Scrabeck at the orphanage where you could be found if your uncle should show up. I need you on this trip. I can't do this without you. And what about Tick? If you don't go with us, he'll be all alone. Please, Phin."

Phin's tough expression crumbled a bit around the edges. If he had any weak spot, it was Tick. He rubbed his chin as if considering the situation. "I guess I could at least help you get the kids to Denver. Nothing says I have to stay there. I could hop a return train to St. Louie and be back here before New Year's."

Eldora's knees went wobbly. She gave Phin a trembly smile and let his hand go. "Thank you, Phin. I knew I could count on you."

❧

Sam helped Yvette to her feet and escorted her to where Aunt Tabitha sat with two children. He almost laughed at the look on Tabitha's face. Her nose twitched like she'd just smelled something foul but was too polite to mention it. "Yvette, sit here with these children for a moment while I talk to my aunt."

Tabitha levered herself up and walked with him a few paces. "What did she want?"

Though he was loathe to spill Yvette's secrets to anyone, he needed Tabitha's help in the matter. "She's going to have a baby."

Tabitha jerked as if he'd slapped her, and he put up his hands. "The child isn't mine."

She relaxed a fraction, but her eyes were wary. "Is there time to tell me the story?"

"Not all of it, but enough. From what I gather, she and her mother are broke, the father of the child has skipped town, and they're about to be evicted from their house. I know it's a lot to ask, and I have no real right to do so, but would you consider helping them out? Investigate her claims, since we both know what a liar she is, but maybe see if you can get them settled in a house somewhere, maybe find a job for Hortense so she can support them?" He dug in his newly reclaimed wallet, happy to see the little thief had left the cash inside. "Give her this." He pressed some bills into Tabitha's hand while the train whistle blew. "I've got to go."

She lifted her wrinkled cheek for his kiss. "I'll look into it. If her claims are true, I'll see what I can do." She folded the bills and tucked them into her bag. "Give my love to the family, and remind your father if he doesn't come visit me soon, he might find me on his doorstep checking up on him."

"I will, and thank you." He squeezed her hand gently in deference to her delicate bones. The young woman from the orphanage approached, her hand on the shoulder of the pickpocket.

"Miss Carter, this is my great-nephew, Sam Mackenzie. Sam, this is Miss Eldora Carter and her charges. She'll introduce the children once you're on the train."

Eldora. The name seemed too old for her. This entire enterprise seemed too much for someone her age. Wrangling a petty thief would be bad enough, but she had two others to manage as well. "Let me take your bag for you."

The older boy—Phin, she'd called him?—snatched the battered valise and glared at Sam. "I can get it."

"Fine." If the boy had his hands full, he couldn't be dipping them into others' pockets. "Shall we?" He took Eldora's elbow. The little boy slid off the bench and took her hand on the other side, and the girl stood up gracefully and adjusted her scarf. She'd be about ten, he supposed, though guessing little girls' ages wasn't something at which he was proficient. Why had no one adopted such a strikingly beautiful child?

"Are we going to the train now?" The small boy might be six or seven. He had a sort of stretched-tight, worn-thin look about him, though he almost quivered with excitement. Maybe a little mountain air and some good food would brace him up, make him a little more robust.

Yvette shot him one last pleading glance, and he had the feeling of wriggling out of a trap as he walked away from her. He'd done the best he could short of marrying her, and that he was not prepared to do.

He held the door for Miss Carter and the kids and ushered them outside, casting a thank you over his shoulder to Aunt Tabitha.

She nodded and joined Yvette on the bench, making a shooing motion toward Sam.

The conductor was picking up his stepstool when they reached the edge of the platform. "Just in time." He replaced the wooden box and offered his hand to Miss Carter, then swung the girl after her.

The little boy scrambled up, followed by Phin and the bag.

The conductor consulted his watch. "You can board here and walk through two cars to get to your private car, Mr. Mackenzie."

Sam nodded and grasped the cold, metal handrail. He'd just see them settled and head to the privacy and peace of the Mackenzie private car. Yvette's condition had shocked him more than he cared to admit, and he needed a little time to sort things out in his mind.

The conductor pointed to the overhead rack tilted out from the wall. "You can stow your bag there or under the seat." He checked his watch again as the train whistle blasted. "You might want to take your seats. We'll be pulling out any minute now." He continued up the car, nodding to passengers, stopping to talk to some.

Two velvet-covered benches facing each other defined a seating area. The smaller boy hopped up to kneel next to the window, his thin face alive with excitement. Phin shoved his hair out of his eyes and tossed the valise under their seat. Eldora ushered the girl ahead of herself. She looked so fragile and uncertain, as wide-eyed as the kids, though she was supposed to be in charge.

"You'll be fine here, right? If you need anything, ask the conductor or have him send someone to my car at the rear of the train." The train lurched, and Sam grabbed the back of a bench. Somehow it felt wrong to just abandon her here, but what else was he supposed to do? His instructions from Tabitha were to see her and the kids onto the train and maybe check in on them occasionally to make sure they were doing all right. Odd to feel this conflicted over leaving her when leaving Yvette had brought only relief. He shook his head. Addlepated, that's what he was.

"We'll be fine. Thank you for seeing us onto the train."

"I won't be far away if you need me. You've got your tickets, right?"

She nodded, patting her pocket. "Your aunt asked me several times."

"All right. I'm going to go now." He turned to Phin. "Behave yourself and watch out for the ladies."

Phin glared back and said nothing.

The smaller boy bounced on the seat, his feet knocking into Phin's leg. "We're moving, Phin. Lookit how fast!" He pointed to the buildings sliding past the window as the train gained momentum. If he was this thrilled by train-yard speed, what would he be like once they got onto the open prairie?

"Tickets, please." The conductor approached, stopping at each set of seats. Sam shifted his weight and decided to remain just long enough to be sure she had the tickets properly punched. When the conductor drew near, Eldora dug in her pocket and produced the pasteboards. Her eyes seemed to swallow up her face, liquid pools the color of caramels, and a tremulous smile touched her lips when she looked up.

While the conductor worked his hole punch, Phin swatted the thin boy's feet off the bench. "Turn around and sit down, Tick. There's no room for your boots up here." He tugged his cloth cap down and folded his arms as if preparing for a snooze.

Eyes narrowed, the smaller child snatched the cap and tossed it onto the floor.

Phin jolted upright and snarled. "Tick, you rat. Pick that up!" He grabbed the boy's wrist and forced it down toward the floor.

Tick squirmed out of Phin's grasp and tripped over his feet, sprawling into the aisle. He popped up and whirled to face the bigger boy. "You're acting like you think this ain't no big deal, but I know better. You ain't never been on a train before. You ain't never been out of the city." He plowed into Phin, elbows jutting, puny fists swinging. "Admit it, you're excited and maybe even a little scared."

In their jostling, they tumbled into the space between the seats and rammed into Eldora and the little girl.

"Phin, Tick, stop it this instant!" Eldora tried to grab a flailing arm as the boys tussled but got an elbow in the chin for her trouble. She rocked back blinking.

Heads turned. The conductor started back their way. "I say, miss, you must control these children. We can't have them brawling in the middle of the car."

Phin struck out and his boot connected with the conductor's shin. The squabble had the attention of everyone in the car.

"Boys, knock it off." Sam reached into the fray, grabbing whatever appendage he could. Little hooligans. He wound up with Phin's wrist and Tick's ankle. Righting the little boy, he pushed both of them back into their seats. In his efforts to get them off the floor and separated, his arm brushed the girl, snagging her scarf and dragging it off. He glanced up to beg her pardon and froze. A quiver rippled through him, and he couldn't look away.

Below the china-blue eyes and perfect porcelain skin, her mouth was a ravaged mess. Where her upper lip should have been, a gaping hole snarled, the edges disappearing into her right nostril. Her teeth jutted at odd angles in the opening. She grabbed the muffler and tried to put it up before anyone else saw, but it was too late.

A woman let out a shriek, and a man gasped.

"Lookit that!" A boy nearly Phin's age hung over the seat ahead of them and pointed. "What a freak!" He doubled over with laughter, and before Sam could prevent it, Phin punched the jeering boy right in the mouth.

Chapter 5

Sam had a fraction of a second to shoot an arrow of prayer for patience heavenward before braving the fray.

Phin launched himself over the back of the seat and pinned the boy. Tick followed suit, shouting, "Stop your laughing, you skunk. I'll beat you to a powder."

Even as Sam hauled both boys off the offender, he marveled at their swift change from foes to allies. Evidently they could beat on each other all they wanted, but nobody from outside was allowed to without consequences.

"Ha, now you've got a split lip, dog face!" Tick took one last weak swing, his face pasty white and his little ribcage working like a bellows. A bluish tinge colored his lips.

The conductor's genial expression fused into a hard mask. "Miss, we cannot allow this kind of behavior on the train. You'll have to control the boys, or they will have to be put off at the next stop." He darted a glance at the little girl who had tugged her scarf over her face once more and whose eyes now brimmed with tears.

Eldora put her arm around the child and drew her into her side. "Sir, please, I am sorry. I'll make them behave. Don't put us off, please. We'll try not to trouble you or anyone else."

It bothered Sam that she should be apologizing for the boys when they should be apologizing for themselves, and that the conductor had nothing to say about the poor manners of the people who gawked and jeered at a little girl with a deformed face. Before he could speak, one of those ill-mannered passengers voiced her opinion.

"Those little hoodlums should be in jail, and that girl should be in an asylum. What's she doing out among decent people with a face like that?" A woman's high-pitched inquiry shot through the car. She hoisted her ample self up and leaned over the seat to glare at the little girl as if everything was somehow the child's fault. "I've never seen anything so awful in all my life. What is the railroad thinking putting brawling children and deformed freaks in with the regular passengers?"

Phin stiffened and then bolted out of his seat. "You fat old sow! Your sour face is worse than a harelip. Celeste can't help her twisted mouth, but you sneer on purpose. Your nasty mug would curdle fresh milk."

"Phin!" Eldora's chin dropped, and she stood.

Sam—though he wanted to cheer and second the boy's opinion—clapped his hand over Phin's mouth and dragged him backward before he could launch himself at the woman. How had a simple errand for his aunt turned into this debacle? They hadn't been on the train ten minutes yet, and already the entire complement of passengers wanted them off. "Enough, Phin." He spun the boy toward the door they'd entered by and gave him a push. "March."

The boy scowled over his shoulder and barely caught the valise Sam tossed at him. Sam sent Tick after Phin, scooped the tearful Celeste onto his arm, and grabbed Eldora by the elbow.

The conductor barred their way. "Sir, where are you going? The next car is full. This is the only passenger car with any room left. I don't have anywhere else for them to go."

"Fortunately, I do." Sam guided Eldora to the door and then turned to face the length of the car. "You all should be ashamed of yourselves, driving these orphaned kids away. I apologize for the fracas, but in one thing Phin was right." He leveled a stare at the woman who had been so rude. "These kids are what they are through no choice of their own. But you all here had a choice as to how you would accept them, and you chose badly." His little group clustered near the door, and he took Eldora's elbow again.

"Where are you taking us?" She sounded like she was being strangled. "You heard the conductor. There's no room for us in the next car."

"Just keep walking." He hitched Celeste higher on his arm and opened the door to the platform. Cold air rushed at him, and the noise of wheels on rails deafened speech. Keeping a good hold on each of them, he transferred them one at a time to the next platform and through the crowded car.

The little boy held his chest, wheezing. Without being asked, Phin handed the valise to Eldora and lifted Tick up.

"I'm not a baby," Tick protested weakly.

"Hush up. You're about done in. Fighting takes it out of a man." Phin shoved the boy's head down on his shoulder and looked to Sam for what to do next.

"Please, Mr. Mackenzie, where are you taking us?" Eldora stopped at the end of the car and faced Sam like a prisoner before a firing squad.

"My private car at the end of the train. There's plenty of room and no one to complain about the children." He opened the door and moved them across to the railed platform at the end of the Mackenzie car. Using his key, he unlocked the door and stepped aside for them all to enter.

Warmth surrounded them, and when he closed the door behind him, the noise lowered. He eased Celeste down onto the closest chair, and Phin did the same for Tick.

Eldora stood in the middle of the salon, clutching the threadbare valise and staring at the rich pecan woodwork, etched mirrors, and gilded metalwork. Her pink lips parted. "Oh my."

Phin let out a low whistle. "Pretty swank. You must be loaded. Who'd you rob to get this palace on wheels?" He ran his hand along the carved back of the chair Tick sagged on.

Sam sighed. "I didn't rob anyone. My family and I own some silver mines in Colorado."

Eldora dropped the valise and half-turned to stare at him. "You're a miner? A mine owner?"

"Yes, Mackenzie Mining Company." He frowned when she shot him an accusatory glare. "Is there something wrong with that?"

≈

Eldora had a moment to imagine her knight in shining armor toppling off his white charger into a clanking pile in the dust. A miner. Not just a miner, but a mine owner. "No, there's nothing wrong with that."

Except that even a poor orphan like her had heard of the Mackenzie Mining Company. He was one of *those* Mackenzies. So far above and beyond anything Eldora could aspire to, it made her cringe. Here they'd been wallowing and brawling in front of him, and now they'd imposed themselves on him like beggars.

A cold wind blew through her, though she stood beside a coal stove, cherry-red with warmth. "Tick, are you all right?" She knelt beside him and touched his cheek.

He opened his eyes and nodded. "Peachy. Just need to catch my breath." He put his hand against his chest and his ribs pumped.

"Lie still for a while." She shrugged out of her shawl and tucked it around him. He looked as if a puff of air would blow him away. Her stomach tightened. The only instructions she'd been given regarding Tick were about keeping him calm and warm. So far she was zero for two.

"Is his name really Tick?" Mr. Mackenzie raised the glass on one of the wall sconces and lit the lamp, bringing more light into the elegant salon.

Eldora smoothed the boy's light-as-air white hair onto his forehead. "No, his name is Michael. But he sticks so close to Phin, the kids started calling him Tick. Now that's all he'll answer to. Isn't that right, Tick?"

"Me 'n' Phin stick together." He puffed up a little and threw a smug look Phin's way.

Phin jerked his chin in agreement.

"Tick arrived on the orphanage doorstep about the same time as Phin. They've been fast friends ever since, though as you saw in the other car they tend to squabble quite a bit."

Mr. Mackenzie nodded and squatted beside her. "Like brothers. My older brother and I have been known to mix it up from time to time." He scrutinized Tick, his brows drawn together.

Eldora glanced at Celeste. Her scarf once again covered the lower half of her face, and she sat perfectly still, feet primly together, hands in her lap, staring at the floor. Everything about her posture begged no one to notice her, and all trace of tears had subsided. She looked controlled and composed. That bothered Eldora. Celeste was too controlled. She should be crying right now, angry and hurt. Instead, because she was accustomed to the cruelty of others, she withdrew even deeper into herself.

"This is Celeste. She's ten." Eldora rose and put her hand on Celeste's shoulder.

The little girl tilted her head and flicked her lashes upward for a quick peek at Eldora's face, then returned to staring at the floor.

"Pleased to make your acquaintance, Celeste." Still squatting, he patted Celeste's knee and then pushed himself upright. Eldora liked the way his voice softened when he spoke to the little girl. "And you're Phin."

"Phineas Bartholomew, at your service." Phin removed his flat cloth cap and bowed low. When he straightened, he swept aside his black forelock and grinned. The smile was not returned.

"Let me have your bag. Leave the children here, and I'll show you where everything is." He turned to Phin. "Keep your hands in your pockets, and stay in this room. Got it?"

"Who died and made you emperor? I won't nick anything while you're gone." Phin made a show of jamming his hands into his pockets.

Why did he always have to choose the hard way to do everything? Couldn't he see how much they were already beholden to Mr. Mackenzie? Eldora sent him a half-imploring, half-exasperated look and followed their host.

He stopped at the first door in the narrow passageway. "I hope you don't mind sharing a room with the little girl." A match scritched and flared as he lit a kerosene lamp beside the door. "When we travel, this is my parents' room." A double bed with an indigo satin spread took up most of the space. "The water closet is next door." He indicated a narrow door into a well-appointed washroom.

A porcelain sink stood in one corner, and a zinc-lined tub peeped from behind a curtain. A whole washroom all to themselves. The image of the ranks of sinks and commodes in the orphanage community washroom came to her mind. "We won't mind sharing. We're used to it." Eldora hadn't had a room of her own since she first came to the orphanage. To share a room with only one other girl would be a luxury.

In the next compartment, two chairs sat facing one another. He lit another lamp. "The boys can stay in here. The chairs fold out into a bed, and another bunk lowers from up there, Pullman-style." He pointed to a brass handle set into the sloping wall above her head.

The paneling gleamed, and everything screamed money and privilege. Even more than the upscale houses where she had been a domestic, this railcar bespoke the wealth and power behind the man so casually showing her about.

He sauntered toward the rear of the car, past a narrow galley, cold and dark, and another bedroom—his own?—and on to another salon, this one doubling as a dining room with a table and chairs in one corner and sofas lining the other walls. Olive-green velvet drapes with gold fringe trim hung from every window, and stained-glass transoms defined the overhead space.

"What kind of mining does your company do?"

He shrugged. "Silver mostly. And lead."

She pressed her hand to her middle. At least it wasn't coal. But did that change anything? No. He still sent men down into the bowels of the earth to bring him treasure. And sometimes those men didn't return. Men like her father.

"The kitchen isn't in use on this trip. I had figured to eat in the dining car with the other passengers, but I can see that won't be possible now. I'll talk to the conductor in the morning about having trays sent in. Let's get back to the children."

He waited for her to precede him up the passageway, something men in her experience rarely did for girls like her. Kindness and consideration marked everything he did. Did those practices extend to his mine workers? And why did she care so much?

Phin stood exactly where they had left him, hands still in his pockets. When she entered the room, he withdrew his hands and flopped onto the settee. "Didn't steal a thing—this time."

"Phin, that's enough." Eldora rounded on him. "We're beholden to Mr. Mackenzie for too many things for you to be so churlish." She wanted to press her fists to her temples and give in to the overwhelming sense of drowning in the responsibilities heaped on her.

"Call me Sam. You're not beholden to me. I'm doing this as a favor to my aunt. She asked me to look after you."

The little knife that had been thrust into her heart when she learned he was a mine owner twisted a half-turn. All his kindness was merely a favor for his aunt. Eldora sagged onto the sofa and chided her reflection in the dark window across the car. She'd been silly to spin daydreams. Her would-be hero had feet of clay.

Chapter 6

Sam awoke to a strong knock on the door. A quick peek through bleary eyes showed no light coming around the window blinds. "Who is it?"

"Mr. Mackenzie, it's the conductor. I apologize for entering your car unannounced, but I need a word with you."

"Can't it wait till morning?" He wanted to stuff his head back under his pillows. Morning wasn't his favorite time, and he liked dead-of-night-before-morning even less.

"I'm afraid not. It concerns one of your charges."

For a moment, he thought the conductor was talking about the dynamite used in the mines. "Charges?"

"One of the children, sir."

Remembrance rushed back to him. The kids. And Eldora Carter. He swung his feet over the side of the bed and scrubbed his hands through his hair. A yawn threatened to crack his jaw. "I'll be out in a minute."

"Very good, sir. I'll meet you in the salon."

Stumbling into his clothes, yawning every few seconds, he managed to drag himself to the end of the railcar. He hadn't bothered to button his shirt all the way nor to find socks and boots. Since he could barely keep his eyes open, he planned to deal with whatever the problem was and then fall back into his bed until daylight.

The conductor—every shiny brass button secured through its corresponding buttonhole—stood in the center of the room.

Phin stood with his back to the wall, hands behind him, chin tucked low, glaring out of the tops of his eyes. "I told you, I didn't steal your watch." The boy's face paled, and his thin chest rose and fell under his threadbare shirt and jacket.

Sam groaned and scratched the stubble on his jaw. "Is that what this is about? Give it back, Phin. I told you to lay off the stealing."

Lifting his chin, Phin braced his legs so hard his muscles quivered, but his hands remained behind his back. "I said I didn't take it."

Rolling his shoulders, stiff from the strange bed, Sam yawned again. "You'll have to forgive my doubts since you managed to light-finger my wallet just yesterday. What are you doing wandering the train in the middle of the night?"

Phin snorted. "It ain't the middle of the night. It's getting on for five o'clock. Or do you rich gents sleep till noon every day? Matron would've kicked you out of your cot a half-hour since if you were at the orphanage."

His sneer grated Sam's skin. As soon as he got the sand out of his eyes, he was going to clobber the little snot. "What're you hiding then if not the watch?"

"None of your affair."

Sam decided he'd had enough. "I'm giving you fair warning. I'm a man to be reckoned with, especially on short sleep. Hand over whatever it is so I can go back to bed, or I'll have to take it from you."

The conductor advanced on Phin. "The truth is I had my watch before I found you in the dining car bothering the attendants, and now my watch is missing. The head waiter told me you were bragging about your pickpocket abilities, and you ran the moment you knew I was looking for you."

Red suffused Phin's high cheekbones. His dark eyes glittered in the candlelight, and his lips set in a thin line. Withdrawing his hand, he opened his fingers to reveal a squashed hunk of bread. "That's all I took."

"I insist we search his pockets." The conductor grabbed Phin by the arm when someone pounded on the door.

"Hold up there." Sam sauntered to the door. "Might as well be back in the St. Louis railway station, what with all the coming and going." He opened the door, letting in a gust of cold air along with a white-coated waiter.

"Suh, you were missing your watch? We found it on your breakfast table." He dangled the golden timepiece from its chain.

"I told you I didn't take your stupid old watch!" Phin reared back and hurled the chunk of bread at the conductor. The crust bounced off the man's wire-rimmed glasses.

Sam lunged for the boy before he could follow the bread with his fist. "Lemme go!"

"Calm down." Sam had his hands full with the wiry boy. "Stop it!" He pinned Phin's arms.

"What's going on here?" Eldora's question sliced through the air, freezing everyone for a second.

Sam whirled, dragging Phin around with him.

Barefooted, gripping a shawl around her slender shoulders, and with her hair in a wispy braid, Eldora looked about fifteen. "Sam, what are you doing to him?"

Celeste peeped around the corner, her mouth hidden by her hands.

Phin took up his struggling again. "He's hurting me. He's going to throw me off the train." His accusations flew like his wiry arms.

"No!" A tow-headed bullet in a short nightshirt launched itself across the room and barreled into Sam's knees. "Let him go! Let him go!" Tiny fists pummeled his leg. Tick butted him and then looked up, blue eyes swimming with tears. He blinked and the tears spilled over; then he backed up and wobbled a couple steps. His face was pale as milk, and his lips gasped like a fish in the bottom of a rowboat. Without a sound, he collapsed onto the carpet.

Sam's arms went limp, and Phin sprang from his grasp.

With a cry, Eldora dropped beside Tick and patted his face.

Phin shoved her aside and straddled Tick. He pressed his ear to Tick's chest. "Nothing!" Before anyone could stop him, he lifted his hand into a fist over his head then dropped it sharply, punching Tick in the chest.

❧

Eldora rocked back when Phin shoved her, and she cracked her shoulder against the wall. A cry burst from her lips, both from the pain and from the shock of seeing Phin hit Tick so hard.

The small boy's body jerked, and Phin thrust his ear down to listen to Tick's chest once again.

Her legs tangled in the hem of her nightgown, and she grappled with her shawl, her braid, and the rocking of the train.

The three men in the room seemed frozen in place, jaws slack, eyebrows high.

She lunged forward to push Phin off Tick, but he evaded her unsteady attempt, keeping his attention focused on the little boy. A lump lodged in her throat, and her heart raced faster than the train. Tick!

"C'mon, Tick!" Phin pounded the boy's chest again. "C'mon!" He jammed his ear against Tick's ribs. Eldora's fright was mirrored in Phin's dark eyes.

Sam seemed to come unstuck from the floor and in two strides crossed the salon to haul Phin upright.

Phin dangled from his grasp, writhing. "No! Lemme go! Lemme go!"

Eldora bent over Tick, noting his blue lips and his eyes rolled back in his head.

Phin shrugged out of his jacket and pounced on Tick once more. He slammed into Tick's chest.

The little boy jolted and took a staggering breath. His eyelids fluttered open, and his glassy eyes tried to focus on her face. He groaned, the sweetest sound Eldora had ever heard, and dragged his hand to his chest.

Sam hauled Phin off again, grunting with the effort.

At Tick's movements, Phin went limp in Sam's grip and blew out a long sigh.

Sam shook Phin. "What do you mean, jumping on him that way? Ellie, is he all right?"

Even in her befuddled state, it registered that Sam had called her Ellie. She'd have to take that out and ponder it later. Gathering Tick in her arms, she stroked his hair and hugged him.

He sank against her, his chest rising and falling rapidly. "What happened?" His voice sounded thin as paper.

"You dropped to the floor, and—" She stopped. "I'm not exactly sure what happened—it all happened so fast."

The conductor advanced on Phin and, shoving his hands against Phin's shoulders, pinned him to the wall. "That boy is a menace! First fighting in the passenger car, then stealing food, and by your own admission"—he pointed to Sam—"your wallet, and now pummeling a defenseless child in the throes of some kind of fit. I won't have him on my train, under your protection or not, Mr. Mackenzie."

The white-coated waiter hovered near the door, the whites of his eyes a stark contrast to his dark face. He stood still, as if charmed like a rabbit watching a rattlesnake, his hand clutching the doorknob.

Sam interposed himself between the conductor and Phin. His eyes snapped fire, and his muscular frame, barefooted and with shirt hanging half open, dwarfed the railroad official. "That will be all. I'll get to the bottom of everything here, and I can assure you Phin will be no more trouble."

Eldora averted her eyes when she realized she was staring at Sam's half-bare chest. Heat bloomed in her cheeks, for she had never seen a man so carelessly attired. That same heat warmed her heart, for he was championing Phin. She took herself severely to task.

Don't go getting any romantic notions about him, or any man, Eldora Carter. Just because he's being kind in taking up for you and the children doesn't mean anything. A plain-as-potatoes orphan wouldn't attract the attention of someone as wealthy and handsome as Sam Mackenzie.

The conductor raised himself to his full height—still several inches shorter than Sam—and puffed out his chest. "If there is one more incident regarding that boy before this train reaches Denver, I'll put him off, even if I have to stop in the middle of the prairie to do so."

Phin leaned around Sam and bared his teeth, giving the conductor what the orphans referred to as "the stink eye." Phin had always proven quite adept at this expression, turning it on the matron at every opportunity.

Eldora lowered her eyebrows and shook her head at him, giving him her best don't-poke-the-bear expression.

The conductor blinked, turned on his heel, and snatched the watch still dangling from the waiter's hand. He all but shoved the waiter ahead of him out onto the platform and slammed the door so hard the windows rattled.

Celeste nudged her arm, giving her a fright. "Yes?" Eldora managed.

The little girl leaned in close and whispered as she always did, afraid someone would hear her garbled speech and poke fun. "Don't be mad at Thfin. He did that wunth before and Thickth heart stharted again."

Eldora nodded and flicked a reassuring smile at Celeste.

The girl retreated to the passageway once more, tugging the neckline of her nightgown up just under her nose.

Sam squatted beside Eldora and peered at Tick. Her heart quickened again to have him so near. His hair stood up, and a fine dusting of reddish-blond whiskers covered his cheeks. She forced herself to concentrate on the boy in her arms.

Sam touched Tick's hand. "How you doing, buddy?"

"Fine. I'm sorry I jumped you. I thought you were hurting Phin. Then everything got black around the edges, and I was gone."

Phin elbowed his way in. "Sorry I had to knock you like that. You dropped like a prizefighter with a glass jaw, just like last time."

Eldora shivered, realizing how close they had come to losing Tick. She hugged him harder until he squirmed. She loosened her hold and realized Sam was staring at her.

"What was the orphanage thinking to send you out with these three? You're barely more than a child yourself." His blue eyes had the same softness as when he'd first seen Celeste.

Bitterness coated Eldora's tongue. Charity. Pity. Benevolent largesse on which they must depend forever to survive. Her spine stiffened, and her jaw tightened. "I'm not a child. I'm twenty years old." A thrust of honesty pierced her. "Or I will be this spring." She helped Tick to stand and pushed herself off the floor, righting her shawl and swinging her braid over her shoulder. "Someone has to take care of these children. Who better than me, who knows what it is like to go through life alone, forced to live on the charity of others?"

He blinked and stepped back.

She wanted to recall her harsh tone. Another shiver raced up her spine. What would they do if he decided to abandon them to the mercies of the passenger car?

He glanced out the window while he buttoned his shirt. "You're going to catch cold standing there in your night things. Everybody get dressed, and I'll see about rustling us up some food." He turned to Phin. "You will not leave this car, is that understood? If the conductor catches you pilfering anything, he'll make good his threat. He's like the captain of a ship. His word is law on this train. In fact, you've antagonized him to the point that he won't have to catch you stealing. He's liable to chuck you off if he so much as catches sight of you."

Phin shoved his hands in his pockets and nodded, staring at the far wall as if he didn't care one way or the other.

Eldora sighed and, with her hand on Tick's shoulder, directed Phin down the passageway to get dressed.

When they reassembled in the salon, breakfast had been laid on the side table. Eldora insisted Tick lay on the settee, and it alarmed her that he acquiesced without complaint. His face was still pale, and his movements a bit shaky. She tucked a rug around him. "Do you want something to eat?" Her brow puckered as his eyelids fluttered closed.

"No. I'm not hungry." His face went lax, and she scrabbled for his wrist to check his pulse. Concern hovered, though she could feel the rapid beats. Tick was always hungry.

She turned back to the table as Sam finished stoking the coal stove and held her chair for her. She wasn't quite sure what to do, since no man had held a chair for her before, but she managed to sit safely and spread her napkin in her lap.

"How is he?" Sam took his seat and glanced over at Tick.

"Sleeping."

"He sure scared me, dropping down like that. I thought he was dead."

Phin barely waited for grace to be said before diving into the food. Celeste sat primly at the table and ate nothing.

Sam frowned. "Why doesn't she eat something? I thought all kids liked biscuits with jam."

Eldora's eyes caressed the little girl. "You may take your plate to our room if you like, Celeste."

Celeste shot her a grateful glance and picked up her plate and cutlery.

"Can you manage?"

Her black curls bobbed, and she disappeared down the hall.

When she was out of earshot, Eldora explained. "She doesn't like to eat in front of other people. With her mouth the way it is, eating isn't a pretty sight. The kids at the orphanage made terrible fun of her until the matron finally consented to let her eat alone."

"Poor kid. I wish there was something to be done for her." Sam tilted the gravy boat over his biscuits. "Phin, you should slow down and chew that food. It would be better if you actually tasted it before swallowing."

Phin looked up, his cheeks bulging like a gopher's. He swallowed a couple times. "I ain't never had nothing but oatmeal for breakfast for about as long as I can remember. Biscuits and jam, gravy, eggs, sausages. . .do you eat like this every day?"

Eldora could identify with his wonder. She was a bit taken aback by the spread herself, though working as a domestic had shown her some of the world beyond the orphanage.

Sam shrugged. "I guess this is a pretty typical breakfast for me."

"It's a wonder you ain't as round as a beetroot eating like this every day." Phin shoved another spoonful of eggs into his mouth.

Eldora choked and grabbed for her napkin. "Phin, how is it you knew what to do when Tick's heart quit?" She hoped to change the subject before Sam's thundercloud expression broke into a storm all over Phin.

The boy shrugged. "I asked the best doctor in St. Louis about Tick's condition."

"How did you talk to the best doctor in St. Louis?"

"I slipped out of the orphanage one day and asked around for the name of the best doctor in the city. Then I waited by his gate until he came out, and I followed him downtown. Wasn't hard to lift his wallet off him on the street."

Eldora groaned, and Sam's hand tightened on his fork.

"Then I followed him back to his house and returned the wallet—made out like I found it on the street—and he invited me in." Phin waved his fork at the interior of the train car. "His place was nearly as fancy as what you got here. Anyway, I told him I had a friend with some heart trouble and would he mind if I asked him a few questions. He asked all about Tick and told me about thumping him in the chest if he ever dropped down and I couldn't find a heartbeat. He said Tick needed some medicine, but I told him we couldn't afford it. Then I hustled out of there because it was getting late and I knew I was already in for a beating with the radiator brush when I got back anyway."

Sam laid down his fork and knife and sat back, staring at Phin. Finally he shrugged. "What were you doing in the dining car this morning?"

Phin stopped chewing, his eyes growing wary.

A tickle of unease feathered under Eldora's breastbone. With Phin you never knew what he might have been up to. She gripped her napkin in her lap.

"I didn't know if we'd get breakfast this morning, so I snitched some bread for Celeste and Tick. Figured me and Eldora could go hungry, but the little kids needed something to eat."

Tears pricked Eldora's eyes.

Sam cleared his throat and passed Phin the basket of biscuits.

Chapter 7

Eldora throttled the handle of her valise as if trying to squeeze the life out of it, numb to the continual rocking and swaying, the clacking and clatter of the train. The falling dusk through the windows revealed the same sodden, flat landscape they had seen for miles.

Tick still slept on the settee beside her as he had all day, rousing every once in a while to drink some broth and give her a smile that was a mere shadow of its usual self. Celeste turned the pages of a *Harper's Magazine* Sam had dug up somewhere for her, and Phin sprawled in a chair, flipping a poker chip he always had on him, making it walk across the backs of his fingers and appear and disappear. Had to keep his fingers nimble, he claimed.

"Salina! Next stop!" The conductor's voice came through the door, still with a cranky edge.

She supposed she couldn't blame him, being subjected to life with Phin, but the boy hadn't budged from the railcar all day. By now the conductor should be over such things.

"Salina!"

Salina, Kansas. Sam had announced after breakfast they would be stopping over there. "I pressed the conductor pretty hard, and he finally said the best doctor between Topeka and Denver was in Salina. Tick should be under a doctor's care. We'll stop there, and you can get him looked at."

His grave expression pressed Eldora's heart until guilt seeped into every corner. Defensive words flew out. "I'm doing the best I can. I know he needs a doctor, but I can't afford one. I have no money for doctors or medicines or staying over in a strange town. I have to get the children to Denver. Maybe they'll have a doctor there who can treat him."

"Tick never should've left St. Louis, as delicate as he is. Didn't the orphanage have a doctor?"

Phin sat up. "No doctors. Sometimes we'd get a dose of castor oil or the like, but I never saw no doctor there. Wouldn't surprise me a bit if old Korbin wasn't skimming the donations and pocketing the cash himself. Be easy enough to do, if nobody was checking up on him."

Eldora shook her head and frowned. "Phin, that's a thoroughly scurrilous remark. You have no proof Mr. Korbin was embezzling funds."

Phin cocked his head to the side and appraised her. "You always talk like you swallowed a dictionary whenever you're mad at me. Why don't you just say things plain?"

"Fine. I'll give it to you plain. Stop talking about things you know nothing about. Keep your mouth shut, and do as you're told." Eldora regretted her sharp tone the instant the words flew out of her mouth. Here she was, scared to death to be dumped in a strange town with no money or means, and she was taking it out on Phin, who was probably not so far off the mark with his assessment of Mr. Korbin's financial finagling.

Sam rose and shrugged into his coat. "I'll be back in a bit." He shot one warning glance at Phin and slipped out the door.

Eldora fretted the entire time he was gone. The little bit of money Mr. Korbin had given her wouldn't last a day, much less cover an expensive doctor's visit. She had nothing of value to sell to gain the funds. Her only recourse lay in spending the coins to send a wire to the orphanage asking for more money. And what would she do if they denied her request? The train would be gone, she would have no money, and they would have to wait two days for the next train before continuing their journey. At least their tickets to Denver would still be good, but how would she feed the children in the meantime, and what about Tick? Sam was right when he said Tick needed a doctor, but right or not, Sam's words wounded Eldora. She was doing the best she could. She'd like to see him do better in her place.

Sam breezed through the door, shaking droplets of water off his coat and hat. "Salina coming up. Are you all packed?"

She couldn't really blame him for wanting to be rid of them. In only twenty-four hours she and the children had erupted into his life like a firework. He'd been involved in several unpleasant scenes and been forced to share his private car. His quiet return home had turned into a traveling circus. "I've got everything." And precious little it was, too. Skimpy, well-worn night clothes for each of them, and an extra pair of stockings for her and Celeste. At least she could clothe Tick in two nightshirts, since Phin scorned nightwear, preferring to sleep in his pants and shirt. They would be indescribably filthy by the time they reached Denver, if they ever did. Eldora was beginning to despair of arriving there with all three children.

The train jerked to a stop in the rail yard.

"I want to thank you for taking care of the children and me. I know we've put you to considerable trouble." She rose. "You've been most kind. I hope you have more pleasant travels on the remainder of your journey." Though she kept her voice calm, panic thrust against her windpipe and accelerated her heart. Cold rain splattered the windows. How was she going to get Tick off the train? Celeste would have to carry the valise, and she and Phin could trade off carrying the boy. Though she hated to ask for anything more, she forced herself, for Tick's sake, to say the words. "Would it be too much to ask if we could take one of the blankets with us? Tick's coat is less than adequate, and I need to keep him warm and dry." Not to mention if they had to spend the night holed up somewhere in a barn or alley, they could all huddle under it.

Sam's eyebrows rose, and he used his thumb to push back his hat. Water droplets dotted the shoulders of his sheepskin-lined jacket and glistened on his ruddy cheeks. "A blanket? Of course he can keep the blanket. What are you talking about? You don't think I'm just going to toss you off at the depot and go on ahead without you?" His raised eyebrows darted down, and his expression darkened. "What kind of man do you take me for? Leaving a penniless girl and three kids to fend for themselves." He stuck his hands on his waist and glared at her. "Give Phin that bag, and take Celeste's hand. I'll carry the boy. We're all heading into town. I've arranged for the railcar to be put into a siding."

"But Mr. Mackenzie, I can't—"

"Don't you think we've gotten beyond formal names? I answer to Sam." He stooped and lifted Tick into his arms. "Make sure he's well covered."

Eldora adjusted the blankets, buffaloed by his commanding manner. She should protest that they couldn't take advantage of his generosity any more, that he'd done enough already, but his set jaw and forbidding stare kept her quiet. She took up the valise and Celeste's hand and nodded to Phin to follow Sam out onto the platform.

"You don't have to do what he says, you know. I can take care of us without him." Phin's dark eyes narrowed, the black lashes almost touching.

Eldora shook her head. "We have to think of what's best for Tick. He needs a doctor. We should be thanking Mr. Mackenzie, not resenting his provision."

"You can thank him all you want, but you wait and see. He'll get tired of playing 'pat-the-head-of-the-poor-orphan' and he'll scamper. Then it will be just us again."

Though she didn't want to agree, she knew from experience that people often tired of good works long before the need for them ended. Benefactors started out on fire, well-intentioned and full of enthusiasm, volunteering and donating. But as soon as anyone started counting on them, they tired of their charitable works and moved on, leaving in their wake needy hearts that grew wary of trusting.

Her thoughts pushed at her like the stiff wind as they left the depot and walked up the street. Phin took the valise and tugged his cloth cap down tight. Celeste anchored her scarf over her face and leaned into the gale.

Rain gusted and pelted them, first from one direction and then another. Sam kept his head bent, checking over his shoulder every few moments.

At last they reached the front porch of a brick building. A sign instructed them to enter and walk upstairs to the doctor's office. The quiet calm of the entryway made Eldora's ears ring. She let go of Celeste's hand, and with chilled fingers, she swiped at the raindrops on her cheeks.

"This way. Hope the doc's in." Sam's boots thumped on the treads, and they all followed him. Tick didn't stir, his face tucked into Sam's shoulder. At the top of the stairs, Sam stepped back to allow Eldora to precede him into the office.

The smell of carbolic and licorice wrapped around them, along with the starchy smell of cotton and the tang of vinegar. Eldora guided Celeste to the settee. "Phin, you can set the bag here by this table. Stay with Celeste while we're with the doctor."

He shrugged and nodded, shoulders slouched.

Sam knocked on the connecting door.

A shadow moved behind the rippled, frosted glass, and the door opened. A young man about Sam's height wiped his hands on a cloth and smiled. "Hello, I'm Dr. O'Kelly. You just caught me. I was about to head for home. What can I do for you?" He noted Tick in Sam's arms and stepped back to allow them to enter. "You and your wife can both come in. How old is your son, and what seems to be his trouble?"

Surprise shot through Eldora, followed by red-hot embarrassment. Her tongue refused to say anything, and she stood there, feeling stupid.

Sam, easing Tick onto the examining table, jerked upright and spun around. "We're not married."

At the doctor's raised eyebrows, Eldora found her voice. "What he means to say is Tick isn't his son. He's not my son either. Tick's an orphan."

"Tick?"

"His given name is Michael, but everyone calls him Tick. I'm taking him from an orphanage in St. Louis to one in Denver, and Mr. Mackenzie has been kind enough to help."

"I see." The doctor peeled back the blankets, and Tick opened his eyes, giving a wispy smile. Then came what seemed hundreds of questions from the physician as he poked and prodded.

Some she could answer; some Tick supplied. Sam remained silent, arms crossed, leaning against a bookcase crammed with books and bottles and jars.

When Dr. O'Kelly listened to Tick's heart, first with his ear against the boy's chest and then with an instrument, his face grew grave.

The clock ticked on the wall and then chimed six times. Eldora's stomach rumbled, reminding her she'd been too anxious to eat anything at lunchtime.

The doctor ignored everything, closing his eyes. Furrows creased his forehead.

Tick's eyes rounded and locked onto Eldora's, and his narrow, bare chest rose and fell like a scared rabbit's. A faint bruise hovered over his breastbone where Phin had hit him that morning. His vulnerability made Eldora want to snatch him up and hold him tight.

Finally, the examination was over. Dr. O'Kelly patted Tick on the head and dug in a jar on his desk, producing a peppermint stick. "Here you go, young fellow. Why don't you climb down and go eat this in the waiting room? I'd like to talk to your"—he stopped and tilted his head toward Sam and Eldora—"to your friends here."

Tick nodded, his hair falling across his brow.

When the door closed behind him, the doctor stuffed the listening tool into his pocket and sat in the chair behind the desk. "Please, sit down."

Eldora's knees felt like putty, but she managed to get to a chair. O'Kelly's grave expression struck fear deep in her heart for the little boy.

"I won't beat around the bush. You've got a walking miracle there. I am surprised that he's gotten to the age of seven without treatment. Tick's got cardiac arrhythmia. Dizziness, weakness, tiredness, the fainting, they all point to it, and from what you say, his heart has stopped twice. That someone has been able to revive him with a heart punch even once is amazing."

"What is cardiac arrhythmia?" Eldora bit her bottom lip.

"In layman's terms, it's an irregular heartbeat. In Tick's case, his heart beats unusually fast, and from what I can tell, not effectively. His heart is beating so rapidly the blood hasn't time to be properly oxygenated before it is pushed through his system. He is often short of breath, and when he gets excited this is exacerbated."

Sam leaned forward with his forearms on his thighs. "What can we do for him?"

"He needs medication. I'm going to prescribe digitalis." He frowned. "The medicine should slow his heart rate and strengthen the heartbeats. Once he goes on the medication, he will need to stay on it. He's had this heart condition for as long as he can remember, so it isn't likely to just go away as he grows. Digitalis is what he needs."

She rolled the strange word around in her head. Though relieved there was some treatment to help Tick, her mind staggered. How would she afford the medication? Would the orphanage be willing to pay for it? And how would Tick ever be adopted? Who would take on a child who needed medication for the rest of his life?

"I've never given digitalis to so young a patient before, so I'd like to observe him for one night, possibly two, depending on the results. I can either watch him at your place of residence or admit him to the hospital."

Nodding, Sam said, "We're fresh off the train, Doc. Haven't even taken time to get rooms at a hotel. Maybe the hospital would be the best place." He looked at Eldora for her opinion.

Her throat closed, and her eyes burned. Hospitals were worse than orphanages. The thought of Tick lying in some high, white bed, all alone in a vast room of sick people, made her chest cave in. But what else could they do? She nodded.

Emerging from the examination room, her steps were wooden. Tick had broken the candy stick into three pieces. Her heart warmed at his generosity. Celeste hastened to jerk her scarf back over her face, but Eldora's quick glance at the doctor showed he had seen her deformity. Phin shoved the last bit of his candy into his mouth and crunched it, releasing a minty aroma into the air.

Sam put his big hand on Tick's shoulder. "Hey kid. The doctor says he's got just what you need, some medicine to help your heart. Trick is he has to watch the dosage pretty close to get it just right, so he wants you to spend the night in the hospital so he can keep an eye on you. I told him you were a brave kid, and a night or two in the hospital wouldn't bother you a bit."

Even though Sam was talking to Tick, he was looking at Eldora, sending her the message that she needed to be brave, too. His strength and surety that they were doing the right thing strengthened Eldora's resolve. She squatted beside Tick and smiled. "Just think, when you have the right medicine you won't be keeling over. Phin won't have to sock you in the chest anymore."

Phin studied the doctor, shoving his hands in his pockets and staring under his hat brim. "Only a night or two?"

"That's right. I just want to keep an eye on him. You're Phin, right?" The doctor held out his hand. "It's a pleasure to meet you, young man. Your quick thinking saved Tick's life, and from what I hear, on more than one occasion. You're to be commended. Perhaps someday you'll be a physician yourself. You've got the instincts."

Phin shook the man's hand, his cheeks flushing. He toed the carpet and shrugged. Eldora hid a smile at his embarrassment. Few people praised Phin.

"Now, I'll take Tick with me. The hospital is just down the street here on Santa Fe. There's a hotel next door, good clean rooms and a restaurant."

Dr. O'Kelly shrugged into his coat and put his hat on.

Eldora tried not to feel as if she were abandoning her responsibilities as they parted ways at the hospital door. The look Tick gave her over his shoulder formed a lump in her throat. She stuck her hand into her pocket and gripped the two silver dollars there, the only money she had.

❧

Sam took Eldora's elbow and Celeste's hand and escorted them across the muddy side street to the hotel porch. Phin trotted beside him, the valise bumping his legs. For the tenth time that day Sam asked himself how he got saddled with a woman and three kids. And yet, he couldn't say he really minded. There was something about Eldora that intrigued him, brought out all his protectiveness. Those expressive eyes, her bird-delicate features, the way she handled the children, with affection but authority, too. So different from Yvette. Yvette took everything he gave her as her due, as his homage to her beauty. Eldora asked for nothing, was even surprised when he provided for her and the children. Her lack of acquisitiveness appealed to him.

And who could help falling for Celeste with her ravaged little face? The world had been unkind to her because of her deformity, but she retained a sweet nature that sought only to be invisible. Not to mention Tick, brave, weak as water, flying to the defense of anyone he thought needed help.

They reached the porch, and Phin thumped the valise down on the boards. The blanket from the train dangled over his shoulder, and he hitched it higher. He appraised the restaurant through the window before him, his eyes sparkling with a lean, hungry look. Sam appreciated his spunk. The boy was extremely loyal to those he considered his family.

They each had their challenges, but each had strengths, too. How did Korbin sleep at night knowing he'd all but cast them out on the street?

"Let's go." Sam set Celeste down and opened the door. Warmth and light and the smell of roasting meat greeted them. His mouth watered, and he sniffed the air. He passed the dining room door and stopped at the desk. With little trouble, Sam procured two rooms and had the bag sent up. He handed Eldora a key.

Lamplight played across her face, revealing her pale skin and the shadows under her eyes. She moistened her lips, and a little sigh escaped her. "I'm not sure the orphanage will reimburse you. We weren't supposed to be stopping at all. Mr. Korbin surely won't pay you back for the hotel." She took the key, but the worry lines on her face only deepened. "And there's the hospital and Tick's medicine. . ."

He wanted to comfort her somehow, to wipe the worry from her face. Though he could do nothing about her concern over Korbin's reaction, nor totally erase anxiety over Tick, at least he could ease her mind about her immediate future. "We'll talk about that later. Right now you need some food and some sleep, and so do the kids. Let's go on up. Phin and I can eat in the dining room, and I'll have a tray sent up for you and Celeste so you can eat in private, all right?" He winked at the little girl and cupped the back of her head to direct her to the stairs.

Her eyes crinkled above her scarf, rewarding him for remembering she didn't like to eat in public.

The hotel rooms were nothing to speak of, but at least they were clean. "Phin and I are next door. I'll have that food sent up as soon as I can."

She looked worn out, and who could blame her after the day they'd had? When he left, she was helping Celeste out of her shabby coat and yawning.

Sam and Phin entered the dining room and found a table near the front window. Consulting the menu, he ordered a tray sent up for the girls and the special of the day for himself and Phin.

Conversation flowed around them in the crowded room. China and glass clinked.

Phin's eyes never quit moving, taking in the patrons, the décor, the table service. He picked up his spoon and looked at his reflection in the back of it. "Steel. Guess you're used to silver, eh?"

Sam took a drink of water, noting the accusatory set of Phin's jaw. The boy was spoiling for a fight, as usual. "My family owns a silver mine. We do have silverware, but when I'm working up at the mine, I have a tin plate and a steel fork like everybody else."

A man at a nearby table dropped his wallet, and several coins rolled onto the carpet.

"Bet there are some good pickings in this lot." Phin took out his poker chip and walked it through his fingers, tilting his head at the customers. "I bet I could live for a couple months on the loose change alone."

"Who taught you to steal?" Sam leaned back as the waiter set a basket of bread on the table. Then he lifted it toward Phin to help himself first.

Phin's lips curved. "My Uncle Myatt. He said I was the best natural-born thief he'd ever seen. Didn't take me but a couple of days to master the seven bells. I was only six at the time."

"Seven bells?"

"Yep, Uncle Myatt tied seven little bells all over a coat and hung it on a tree. If I could get the wallet out of any of the pockets without ringing a single bell, then he knew I was ready to take to the train station or the fair or the market."

What kind of man taught his nephew to steal? Not only taught him but also boasted about the boy's ability? "You do know that stealing is wrong, even if you are good at it?" Sam tore open a roll and spread it with butter.

Phin scoffed. "So's beating orphans and giving them skimpy rations and not letting them see a doctor when they're sick. It's wrong to throw kids out just because their hearts don't work right or they were born with twisted lips. It was wrong for that rich lady to throw Eldora out on the street just because she wouldn't let the son of the house put his filthy paws on her. There's plenty of wrong in the world. I don't steal stuff to get rich. I steal to survive, to get food for the kids, or to make things easier for them." He crammed the bread into his mouth and reached for another. "You're sure," he spoke with his mouth full, "that Tick's gonna get fed in that hospital?" His eyebrows took a guilty tilt.

If Sam hadn't been watching closely, he never would've seen Phin slip a dinner roll into his pocket. "Tick's being fed, and so are the girls." He pursed his lips. "Go back to what you said about Eldora. She got thrown out?"

Phin shrugged. "Sure, more than once. The oldest orphans are farmed out to work wherever they can. Korbin placed her as a maid in three different houses, and every time something happened that got her sent back. The last place, one of the gents that lived there wanted to get fresh with her, and she slugged him for it." Phin shook his head. "There's those in this world that believe they can treat poor people any way they want to, and the poor people just have to take it, but that's wrong. Eldora has the right not to be bothered by the likes of him. Wish I'd have been there. I'd have done more than slap his face, I can tell you." His hands fisted on the edge of the table. "Eldora's tough, but she deserves to be protected." Phin directed his glittery black glare at Sam. "Don't you get any funny ideas about her either, or you'll have to deal with me."

Sam blinked, both amused and irritated at the boy's declaration. "I have no notion of getting embroiled with another female. I just slipped my neck out of that noose. My motives in helping you all are pure. As a favor to my aunt, who is a new board member at the orphanage, I'm just looking out for you on the trip, that's all." And based upon the information he'd gathered from the kids so far, he had a long letter to write to Aunt Tabitha about what happened at the orphanage. She couldn't possibly be aware of the plight of the children, or she would do something about it and Mr. Korbin. "Eldora said she was almost twenty. Sometimes she doesn't seem much older than you."

"By rights she shouldn't have come back to the orphanage at all when she got fired, since she's too old now, but she didn't have any place else to go. I guess Korbin figured he'd get rid of her and us three all at the same time."

The waiter brought their food, and Phin ate as if it might be his last meal.

181

Sam toyed with his fork. How many times had the boy missed a meal or gone without so Tick and Celeste could have more? How often had he wondered where his next meal would come from?

"What did the doc say was wrong with Tick, and how long does he have to stay in the hospital?" Phin managed the questions between huge bites of potatoes and peas.

Sam, eating more slowly, explained what he understood about the diagnosis. "Doctor says he needs some medicine called digitalis, and that he'll need watching to make sure the dose is right. Might take a couple of days."

"Will the medicine cure him?"

"I don't know that there is a cure, but the medicine will help him out. It's something he's going to need for the rest of his life, I gather."

An arrow formed between Phin's black brows, and his chewing slowed. "Is it expensive?"

"I don't know. Some medicine can be very costly. I didn't ask about the stuff Tick needs."

When Phin couldn't possibly eat another bite, Sam sent him upstairs. "I'm going to check on Tick, and I'll be back soon." He lowered his head to stare Phin right in the eye. "Don't get into any trouble while I'm gone."

The hospital windows were mostly dark when Sam arrived. Only a faint glow showed here and there. A nurse led Sam up the stairs to the ward.

Tick lay in a high cot, half in shadow with the lamp turned down low beside him. Rain pattered on the windows, and the strong smells of carbolic and vinegar hung in the air. Tick opened his eyes when Sam drew near.

"Hey there, Tick. How're you feeling? Did they feed you?" Sam eased onto the chair. Tick's bed was so high they were almost eye-to-eye. "No, don't try to sit up. Lie still."

"They fed me oatmeal." Tick made a face. His freckles stood out in his thin face like flecks of black pepper. But he had a little color to his cheeks, and his eyes were brighter. Perhaps the medicine was working already.

"You don't like oatmeal?"

He shook his head on the pillow. "You wouldn't either if you got it twice a day, every day."

"Twice a day?"

"Yep. Morning and noon. And salt-pork for supper." He stuck out his tongue. "The candy from the doctor was nice today. I like Dr. O'Kelly. But I don't like the medicine much. It doesn't taste so good."

"I don't imagine it does, but it appears to be helping you."

"It is." The doctor's voice surprised them both, and Sam turned in his chair. Dr. O'Kelly, wearing a white coat, stepped out of the shadows by the door. "I've come to check on you again, young man. Then you need to get to sleep."

Sam rose and backed up to give the doctor room.

After listening to the boy's heart for what seemed a very long time, the doctor straightened and smiled, rubbing Tick's head. "Better. Much better. Now, you snuggle down and sleep." He held the blanket up for Tick to wriggle farther under and tucked it in beneath his chin. "If you need anything, the nurse's desk is just outside the door."

"See you in the morning, Tick." Sam followed the doctor out the door and down to the first floor. "Doc, is he really better?"

"Yes, his heart rate has slowed, and his pulse is stronger. I'm going to increase the dosage in the morning by a few grains and see what effect that has. I'm very pleased with his reaction to the medicine so far. I'd like to see him get some meat on his bones though. Wherever you're headed, make sure he stays under a doctor's care. The dosage will have to be regulated as he grows and his activity levels change."

How likely was it that Tick would be under a doctor's care at an orphanage in Denver? The muscles in the back of Sam's neck tightened, but he nodded that he understood. "There's something else I wanted to ask you about." A nurse bustled by with an armload of linens. "In private."

Dr. O'Kelly's eyebrows rose, and he motioned for Sam to step into a side room. "This is one of the exam rooms. No one will bother us in here tonight." He took the chair from the corner and offered it to Sam, then leaned against the counter and crossed his arms. "What can I do for you?"

"It isn't about me. It's about the little girl who was with us today in your office."

O'Kelly nodded. "Remarkable blue eyes."

"She's real pretty and well-mannered, too. It's just such a shame about her lip. I was wondering if there wasn't something that could be done about it."

"She'd need a thorough examination to determine the extent of the deformity, but doctors have been operating on cleft lips for decades. Has she ever seen a surgeon about it?" He frowned and put his index finger along his upper lip. "No, I imagine she hasn't, not if she lived in the same orphanage as the little boy upstairs. Their neglect is criminal. Someone should report them to the proper authorities."

A spark of hope for Celeste burned in Sam's chest. How different would her life be without that gaping hole where her lip should be? "Don't you worry about that. I intend to see that the city of St. Louis knows what kind of treatment the orphans are receiving. Do you think you could take a look at Celeste in the morning? And how long would it take for the surgery and for her to recover?"

The doctor held up his hands. "Wait. I didn't say I could do the surgery.

You need a surgeon who specializes in children's operations. I have a friend who would be just the man to treat Celeste. We went to medical school together. The trouble is he lives in Chicago now."

"Chicago, huh? Know anybody in Denver?"

"I can make inquiries. Bring the little girl to this room tomorrow morning at eight, and I'll take a look at her. Then I can write up some case notes to send with you." He frowned. "I was under the impression you were merely helping to get these children from one place to another. From your questions, it almost sounds as if you're considering taking on more than that."

It did sound that way. Sam studied his hands and pursed his lips, then shrugged. "I'm not committing to anything. I just wondered if there was anything you could do for the kid." He chuckled. "She hasn't said a single word to me. Quiet as can be. Just looks over that scarf at me with those big, blue eyes." He stood and started for the door.

The doctor followed him out into the hall toward the street entrance.

Sam held out his hand. "Thanks for everything you're doing, Doc. I'll see that the girl is here tomorrow morning for you to examine. Then, if you could give the case notes to Miss Carter, that would be fine. She's the one in charge of the kids. I'm just sort of helping her along a little. They're not really my concern."

The front door flung open, crashing into Sam's shoulder and sending him reeling backward into the wall. Dr. O'Kelly's eyes widened and he stepped back.

Eldora stood in the doorway, water streaming down her face and dripping off her clothes. She gasped, her chest heaving.

"What's wrong?" Sam asked.

She hadn't even taken the time to put on her shawl. Her dress clung to her, saturated with rain. "Sam, hurry. It's Phin." Her teeth chattered, whether from cold or from upset he couldn't tell.

"Is he hurt?" Sam slipped out of his coat and wrapped it around her shoulders, trying to ignore the pain screaming through his upper arm from the abrupt contact with the door.

She appeared not to notice when the heavy material closed around her, swallowing up her slight frame. Her icy hands gripped his, and she clung to him. "No, he's not hurt." She shook her head, sending droplets flying from the rats' tails of wet hair around her face. "At least I don't think so." Her teeth chattered.

"Then what?"

"He's been arrested."

Chapter 8

I can't turn my back on you for two minutes. What were you thinking?"
Eldora threw her hands up and paced the narrow space before the cell.
Phin sat on the edge of the wooden bunk, staring at the floor. His
stony silence pushed Eldora closer to the brink of tears.

Weak morning sunlight, cold and clear after last night's rain, came
through the window. She could see her breath and Phin's in the frosty air.
The smells of damp wood, mud, and unwashed humanity assaulted her
nose. How had Phin endured a night in this unheated cell with only a
single, thin blanket for cover?

"This entire trip is like a raveled sweater. Every time I pull on a string,
more comes undone." She blinked hard. "Tick in the hospital, Celeste's
tantrum about seeing Dr. O'Kelly this morning—I had no idea such a
well-behaved child could throw such a spectacular fit—and now you in jail
for stealing." Hot tears pricked her eyes, but she quelled them. Tears were
useless. Life just rolled right over her, in spite of tears.

Phin rose and crossed the narrow area between the bars and the far wall.
"What did the sheriff say?"

"He said if I paid your fine he would release you."

"You are going to pay it, right?"

"With what? Air? The fine is ten whole dollars. I have exactly two. Two
dollars to get four people to Denver. You tell me where I'm supposed to
get ten dollars to pay a fine you never should've incurred in the first place."

"So what happens if you don't pay the fine? How long do I have to stay
in here?"

She searched his countenance for a single shred of repentance or fear or
even chagrin but read only defiance and stubbornness, and if she wasn't
mistaken, a glint of pride.

"Sam's talking to the police officer now to find that out. Phin, why? And
don't tell me it was for food. Sam said you ate enough for two grown men
at supper, and the police found three dinner rolls stuffed in your pocket."

"I wasn't stealing food. Not that time."

"A wallet? A purse? You do know that stealing is wrong."

Phin stared at the wall behind her shoulder.

"Why, Phin? Why do you do it?"

"You're so smart, why don't you tell me?" He glared at her. "Always trying to boss me around, thinking you know what's going on in my head. You tell me why you think I steal stuff."

She'd had it with him. His stealing, his unreliability, his making her job harder at every turn. Leaving him here to learn a lesson appealed to her like it hadn't before. "I'll tell you why I think you steal. I think you're trying to get even with people for what your uncle did to you. I think you take your anger out on those around you, blaming them because you're an orphan."

"Don't talk about my uncle. He's going to come for me someday. I'm not an orphan like everyone else. I have family. And I don't plan to stay in Colorado. I only came along to get away from Korbin. If he thinks I'm in Denver, he won't be looking for me when I get back to St. Louis. I'll find somewhere in the city to hide and wait until my uncle comes back for me." He stopped pacing and tossed his hair off his forehead. A defiant gleam lit his eyes. "Then we'll be a family again."

Eldora prayed for patience and then promptly let fly. "Phineas Bartholomew, when are you going to get it through your thick head that your uncle isn't coming back? He dumped you in the orphanage to be rid of you the same way Celeste's family and Tick's family did. Too much time has passed for you to still cling to this stubborn hope that he's somehow going to waltz in and rescue you. The sooner you get over this notion, the better, because I'm sick of hearing it. You're an orphan like the rest of us, no better."

Red suffused his cheeks, and his fingers balled into fists. "You don't know what you're talking about." Tremors shook his rigid frame. "You're just jealous that I have family that's still alive and yours is dead. Uncle Myatt promised me he'd come back. He gave me his word."

"The word of a thief—someone who trains children to steal—isn't exactly gospel, you know. He lied to you so you wouldn't put up a fight when he left you, so you wouldn't try to follow him wherever he was going." She hated battering him this way, but someone had to make him see how things really were. His delusions were harming himself and those around him, and they had to stop. "Phin, I'm sorry, I really am. I wish your uncle had come back. I wish Tick's and Celeste's families had wanted them and loved them like they deserve. I wish I wasn't standing in a freezing jail worrying about all of you and trying to think of a way out of this mess. Mostly I wish you'd stop stealing and help me instead of making my job harder."

Inhaling sharply, his nostrils thinned, and he glared at her. "I was trying to help you."

"By breaking into a store? How would that help me?"

"I did it for Tick. Sam told me what kind of medicine he needed. I broke into the drugstore to get some."

Shock trickled through Eldora like little spiders. "But Phin, the doctor was going to provide us with enough medicine to get to Denver. You didn't need to steal any."

"Just like a girl. You never think ahead. So we have enough to reach Denver. Then what? Sam says Tick will need the medicine for the rest of his life. Where do you think that's going to come from? The orphanage?" He spit out the word. "Nope, the minute we walk through those doors, Tick's medical treatment will quit. We'll be on our own again. Sam won't be there to pay for things and make people take care of us."

He wasn't saying anything Eldora hadn't feared, but hearing the words made the fear real. But what could she do? She could only cling to the truth she knew in her heart. "God will provide a way for us. He'll light the way for us, and His way won't involve breaking a commandment."

Phin snorted. "I can't see that God has bothered too much with us to this point. We're as alone now as we've ever been."

"You're wrong. He's with us. He brought Sam to us. Where would we have been without Sam? You got to ride in a private car, got served nice food off fine china, and Tick's being looked after properly at last. You would've had a nice warm bed last night, too, if you hadn't been so stupid."

"You're addle-brained if you think Sam is going to hang around after we get to Denver. For all the time you've spent telling me to quit holding onto a dream, you're spinning a few yourself. I see the way you look at him, like he was the president or a prince or something."

His words stung. She'd tried hard not to spin romantic notions about Sam, bracing herself for when he walked away, but he'd been so kind, it was hard. Shaking her head, she rallied. "I do nothing of the sort. Stop lashing out at me because you're mad. I told you a few truths you needed to hear. You need to get a grip on your temper and your bitterness before both land you in real trouble. You're in enough of a jam as it is. What Mr. Korbin will say, I don't know."

She rubbed her cold hands together. She had a fair idea. If Mr. Korbin were here right now, he'd say she was an incompetent fool and that Phin was getting exactly what he deserved.

"Who cares what that skunk would say? I'm better off in jail than any-where near him. At least no one here has belted me." He sank onto the bunk and lay down, putting one knee up and throwing his arm over his eyes. "I still think you're an addle-headed girl."

"At least I'm not in jail."

❧

Sam clenched and unclenched his hands, trying not to imagine them around that little scamp's throat. How could he upset Ellie like this? At least in jail Phin couldn't do anything else stupid to upset her.

Sam glanced at the door to the cells, wondering what she was saying to him. Probably coddling him, telling him everything would be all right, that she was sure he didn't mean to steal. Eldora Carter had a tender heart, and Phin took advantage of it at every turn.

Well, no more. The image of her soaking wet, cold right through, and desperately clinging to him out of fear for Phin rose in Sam's mind. The kid needed to learn that his misdeeds had consequences. She might coddle him, but that didn't mean Sam would.

"Ten dollars or ten days." The policeman crossed his arms and leaned back in his chair. "That's the standard fine for petty theft around here. Since he's a kid, and just passing through, we won't bother with a trial, not for something so small. He didn't even break a window to get in. Picked the lock as pretty as you please."

Sam didn't miss the admiration in the officer's voice, though he didn't share it. "I need to be on the train in three days if I'm going to make it home for Christmas. I could just pay the fine, but I'm not inclined to do that. What kind of lesson will he learn if I bail him out?"

The lawman pursed his lips and rubbed his mustache. "Christmas. That's rough." He leaned forward and shuffled the papers on his desk. "Tell you what. He can work it off. If he works today and tomorrow for the city, I'll release him to get on the train Sunday morning. Can't do better than that."

They shook hands on the deal, and Sam followed the officer into the next room.

"Well?" Phin bounded up, grabbed the bars, and thrust his thin face forward. "When can I get out of here? Did you pay the fine?"

Sam studied Eldora. Her cheeks were flushed, but she didn't look like she'd been crying. Her delicate throat worked and she exhaled, her breath showing in a puff of crystals. That thin shawl couldn't be keeping her very warm, and he was conscious of the weight and warmth of his own heavy coat. His jaw set. "No."

She turned those big eyes on him, and he felt like a worm. Her eyebrows arched, and she blinked. "No?" Her lips remained parted.

Sam shoved his hands in his pockets. "The officer and I feel it would be best for Phin to work off his fine."

It was Phin's turn to gape. "Work it off? How?"

Keys jangling, the policeman stepped forward. "You'll be sweeping sidewalks, cleaning the streets, and emptying the spittoons in the public buildings." He inserted one of the keys and cranked it over, opening the door. Withdrawing a pair of shackles from his belt, he slipped one on Phin's thin wrist and let out a piercing whistle.

Eldora jumped a foot, and Sam put his hand on her arm to steady her.

A burly constable shouldered his way into the cell area. "You want something, boss?"

"I do. Take this young man out to do some service for the community. Start with the courthouse. He can sweep the floors and empty the spittoons."

"Sir," Eldora asked, "are the shackles necessary?"

"They are. If he's out of the cell and not actually working, he'll be cuffed to the constable here." With a snap, the cuff closed around the young officer's wrist.

Phin scowled at Sam. "This is the best you could do? I thought you'd pay the fine."

"You thought wrong. You know, you're a rotten thief. I've only known you a few days, and you've been caught stealing three times."

Phin's mutinous glare turned into a smirk as the constable headed him out the door. "You don't know how many times I *don't* get caught."

Sam didn't know whether to laugh or yell, so he gritted his teeth. Phin was the epitome of unrepentant arrogance. A little time cleaning spittoons and sweeping up the dung on the streets would do him a world of good. In the meantime, Sam didn't intend to go another hour without taking care of another problem that needed tending to.

"Let's go check on Tick. The nurse said Celeste could sit with Tick for a while, but I'm sure she's getting restless." He put his hand under Eldora's elbow and steered her out. "I never would've suspected Celeste could be so. . ."

"Strong-willed?"

"Yes. I never thought she'd break down like that. Poor kid. How did you convince her finally to let the doctor at least look at her lip?"

"I had to promise to hold her hand through everything, and I had to promise that he wouldn't laugh or make fun of her or hurt her in any way. Dr. O'Kelly was so kind and matter of fact. He didn't recoil or even talk about her lip the whole time he examined her. He talked about his new puppy. It seems he got a new spaniel pup a couple of weeks ago, and he told her all about the dog's antics and made up a few adventures about him, too. In the end, she forgot to be afraid or self-conscious, though she refused to answer any of his questions. He promised to bring the puppy to the hospital for her and Tick to see this afternoon."

They crossed the street and walked up the two blocks to the hospital. The wind whipped her skirts and tugged her hair from its braid. She clutched her shawl under her chin and leaned into the breeze. He held her elbow with one hand and anchored his hat with the other. When they reached the calm of the hospital foyer, she blew on her hands and shivered, then tried to tuck wisps of wayward hair behind her ears.

"Run up and get Celeste, and then we have an errand or two to see to." He waited at the bottom of the stairs, eager to get going now that he'd made up his mind what he wanted to do.

When the girls reached the bottom of the stairs, he took Celeste's hand and Eldora's elbow and led them back out into the wind. Good thing the Emporium was only in the next block.

The bell overhead jangled when he opened it, and they stepped inside.

Celeste gave a gasp, and her blue eyes widened. Eldora wasn't much different, trying to see everything in the packed store at once. The little girl dropped his hand and took Eldora's, pointing to a glass case full of jars of candy.

Eldora seemed to remember her manners and turned to him. "Was there something you needed to pick up?"

"I need quite a few things, actually. Hopefully you can help me."

"Of course." She let her fingers drift across the polished wood on the edge of the counter. "I don't have much experience shopping, but anything I can do to help I will."

"I haven't the slightest doubt that you'll be more than up to the task." He nodded to the sales clerk headed their way.

"How can I help you?" The woman tucked a pencil behind her ear and brushed the front of her white apron. "My, what a pretty young'un you have." She tilted her head to one side. "I'm trying to decide who she favors. Must be you, sir, with the blue eyes."

Sam didn't bother to correct her, giving the girls a wink when the clerk turned her back to straighten some boxes on the shelf behind her. "You seem to have a nice selection of ready-made clothing available. I'm looking for new clothes."

Eldora's eyebrows rose and bunched, but she still didn't ask her questions aloud. The saleswoman nodded and pulled a tablet toward her. "What size?" She flicked a glance at him, appraising his build.

"Several sizes. The clothing isn't for me. It's for Miss Carter and Celeste here. Also for two boys, one about seven and one around thirteen." Sam held his hand level with his waist and then raised it to mid-chest. "About so high for each of them."

"Sam," Eldora breathed, "you don't—"

"Don't argue." He took her hand and tugged her away a few steps. "Celeste, you stay right there." When they were at the far end of the store, standing among the garden tools and hardware, he stared straight into her eyes. "You all need new clothes, warmer clothes. I feel like a cad in my heavy coat when you're getting by with nothing but a shawl." He gestured to the frayed edge.

Pink flooded her cheeks, and her lips flattened. "I'm sorry if we shame you." Guilt stabbed him. He'd said the wrong thing. "No, no. I'm not in the least ashamed of you." He squeezed her chilly hands. "You've done more with less better than any person I've ever met. It's just that I have so much, and you have so little. Please, let me do this for you and the kids. It won't do Tick much good to come out of the hospital and get a chill because his coat is too small and worn out to keep him warm. And Celeste's wrists stick out of her dress. They'll be better off with clothes and shoes that fit and function." He tilted his head to the side and entreated her.

"You know the orphanage won't authorize the expense. They won't reimburse you."

"I'm not worried about that."

She stared at their joined hands for a long time without speaking.

"Is it such a difficult decision?"

"If it was only for myself I would refuse, but you are right. The children need warmer clothes."

"So do you."

"No." She shook her head. "The children's needs are one thing. I can't let you buy anything for me. It wouldn't be proper." She bit on her lower lip. "I wouldn't feel right knowing I could never repay you."

He released her hands and shook his head. Rubbing his palm on the back of his neck, he contemplated her. Yvette had taken with both hands, though she had no real need of the baubles and fripperies he'd bought for her, and here stood Ellie in threadbare clothing and worn-out boots, refusing necessities for fear of owing a debt she couldn't pay.

"I tell you what. You can consider it an early Christmas gift. It's rude to refuse a gift, and if you don't pick out the stuff yourself, I'll have to do it. Now, stop arguing with me and start shopping." He stepped aside for her to walk up the packed aisle, hoping she'd acquiesce to his authority.

Another thought occurred to him, something Phin had shared at dinner the night before. He reached for her hand once more. "I assure you I'm not looking to be repaid for anything, not with money and not any other way." He waited until understanding dawned in her brown eyes.

Again pink raced up her cheeks, and she nodded.

Chapter 9

Though she was grateful to be getting back on the train and continuing their journey after so many days in Salina, Eldora couldn't help but feel it was wrong to be traveling on a Sunday morning. The rain from the past few days had turned to sleet in the night, coating every surface with a layer of glittering ice. Her brand-new shoes slid on the frozen ruts of the rail yard, and she lurched.

Sam's strong hand came under her elbow and steadied her. "Whoops. A little slippery." He winked at Tick, high on his other arm. "At least the sun is finally shining."

The Mackenzie railcar, its dark green paint and brass rails gleaming, stood just ahead, the last in the train. Frosty crystals hung in the air, shreds of the clouds of steam emanating from the hulking engine far to their right up the line ahead of the passenger, freight, and mail cars.

Entering Sam's private car felt familiar and yet strange. Like her new clothes. She squeezed her shoulders together inside her new wool coat, luxuriating in the warmth and heaviness but uneasy at taking so much from him.

Phin shucked his coat to reveal a smart new tweed jacket and pants. He'd been even more reluctant than Eldora to take anything from Sam, but in the end, Sam had his way. Though Phin pretended not to be impressed with the new outfit, Eldora caught him fingering the edge of his jacket or the sturdy buttons on his shirtfront several times.

A porter carried their bags, the old, beat-up valise and a shiny, new leather case, to their rooms.

Sam waited for a second porter to bring his bags before letting Tick slide down until he landed on the settee. "Don't take your coat off yet. Let it warm up in here a bit. Once the engine gets going, the radiators will heat up." He ducked outside to speak to the conductor, a different man from the martinet on the last train.

Celeste sat beside Tick, her feet together in her glossy black boots. She stroked the edges of her cape, seemingly unable to stop touching the soft fur. Her black hood framed her face, and the blue scarf Sam had chosen for her made her eyes even more brilliant.

Tick bounced on his seat, his cheeks pink from the cold and better health. He knelt on the upholstery and peered out the window at Sam.

"Eldora, he's pretty swell, isn't he? New clothes for us, and food and medicine and candy." He flashed a grin over his shoulder, a faint ring of stickiness testament to the peppermints he'd consumed that morning.

Sam *was* pretty swell, to use Tick's description, but Eldora knew she must steel her heart against him. A headache pinged behind her eyes, reminding her of her sleepless night, tossing and turning, worrying about the children, being squashed under the responsibility she bore and tortured with thoughts of Sam and the mounting debts she owed him.

She heard once again the cautions of a kindly woman who had come to teach a Sunday school for the orphan girls once. *"You are so vulnerable, more than most. Without fathers and brothers to look after you, you're easy prey for men once you leave here. If you aren't taken advantage of, then you're in danger of giving your heart too easily to the wrong man. Starved for love and affection as you are, any kindness or flattery might turn your head. I know from experience, for I was once a girl newly turned out of an orphanage. I married the first man who came along, and I have lived to regret it. So, beware, all of you. Don't spin dreams about romance and rescue. You'll wind up hurt and more alone than ever before."*

Though Eldora hadn't understood at the time everything the woman was trying to caution them against, she had come to realize the truth and wisdom in the warning. Too many of her fellow orphan girls, once released into the world, had become street walkers or virtual slaves in the workhouses, or had married men who abused and mistreated them. Even those like Eldora who had found work as domestics were considered easy pickings for the male members of the households, as she had encountered firsthand.

But was Sam like that? He claimed to want nothing in return for his kindness. In every way, he had behaved as a gentleman should. But why? What did he have to gain? What did he want from them, *from her*, in exchange?

She couldn't deny that every time she was near him her breath came a little faster and her heart began to trip and stall. The way he had with the children, even the prickly Phin, made her middle feel mushy and warm, and sometimes when he looked right at her she forgot to breathe altogether.

Stop it, Eldora. You're in danger of making a complete fool of yourself. A man like Sam Mackenzie would never be interested in an ugly duckling like you, poorer than a muskrat, with no proper schooling. If you let yourself dream romantic notions about him, you're just going to get your heart broken when he leaves you in Denver. Get through the next two days with your wits and your heart intact.

Something tugged her sleeve. She looked down into Tick's face.

"I said, 'He's pretty swell, isn't he?'"

She smoothed his fair hair out of his eyes and nodded, a lump in her throat. "Yes, he's pretty swell, but Tick. . ." She wanted to caution him against hero worship, against giving his little heart to someone who would walk away from them, but somehow she couldn't do it, couldn't rub the bloom off his obvious admiration for Sam. He'd know heartache soon enough without her hurrying it along.

The train shuddered, and Sam swung up onto the platform and entered the car. He braced his legs as the train jerked and then slid into motion. "Two days to Denver." He took the seat beside Eldora. The smells of coal smoke, cold air, and shaving soap clung to him.

She slid down the settee and fussed with helping Celeste remove her cloak and hood.

"Kids, there's some hot cocoa and cookies down in the dining room." Sam pointed to the rear of the car. "You head on back there. I want to talk to Eldora for a minute, and then we'll join you."

Eldora's palms prickled, and her throat went dry. She had to get over this silly-girl attraction to him. Securing a polite expression on her face that she prayed gave nothing away, she waited.

Tick and Celeste went without having to be asked twice, but Phin remained, his hands in his pockets. The suspicious tilt of his eyebrows and the set of his jaw both touched and exasperated Eldora. "Go ahead, Phin. We'll be right along."

Sam tugged off his gloves and stuffed them in his pocket. "He can't quite bring himself to trust me, can he?"

With her hands folded in her lap, she shrugged. "He doesn't really trust anyone. You'll notice he's not speaking to me. I'm afraid we had some harsh words when he was in jail, words he needed to hear but that I spoke in anger." Heaviness dragged at her. "What was it you wanted to speak to me about?"

"Quite a few things, actually. We hardly ever seem to be alone, what with one crisis with the children or another. Now I guess I know how a parent feels." He chuckled, and a spark of longing flared in Eldora. "I wanted to tell you what the doctor said about Celeste." He dug in his inner coat pocket and pulled out some folded papers. "He wrote some notes up for you to give to the doctor in Denver, both for her and for Tick." The pages crackled as he smoothed them out. "He seems to think she's an excellent candidate for surgery to correct her problem. Said she'd have a small scar where that gaping hole is now, and she'd be able to eat normally, breathe better, talk clearer, and would probably have fewer problems with her ears and with catching colds."

Hope clashed with reality in her breast. She took the papers, not seeing the words. He just didn't get it. In his own way, he was in as great a need to hear and resign himself to the truth about these kids' futures as Phin had been about his uncle. "Sam, you've been very good to us, and I thank you for all you've done, but you need to understand something. Celeste won't be getting surgery. Tick most likely won't have another dose of medicine once the supply the doctor gave us runs out. When we get to Denver, we won't be going to nice homes. We'll be going to an orphanage. Probably one that has all it can do just to keep kids fed and clothed. There's no extra money for medicines and surgeries. Without adoption, their future is hardly secure, and who will adopt any of them?"

She couldn't sit still any longer. The fears and knowledge she had wrestled with all night spilled out, and she had to move away from him. The train swayed, but she caught the rhythm and paced to its roll. "Who would adopt Celeste, with her face like that and knowing an expensive surgery is needed? If she got adopted, it would most likely be by someone who only wanted to abuse her or work her to death. Once she is too old for the orphanage, she'll be turned out, and how can she hope to get a decent job? Then there's Tick. No one will want him, knowing of his heart trouble and that a lifetime of drug expenses lies ahead. If he lives to be an adult—and what are his chances without the medicine—what kind of work can he do? Nothing physical, and his education thus far is pathetic." She swung her hands, trying to make him see her point. "Not to mention Phin. He's destined for prison, the way he's going. Who would adopt him, knowing they'd have to nail down everything in the place to keep him from stealing it? I'm responsible for them, and I can't do a thing to help them." Panic welled in her chest and choked off her airway. She tried to close her eyes and ward it off, but that disrupted her balance. Lurching against a table, she pushed aside his steadying hand. "What's going to happen to them?"

Sam grabbed her arms and tugged her against him. His large hand came up to cup the back of her head, and she realized she was on the verge of sobbing. "Shhh, Ellie, I'm sorry. I didn't mean to upset you. I understand you're scared, but everything will be all right."

His kind words coupled with the strong, protective feel of his arms around her broke through the tissue-thin walls she'd tried erecting around her heart. Swaying with the movement of the train, she tilted her head back to look into his eyes, but her gaze got caught on his lips. Finely molded, gently curving. . .

The instant she knew she wanted him to kiss her, she jolted backward out of his grasp. "What can a rich man like you know of our troubles? You snap your fingers, and whatever you desire comes to pass. Your life is light and freedom. Ours is darkness and no choices." Words sprang out of her mouth, stupid words hurled at him to try to dodge the guilt and fear stabbing her. "The children adore you, even Phin, though he's trying hard not to show it, but what happens to them when you leave us—I mean...them? Where will they be then?"

Where will I be when you leave me? Her insides turned to a quivering mass as the reality of her feelings hit her.

"Ellie, please—"

"Don't call me Ellie!" Pain cleaved her heart, knowing she had been foolish enough to fall in love with him and knowing there was no hope along that path. To her mortification, the tears slipped over her lashes, and a strangled sob exploded from her throat. She fled into her sleeping compartment, slammed the door, and threw herself across the bed.

꙳

Sam's shoulders slumped, and he sank into a chair, as battered as if he'd fallen down a mineshaft. Here he'd meant only to encourage her with his good news about Celeste, and she'd detonated like a pint of nitro. The memory of her tears lashed him like a whip.

At least they were real tears, real emotion spawned by real problems. Her choking cries, muffled through the wall behind him, made him close his eyes and fist his hands, leaning his head on the paneling.

Yvette had cried prettily, dabbing at her lashes with a lace handkerchief, darting sidelong looks at him to gauge his reaction and coming out of her sorrow the instant she got what she wanted. Manipulative minx, and he, like a first-class chump, had fallen for it for a time. A scowl twisted his mouth. Why was he thinking of Yvette now?

After a few minutes, the crying sounds ceased, or at least grew so faint he couldn't make them out. He rose and edged down the narrow passageway to listen at her door. Should he tap? Perhaps she was asleep. The shadows under her eyes this morning made him wonder if she'd slept at all last night, and who could blame her? She'd certainly been under a lot of strain, and the glimpse she had given him into the children's futures would have kept him awake under the circumstances. He decided not to disturb her, knowing he wouldn't have any idea what to say to her if she answered the door. He'd best check on the kids.

Tick and Celeste sat at the table, Phin leaned against the wall, and none of them were eating the cookies. Phin's glare could've set Sam's suit on fire.

"What?" Still tender from the scene with Ellie—Eldora—he was in no mood to deal with anything from Phin.

"We heard you. We all came to get you, because Tick didn't want to start in on the cookies without you and Eldora."

Tick's lower lip jutted. "You made her cry."

Fear that they might've heard the discussion of their futures clawed up his chest. "What else did you hear?"

Celeste had tucked her scarf up again and leveled an unnaturally mature stare at him. Phin shoved away from the wall and flung himself into a chair. "Nothing we didn't already know, and nothing you shouldn't have figured out. Why do you think we're on this train? Because nobody will adopt us in the whole city of St. Louis, and Korbin wanted to get rid of us. He's making us someone else's problem."

Their resigned acceptance of their lot in life tore at Sam. His own childhood, so secure in the love and care of his parents, mocked him. Ellie—Eldora—was right. He knew nothing of the suffering they'd endured, the uncertainty, the lack of affection and security. He had thought getting them to Denver would be enough, that he'd leave them at the orphanage, fulfilling his promise to Aunt Tabitha and doing his good deed. But the notion of leaving them there—especially knowing how precarious their futures would be there—didn't sit right with him. But what could he do?

"Why doesn't she like to be called Ellie?" The question was out before he realized it.

Phin rolled his eyes. "She told us she used to be Ellie—that's what her dad called her—but when she came to the orphanage, the matron called her by her full name, Eldora. She says Ellie is for the happier times, when she had a family. Eldora is her orphan name."

"Like Tick's mine." The little boy nodded as if this made complete sense. "I ain't been called Michael in a long time, but if I was ever gonna get a family someday, I'd let them call me Michael. I don't guess Eldora will want to be called Ellie until she has a family again."

"Does everyone have two names?"

Phin shook his head. "Nope, not when they're foundlings. The women in the orphanage nursery name the kids who show up as babies. She"—he jerked his thumb at Celeste—"got dumped on the orphanage doorstep on a clear night with lots of stars, so they named her Celeste. One of the schoolteachers we had for a while, Mr. Plimpkin, told her it meant 'from the heavens' or 'from the stars' or something silly like that."

Sam raised a smile for the little girl. "I don't think that's silly at all. It's a beautiful name, and she wears it well." He fingered the edge of the tablecloth where it fell against his leg. So, Ellie was for the happy times. He fervently hoped someday she'd get to use the name again. She deserved to be happy.

"I'm going to find the conductor and see about getting some food ordered in for lunch. You kids stay here, and don't disturb Eldora. She'll come out when she's ready." He rose. "Phin—"

"I know, don't leave the car."

As he headed up the passageway, Tick's piping little voice reached him. "Phin, is what Eldora said true? Will Sam leave us when we get to Denver?"

Sam froze.

"Of course he will, you twit. He's just looking after us as a favor to that dried-up old aunt of his that we saw at the station in St. Louis. What did you think? That he was going to adopt you or something? You're worse than a girl for pipe dreams. He'll drop us like a hot rock as soon as he can."

Stung and not wanting to hear whatever other aspersions Phin might cast on his character, Sam stalked away. How had Phin struck so close to the truth?

Chapter 10

I sent a telegram from the last stop so transport will be waiting when we arrive." Sam slid his watch out of his pocket. "We should be pulling into the station soon."

Eldora nodded. Her skin stretched taut over her cheekbones, and the dark smudges hadn't left the hollows under her eyes.

Several times over the past two days he'd tried to engage her in conversation, but she remained aloof. Though he knew he'd hurt her, he didn't have a clue as to what he had done that was so terrible. Provided them with food, safe and comfortable travel, medical care, kindness. He clenched his back teeth.

Phin and Tick's accusatory glares didn't help the situation either. At least Celeste wasn't shooting daggers his way with every glance. No, she just avoided looking at him altogether.

"If it weren't dark, you could see the mountains by now."

No one responded.

Eldora dug in her handbag and produced the box from the drugstore. She lifted one of the twists of paper out and emptied the contents into a cup of water. "Here, Tick, time for your medicine."

The youngster made a face but gulped the stuff down, swiping his mouth with the back of his hand and giving the cup back to Eldora. "Thanks."

Tick, one good change. Each day he seemed stronger, had more color in his cheeks, and he certainly had an appetite. The child could eat more than Sam and Phin combined, it seemed.

With almost imperceptible slowness, the train decelerated as they neared the Denver depot. Hundreds of train cars slid by the windows—boxcars, ore cars, and passenger cars. Lights and buildings. "We'll have to cross over several tracks to get to the depot, so everyone keep hold of a hand." The last thing he wanted was to lose someone in the dark rail yard or in the busy depot. "We'll climb a flight of stairs to get to street level. That's where Buckford will meet us with the sleigh."

They rose as one and lined up by the door. Prisoners going to the dock. Why did he feel like an executioner? His promise to his aunt was almost fulfilled. Soon he'd be having supper with David and Karen, and tomorrow he'd be on the train to Martin City, home in time for Christmas.

The snow was a foot deep in places, so he picked Tick up. Two porters and Phin carried the bags, and they wove their way along with the other passengers to the brightly lit platform.

The instant their feet hit the boards, Tick wriggled to get down. He marched over to Eldora and took her hand, staring hard at Sam to be sure everyone knew where his allegiance lay.

"This way." Their footsteps crunched on the damp concrete stairs leading to the street. Voices echoed off the tiled walls and were swallowed up when they reached the high-ceilinged waiting room. The smell of damp wool and wood smoke, people and cold weather, wrapped around him. Ushering his little group to a backwater corner where they wouldn't be jostled, he scanned the crowd for a familiar face.

"Lookit that." Tick pointed. Every window and wall was festooned with garlands and ribbon. Red and silver ornaments glinted in the gaslight. In the far corner, near the huge fireplace, a quartet broke into a Christmas carol. Each time the doors opened, a gust of wind brought in the tinkling sound of sleigh bells.

"Wonder what Christmas is like at this orphanage. In St. Louis, we got to eat ham, and every kid got new socks or gloves or something." Phin kicked his heel against the wall, his hands shoved deep in his pockets.

Eldora's eyes were huge. "I'm sure it will be nice. Maybe there will be some decorations, or even some toys." She didn't sound as if she believed what she was saying. And what kind of Christmas was it for a kid without toys?

The crowd parted a little, and he spied Buckford waiting by the door. Swinging his arm overhead, Sam flagged the friend and family butler.

Impeccably dressed in a wool topcoat and bowler, Buckford clasped Sam's offered hand. "Hello, sir. Good to see you back again."

"Hello, Buckford. Glad you got my message. You brought the big sleigh?"

"Yes sir."

"Good. Buckford, this is Eldora Carter, and these are her charges: Phin, Celeste, and Tick. We're driving them out to the orphanage."

"Very good, sir." Not so much as a lift of the eyebrow or a twitch of the lip. For as long as Sam had known Buckford—and that was most of his adult life—he had been unable to crack the butler's shell of decorum. He looked each one over, a polite smile on his seemingly ageless face, and bowed to Eldora. "I'm pleased to meet you. It's quite an endeavor, traveling across the country with children. I hope you had a pleasant journey."

Eldora blinked and nodded. "Thank you. It was fine. Mr. Mackenzie was most helpful."

"His mother will be pleased to hear it." A twinkle lit Buckford's eye, and he turned to the children.

Phin stuck out his hand—Sam watched closely, knowing Phin's proclivities—and shook Buckford's. Tick copied the older boy, pretending bravado, but his cheeks were pale.

When Buckford's gaze landed on Celeste, he stopped, took a second look at her pretty eyes and roses-and-cream complexion, and bowed deeply. "Miss Celeste, it is my pleasure."

The sound that came from the little girl could only be described as a giggle, the first Sam had heard her utter. Hmm. He blinked. How had Buckford managed that?

The butler chucked her under the chin and patted her head. And, of all things, when he held out his hand, Celeste took it, her nose wrinkling in a grin above her scarf.

Eldora seemed taken aback by this instant rapport as well, staring from one to the other, her lips parted.

Buckford led the way outside to the waiting sleigh, holding the little girl's hand and leaving Phin and Sam to wrestle the luggage.

Sam piled kids and bags in and tucked buffalo robes around them. He handed Eldora in as if she were spun glass and received a whispered thank you, then vaulted himself up onto the front seat to ride beside Buckford. With a clash of bells, the horses took off.

They traveled several blocks before Sam couldn't stand it anymore. "Aren't you going to ask me about them?" He ducked his head deeper into his collar to shield him from the wind their quick passage created.

"Do you want to tell me, sir?"

"I'm watching out for them as a favor to Aunt Tabitha." Buckford had worked for Tabitha Mackenzie before coming to Sam's parents' employ. Now he worked for Sam's brother and his wife, mostly at their town house here in Denver. "I'm supposed to see they get to the orphanage here without trouble."

"And have you had trouble? Your brother expected you several days ago. They've delayed traveling to Martin City, waiting for your arrival."

"He got my message, didn't he? About stopping over in Salina?"

"Yes."

"How's Karen feeling?"

"Doing well. Anxious for Christmas. She's looking forward to seeing your parents again. As am I." Buckford steered the horses around a corner and headed toward the south end of the city. "David hovers and fusses, and she pretends to like it. They're both very excited about the little one."

"Almost as excited as my parents, I bet. The first grandchild." Sam grinned. "I bet Dad is hardly fit to live with."

"Mr. Mackenzie even sent me a cigar, though neither of us smokes."

"That sounds like him."

They rode in silence, and Sam checked over his shoulder every few blocks. The kids were all eyes, watching the houses and buildings flash by. Eldora seemed not to see any of it. She kept her eyes straight ahead and appeared lost in thought—or worry, if the crease between her eyebrows was any indication.

The buildings and houses grew farther apart as they left the city center, and eventually the only thing on the horizon was a black, square-shaped edifice alone out on the east face of a foothill. "Is that the place?"

"Yes." Buckford slapped the lines.

"Why is it so far out of town?"

"Cheap land, most likely. That and there's room to expand."

"More like they want to keep the whole thing out of sight."

The closer they got, the uglier the building grew. In a complete revolt against graceful architecture, the solid stone walls and blank rectangular windows looked more like those of a prison than a home for children. Cold seeped into Sam's bones that had nothing to do with the outside temperature. Well, maybe it was more cheerful on the inside. At least those thick walls would keep the wind out.

Buckford pulled the sleigh onto the horseshoe drive, passing between the gateposts and beneath the iron sign declaring this indeed to be the Denver Orphanage.

Since when did doing exactly what he was supposed to do fill Sam with such dread?

❧

Eldora's throat closed, and her hands ached from clenching them beneath the heavy buffalo robe. The orphanage looked much worse than it had in her mind. Cold, imposing, unfriendly. Home to the children now and home for her if she could get them to hire her on. She'd decided, after sobbing her heart out on the train, that she couldn't leave the children here alone and go back to St. Louis as if she didn't care. Mr. Korbin would be as relieved to be rid of her as he was the children. She could clean or do laundry or sew or even care for the babies in the nursery. Surely somewhere in this hulking building they could find room for her.

The sleigh pulled to a stop with a final clash of bells. Eldora clambered down without waiting for Sam's help, determined to take charge of the situation and stand on her own two feet. The past two days, being with him in the close confines of the railcar and knowing their time together was getting small, had been torture. She knew she had been distant and unkind, but it was the only way she knew to deal with the pain. His puzzled glances and halting efforts to draw her out of her shell only made her retreat faster.

Weights pulled at her legs with every step across the snow-packed drive. They mounted the stairs, Celeste clinging to Buckford's hand in a thoroughly uncharacteristic way and Phin and Tick dragging their feet. Sam held the door. Once in the foyer, the children lined up along the wall in a formation all too familiar to Eldora for having performed it so often herself. Their faces lost all the animation and life they had displayed on the journey.

From the end of the long hallway, the sounds of cutlery and plates clattered. The smell of cooked cabbage, as familiar to her as the lining up of children, assaulted her nose. Dinner in full swing.

She tugged off her gloves and smoothed her hair as best she could. At least, thanks to Sam's generosity, they all looked respectable in new clothes. "You children wait right here. I'm going to see the matron or the superintendent or whoever is about at this hour. Phin, keep an eye on the younger kids and don't stray."

Bracing herself, she turned to Sam and held out her hand. "Thank you for all your help in getting us here. We are most appreciative. I don't know what I would've done without your assistance." She kept her tone and her words as formal as possible, in spite of the overwhelming feeling of despair and abandonment that threatened to swamp her. "I'm sure you want to be on your way to your relatives' house, so we won't keep you."

Sam shoved his hat back, a puzzled expression on his face. "If it's all the same to you, I'll talk to the superintendent. I'd like to satisfy myself that the kids will be taken care of." He reached out his long arm past her and rapped on the office door.

On the staircase above them, someone cleared her throat. "Excuse me? May I help you?"

Eldora stepped out so she could see better. A thin-faced woman with pale yellow hair shot through with gray leaned over the banister. The light from the lamp she carried cast a golden glow over her features.

"I'm looking for the superintendent or the matron." Eldora unbuttoned her coat to get at the papers Mr. Korbin had sent.

"Mr. Korbin and Mrs. Phillips are at dinner."

"Mr. Korbin?" Eldora stopped.

The woman came down the stairs. "Yes, Mr. Finlo Korbin. He's the super here."

Sam stepped closer and whispered to Eldora, "Maybe he's a relative?" Then he turned to the woman, smiling and charming. "Miss, would you please tell the superintendent we want to see him? These kids have come a long way, and they're tired and hungry."

"Of course. I'm Miss Templeton." Her smile changed her face from plain to pretty in an instant, responding to Sam's friendliness. She set the lamp on the hall table and hurried away, eager to do his bidding.

Eldora clamped her lips shut. So much for taking charge and freeing Sam from his self-assumed responsibilities.

A lean man in a dark suit strode down the hallway, dabbing his lips with a napkin. One glance told her he must be related to Conrad Korbin.

"You wanted to see me? I'm Finlo Korbin, superintendent of this orphanage." He ignored Eldora and offered his hand to Sam. "What can I do for you?"

"Can we step into your office?"

"Of course." The super studied each of the lined-up children for a few seconds and then turned and opened the office door. "Miss Templeton, light the lamps."

Wanting to exert the little authority she had, to show her competence before the super so that he might look favorably on hiring her, Eldora put her hand on Sam's arm. "I will take care of things. You don't need to stay."

"Don't be ridiculous."

"Please, Sam. I need to do this myself. At least wait here with the children while I speak to Mr. Korbin."

With a frown, he backed up and let her enter the office alone.

Miss Templeton put matches to lamps and brought a very utilitarian room to light. Immense desk, straight-backed chairs, rank of filing cabinets. No pictures, no adornments of any kind. Eldora gathered her courage, stepped forward, and laid out the paperwork on his desk. "My name is Miss Carter, and I've come from the St. Louis Children's Home. Mr. Conrad Korbin sends his greetings."

"My brother?" He reached for the papers and unfolded them.

So that was the relation. Eldora laced her fingers at her waist and waited for him to finish reading the letter explaining the arrival of the children and her.

Finlo tipped the pages toward the light, and as he read, his face hardened. Slowly, he lowered the pages. "Is this some kind of joke?"

A sinking feeling trickled through her. "No sir." She swallowed.

"Impossible. There is no room here for these children. We're at capacity now. Over capacity." He tossed the letter on the desk, his lip twisted in contempt. "I will not allow my brother to foist his problems off on me. You can go right back to St. Louis and tell him I said so. How dare he? Without so much as a telegram." He sprang up and shoved his hands into his pockets. "Conrad's a sneaky one."

"Please, sir, we don't have the funds to return. Mr. Korbin—your brother—didn't pay for return tickets. He never thought we'd need them."

"That isn't my problem. These children were perfectly fine where they were, and knowing my brother, it was more than random overcrowding that made him pick these three." He glanced sharply at her. "Ah, I see by your guilty start that I'm on to something. Tell me, what's wrong with them?"

"Nothing, really. They're wonderful children. It isn't their fault. A few physical ailments—"

"Aha!" He pounced before she could continue. "I knew it. What is it? Consumption? The state is overrun with lungers now trying to take the altitude cure. We can't have them mixing with the healthy children in this orphanage. You'll have to take them to one of the asylums."

"No sir. They're not consumptive. The little one has a bit of a heart ailment, but with medication—"

Again he interrupted her. "Medication? Conrad must think we're made of gold. There's no money for medicaments beyond the occasional dose of castor or cod liver oil. If the child is ill, he should be in a hospital, not an orphanage. What about the other two?"

A hard lump formed in Eldora's throat. "A doctor has written up some case notes. You have them before you there. The little girl, Celeste, is in need of an operation to correct a facial deformity. She's got a harelip, but the doctor seemed to think surgery would put things right."

"Ha!" His bark of laughter made her flinch. "Surgery. Who are you trying to kid? What about the other one, the older boy? What's he got? Pneumonia? Typhoid?"

"No, he's perfectly healthy." The superintendent's derision put some steel into her spine. "There's nothing wrong with Phin that a little love, attention, and kindly discipline wouldn't cure."

"Well, he's not going to get it here. As I said, we're overcrowded and not taking anyone in."

"Please, sir, they've nowhere else to go. Even if you can't afford the medicines or surgery, you can't turn them away." She gripped her hands until they shook.

"Take them back to St. Louis. If I allow them in here, everyone else will have to get by with less, and we're strapped as it is. This is a private establishment that relies on donations and benevolence to survive, both of which seem to be in short supply at the moment. I'm turning away children every day, and the minute any of the children here turn fourteen, they have to leave to make room for more. There just isn't space. I know you think I'm being cruel, but that's the way it is. It was wrong of my brother to send you here in the first place. How long have you worked for him? You don't look much more than a child yourself."

"I'm nineteen." She lifted her chin. "Perhaps we can reach a compromise. I would be willing to work here for you for just my keep if you would take these children in. I'm well-versed in orphanage life. I can clean, cook some, sew, and do laundry." Impossible to keep the pleading from her voice, but she tried to steady her tone and at least appear professional. "Please, don't turn us out."

His face softened, and for a moment she knew hope, but he shook his head. "I told you it was impossible. You'll think me an ogre, but I've got children sleeping on the floors right now. We're barely getting by for food, and I've got an overabundance of girls here working for their keep as it is. I'm sorry, but there just isn't room. I apologize for my brother getting your hopes up that there would be a place for you here and that he sent you on this hiding to nowhere. Now"—he rose, folded the papers into a tidy bundle, and handed them to her—"if you will excuse me, I've got things to see to."

She found herself ushered out of his office without much ceremony. Five expectant pairs of eyes met hers, and she didn't know what to say. How could she tell these little ones that not even an orphanage wanted them?

"Good night, Miss, er, Carter, was it? And again, I'm sorry I couldn't help you." Mr. Korbin nodded and strode down the hall toward the dining room.

"What does he mean he couldn't help you?"

Eldora clutched the papers in one hand and pinched the headache forming between her eyes. "He says they are full up. There's no room here for us." Her shoulders sagged, and her mind refused to form a single coherent thought.

Phin scowled and shrugged, as if he'd known it all along, and Tick's eyes got round. He slid close and tugged on her hand until she lowered it. He slipped his fingers into hers and gave her a look full of questions. Celeste said nothing, just waited patiently for more of life to happen to her.

"That's ridiculous. I'll be right back." Sam yanked off his hat and marched away, his boots ringing on the hardwood floor.

Buckford's brow furrowed. "I didn't know an orphanage could turn away children in need."

"Apparently they can, especially since this is a private establishment. There's no room and barely enough money to keep food on the table as it is."

Tick squeezed her hand until she looked down at him. "What are we going to do then? Are we getting back on the train?"

She smoothed his fair hair and tried to smile. "We're not getting back on the train. Don't worry. I'll think of something." Though she hadn't a clue what.

Sam came back, his face a thundercloud. "That's it. Grab the bags, Buckford. Phin, give him a hand." He bent and picked up Tick and took Eldora's elbow.

"Where are we going?" She anchored her hat and tried to keep up.

"We're going to my brother's house. I wouldn't leave a dog I didn't like in this place."

Chapter 11

Buckford guided the team to a halt, and Sam looked up at the lighted windows of his brother's town house. How would David and Karen react to him showing up with four extras in tow? He braced himself and jumped down. Only one way to find out.

"Come on, kids. We'll have you warmed up in a minute. How does some hot chocolate sound?" He made his voice as jolly as he could, knowing he couldn't make up for their being rejected again. None of the four had said a word during the ride, and he didn't know what hurt worse, the dejection on Tick's and Celeste's faces or the resignation on Phin's and Eldora's.

He shouldered his way through the door, dropping the luggage on the floor by the hall tree. "Karen? David?" Dropping his hat on the newel post at the base of the stairs, he turned to Buckford. "Can you rouse the housekeeper for some hot chocolate?"

Karen appeared at the head of the staircase. "Sam, you're back. I was afraid you might not make it before we left in the morning for Martin City." Carefully, one hand on the rail and the other on the mound of her expectant motherhood, she descended. Before he could make introductions, she held out both hands to Eldora. "You must be Yvette. Welcome to the family." Karen kissed a bewildered Eldora on the cheek. "And who are these young people?"

Sam's innards squirmed. "Karen, I figured Aunt Tabitha would've wired you by now with the news. This is Eldora Carter, and these children are. . . I guess they're her wards. They need a place to stay tonight. I hope you don't mind. If it's a problem, I can put them up in a hotel." He tilted his head and gave a half grin. Weariness had set up an ache in his muscles, and he lost a moment thinking of how good it would feel to sink into a bed that wasn't rocking and swaying.

A small furrow appeared between Karen's brows. "Of course they're welcome here. We'll find beds for everyone. But where is Yvette?"

"Can we talk about that later? The kids are tired and hungry, and I'm worn clean through. Where's David?"

He and Karen measured glances, and she patted his arm. "We'll talk later. David is in the sitting room. Why don't you take your guests in and make introductions, and I'll see about some supper?"

When she'd disappeared, Eldora put her hand on his arm. "Are you sure about this? I feel terrible, crashing in without warning. Perhaps it would be best if we left."

"Where would you go? Don't worry. Karen and David will welcome you. They're nice people. They'd never turn away three kids in need, especially when they hear what happened at the orphanage."

Sam helped Eldora out of her coat and hung it beside his, then ushered everyone into the warm sitting room. A healthy fire glowed in the fireplace, and the smells of pine boughs and cider wrapped around them. David sat in a chair, his head back on the antimacassar, a heavy book open on his knees.

"Hello, David. I'm back."

His brother sat up, scrabbling for the book before it hit the floor. "Sam? I'm afraid I dozed off. It seems like ages since Buckford went to get you. Welcome back." David set the book on the table beside him, rose, and held out his hand.

Sam grasped it, taking in the content expression and wide smile. A year ago, he wouldn't have given short odds on David's future happiness, but after quite a struggle, it appeared that he and Karen were on a sure footing, at peace and much in love. "Thanks. It's good to be back in Colorado."

"And where is your lovely bride? Karen and I have been so anxious to meet Yvette ever since we got your letter about the engagement. I have to say, you're a fast worker."

Sam squelched a sigh. He should've cabled, but it wasn't something he'd wanted to put in a telegram, and he'd figured Aunt Tabitha would've let folks know. "The wedding didn't come off. But I did bring someone with me."

"How come this book doesn't have any words in it?" Tick turned the heavy cream page. "The paper's all bumpy."

David turned to the voice. "Who might you be?"

"David, these young folks are Tick, Phin, and Celeste. Also with them is Miss Eldora Carter, who is looking after them."

"How do you do?" A hundred questions lingered in David's voice, but he didn't voice them. "And to the one who asked the question, the book has words, but you can't see them. I read with my fingertips, not with my eyes." He smiled. "I'm blind. The little bumps tell me what the words are."

"You can't see anything?" Phin's eyebrows rose. Then he glanced about the room, as if appraising the décor. He shoved his hands in his pockets and looked away when Sam sent him a warning glare.

"I'm afraid not. But I try not to let that slow me down too much." David indicated the chairs before the fireplace. "Miss Carter, won't you sit down?"

Celeste appeared not to notice anything else, having dropped to her knees beside a low table. In the center of the table, a small crèche stood, surrounded by carved nativity figurines. The little girl had her hands clasped beneath her scarf-wrapped chin, and her eyes were round as pennies.

Eldora perched on the edge of her seat as if she expected someone to yank it out from under her. "I'm so sorry for barging in like this. Sam said you wouldn't mind, but I realize what an imposition it is."

David resumed his seat with a chuckle. "We're used to the unexpected where Sam is concerned. Tell me, how did you two meet?"

Before she could answer, Karen came in with Buckford. The butler smiled at Celeste and winked at Tick. Karen eased down onto the arm of David's chair and took his hand. "Buckford is going to take the children into the kitchen to eat. That way we can visit without interruption."

When the children had followed Buckford out of the room, Sam leaned forward and put his elbows on his knees. "To answer your question, Dave, Eldora and I met at the orphanage in St. Louis. I was there to pick up Aunt Tabitha. Eldora was put in charge of these kids, getting them to Denver, and Tabitha asked me to look out for all of them. You know she's recently joined the board of the children's home in St. Louis? Anyway, due to one thing and another, we got delayed halfway across Kansas for a few days, but we finally made it into town tonight. When we showed up at the Denver orphanage, they wouldn't take the kids. So I brought them here."

Eldora's eyes were bright in the firelight. "I am so sorry, Mrs. Mackenzie. As I told your husband, I realize what an imposition this is. I begged the superintendent to take us in, but he was adamant. They didn't have the room or the money to feed any more children."

Karen nodded her understanding. "Don't worry. Sam did the right thing bringing you here. They just built that new orphanage, and it's already full to bursting. There's talk of adding two new wings come spring. With all the consumptives pouring into the state, and most of them not getting well, the orphanages are filling up quickly." She glanced over at Sam. "Your mother has been approached about starting an orphanage in Martin City. With the central location, it would be ideal for the mining communities. You know how quickly disaster can strike up there."

"That sounds perfect for Mother. You know how she likes organizing people."

Eldora stood. "Mrs. Mackenzie, I should go supervise the children. I don't like leaving them alone. You never know what mischief they might get up to"—she grimaced—"though they are biddable children for the most part. Will you please excuse me? And thank you for taking us into your home tonight. I'll do my best to find a place for us tomorrow." She bobbed her head like a servant.

Sam stood, but his good manners went unnoticed, for she hurried out of the room without a backward glance. He eased down, at a loss to explain her sudden departure.

"Sam, what happened with Yvette?" Karen took Eldora's vacant seat. "We thought you'd be bringing us a bride, and you've brought us three children and a caretaker instead."

A sigh built in his lungs, and he pushed it out. "Yvette turned out to be a beautiful gold digger. She wanted the Mackenzie name and money and didn't care a nickel about me. I was a sucker, fell for her in a big way, and I made a lucky escape, finding out what kind of girl she was before we walked down the aisle." He smiled, trying to make light of it, but it stung like salt in a wound.

David shook his head. "That's too bad. Your letters were—" He stopped, as if not knowing how to say it without making Sam feel worse, and spread his hands, palms up.

"I know. I let myself go on about her, but when I found out what she was really like, all that outer beauty soured. All I could see was the grasping, money-grubbing dollar signs in her eyes. At that, I don't know who was worse, her or her mother. Hortense Adelman makes a squanderer look like a skinflint. As it is, they weren't just after the money. Yvette came to me at the train station and made one last plea. She's—" His collar tightened, and he grimaced. A bad taste entered his mouth, talking about her this way, but it had to be told. The family deserved to know why the wedding had been called off. If only there was some way to tell it without making him seem such a thickhead. He sighed again. "She's in the family way. The baby isn't mine, I assure you. The father of the child refused to marry her."

The indignant expression on Karen's face gratified him. "You sure made a lucky escape. Imagine if you'd married her." Her scowl softened. "But I have it in me to be sorry for her, too. What will happen to her now?"

"I left her in the care of Aunt Tabitha. If anyone can sort things out, it's her. I imagine she's tracking down the previous suitor, and she'll make him do right by Yvette. Hortense will be appalled, but"—he shrugged— "she's no one to blame but herself, really, raising her daughter to be so acquisitive."

"And how are you taking it? You sound right enough, but it had to hurt." David rubbed his finger along his jaw.

A chuckle escaped Sam's lips. "Truth be told, I've hardly had time to think on it much. Tabitha pitchforked me into looking out for Eldora and the kids, and it seems to have been one crisis after another. There're issues with all of the kids that make them less than ideal for adopting, and all of them came to the fore on the trip."

"What issues?"

"The little boy has heart trouble, which reminds me, we need to get to a drugstore first thing in the morning for more medicine. The little girl—David, she wears a scarf over her mouth all the time because she's got a harelip. It's bad enough that you can't help but be startled by it, but I spoke with a doctor in Kansas who said it was operable. The thing is nobody will adopt kids with problems like that. That's why the director in St. Louis was shipping them out. Seems he was looking for a quick way to get rid of all of them."

"What about the older boy?" Karen rubbed her stomach with her fingertips, a light in her eyes that bespoke maternal feelings.

"Phin. He has a tendency to swipe things that don't belong to him. He's good at it, but not as good as he thinks he is. He gets caught often."

"And Eldora?" A smile played at the corners of Karen's mouth. "She seems nice, and a bit awestruck, if you don't mind my saying so. She never took her eyes off you. Is there something between you two?"

Sam pondered her words. Was it true? Did Eldora watch him? Would he mind if there was something between them? The warmth around his heart mocked him. Though he could easily fall for someone like Eldora, he wasn't minded to play the fool again. And Karen's matchmaking gleam chafed. If he was to court another woman, he wanted to do it himself, not be pushed into it like he'd been shoved around by Yvette and Hortense. Better to disabuse Karen's mind. "There's nothing between us. Yvette cured me of that nonsense by trying to marry me for my money. If I marry someone, it will have to be a girl who is as rich as an empress. Then I'll be sure of her motives. I have no plans to be duped like that again."

A gasp caught his attention, and he looked up from his hands and right into Eldora's big, brown eyes.

&

It wasn't supposed to hurt this badly. Especially since she'd warned herself not to fall for him, not to cherish any hopes. She assumed her "institution mask" and stepped into the room, determined that he would never know of her foolishness.

"Have the children finished their meal already?" Karen Mackenzie levered herself out of her chair. At Eldora's nod, she approached and took Eldora's arm. "I'll show you upstairs. I can imagine you're tired out after all your travels and troubles. Sam has been sharing with us some of your adventures."

"It's been a long trip." The tiredness wasn't just of the body but of her spirit, which threatened to collapse altogether under the weight of responsibility and disillusionment. She kept her voice neutral and didn't look in

Sam's direction. It mortified her to think that in only a few minutes Sam's sister-in-law had tumbled to Eldora's affection for him. Did Sam know? Was his comment to his family his way of warning Eldora off?

They gathered the children, and Karen showed them upstairs. "You and Celeste can share this room, and the boys can have the room across the hall. Sam will have to bed down on the sofa in the office."

Eldora winced. "I don't want to put him out of a bed. Perhaps Celeste can have the sofa in the office, and I could bed down on the floor?"

"Nonsense. Sam wouldn't hear of it, and neither will I. Believe me, Sam's slept rougher than this." Karen set her lamp on the table beside the door. "The washroom is across the hall next to the boys' room. Why don't we run the kids through there first; then you can have a nice, hot bath."

Phin made short work of his washing up, and Tick followed suit. While Celeste had her turn, Eldora gave Tick his last dose of medicine. Where would she get more for him? If she'd heard correctly, the Mackenzies were all leaving in the morning for the family home in the mountains. Where did that leave her and her children? She'd have to find someplace for them first thing tomorrow.

Tick swallowed down the last drop and swiped his hand across his lips. Even in a few short days, the difference in the little fellow was remarkable. Pink tinged his cheeks, and he didn't stop to rest nearly as often. His eyes sparkled, bright as a bluebird's. He still needed to gain some weight and muscle, but he was making progress. How quickly would that reverse now that they were out of medicine?

"Scamper into bed now, before you catch a chill."

Lying side by side, freshly scrubbed and in warm nightshirts, Phin and Tick snuggled down against real feather pillows for the first time in their lives. "This sure is nice, ain't it?" Tick lifted his chin for Eldora to tuck another blanket in. "What're we going to do in the morning?"

Phin's dark eyes echoed the question, and having had more experience of the trials of life than Tick, those same eyes were clouded with doubts and worry.

Eldora swallowed. "Let me listen to your prayers, and don't worry about tomorrow. The Lord's been taking care of us so far. I don't imagine He'll quit now. Something will turn up." She hoped she sounded surer than she felt. Then guilt pounced on her. Who was she to doubt the Lord's provision?

Tick folded his hands under his chin and closed his eyes. "Dear Lord, thanks for bringing us to such a fine place and for the food we got to eat and for this nice soft bed. Bless Sam and his family for being so nice to us. Watch over us while we sleep, and when we wake up, too. Amen."

Eldora opened her eyes and looked at Phin without raising her chin.

He scowled back and made a big show of dragging his arms from beneath the covers and lacing his fingers. "What Tick said, I guess. Amen."

She shook her head, her lips pressed together, and then rose and tucked the covers around them once more. "Good night, boys. I'll see you in the morning."

Karen met her in the hall with an armload of fluffy towels and her valise. "I'll just set these in the washroom, and then I want to show you something." Her eyes sparkled. She took Eldora's arm and led her to the bedroom door. Karen put her finger to her lip and peeked around the doorframe.

Eldora peeked too, mystified.

Celeste lay in the high bed, surrounded by a mound of pillows, and in a chair beside her sat David Mackenzie, a book open on his lap, his fingers inching across the pages. "'The princess pricked her finger on the spindle, and she dropped into a deep, deep sleep.'"

Eldora swallowed the lump in her throat. The blind man reading a fairy tale to the little girl was reason enough to choke up, but the tears burning Eldora's eyes were because Celeste's face was bare. The scarf lay folded neatly on the bedside table, and a look of such contentment and joy rested on the child's face as to minimize the shock of her upper lip.

Withdrawing as quietly as she could, Eldora groped for her handkerchief. Karen dabbed at her eyes as well. "Isn't it amazing? Sam said she never takes that scarf off."

"And she never warms up to strangers, but both Buckford and now David have somehow put her at ease. It's uncanny. She didn't unbend for Sam, no matter what he tried, the entire train trip, but here she is completely comfortable with David in only a few minutes."

"It must be because of his blindness. Maybe she feels that because he can't see her face, she's safe to let him get to know her."

Eldora pondered this. "I think you're right. She tries so hard not to be seen, it must be a relief for her to be with David. Maybe she feels he can see the real her instead of being put off by her appearance."

Karen sniffed and dabbed her eyes again. "It's so wonderful to see David like this. One thing he worried about when we first married was what kind of father he would make. Not that he's not thrilled and excited about this baby." She caressed her stomach. "But he's been a little apprehensive. Such a positive response from Celeste will give him confidence." She laughed. "Here I am blathering on, and you must be ready to drop. Have a good soak in the tub and relax a little."

Parting from Karen at the washroom door, Eldora closed herself in the small room and leaned against the door with her eyes closed. Steam rose from the large bathtub, and the smell of roses filled the air. A bottle of bath salts sat on a shelf behind the tub, pink blossoms painted on the label. Bath salts, for an orphan girl?

Bemused, Eldora tied up her hair and slipped into the steaming water of the tub. Immediately, the hot water soothed her tired muscles and leeched some of the tension from her shoulders. A sigh eased from her throat and rippled the water. Never in her whole life had she felt such luxury. Baths at the orphanage were sketchy affairs with tepid water and not much time to wash properly. This was positively decadent—hot scented water up to her chin, room enough to stretch out in the claw-footed tub, a pile of towels waiting.

"Lord, I echo Tick's prayer." She kept her voice to a whisper. "Thank You for keeping watch over us thus far. I admit I don't know what will happen tomorrow, but thank You for a warm place for the children to sleep tonight." A cold stone of heaviness sat just over her heart. "Thank You, too, for opening my eyes to my folly where Sam is concerned. He's made it clear he wants to marry a rich woman and that he would never be interested in someone like me. I knew this with my head, but my heart wanted things to be different. Help me remember to seek Your will and to be content with You. Guard me against the danger of seeking love and approval in the wrong places. Light up the path where I'm supposed to go, and keep me off the paths You know aren't good for me."

Though the prayer was painful, she forced herself to pray it. If only Sam's heart wasn't the wrong place to seek love and approval. She loved everything about him—his smile, his laugh, his protectiveness. The way he treated the children, the way he stood up for them. The memory of his comforting arms around her was something she would treasure always. Realizing she was in danger of turning right back where she had been, she bolted up, sloshing water over the rim of the tub.

Eventually slipping into bed beside the slumbering Celeste, Eldora rolled onto her side and punched up the strangely soft pillows. *Wake up early, girl. You need to find somewhere for you and the kids first thing in the morning.*

Chapter 12

So of course she slept late. Weak winter sunlight streamed through the window when her heavy eyelids opened. For a moment she didn't know where she was, and then the events of the previous day flooded in. A glance at the clock over the fireplace told her it was after eight. She couldn't remember ever staying in bed so long.

Flipping back the covers, she cringed when cold air hit her. Celeste's side of the bed was empty, and her nightgown lay folded on the chair beside the bed, as she had been taught since birth at the orphanage. Eldora hurried, buttoning buttons, pinning up her hair, making the bed. How could she have been so lax? The Mackenzies would be preparing to leave town this morning, and here she was, lazing away. Her stomach rumbled, reminding her of how she'd picked at her food last night.

She poked her head into the boys' room and found it tidy and empty of children. From the first floor, happy voices reached her. Almost tripping in her haste, she made it across the foyer and stopped in the doorway to the sitting room.

Celeste sat on the floor in front of the wooden nativity figurines. She lifted a donkey and put it in David's hand where he sat in the chair beside her. She followed this action by climbing into his lap and whispering in his ear, lowering the scarf just a bit and then tucking it back up over her nose. David smiled and nodded at whatever she said, and squeezed her before letting her slip back to the floor.

As if this weren't shock enough, Sam and Phin knelt across from each other on the floor, a string circle between them. Marbles littered the carpet, and Phin shot another into the circle.

Tick jumped out of his chair when he spied her, clutching a book of photographs. "She's awake! Eldora, lookit this!" He hefted the book for her to see. "Pictures of Sam and David and Karen and even Buckford."

"Good morning, Eldora. You look well-rested." Sam sprang to his feet and smiled down at her. "We decided to let you have your sleep out rather than wake you."

Heat tinged her cheeks, and she advanced into the room. "I'm sorry. I meant to rise early. We've imposed on you long enough. Children, please go fetch your things so we can go."

Phin rose slowly and shoved his hands in his pockets, and Celeste's eyes filled with tears, another shock. Celeste never cried. The little girl blinked hard and set the donkey back on the table as if it were made of spun sugar. Both moved to obey her, but Tick held his ground. He clutched the book like a shield and shook his head. "I don't want to go. I want to stay with Sam."

So did she.

Just the sight of Sam, so strong and kind, affected her. She swallowed. "Tick, please. We've imposed long enough. We have to go now."

The little boy dropped the book and belted across the carpet to throw himself against Sam's legs. His sobs rent Eldora's heart, but what could she do? Phin's dark glare accused her, and Celeste edged closer to the door with shuffling feet and bowed head.

Sam bent and lifted Tick into his embrace, and Tick threw his wiry arms around Sam's neck. "Please, Sam, can't we stay with you? Just for a little bit longer?"

"Well now, sport, you've stolen a march on me. I was going to tell you later, but David and Karen and I sat up late last night talking it over. Christmas is only a few days away, and we thought it would be nice if you spent the holiday with us. How's that sound?"

The room reeled, and Eldora clutched the doorframe. Sunbeams shone through Tick's tears, and he hugged Sam so tight his little body shook. Celeste's feet flew, and she threw herself into David's arms with a squeal. David recovered his surprise and patted her back. Even Phin couldn't conceal a grin, toeing the edge of the carpet and ducking his head.

How could she dash their hopes? Each child looked to her for approval, and even more powerful, Sam's gaze pled with her.

He eased Tick down with a pat on the head and approached her. "Let's go out in the hall and talk." He took her elbow and directed her into the foyer.

Wild thoughts, hopes, and guilt skittered around her head until she didn't know which way to hop. Sam had kept her off balance since the moment she'd met him. On the one hand he didn't want someone taking advantage of him, and on the other he repeatedly proved his generosity. It was as if he couldn't help himself. His protective nature *would* come to the fore.

"I know we should've talked to you first, but it seems the perfect solution. You don't have anywhere else to go, and we've got plenty of room at the house in Martin City. My parents would love to have you all. Christmas is always better with children in the house. And think what it would mean to the kids. A real Christmas, not an orphanage one."

"That's very kind of you, but we don't want to impose. We've taken so much of your time and money already. I've no way of paying you back for your generosity. We've been burden enough." Determined, she put force into her words. "We cannot go to Martin City with you. How do you think we would feel, crashing in on a family holiday celebration? And what would your parents say? You think they would love to have us? You can't know that. Bad enough that your aunt foisted us upon you for the trip."

He frowned and tilted his head. "Nobody foisted you on me. And I do know what my parents would say. My mother would have my hide skinned and stretched on the barn door if I didn't bring you and the kids home with me. David and Karen are so excited about the idea. You'd do us out of this pleasure just for your pride?" Furrows formed on his brow. "Anyway, where else would you go?"

She tugged at her bottom lip. With all her heart she wanted to throw herself into his arms and beg him not to let her go away from him, but she wouldn't. She couldn't. She wouldn't take advantage of him like Yvette had. "I had thought to go back to the orphanage and try to get Finlo Korbin to see reason. If I couldn't persuade him to change his mind, then I thought to try some of the local churches. Then I was going to look for a job."

"A job? Just days before Christmas? Taking care of the kids is job enough. Please, they've got their hearts set on it now." He took her hand and rubbed the back of it with his thumb, sending a quiver through her. Ducking his head, he locked his blue eyes onto hers, entreating her with an engaging, boyish smile. "I do, too."

With a sigh, the resistance fled. "All right, but only over Christmas. Then I have to find some work and a place for the children."

Sam straightened and swung her hand. "Great. We'll sort everything out after Christmas. For now, just relax and enjoy yourself. I have a feeling you haven't had much enjoyment in your life. But you'll see. Problems just melt around my mother."

Corralling the children when Sam broke the good news to them proved nearly impossible. Phin relaxed his guard enough to whistle a Christmas carol while carrying bags. Buckford was dispatched to the closest pharmacy for Tick's medicine, and the housekeeper plied everyone with hot cider and holiday sweets.

Celeste wouldn't be parted from David and insisted on riding with him and Karen to the station in one sleigh while Eldora, Sam, and the boys piled into another. Harness bells crashed and jangled, and Eldora felt as if she were sitting in the midst of a tornado. Buildings flashed by, and in an incredibly short period of time, they were back on the train ensconced once more in the private luxury of the Mackenzie railcar.

The children made themselves at home. Eldora kept watch, wondering what Karen and David would say to their lack of inhibitions. Tick knelt on the sofa and watched out the window, commenting on everyone and everything. Phin dropped into a chair and stretched his feet out, lacing his fingers across his middle and grinning like a cat. Celeste stood beside David's chair.

"Karen, you should get some rest." Sam emerged from helping Buckford stow baggage in the front stateroom. "You've been running around since dawn, and we'll be up late. The train won't pull into Martin City until after ten tonight."

"Karen?" David sat upright, his dark brows bunching. "Are you all right?"

Karen patted David on the shoulder. "I'm quite fine, though a nap sounds lovely. I wonder if I'll be able to sleep though. I don't remember the last time I was so excited for Christmas to come."

Eldora eased Tick's boots off the upholstery, trying to ignore a pang of guilt. Karen had been on her feet all morning, packing, seeing to last-minute details, all added to because of Eldora and the children. "I'll try to keep the children quiet."

"Don't worry about that. The noise of the train covers most everything else, and even if it doesn't, there's nothing better than happy children's voices." Karen disappeared into the front stateroom.

Turning to the children, Eldora held up a warning finger to her lips. "Regardless of Mrs. Mackenzie's kind words, you will be quiet."

Sam's eyebrow quirked. "Why so chippy? Didn't you sleep well last night?"

She folded her arms. "It won't do for them to forget that they're here on sufferance. They've grown entirely too wild and free on this trip, and though I'd love to see them lose some of their restraint, it doesn't bode well for them in the future. The minute they return to institutional life, they'll be slapped back into place."

His sigh told her he was being patient again. If anything could grate on her nerves like pumice, it was someone being obviously patient and patronizing with her. "You sure are a gloomy Gus this morning." He looked at Phin and Tick. "How's about we let her rest on the sofa, and I'll tell you about Christmas in the Mackenzie house?"

Tick nodded so hard, Eldora thought his head might come off. His slight frame bounced on the seat, barely denting the horsehair upholstery. Phin shrugged, as if he didn't care, but his eyes brightened, and he slid over to make room for Eldora. Celeste perched on the arm of David's chair.

"Now, Dave might have to help me remember some things, but I can tell you, Christmas is quite an event at our house. Our pa is like a big kid. He loves buying presents for people, and for a couple weeks before the holiday he sneaks around wearing a cat-who-got-the-cream grin."

Tick's eyes grew round, and he tucked his hands between his knees and hunched his shoulders.

Eldora bit her lip. Had she done the right thing, allowing the children to have Christmas with the Mackenzies? Not that she'd had a lot of choices. An event like this in their young lives could go one of two ways. Either they would live on the experience and it would help them get through the hard times, or it would start up a hankering in them for the finer things and they would grow bitter at being deprived of them.

She watched Phin, who seemed to feel the injustice of inequality the most and tried to even things up by stealing from those who had more than he did—which was just about everybody. Though he hadn't stolen anything since trying to get medicine for Tick. Or at least he hadn't gotten caught.

"On Christmas Eve, we take the big sleigh with the harnesses all strung with bells, and we drive to the church. There will be candles in every window, and the snow will be deep and make everything seem quiet. If it's a clear night, you'll imagine you can almost reach up and pluck a star out of the sky to keep in your pocket." He made a picking motion over his head. "We'll sing carols and hear about the reason for Christmas, and we'll all walk outside hushed and reverent."

"When we were kids, we'd hurry to bed as soon as we got home, so the night would go faster and Christmas day would get here sooner." A smile played across David's lips, and for the first time Eldora saw a resemblance between the brothers.

"And I'd lie awake for hours, too excited to sleep," Sam said. "Then it would be morning, and we'd race downstairs to see what was in our stockings. Whew, the storm's really blowing now." He glanced out the window.

Snow had begun to fall almost the minute the train had pulled out of Denver, and as they rose in elevation, the storm had worsened. Heavy, fat flakes of wet snow had given way to sand-fine particles of ice that scoured the windowpanes and whipped around in the wind.

In the warmth of the railcar, it was easy to push aside the storm and imagine what life must've been like in the Mackenzie household at Christmas. A lump formed in Eldora's throat as she remembered Christmas with her parents in the company-owned house they had shared. . . before her mother had gotten sick and before her father had been killed in the accident at the mine.

"Tell them about the food." David leaned back in his chair, his arm around Celeste to steady her.

"Oh, the food." Sam grinned and patted his stomach. "The house smells so good. There's roast goose and all the trimmings, and pies and cake and candy. Eggnog and hot cocoa. Christmas breakfast is the lightest, fluffiest pancakes you ever saw, drowning in maple syrup and melted butter. And hickory-roasted bacon and ham all the way from Virginia. And just wait until you taste Mother's gingerbread, slathered in whipped cream, warm and spicy. You kids are going to have a wonderful time." He breathed deeply, closing his eyes.

Eldora almost laughed to see all three children and even David doing the same. She had to admit, her mouth watered at the thought of all that wonderful food.

Phin recovered first. "After breakfast what will we do?"

"Well, we'll dig out some of the games David and I used to play when we were kids, and after our dinner has settled, I imagine we'll go tobogganing. When we get back, all cold and wet and tired, Mother will greet us with hot chocolate, and then we'll start receiving guests. Lots of visiting on Christmas evening. After supper, which is leftover bits from dinner, we'll gather around the piano in the parlor and sing Christmas carols. And best of all, Father will read us the Christmas story."

A father reading the Christmas story. Sam's eyes collided with hers, and she bolted for the passageway before she embarrassed herself fully.

❧

For two hours, Sam debated about whether to follow Eldora or give her privacy. He sent Phin back to check on her, but when the boy returned, he said Eldora had fallen asleep on one of the settees in the dining salon. She must be as all in as Karen, who slumbered away in the front sleeping compartment.

The snow continued to blow, and the wheels slipped on the icy rails. Sam whispered into David's ear that the storm seemed to be picking up strength. "Hope they topped up the sand domes. They'll need to sand the tracks, the way it's coming down out there."

David nodded, his face grim. "Surely they'll have the snowplows out on the line as well. The real danger is an avalanche, but they wouldn't have sent us out from Denver if the line were blocked."

Sam scowled out the window while Phin and Tick set up for another game of checkers. "Unless a snow slip happened after we pulled out. I can feel the train plowing through drifts on the track already. If this snow keeps up, we'll be late getting in."

Buckford and a porter entered, each carrying a lunch tray. Fat flakes dotted their shoulders, and icy wind blew in with them.

Sam tossed his paper aside and rose. "I'll get the girls."

"If Karen's still sleeping, don't wake her. She can eat later. I'd rather she got some rest before we get home. You know how it is over the holidays, one event after another." David set down the domino he held and smiled at Celeste. "We'll finish our game after lunch."

Sam found Eldora at the rear of the car, staring out the glass pane in the back door at the caboose. Not much of a view, mostly clouds of snow. She had one arm crossed at her waist, with the other elbow perched on it, her hand across her mouth.

He stopped in the doorway. "Lunch is here. Late, I know, but this way we won't be starving for dinner before we reach home."

She nodded but didn't move.

"Is something wrong?"

"No." The word sounded squeezed tight, like she was barely holding on to control. Just like a female. Something was obviously wrong, and he was supposed to figure it out on his own.

"The kids are pretty excited. Celeste and David are playing dominoes, and Phin and Tick are wrangling over checkers." He shoved his hands into his pockets and braced his shoulder against the passageway wall. Cold air flowed off the bank of windows on his right. Gusts rocked the train, and he ducked to look out under one of the window blinds. "Looks like our white Christmas is guaranteed, not that there was any doubt."

"White and cold."

"But warm and cozy in the house. Mother will love having the kids for Christmas, and Father will be over the moon. David wired ahead and let them know you would be coming with us." He stepped into the room. "You didn't say what upset you back there. Are you still mad about having to come with us?"

She shook her head. "I'm not mad. I just hope I'm doing the right thing. You've filled the children's heads with such grand ideas. Even a simple celebration would've been more than they could've imagined, but the holiday you describe. . ." She turned from the door and hugged her middle. "Reality is going to come crashing in pretty hard in the New Year."

"Maybe, but does that mean they should never have any fun, never have any good times, just because the future might not be so rosy? And who's to say the future might not be brighter than you think?"

"Rosy futures don't happen to orphans very often, especially not these three. This train trip marks the end of your destination. You're coming home, but we're just marking time. You've convinced me to accept your hospitality for the holiday, but after Christmas I still have to find somewhere for these children and myself. The best I can figure is maybe I can get a job as a laundress somewhere—I have plenty of experience as a laundress—and maybe I can find a cheap place to rent—"

The lines on her forehead and the way she twisted her fingers together tore at him, reminding him again of how blessed he had been. "Don't worry about that now. I told you, things will work out." He took her hands and drew her to the cushioned bench along the wall. "What else is bothering you? Maybe talking about it would help."

She lifted her chin in an all-too-familiar gesture that told him he was about to be rebuffed. Again. Then, to his surprise, her eyes glistened, and she ducked her head. Candlelight raced along the coil of her hair, and he wanted to gather her into his arms, to promise her that nothing and no one would ever hurt her. The strength of his protective feelings caught him so off guard he almost missed what she had to say.

"It was when you said your father would be reading the Christmas story." She whispered, barely audible above the clack of the train and the howl of the wind. "My father used to do that on Christmas Day. It's one of my most vivid memories of him."

She turned those big, brown eyes on him, and his heart raced until he thought he might need a dose of Tick's medicine. "How old were you when you lost him?"

"Ten. I was devastated. I'd already lost my mother to sickness the previous year." She shook her head and tucked a loose hair behind her ear. "We lived in Pennsylvania."

"Pennsylvania? How'd you wind up in St. Louis?" He rubbed his thumbs across the backs of her chilly hands, grateful that she hadn't withdrawn from him.

"Overcrowded orphanages are a fact of life. When there was no more room in the Pittsburgh orphanage, they put us on a westbound train. At every stop, they'd get us off, line us up, and people would look us over for who they would want to adopt." Her delicate throat lurched, and she shrugged. "Nobody wanted me. At ten I was too big to be someone's baby, but I was too small to be of much use around the house. Like Tick, I was skinny and small for my age, and. . .ugly."

"Ugly?" He jerked. "Who told you that?"

"The matron at the first orphanage I was sent to. She said I was all eyes and knees and sallow skin, and who would want a child so morose and difficult anyway? Hair that can't decide whether to be yellow or brown, and dirt-brown eyes don't exactly shout 'beautiful' to anyone." She freed one of her hands from his, touched her hair, and shrugged, but the hurt of those words lingered in her eyes. "When we got to St. Louis, I was the only one who hadn't been adopted, so I was dumped in the orphanage there. The matron didn't think I'd amount to much either, and she was right." Red tinged her cheeks, and she ducked her head. "I can't seem to hold a job, and

I can't seem to find a home for these three kids, not even an orphanage."

Her casual acceptance of the matron's summing up of her looks and worth disturbed him. "I don't know what you looked like at ten, newly bereaved and being toted across country, but I can assure you, you're no ugly duckling." Sam tugged on her hand to get her to look at him. Again her magnificent eyes sent a jolt through him. "You're beautiful."

She shook her head. "That's silly. I saw Yvette Adelman at the train station. *She's* beautiful. Porcelain skin, china-blue eyes, and that magnificent auburn hair. She turns heads everywhere she goes. She turned yours. Karen told me about it this morning while we were packing."

His collar tightened, and when she would've withdrawn her hand, he held on. "That was momentary foolishness. I won't gainsay that Yvette is nice to look at, but that's all. She's calculating, scheming, and has an eye to the main chance. She only wants what she can get out of a man, and she's selfish to the core. I feel sorry for her. I'm sorry she got herself into the family way, but I'm not going to marry her just to salvage her reputation."

Eldora's jaw dropped. "You utter cad!" She reared back, yanking her hand away. "What kind of man—"

"Ellie, stop it!" Sam lunged for her and clamped his hand over her mouth. She writhed in his embrace. "No, stop it. You're going to hear me out." Her movements stilled, but her eyes shot sparks. He eased his hand away from her lips, wary that she might burst into scalding speech before he could explain himself. Her nostrils flared with her indignant breathing and she quivered. Momentarily distracted by her nearness, by her pink lips and flushed face, he had to force himself to concentrate.

"I told you not to call me Ellie."

"So you did, and I apologize, but you are going to listen to me. You've had the wrong idea about Yvette from the start." Though he didn't want to, he let his arms fall away from her. "No man likes to speak ill of a woman, but you have to know the truth. Yvette *is* expecting a child, but it isn't mine. I know I can offer you no proof but my word, but I assure you it is *impossible* that the baby could be mine." He stared into her eyes, willing her to understand his meaning and to believe him.

She drew a deep breath and nodded, but doubt lingered, forcing him to go on and admit the entire humiliation of his error in judgment.

"I didn't even know about the baby until Yvette came to the station. From the very beginning she set out to try to trap me into marrying her because I'm wealthy. Her mother brought her up to marry a rich man, and when Yvette found herself with child by a poor man, they locked onto me as the scapegoat, or should I say scape-sheep. I overheard her and her mother summing me up as a dumb sheep, led to the slaughter." He spread his hands. "I admit I was a gullible fool, taken in by her good looks and flattery, but even before I knew what a schemer she was, the engagement was proving to be more pyrite than gold."

"I'm sorry. That's a terrible thing for you to overhear."

"I'm not sorry. I'm grateful. Better a broken engagement than a broken marriage. I only regret being such a mug and getting hornswoggled by their trap. You and Yvette couldn't be more different. She took everything I gave her and expected more—trinkets, flowers, candy. You, on the other hand, won't take so much as a new pair of shoes without fighting me every step of the way." He tilted his head and smiled ruefully.

Eldora rose and went to stand by the windows. By now the snow was so thick and the light so poor it was impossible to make out anything more than a few feet from the train. "You don't know what it's like, always living on sufferance, forced to take charity, knowing that eventually those who are doing their good works toward you are going to abandon you for something else. We learn not to count on others, to rely on ourselves, because in the end that's all we have."

"What about your faith?"

A smile touched the corner of her lips. "Faith's important. Who do you think brings us through when people fail us as they always do? I've been holding on to my faith with both hands this whole trip. I don't know when I've prayed harder."

"You do realize that God uses people to fulfill His purposes, right? If you're praying for help, that help is most likely going to come through someone God brings into your life."

She squirmed and flung her hand out. "I know. I don't—"

Her words were cut off as the train lurched. A shudder rippled through the car, and a horrible grinding noise came from the undercarriage. Sparks illuminated the air beneath the window.

Eldora grabbed a chair, but it gave way under her hand, sending her tumbling into Sam's arms. He held her tight as the coach lurched and rocked, bracing his feet against the floor and his back against the sofa.

Metal screeched and a sound like gravel in a sluice blanketed them. Glass broke and chairs tumbled, and the lamp went out.

Chapter 13

Eldora was conscious of cold air flowing over her and the rise and fall of Sam's chest under her ear. She fought to unscramble her brain and her limbs.

"What happened?" Hunks of snow and ice bit her skin, and when she tried to roll off Sam, shards of glass tinkled.

He grabbed her. "Be still. I think the window broke. I don't want you getting cut." Wood clacked as he shoved aside a chair and stood, bringing her with him.

Glass trickled off her hair and shoulders, and her hip throbbed where she'd knocked it against something. "We've stopped. Is the car tilting?"

"I think we derailed. Are you hurt?" A match scritched and flared, bringing his face into golden-yellow sight. "We're lucky that lamp went out instead of exploding." Before the match burned too low, he climbed to the opposite side of the car and took down the kerosene lamp. The globe had come off and broken, but the bowl and wick seemed intact. He touched the match to the cotton wick and jerked his hand away as the match burned out. "Ouch." Holding the lamp high, he surveyed the room.

"We've got to get to the children." As she turned to head toward the front of the car, the sound of movement reached her.

"Karen? Sam? Eldora?" David's voice came down the passageway. "Karen? Are you all right?"

"Dave, we're back here. Stay put until I can get to you." Sam took Eldora's hand and helped her along the leaning hall.

"Check on Karen first. The kids and I are fine, just shaken up a little."

Relief coursed through Eldora as she followed Sam. They reached the door to the stateroom where Karen had been napping, but it was wedged shut.

"Karen? Are you all right?" Sam pounded on the door and then handed Eldora the lamp.

"I think so. What happened?" The wooden panel muffled her voice. "I can't get the door open."

"Get back. I'm going to see if I can force it." Sam braced his back against the window frame and kicked his boot upward, crashing it into the brass hasp. The wood around the hasp cracked and splintered. Once more he kicked, and the door broke free of the latch. Using his shoulder, he shoved the pocket door to the side and reached in for Karen.

Her hair tumbled down her neck, and her eyes shone in the lamplight. "Is David all right? And the children?"

They assembled in the front sitting room, taking stock. Eldora's heart gave a pang at the tender embrace shared by David and Karen as they reassured each other that no harm had been done. What must it be like to be cared for that much?

More glass had broken in the front salon, and snow and cold rushed in. Sam shook out Celeste's hood and cloak and handed them to her. "Everybody put on your coats and hats. David, keep everyone here while I go forward and assess the damage. Where's Buckford?"

Phin shook Tick's coat free of glass and helped the little boy into it. "He said there was one more tray to bring from the dining car."

Sam headed for the door. "I'll find him and see how bad the damage is. If it's just our car and the caboose, we'll probably uncouple them and go on."

Eldora tugged on her mittens, trying not to give in to the fear pounding on her chest. If it wasn't just the private car and caboose, what then? They were high in a mountain pass with the snow piling up and pouring in.

She couldn't just sit here and do nothing. "We should marshal our resources here. There might be other people who were hurt. Phin, find as many lamps as you can that didn't get broken and bring them back here. Wedge this table so it is fairly level. Celeste, gather blankets from the beds and be sure to shake them out well in case any glass got on them. Tick, stack these bags up." She pointed to the jumble of suitcases and valises that had tumbled from the overhead rack.

Karen handed David his muffler and slipped her arms into her coat sleeves. "I'll get the medicine kit from the washroom. Eldora, where are you going?"

"I'm going forward to see how bad things are. When I find Buckford, I'll send him to you."

The thin afternoon light had faded toward dusk, but when she emerged from the private car, she could still see the devastation before her. The private car and caboose had uncoupled and lay several yards back from the rest of the train. Through the snow, she made out the back of the passenger car, but it leaned off-kilter, half hanging over the downhill slope to her left. The baggage car appeared to have burst, and parcels and bags littered the mountainside below the train. Where the engine and tender should have been, a mass of snow, rocks, shattered trees, and debris covered the tracks. Sam waded knee deep in the drifts, battling to get to the passenger car. Dark forms emerged through the tilted door, reassuring her that others had survived beyond themselves.

Eldora blinked, barely able to take in the scene. The wind buffeted her, and she ducked her head into it. The cold sucked her breath from her lungs and tingled against her cheeks. She stuck her head back into the private car. "There's been an avalanche. The engine is buried, and the passenger car is off the tracks. I'm going to help Sam. Phin, you stay here." She held up her hand when the boy started toward her. "David and Karen will need you here."

Floundering in the snow, she fought her way up the incline toward where Sam now handed passengers down to those waiting to receive them. Gasping, she joined the growing group at the rear of the car. "How many passengers are there?" She tried to wipe the snow from her face but only smeared it with her coated mittens.

"Eldora, what are you doing out here? Go back!" Sam scowled at her and tugged his hat on tighter.

"I want to help. Is anyone seriously hurt?"

"It doesn't seem so, though we won't know until we do a head count and assess things. Now stay back. We've got to get them out of this car in case it decides to slide farther down the slope. Help get folks to our car. It's tilted, but it's more secure than this one."

A woman emerged from the back door, and strong hands lowered her to the tracks. Eldora took her arm. "Are you injured? Can you walk?"

White-faced and round-eyed, the woman could only shake her head. "Take my arm." Eldora steadied the woman.

"I'll help you." Eldora looked up into the dear face of Buckford. He had a gash on his temple and a split lip, but he smiled. "It's nothing serious. What about David and Karen and the children?"

"Rattled, but no injuries, thankfully. The private car is the only one that appears to still be intact and reasonably unharmed. A miracle."

"Has anyone seen the conductor?" Eldora let Buckford take the lead, stamping along the path she and Sam had already tread. The woman they helped seemed as frozen as the landscape. When they reached the private car, Buckford directed Eldora to precede him and then handed the woman up the steps.

"I suggest tacking some blankets over those windows and checking the coal stove. Make people as comfortable as you can. Rip up the sheets for bandages if need be." He turned to go.

"Wait! I'm coming with you."

"No, miss. You'll be of more use here."

She knew he spoke the truth, but everything in her wanted to be with Sam.

By the time the passenger car was cleared, they had seventeen additional passengers crowded into the private car. Every chair, sofa, and bed was occupied. Several cuts, many bruises, and one broken arm comprised the injuries. Still missing were the engineer, the brakeman, the fireman, and the mail clerk from the baggage car, all presumed dead.

Sam and the conductor were the last to enter the Mackenzie car, and one look at his face told Eldora that things were even worse than she'd feared.

Sam wanted to slam his fist into the florid man's face, but he refrained, clenching his jaw. "You don't get it, do you?" How many times did he have to spell it out before these people would see reason? "There's been an ava- lanche—albeit a minor one. We can't clear the track ourselves. It's going to take a snowplow from the other direction and an army of shovelers. Every car in this train has derailed to some extent. We'll need a crane to lift them upright again. This train isn't going anywhere under its own power, but it might go right down this mountainside if the rest of that snow shelf up there lets go." He pointed to the up-mountain side of the car.

"I say we wait right here until they can dig us out." The spokesperson— self-elected—from the passenger car crossed his arms and puffed out his chest. His enormous red side-whiskers jutted from his paunchy cheeks like porcupine quills.

"Do you see that snow out there?" Sam waved toward one of the unbro- ken windows. "At the rate it's falling, we'll be lucky if we don't get buried alive. And the chance of another avalanche grows by the hour."

Crowded into the car like a bunch of canned oysters, shaken and terri- fied by the crash and the implications, it hadn't taken long—less than an hour—before people began to crack under the strain. Arguments, tears, and now a standoff. The conductor was useless—dazed and silent—and no other train employee appeared to have survived the initial wreck.

Florid-face wasn't done yet. "We've got shelter and some food here and a fire. There are injuries and women and children. We're miles from the nearest stop. We're past due already. Help is probably already on its way."

Sam looked from face to face. Karen and the children huddled close to the stove. Eldora stood in the passageway door, her hand bracing herself against the tilt of the car. "What do you suggest, Sam?"

"The risk of another avalanche aside, there's the issue of heat. We have one hod of coal left for this little stove. The coal tender for the engine is buried in snow and ice. There's not much food aboard, and with more than twenty people it won't last us more than a meal or two, even if we go sparingly. I think we have to try to make it out on foot."

The large man snorted, and his hands flew out in an exasperated arc. "On foot? Have you lost your mind? Do you even know exactly where we are?"

"We're in Shadow Peak Pass. As the crow flies, we're less than ten miles from Martin City."

"Ten miles might as well be a hundred. We'll freeze to death or get lost in this blizzard."

Several nods and frowns. Those who stood more than a few feet from the stove blew out puffs of frosty air, and the wind howled, flapping the meager blankets tacked over the shattered windows. The temperature continued to plummet.

"We can't leave in the teeth of the storm, I agree. But with the lack of provisions and the imminent threat of another avalanche, I strongly feel that we must go first thing in the morning. There are more men than women, and we can help the weaker ones and the children. In the meantime, some of us should go to the passenger car and see if we can find anything to burn in the stove through the night."

David caught Sam's arm and tugged him close to whisper. "There've been a couple of thaws in between these heavy snowfalls the past week or so. That snow pack will be unstable with sheets of ice between the layers of snow. I'm half-surprised they didn't close the line, but I was so eager to get home, especially for the sake of the children, that I put it out of my mind."

Sam took in his brother's bunched brows and tight lips. "You couldn't have known this would happen. Just be ready to move out as soon as we can. It won't be easy, but I know you're up to it."

"I'm not worried for myself." His grip tightened on Sam's coat sleeve. "What about Karen and the children? I'd never forgive myself if something happened to Karen or the baby or those kids."

Sam squeezed his brother's shoulder and edged his way to Eldora's side. Her eyes bespoke her worry and understanding of their peril. In that instant, Sam knew how David felt. If anything happened to the women and children—to Eldora—as a result of his actions, he'd never forgive himself. He took Eldora's hand, wishing neither wore gloves so he could feel the warmth of her palm against his and draw comfort from her touch.

She curled her fingers around his for a moment. "I'm worried about Tick. Look how pale he is."

Sam craned to see the little boy. His eyes stood out in his pinched face. "You think his heart is playing up again?"

"The doctor warned us about stressful situations. I don't know what to do. Should I give him more medicine? Less?"

Would moving him from the train pose a greater peril than a possible avalanche? Would the boy be up to a trek over the mountain? Heaviness settled into the pit of his stomach. "I'm going over to the passenger car. I'll be back soon. See about sorting out what foodstuffs we have, will you?"

She nodded. "Be careful."

"And gather the kids and Karen. Put on as many layers as you can. It's going to be a cold night." He gripped her hands. "And a colder tomorrow."

Chapter 14

I'm asking you to reconsider." Sam tested the ropes on his improvised pack. "You heard the smaller slides during the night. It's only a matter of time before a big one wipes this train right off the tracks and into that ravine." He jerked his thumb toward the windows behind him that faced the chasm.

"You're the one who should reconsider. It's beyond criminal to take children and women—especially a woman so obviously delicate—out in these conditions." Sam's chief antagonist throughout the past night once again reiterated his case.

"Do you think I haven't wrestled with this from every angle? If I didn't think we were sitting in a death trap here, I wouldn't budge so much as a foot until the snowplows came. But we don't know how many snow slides there are between here and the next stop. They might be days getting to us. With the minor slides now blocking us from the rear, we're well and truly boxed in. No food, not much fuel left, and that ledge overhead ready to let loose at any minute? We can't stay here."

"When one of those children or women dies as a result of your foolishness, I'm going to see to it that you're brought up on charges." The red-faced man, Talbot, crossed his arms and scowled.

Sam turned away, lifting the pack. "Take care, and if you do decide to walk out of here, make sure every group has a lantern and some matches. When we reach Martin City, we'll send out a rescue party."

Seven people waited for him, looking to him to lead them to safety. David, Karen, Buckford, Eldora, and the children. Not another single person from the passenger car had decided to join them. He ducked to peer under the window shade. Snow continued to fall, but the wind had died down. Heavy clouds obscured the sunlight, which would be in short supply in winter in any case, surrounded by peaks as they were.

"Buckford, I'm putting you in charge of Karen. Help her all you can."

The older man's face set in determined lines, and he nodded, putting his hand under her elbow.

Sam turned to Karen. "You'll be sure to tell us when you get tired?"

"We'll be fine." Her tight smile and anxious eyes pierced him.

"David, I'm going to give you the pack to carry. It's not heavy."

"I can take it, Sam."

"I know." He slid the straps onto David's shoulders. "Tick's medicine is in there. Phin, you help David. Let him put his hand on your shoulder as you go ahead of him."

He patted Phin on the head, and for once, the boy didn't scowl and shrug away. His face bore the same determined lines as Buckford's, a mature look that said, "You can count on me."

"Eldora, you take Celeste's hand." He slipped a small packet to her and whispered, "Here are some matches and some of Tick's medicine. I gave some to Buckford, too, just in case something happens and we lose the pack. Better not to have all our ore in one cart, you know?"

Eldora took the bundle and shoved it deep into her coat pocket.

He winked at her and chucked her under the chin. "Don't worry. It will turn out all right."

She nodded, her eyes wide in her heart-shaped face. The trust in her expression both gave him courage and increased the burden of responsibility already weighing on him.

He took up the coil of rope he'd prepared the night before and stuck his head and arm through it so it lay crossways on his chest.

"Now, young fellow. I'm thinking those snowdrifts will be higher than your head. You'll do better if I take you up on my back." Sam lifted Tick onto the edge of a chair and turned around. "Besides, we can help keep each other warm this way." He grinned over his shoulder as Tick clambered up, wrapped his arms around Sam's neck, and tucked his hands under Sam's muffler. "Poke your leg through the rope. It will help you stick on." The boy weighed next to nothing, even bundled as he was. *Lord, please don't let his heart play up.*

Talbot barred the door with his large frame. "I'm asking you not to go. Or at least to go alone and send back help."

Sam blew out a breath and held on to his temper. "I'm not forcing anyone to go with me. They want to go. They understand the dangers. Now, let us pass."

They stood toe-to-toe for a moment, but Sam held his ground, and Talbot stepped aside. Trying not to let his relief show, Sam opened the door and took the first blast of frigid air into his lungs. He picked up the lantern from beside the door, hooked it to his belt, and headed down the stairs. When he stepped off the bottom tread, he sank into the snow up to his knees. "Tick, you're going to have to hang on tight. I'm going to need my hands free most of the time."

"I can walk if you need me to." His voice came through the folds of scarf Eldora had wound around his face.

"Naw, better for you to ride for now. Just keep hold." Sam turned and helped first Karen and then David down the stairs. Buckford and Phin followed and took up their charges. "I'll go first, then you, Buckford, with Karen. Phin, you follow next with David behind." Eldora emerged onto the platform with Celeste. "Girls, you come last. If you start to fall behind, holler. We don't want to get separated. I'll try to break the trail for you as best I can. If you feel yourself start to slip, drop down on your backside and ride it out."

He stood for a moment on the edge of the railroad bed and surveyed the best way to get to the valley below. His greatest fear was starting an avalanche that would send them shooting down to be buried in drifts. "We're going to angle down and switch back. Stay in my footsteps as much as you can. We'll have to keep a little room between us, just in case one of us does go down, so we don't take the whole party with us. But don't lag too much. Stay within earshot."

With the lantern clanking against his hip, he picked up the length of wood he'd pried off one of the door jambs of the wrecked passenger car to use as a walking stick. As he took the first few steps, he whispered a prayer. "Lord, help us make it down. Keep the snow on the mountain, and please send help for those who wouldn't come with us before it's too late."

Frosty clouds of breath mingled with swirling snowflakes, muffling sound. His boots sank into the drifts, and he probed for good footing before each step. One question bombarded him. Was he leading them away from danger or straight into it?

❧

The exertion of trying to stay upright and keep hold of Celeste's mittened hand warmed Eldora up to the point where she wanted to take off her coat. Floundering in the deep snow, she tried to watch where she put her feet while at the same time keeping her eyes on David's broad shoulders ahead of her. Occasional rocks jutted through the snow that had to be navigated with care, and several times her feet sank down into a thicket or bramble holding up the snow. The branches grabbed her ankles and held fast, forcing her to stop and untangle herself.

"I wish we were wearing dungarees, Celeste." She panted as she freed her skirt yet again from a hidden shrub. They had been picking their way down the mountain for over an hour. When she paused to look back and up, she could no longer make out the shape of the train through the falling snow.

"How are you making out?" David called back. "Is Celeste all right?"

"She's doing better than I am." Eldora blew out a breath and hurried to catch up. "I seem to find every hole and pocket under the snow to fall into."

"Sam!" David called ahead. "I need a rest."

Eldora suspected David wasn't overly tired yet but that he wanted a rest for the women and children. His face had drawn into severe lines. How he must be suffering, unable to see for himself how his wife was doing. And how much trust he had in Sam, and in Phin, too, to lead him safely down the mountain.

Thirty yards ahead, Sam halted and turned to look back up at them. Buckford and Karen reached him, and Karen sagged to the snow with Buckford's help. Tick slid off Sam's back, and Sam jabbed his walking stick into a drift. Phin picked his way down the slope toward them with David on his heels.

A thrust of what could only be maternal pride shot through Eldora. Phin had shouldered the responsibility of helping David like the man he was becoming. His scowls and slouched shoulders had vanished, replaced by confidence and a tender care that made Eldora's eyes smart. The influence of godly men in his life, even after only a few days, was already changing him, opening his eyes to a different way of behaving. If only it could continue past the holidays. How different his life would be if she could find a family like the Mackenzies to adopt him.

Finally, she and Celeste joined the group. Chests rose and fell from the exertion of staying upright, and snow clumped and clung to every fold and wrinkle of clothing. Sweat trickled from her temple, and her knees wobbled. Though used to hard work every day of her life, she'd never exerted herself like now, tramping through thigh-deep snow on such a steep angle, all the while worried about slipping and being hurled down a mountainside.

"We're about level with the treetops now. Soon we'll be in among the trunks and branches." Sam brushed snow from his shoulders and took his hat off to whack it on his thigh. "Good news and bad. There will be better handholds to help us get down, but if we do slip, there's real danger in plowing into one of the trees. You could break a limb or bash your head. Take extra care." He glanced skyward into the falling snow. "It's taken longer than I thought to get this far. At this rate, we might have to camp out. I want to make it down this side and up that ridge before dark." He pointed across to the next peak. "Martin City is on the other side."

It sounded so easy. Their destination lay on the other side, just out of sight. Buckford reached into an inner pocket and pulled out a bundle wrapped in a napkin. "I brought these. Perhaps now would be a good time to enjoy them." Opening the cloth, he revealed four fat oatmeal cookies, a little squashed for being in his pocket.

Tick's eyes glowed, and he tugged down his muffler. "How beaut!"

"Tick can have my share, and Celeste." Phin shrugged and straightened his shoulders, as if trying to appear bigger and tougher than he was.

Eldora's heart went out to him, wanting to hug him but sensing he would be embarrassed.

Sam shook his head. "That's a fine gesture, Phin, but I think everyone should have a bit. There's enough for half a cookie each, and we'll all need every bit of our strength to get where we're going. You eat your share, and don't feel guilty."

Buckford broke the treats in half and passed them around. Tick devoured his in three bites, while Celeste turned her back and broke hers into bites. She tugged down her scarf, popped in a piece, and covered her mouth again to chew. Phin, his brows arrowing toward one another, waited until Sam took a bite of cookie before starting on his own.

Sam tilted his head to Eldora, and with his body shielding his movements from the children, he gave Buckford back half of his portion. Eldora broke hers in half and secreted part back to the butler and nodded when Karen followed suit with her portion and David's.

Tick licked the last crumbs off his fingers and wilted, his shoulders hunched. Though he'd ridden on Sam's back all the way thus far, his skin resembled the snow banks around him, and his freckles stood out like pepper flakes. His breath came in quick, shallow puffs.

"Tick, are you all right? How are you holding up?" Sam squatted and looked into the little boy's eyes.

Tick straightened a little. "I'm fine. I can walk if you need me to. I gotta be getting heavy."

"I barely feel you. Don't waste any worry on me. Better spend the time wondering what you might get in your Christmas stocking in a couple of days. My father is going to love having kids in the house again. He'll probably bury you in toys and goodies." Sam glanced again at the sky. "We'd best push on. Thanks for the cookies, Buckford. They hit the spot."

Buckford nodded and tucked the napkin into his pocket with a private little smile.

Eldora braced herself and took Celeste's hand.

Sam hoisted Tick once more, tucking his leg through the rope. "If you think you're getting too tired to hang on, we can fix up some way to tie you on so you can sleep."

"I'm not sleepy." Tick's heavy eyes belied his words, but she had to admire his courage. "I can stick on."

They set off once again in their straggling line. Following along was hard enough. She didn't know how Sam could continue breaking the trail all by himself. He seemed to have unending stamina and strength. How much would they all need to draw on that strength before they reached Martin City?

The gloom under the trees made it feel like night would soon be upon them, though it was not quite midday yet. Though they no longer switch-backed down the slope, their time didn't improve much due to the sharper incline and the dangerous trees. Sam led them in a straighter line, easing from tree to tree.

After nearly another hour as far as she could guess, Sam halted at the edge of a drop-off. "It looks like this is the best place to go down, but it's going to be tricky. We'll need the rope." He slid Tick to the snow and removed the coil. He tied one end securely around his waist, looped the rope around a tree, and tossed the loose coils down the cliff. "I'll lower you one at a time. Buckford, go first and find a good place for everyone to wait."

Eldora wasn't sorry for the chance to rest, but the thought of dangling down a cliff like bait on a fishing line made her queasy. She couldn't see how far it was, but it seemed an age before Buckford hollered up that he'd reached the bottom.

Sam reeled in the line, and it was Tick's turn. "Sit into the rope, and hold on with both hands. Use your feet to keep you off the rocks as much as you can."

Tick pressed his lips so tightly together they disappeared into a thin line. Sam leaned back against the pull of the rope and played a little out. Tick inched down, out of view.

Eldora held her breath until Buckford's call that the little boy was safely down.

One by one Sam lowered each member of the party over the cliff. Dots of sweat formed on his brow, and his legs shook from the effort of lowering his brother—nearly the same in height and weight—to the arms waiting below to receive him.

Eldora let go of the tree she clutched and inched down the slope toward him. Bracing her feet against the trunk Sam was using for the rope, she grasped the rough hemp.

Sam's jaw tightened. "Take care."

She anchored her boots against the base of the tree and leaned back against the rope, letting it out slowly. Even through her damp gloves the rope made her hands sting. Her shoulders tugged and ached with the strain, but finally, the rope went slack when David reached the others.

Sam used his thumb to swipe at the sweat on his brow. "Your turn next, Ellie."

For once, she didn't correct the use of her name. Drawing a shuddering breath, she allowed him to help her slip into the rope seat.

"Don't look down. Keep your eyes on the rocks in front of you, and try to keep your feet braced. Sit down into the rope." He winked and reached out to touch her cheek. "I won't let you go, Ellie-girl."

With a flash she realized she wished he meant it forever. That he would never let her go out of his life. Afraid her heart showed in her eyes, she closed them. His hands grabbed her arms and gave her a shake. Her eyes popped open to see him nose-to-nose with her.

"Don't go wobbly on me now. You can do this. Are you ready?"

Grateful he took her behavior as fear rather than trying to hide the wave of love for him that cascaded over her, she nodded. Her trust in him was complete. If they survived this nightmarish trek through the mountains, it would kill her to have to leave him after Christmas.

Chapter 15

After hours of climbing up the other side of the ravine, Eldora knew Sam wasn't trying to be a brute, that he pushed them on out of necessity, but it was hard not to lash back or just sink into the snow and refuse to go on when he urged them to move faster. Her muscles ached, the cold had seeped so far into her bones she wondered if she would ever be warm again, and her mind had long ago grown numb with the never-ending trudging through the drifts.

She thought they would never reach the shoulder of Shadow Peak that they must traverse to descend the slope into Martin City. Everyone needed to rest, but daylight was fading. At least the snow had finally stopped, though the rising wind whipped what had fallen, swirling it around them before gusting on by.

They were just short of the summit when a low growl feathered across her hearing. She stopped and cocked her head, concentrating. The growl grew to a rumble and then a crashing roar. Everyone froze and turned to look back across the valley they'd taken all day to traverse.

Eldora's heart flipped. The enormous snow shelf on the top of the opposite peak wavered. She blinked as it appeared to quiver in the fading light of sunset. Then, with an inevitable horror, it rushed downward, gaining momentum and sweeping everything before it. Cracking, grating, roiling, the gray-white mass made matchsticks of trees and playthings of boulders. Though she could not see the spot where the train had halted on the tracks, Eldora was certain the avalanche hadn't missed.

Karen cried out and sank to the snow, and David groped his way to her side, cradling her against his coat and rocking her. Phin let out a low whistle, and his gaze collided with Eldora's. All those passengers, so scared but refusing to move. The avalanche would have swept the private car off the tracks like a cougar swatting a mouse.

Celeste stood by David, her hand on his shoulder. Karen glanced up, her face wet with tears, and opened her arms to draw the little girl close. David wrapped his arms around them both. Buckford struggled past them on the path and lifted Tick from Sam's shoulders.

The cascade continued for what seemed a long time, and it wasn't until the stillness rang in her ears that she realized Sam had come to stand at her side. Without a word he slipped his arm around her waist. She put her head on his shoulder, too tired and too numb to cry.

"Those poor people. They were so scared. Why wouldn't they come with us?"

He hugged her and rested his chin on top of her head. "I suppose, for them, the danger of staying wasn't as scary as the danger of going. Some people are afraid to step out along a path when they aren't sure what waits down the road."

"Should we try to go back? To see if anyone survived?" Even as she asked the question, she realized how impossible that would be.

"We have to press on. There's no going back. We're not safe ourselves yet." Weariness and responsibility wrapped his every word. Three children, two women, one of them pregnant, a blind man, and an old man—it was God's grace they'd gotten this far.

"How much farther do we have to go?"

Gently, he turned with his arm still around her. "Look there. Do you see the lights?" He pointed down the slope toward Martin City. "Those lights will lead us home. That's Martin City. The worst of the journey is over. Just keep your eyes on those lights."

"I've never been so tired in all my life. I can't imagine how the others are feeling." Though reluctant, she stepped out of his embrace and went to Tick, who sat on Buckford's lap with his eyes closed. "Tick, it's time for some medicine. How're you making out?" She tugged down his scarf. His skin had a bluish pallor that struck alarm.

Sam lit the lantern while Eldora dug in the pack for a spoon and Tick's medicine. Melting snow in the spoon over the heat from the lantern, she sprinkled in the powder from a twist of paper. "Take this, Tick. You'll feel better soon." She prayed she was telling the truth. The cold seemed to sap all his strength and energy. His movements were slow and clumsy, and she wound up holding his head steady.

Buckford gave the remaining cookie pieces to the children, winking to forestall Phin's comment. He insisted that Karen take the leftover piece.

"We've got to get moving. As tired as we are, we're liable to fall asleep here, and that would be deadly. The sooner we get down this slope, the sooner we can get warm and dry." Sam kept his voice low. "I'm worried that if we wait much longer we won't be able to go on at all."

They formed a ragged line again. Here on the less-severe slope, the snow was deeper, drifting into piles and heaps. Sam forged ahead, making a path for them to follow. The light from his lantern made dots on the blue-white snow. The clouds parted to reveal an indigo sky sprinkled with stars, and over their shoulders a winter moon rose and bathed the mountainside in soft, white light.

More encouraging, the lights of Martin City lay below. Warmth, comfort, food. A respite from worry.

A toboggan would be nice about now. The final trek to the Mackenzie house down the gentle incline of what the locals called Sluice Box Hill brought back fond memories of sledding parties that Sam had attended as a youth. How nice it would be to sit down on a toboggan and let it slide them all the way to the base of the hill, as he'd done a hundred times before.

Sam's lungs burned, and he forced his legs to move forward. Several times they stopped to rest, but after only a few minutes, he goaded them on, feeling like an ogre but knowing they couldn't quit until he had them all safe.

He could make out the outline of his parents' home, his memory filling in the details that were too dark to see. Gingerbread trim, turrets, balconies, the widow's walk on the mansard roof. Lights blazed from the lower-floor windows, drawing him forward.

"We're almost there, David. I can see the house." Karen's voice, encouraging her husband even though she must be ready to drop, drifted through the night air. Sam's already-considerable admiration for his sister-in-law grew. Not once on this horrific journey had she complained.

But that could be said of all of them. If kids came any tougher than Phin, Celeste, and Tick, he'd never met them. They soldiered on doggedly, manfully in Phin's case, helping David over tricky bits, taking orders without argument or sulks. Life was like that sometimes, offering watershed moments or experiences that set people on the paths they were going to follow all their lives. Sam knew that with the right influences, Phin would be a son to be proud of.

He nearly tripped at that thought. *A son to be proud of.*

And what of Tick? So sick and yet always optimistic, always sunny. Lying in a hospital bed or enjoying his first piece of candy in months, the same smile. Bravely clinging to Sam's back as they wallowed in snow or skidded down a slope. Taking his medicine without complaint, and never once questioning why God allowed his health to be so fragile. A family was missing out on a gem by not adopting Tick.

Sam cast a glance back to check everyone's progress. Buckford fought his way along Sam's trail, easing the way for Karen to follow. Behind him, Phin picked his route, searching in the moonlight for the gentlest path. David's hand no longer lay on Phin's shoulder. Instead, Celeste— abandoning Eldora somewhere along the way—walked beside him, helping him and probably drawing comfort at the same time.

The bond between David and Celeste was beautiful to see, the blind man and the scarred girl. Might that not be an answer? If David and Karen had truly lost their hearts to the little girl, Sam couldn't see them letting her go to an orphanage. In spite of the aching cold and exhaustion mauling him, Sam smiled. He might've gained a niece on this trip.

Behind them all, Eldora trudged along, her head down. Even from here he imagined he could see the stubborn tilt of her jaw, the light of independence glowing in her brown eyes. How he longed to batter down those defenses, to make her see herself as he saw her—not as a charity case or an ugly duckling, but as a brave, selfless, beautiful woman.

"We're almost there." Less than a quarter mile to the house. Tired as he was, renewed energy surged through his muscles when he mounted the last ridge of snow and dropped onto the packed ruts of the plowed road. He lifted the lantern higher to light the way.

Finally, Sam led them through the gate and up to the front door. He was so cold not even the rush of warm air that gusted against his cheeks when he opened the door penetrated. The lamplight made his eyes sting, and he blinked. "Mother? Father? We're home."

"Sam?" Mother's voice from the parlor. Something thumped, her skirts rustled, and her footsteps pattered.

His shoulders relaxed, and he eased Tick down onto the chair in the foyer. He braced himself for Mother's embrace, though he was so stiff with cold he could barely raise his arms.

Mother hugged him. "How—where—we thought—" Tears cascaded down her cheeks. "You're alive?"

He stepped to the side, taking her with him. "Not just me. . .look." One by one, the rest of the group dragged in, snow encrusted and cold numbed.

"Karen, David. . .Buckford!" She blinked, sending fresh tears over the edge, and she clung to Sam as if her knees were giving way. Trembling, her gaze swung back to his face. "Praise God. Your father is in town trying to gather men to form a rescue party."

"We're here. Cold, tired, and hungry, but we made it. There was an avalanche, took out the train. But we can talk about that later. First, there are some folks you need to meet. These are the kids David telegraphed you about, and this is Eldora, who is taking care of them."

"Of course." Mother shook her head and pushed out of his arms. "Where are my manners? Come in, all of you." She called for Mrs. Morgan from the back of the house. "Start running the bathwater and preparing a meal. Then I want you to send one of the maids into town and rouse the doctor. He can check everyone over, especially Karen and these children." Mother burst into action.

On her way up the stairs ahead of Mother, Eldora looked back at him over her shoulder, her eyes filled with thanks but loaded with questions, too. Right now he was too tired to formulate any answers. It was enough that they were safe and soon to be warm.

Chapter 16

"Eldora, wake up! Wake up! It's Christmas!" A small hand pressed against her cheek and then shook her shoulder.

She cracked one eye.

Tick.

She stretched, her muscles still aching from their snowy ordeal. Pressing her elbows into the mattress, she levered herself up.

"Come on! We're waiting!" Tick tugged on her sleeve, jostling her when she went to rub her eyes.

Phin and Celeste waited at the half-open door, each bundled into a wrapper and slippers. "I've had my medicine and everything. Sam sent us up to get you."

Sam. Her heart beat thick and fast. The man who had saved all their lives had been conspicuous by his absence. When he did return to the house, most of his time was spent with bent heads and private conversations with his brother and parents.

"How is Karen this morning?" She sat up, holding the bedclothes to her chin, luxuriating in the feather-tick and down comforter a moment longer.

"She's downstairs, too. Wait till you see the tree. There's a whole tree right in the house." Tick's eyes glowed like candle flames, and a flush decorated his cheeks. Jesse Mackenzie's surprise was paying off in delight already.

"All right." She grinned and mussed his hair. "I'm coming. Scram so I can get dressed."

With chilly fingers she shoved buttons through buttonholes and put up her hair. The past couple of days had been a time of drifting, of recovery, and this morning belonged to the children, but by this afternoon she would need to make some sort of plan for their future. She drew a breath against the anvil of anxiety sitting on her chest and opened the door.

Tick grabbed her hand and tugged her down the hall. Phin and Celeste hurried ahead. All four stopped in the parlor doorway. A fir tree, taller than she was, sat in the corner, festooned with paper chains and candles and ropes of popcorn and red berries. Its piney scent reached her, mingled with the spicy aroma of apples and cinnamon.

"Good morning." Sam's mother rose and came toward her. "I wish we could've let you sleep longer, but the children are near to bursting as it is, not to mention Jesse. I'm not sure who is most excited."

Their generosity overwhelmed her.

Sam leaned against the corner of the mantel, a cup of cider in his hand. His cheeks creased in a smile. "Happy Christmas, Eldora."

"And to you." Seeing him, knowing their time together was growing small, was bittersweet, but she vowed not to let it show, to enjoy the morning and face the future when she had to. If their trek down the mountain had taught her anything, it was that God would light her path when the time came. There was no need to borrow trouble.

Karen, bundled from neck to toes in a thick robe and slippers, sat beside David on the settee.

Eldora took the chair next to her. "How are you this morning?"

"Fine. Still tired, but the contractions have stopped. I was worried there for a while, but the doctor says it was the overexertion. If I take it easy, things should be fine. David and his mother have fussed over and cosseted me so much, I haven't lifted a finger since we got here."

David took her hand and raised it to his lips. He leaned close and murmured something against her hair that made her eyes sparkle.

"Now that everyone is here, we can begin." Jesse's voice boomed with good cheer. "We're so thankful that all of you are with us today, we decided to do things a bit out of order for us and start the festivities with the reading of the Christmas story instead of waiting until this evening." The children clustered at his feet as he opened his Bible.

Nostalgia and longing swept over Eldora, taking her back to when she had been a child at her father's knee, hearing him recount the nativity on a snowy Christmas morning. Back before the orphanage, before the responsibility of these three children, before Sam. Back when she was part of a family.

When she was loved.

When she was Ellie.

At the conclusion of the reading, Jesse prayed a blessing on each one in his household. Then, like a boy, he clapped his hands, rubbing them together. "Who's ready for some presents?"

The gifts rained down. Toys, clothing, books, candy. Her debt to this family increased with each happy squeal. And yet, how could she deprive the kids of this joy when their future was so uncertain? They might as well store up a few happy memories against the time when they must leave here.

It puzzled her that the adults didn't exchange gifts, while at the same time it was a relief, as she had nothing to contribute. Her life in miniature, always receiving, never able to give. Perhaps they withheld their gifts to one another out of deference to her inability to reciprocate. Another kindness from this remarkable family that made her throat thicken.

Each time Jesse handed a gift to Celeste, she took it right to David and Karen, opening it on David's lap and whispering her thank-yous into their ears. Tick bounced between Phin and Sam, too excited to sit still, while Phin kept shaking his head as if he couldn't quite believe what he was seeing. Every so often he would look Eldora's way, as if asking her how to deal with such bounty. She could read in his eyes the same doubts she felt, as if all this was a temporary dream and reality would come crashing in at any moment. If only she could shore up his confidence.

Sam stayed by the fireplace until the last present was opened and exclaimed over. Shoving himself away from the mantel, he came to stand before the tree while Matilda handed out cups of cider. Sam raised his glass. "Happy Christmas to you all."

Everyone responded in kind and raised their cups.

Eldora sipped the warm cider, breathing in the heady aroma of spiced apples and savoring it on her tongue.

"Now, David, I believe you and Karen have an announcement."

David rose, holding Karen's hand, and reached out for Celeste's. "That's right. Karen and I, with Eldora's permission of course, would like to adopt Celeste as our daughter." He turned his face toward the little girl. "Celeste, would you like that? Would you like to come live with us and be our girl?"

If he could've seen her face, he wouldn't have needed to ask the question. Her china-blue eyes went round, and her lashes flicked over them a few times. She dropped his hand and threw herself against him, staggering him.

A wide grin spread over his face, and he hugged her tight.

Karen wiped her eyes. "I know we should've asked you first, Eldora, seeing as how you are her guardian, but we wanted it to be a Christmas surprise. You don't have any objection, do you?"

Eldora scrabbled for her handkerchief. "Of course I don't. This is wonderful. I wondered how I was going to pull her away from you both."

They clasped hands, crying and laughing at the same time.

"You know we'll see to it she has the surgery Sam told us about. We'll do everything we can to see she has a normal, happy life. I'm still amazed at how quickly I fell in love with her, but even more amazed at the bond she and David formed almost immediately."

"I know. She's never opened up like that before. I have no qualms about you adopting her. You'll make a wonderful family." A pang ripped through Eldora's heart, and she glanced at Tick and Phin to see how they were taking the news.

The wistful longing in Tick's eyes made her feel hollow and inadequate.

Phin had his hands shoved in his robe pockets, and he toed the carpet with his shoulders hunched.

She set down her cup to go to them, but Sam forestalled her. "Glad to know I'm getting a new niece." He raised his cup to Celeste. "And that you're getting a new grandchild sooner than we thought." A nod to his parents, who beamed. "I have a little announcement of my own to make."

Everyone stilled.

"For a while now, I've felt that something was missing in my life. I thought I had found that something when I met Yvette Adelman, but I soon realized what a mistake I was making. When I broke my engagement, I thought I'd just have to live with that empty feeling. Then Aunt Tabitha stepped in." He grinned and rubbed the back of his neck. "When she asked me—or should I say ordered me—to look after a woman and three children on the train from St. Louis to Denver, I thought, 'How hard can it be?'" Spreading his hands wide, he shrugged. "Fights, fainting, arrests, hospitals, jails, avalanches, and treks up and down snowy mountains later. . ."

Eldora pressed her hands together in her lap. Where was he going with this?

Then he handed his mother his cup and squatted between Phin and Tick, putting his hands on their shoulders. "It was when we were almost to Martin City, after climbing and slogging and nearly killing ourselves out there in the snow, that I realized how blessed I was. Part of that empty place in my heart had been filled. Feeling your arms around my neck, Tick, knowing you were fighting to hold on and that you were counting on me. And seeing you, Phin, helping David and Karen and looking out for Celeste whenever you could. I realized here were two boys a man could be proud to call his sons. So, if you're both willing, I want to adopt you. You'll be brothers, and I'll be your pa."

Both boys yelled and flung themselves at him, toppling him backward and making the tree shake and waver. Good thing Matilda had blown out all the candles, or they would've set the house on fire!

While they rolled on the floor giggling, tickling, expressing their joy, Eldora hurried to get out of the room before sobs overtook her. She nearly collided with Buckford in the foyer.

"Happy Christmas." He smiled broadly and shook his head at the laughter and commotion going on in the parlor.

"Thank you, Buckford." She squeezed the words out. "And to you."

Not knowing where else to go, she fled across the foyer and found herself in a dark-paneled study. The windows beckoned. Drawing aside the heavy drapes, she looked out on the snowy landscape. Fresh snow drifted down, adding to the mounds already shrouding the lawn and trees.

Sam was adopting Phin and Tick. They were safe, secure. She should be joyful. She should be in there laughing and shedding happy tears and wishing them well. Her head dropped. Sam had filled the empty place inside of him. But what about the empty place inside of her heart?

Pull yourself together, girl. Don't begrudge those boys their happiness. Crying isn't going to change anything.

Evidently a stern talking-to wasn't going to change much either. She had thought she was alone in the world before, but now she had nobody. Not even three children who needed her.

The door opened behind her, and she straightened, scrubbing her cheeks. "Eldora?"

Sam.

"Are you all right? You lit out so quickly. You aren't upset because I didn't ask you first, are you?"

"No." Her voice cracked, and she tried again. "No, of course not. You'll make a wonderful family. I couldn't wish anything better for them."

He crossed the room to stand beside her. His very nearness when she had lost him—when he had never been hers to begin with—burned.

She moved away, pretending to concentrate on the landscape through the glass. "They're going to be very happy here. Your family is amazing. First David and Karen adopting Celeste, now you taking the boys. You've made all their dreams come true."

"They're great kids. I meant what I said. Any man would be proud to call them his sons."

"I'm glad you filled that empty space in your heart."

"Did I say that empty space in my heart was full? I said a *part* of it had been filled."

She shrugged. "It won't be empty forever. I venture that someday soon you'll find that rich woman you're looking for."

"Rich woman?" His brow furrowed. "What rich woman?"

"You told David and Karen that if you did marry it would be to a rich woman so you would know you were being married for yourself and not your money. *That* rich woman."

He scrubbed the top of his head. "You have an amazing memory. Are you always going to hold the foolish things I say against me? The girl I've fallen in love with doesn't have a dollar to her name." His hands came up and cupped her shoulders. "But this girl isn't anything like my former fiancée. *This* girl has fought my generosity every minute since I met her."

His grip on her shoulders tightened, forcing her to look up at him.

"Eldora, you left the celebration in there before I could finish what I wanted to say. The empty place inside me won't be filled until you say you'll marry me and make us a family. You're the center of our world, mine and the boys. But it isn't just the boys who need you."

Bewildered, fearing she was somehow dreaming, she stared hard into his eyes. "You've fallen in love?"

A rueful grin teased his lips. "I didn't mean to, but I did. Head-over-heels, don't-care-who-knows-it, can't-stop-thinking-about-her in love." He gave her a little shake. "I want you to forget what I said about marrying a rich woman. That was plain foolishness said to Karen so she wouldn't realize how I was coming to care for you. I don't want a rich wife." He stopped short. "No, I take that back. I *do* want a rich wife."

Her heart plummeted. She *had* been dreaming. Everything went dark inside her, like a candle snuffed in a high wind. She sagged against his grip, but he wasn't through.

"I want a wife so rich in love that she fills our home with laughter and caring. I want a wife so rich in respect and integrity that I'm a better man just for having her in my life." He warmed to his topic, fanning hope with every passing second. "I want a wife so rich in friendship that our years together will fly by, so rich in generosity"—his dear face split in a grin—"that she fills my home with children. The two boys we start with and however many more God blesses us with."

Her whole future shone from his eyes. Light filled every corner of her mind and heart.

"Yessiree, I want a rich wife. You have all that and more to give. I want you to be Ellie again, and I want the chance to show you how much I love you. When are you going to admit that you love me and that we should be together?"

Waves of happiness broke over her. She laughed. "Maybe when you give me a chance to get a word in edgewise. You haven't changed your tactics a bit. Still bullying me with your generosity." With a boldness she wouldn't have believed only a few minutes ago, she twined her arms around his neck and stood on tiptoe. "I want to be Ellie again, too."

His lips came down on hers, demanding and sweet, giving and taking. She responded with everything in her heart—reborn, renewed, loved, and cherished. When he withdrew, reluctantly, a little at a time, she stared into his beautiful blue eyes and returned his smile. Warm tingles shot through her, and she shook her head, unable to believe how quickly she'd gone from despair to delight.

"Are you two done?" Phin's disgusted voice came from around the door. "Me 'n Tick are hungry."

Sam laughed and hugged her tight. "Let's go, Ellie. Our family is waiting."

STARS IN HER EYES

Dedication

For Katie Ganshert.
We need another field trip to Galena.

Chapter 1

Pastor Silas Hamilton had become adept at dodging matrimony-minded maidens and their matchmaking mamas, but he'd never encountered a mother as determined as Mrs. Drabble.

Beatrice Drabble had proven resourceful in finding ways to throw her daughter Alicia into his path, and he'd nearly exhausted all valid excuses. Not that he was against marriage, and Alicia Drabble was nice enough. But she wasn't the girl for him.

"I do hope you'll accept our luncheon invitation *this* time." Mrs. Drabble tilted her head back to peer up at him from under the feather-adorned awning she called a hat. Her button-black eyes bored into him like a rock drill. "You've been previously engaged for three weeks straight. Alicia has been so disappointed. She does enjoy your company. And we have a new set of pictures for the stereopticon. Natives from Africa. I thought you'd be interested, since you've been encouraging your parishioners to support African missions. . . ." She left the statement hanging, arching her dark eyebrows at him and drawing her lips into their habitual pucker.

He swallowed, his insides squirming. Invitations made under the guise of church work were always the most difficult to evade.

Conversations buzzed around them as people filed out of their pews and stood in line to shake his hand before heading home to a hot meal and a quiet afternoon. Spring sunshine streamed through the brand-new, stained-glass windows that marched down the sides of the church, throwing blocks of color on his congregation as they milled and chatted. The installation of those windows—special ordered all the way from Germany—marked the end of the first major tussle he'd encountered in this, his first solo-pastorate position. Mrs. Drabble had been at the center of that little maelstrom, too.

Alicia Drabble stared over his shoulder, a faint pink tinting her cheeks. China-blue eyes that rarely met his, golden ringlet curls, porcelain skin, and an air of fragility—nothing at all like her mama, whose physique tended more to the cider barrel shape.

He shook Alicia's limp hand and turned back to her mother. "I do thank you, but I'm afraid I will have to decline once more. I've already accepted an invitation to lunch at the Mackenzie home." And grateful he was, too.

The Drabble matron's face hardened, and the creases at the corners of her lips deepened. "I see." She tugged at the hem of her bodice and shifted her Bible to her other arm. "You do realize your first annual review as our pastor is coming up soon. The district supervisor is a very good friend of mine, and it would pain me to have to tell him you were playing favorites amongst your congregation."

The barb in her voice nicked his conscience, and he did a quick gallop around his social calendar to see if she might be correct. Had he been showing favoritism to some over others? The last thing he wanted or needed was a bad report sent to the home office, and until recently, he'd not feared one. But the drawn-out discussions that bordered on arguments over something as simple as new windows for the church had set up a distant warning gong in the back of his mind. In the front of his mind was the knowledge that his father, as the home office director, would be sure to read any report and know his son wasn't living up to his exceedingly high expectations.

Matilda Mackenzie appeared at his elbow as if she had somehow sensed he could use rescuing. "Silas, we're looking forward to your visit today. David and Karen want to show off the little one and talk about a dedication service here in a few weeks."

Mrs. Drabble's severe expression melted into a smile, and she held wide her arms. "Matilda, so lovely to see you." Embracing the smaller woman, she kissed the air beside Matilda's cheek. "Congratulations on that little granddaughter. I hear she's quite a beauty. I can't wait to see her."

Matilda extricated herself. "Thank you, Beatrice. Karen felt it would be best not to bring the baby out in public for a few weeks. It's been such a cold spring. We'll serve dinner at one, if that suits you, Silas." She patted Silas on the arm and strolled toward the door without waiting for an answer.

Beatrice's lips twitched. "I can never get over parishioners calling a pastor by his first name. I guess it was the way I was brought up, proper and all, but using a pastor's first name..." She gave an I-don't-know-what-this-world-is-coming-to shrug.

Silas held in a sigh and vowed to be polite, long-suffering, patient, enduring all things.... "Mrs. Drabble, I did give the adult congregants leave to use my first name if they wanted to."

"And you'll remember I told you I thought it improper. As the spiritual leader of this flock, you can't maintain your dignity and position if you allow people to call you by your given name. If you ask me, even the term pastor is rather. . .common. Reverend"—she traced an arc as if the word could be read across his chest—"is much more ministerial and fitting for the office."

Two young men edged around them, heading for the door. Silas nodded to Kenneth Hayes and his friend. The young man had installed the new windows, and a fine job he'd done, too. Silas didn't miss the black look Beatrice shot Kenneth or the way his shoulders ducked and hunched. Poor Kenneth. She'd criticized and hounded him during the entire construction.

Kenneth's friend elbowed him in the ribs. "You going to the grand opening, or you going to wait?"

He shrugged. "I'll wait a couple weeks till the crowds thin some. Can't say I'm all that interested in the play they're putting on, but I wouldn't mind a gander at the inside of the new theater." Kenneth lifted his chin in greeting to Silas, edging past Alicia who stiffened and lowered her lashes when their arms brushed.

The friend's face split in a grin. "I want to get a gander at that actress. My cousin saw her in Denver this winter. If she's as pretty as he claims, it won't matter what play they're putting on. He said she looked better than a summer sky, and her eyes could make a man feel like he'd been gut-punched."

Silas smiled. All winter the town had buzzed about the new Martin City Theater set to open next week. In a race to keep up with Denver, Leadville, and other Colorado boomtowns, several affluent miners and businessmen had partnered to erect an edifice they felt would elevate Martin City to the status of cultural center. He looked forward to enjoying some of the entertainments himself. It had been a long time since he'd seen a play or listened to an orchestra.

Mrs. Drabble tapped Silas's arm, dragging him back to her. "Don't you agree?"

Uh-oh. He had no idea what she'd even asked him.

Someone whacked Silas on the shoulder. "Great sermon today, Silas. You hit hard and fair."

Silas grinned and shook Jesse Mackenzie's hand, trying not to wince as his palm compressed in a bear-trap grip. "I just open the Word. I let the Spirit do the teaching and convicting."

"It beats all how you can take a familiar passage like the command for husbands to love their wives like Christ loves the Church and bring out something new I hadn't thought of before."

Mrs. Drabble sniffed. "I would think it would help your ministry immensely, help you preach those types of passages better, if you were married yourself, Reverend Hamilton."

Silas didn't miss her treading heavily on the word *reverend*.

She glared in Jesse's direction. "I believe I mentioned as much to the search committee when Reverend Hamilton was presented to the church as a candidate. We've never had an unmarried minister before, especially not one so young."

Jesse laughed. "Time will cure the young part, and I imagine if we give Silas here a little time, he'll work out the married part, too."

"Not in time for his performance review, I imagine."

"Say"—Jesse checked his pocket watch—"we'd best be moving along. We want to have lunch over by the time the baby wakes from her nap."

Silas didn't miss Mrs. Drabble's parting shot. "It's high time he was married and setting up his own nursery. He owes it to his congregation."

❧

Willow Starr followed her sister Francine up the center aisle of the Martin City Theater. Weariness pulled at her limbs and tightened the band around her forehead, though it felt good to stretch her legs after sitting on the train all afternoon. If only she could escape to the little creek she'd glimpsed from the train window. From long experience, she knew only solitude would allow her to return to the theater refreshed and ready to work.

"At least it's a decent size, though I never would've chosen navy blue for the chairs and drapes. It makes it much too dark in here." Francine poked one of the new, velvet chairs with her folded fan. "Positively saps the light. We'll have to adjust the footlights and our makeup or we'll all look positively ghastly."

Philip shoved his hands into the pockets of his narrow, striped trousers and rocked on his heels. "Hello! 'Alas, poor Yorick!'" His voice filled the empty theater. "Wonderful acoustics."

Francine's mouth pinched. "You're no Edwin Booth. Now *there* is an actor. My mother played opposite him, you know. The greatest production of *Hamlet* ever seen outside the Globe Theater."

Willow smothered a smile as the three stagehands behind Francine pantomimed this well-worn phrase. Her sister brought up her acting pedigree at every opportunity, as if being the daughter of the woman who played Ophelia to Edwin Booth's Hamlet made her a great actress, too.

Francine continued up the aisle, the skirts of her ornate traveling gown falling behind her to a train that brushed the carpeted floor with a whisper of satin on wool. "I see they have ample balcony boxes. After that shack we were booked in at the last town, it's nice to see a place with some class."

Willow separated herself from the gawking actors and wandered over to one of the pillars supporting the balconies above. She leaned against the solid post and closed her eyes, wishing away her headache and anticipating getting settled into her room at the hotel and having some peace and quiet. Finding time to be alone had been particularly difficult lately, and she felt like a rag doll with the sawdust drained out.

"Willow, you're going to ruin your posture slouching like that." Francine sounded so much like their late mother, Willow snapped to attention before she realized what she was doing. "We need to inspect the dressing rooms and see that our costumes have arrived."

Philip Moncrieff made his way through the actors and offered his arm to Willow as she approached. "Allow me." His mouth twisted into an oily sneer under the pencil-thin mustache. With his back to everyone, he didn't bother to hide his bold leer.

Her throat tightened, and she stepped back. Though she'd suspected from the first time she'd seen him that Philip might be trouble, she hadn't anticipated how much. Nearly old enough to be her father, he had made a game of pursuing her this past winter, always covertly, laughing at her blushes and evasions and getting closer and closer to outright insulting behavior.

"Philip?" Francine cut through the chatter. "Let's go see what the dressing rooms look like."

He rolled his eyes, pulled his lips into a pleasant smile, and turned on his heel, but not before winking at Willow and whispering, "Perhaps later, my dear."

She swallowed the distaste on her tongue. Walking to the stage, she didn't miss the whispers from the rest of the troupe. Her sister's possessive attitude toward Philip was common knowledge. Willow, having no designs on the lecher herself, was grateful. If Francine kept him dancing attendance on her, he wouldn't be free to make things difficult for anyone else.

Willow followed, pausing to caress the velvet curtains. Even in low light the narrow boards of the maple stage gleamed with wax and elbow grease. Her shoes echoed as she crossed in front of the footlight reflectors.

A familiar form slipped into the theater in the back, and she smiled. Clement Nielson, director and friend, and the only person in the troupe with the clout to override her sister's demands. He waved and cupped his ear.

Her shoulders straightened, and she tightened her abdomen. "'Life appears to me too short to be spent in nursing animosity or registering wrongs.'" The line from their upcoming play, *Jane Eyre*, flowed out to the corners of the auditorium. Though Willow was aware of Francine's snort of disapproval coming from the wings, she didn't acknowledge it.

Clement nodded and made a damping motion.

Willow dropped her voice to a whisper. "'I am no bird; and no net ensnares me; I am a free human being with an independent will.'"

"Bravo, child." He strode up to the stage, planted his hands on his lean waist, shoving back his jacket, and looked up at her. "I knew this part would be perfect for you."

Francine glided over, a ship in full sail. "Clement, I hope you're not making a dreadful mistake. It isn't too late, you know."

Willow's fingers tightened in the folds of her skirt, waiting for a repetition of the histrionics Francine had gone into when Clement first announced the cast for the upcoming production of *Jane Eyre*. The thrill of being awarded her first starring role had been snuffed under an avalanche of protests, tantrums, and petulant criticism, to the point that Willow had been ready to beg Clement to let her sister take the part.

Especially since creepy Philip would be playing Mr. Rochester. The hours she would spend in his company pretending to be in love with him would surely tax her acting ability to the limit.

"The cast is set, Francine. Willow is more than ready. She'll be a sensation. You've read the reviews from this past winter. Even in her supporting roles she's garnering attention." Clement bounded up the stairs, energetic as always, and touched Willow's chin, lifting it slightly. "I've never seen a more perfect ingenue. With that face, form, and ability, they'll be clamoring for her in New York, San Francisco, Paris, London, Berlin. . . ." He smiled, white teeth flashing, and feathered his fingers through his thin, pale yellow hair. "I've only held back until now, waiting for a bit of wisdom and serenity to appear in those marvelous gray eyes. She only lacked a bit of maturity to her carriage and voice." He clucked his tongue. "It was that tip-tilted nose. Gamine, pixie-ish, and alluring, but without a bit of maturity to counter it, she appeared too young. Until now."

Willow kept her gaze steady on the director, well used to being discussed as a commodity, an object with pros and cons. With Clement it wasn't personal. He spent a great deal of energy and time cataloging his cast and using everything at his disposal—costumes, lighting, makeup, positioning, props, sets, the lot—to bring out the best performance possible. He knew his actors inside out.

Or so he thought. Clement knew the public her, the actress who could pretend to enjoy the crowds, the demands, all the people pushing and prodding her to do what they wanted. But there was another Willow, intensely private, needing solitude, longing for stability in a life that had them moving every few weeks, longing to put down roots, fall in love, marry, and raise a family.

Only once had she dared to let that part of herself show, had she dared to give voice to her own desires and dreams of love and marriage, and Francine had squashed her dream flatter than dropping a sandbag on an éclair. "Ridiculous. Mother raised us both better than that. The daughters of Isabelle Starr deserve better than to be shackled to a cookstove, caring for the squalling brats of a dirt-poor farmer or miner. She'd turn over in her grave."

Clement clapped his hands, drawing Willow back to the present. "For now, I say we start making ourselves at home. We'll be here for the next two months, so feel free to unpack over at the hotel. Dressing rooms are over there." He waved to the wings. "Name cards are already affixed, and no sniveling as to the assignments." His brown eyes panned the cluster of actors. "Costume trunks should've arrived from the depot by now." He indicated the woman in charge of costuming. "Make sure everything got here in one piece. I'll get together with you and the prop master tomorrow for any last minute issues." He raised his voice. "We'll do a read-through rehearsal tonight at six, so don't be late."

Francine's brilliant green eyes glittered, and her jawline tightened, but she didn't challenge Clement's casting decision further.

Willow followed her off the stage, around the ropes and rigging for the curtains and backdrops, and down a narrow hall to the dressing rooms. She winced at the white card tacked to the center of the first door. WILLOW AND FRANCINE STARR.

Not that she wasn't used to sharing a dressing room with her sister, but to Francine Starr, billing was *everything*. To be listed, even here in this dim hallway, second to her younger sibling. . .

Bracelets clanked but didn't drown out the snort as Francine snatched the card, crumpling it and tossing it to the floor. "Now that we know which room is ours, we don't need the card." She twisted the knob and shoved the door open.

Willow set her features into a pleasant expression and stepped into the dressing room. Clement needn't worry about her acting abilities on stage. Anyone who could pretend to be at peace in the company of Francine Starr in a temper was a fine actress indeed.

Chapter 2

She's a beauty, just like her mother." Silas cradled Miss Dawn Matilda Mackenzie, gazing down into her tiny face. "You're a blessed man, David." He only hoped he didn't drop her or break her.

David eased himself into a chair in the drawing room, his wide smile creating deep creases in his cheeks. "I try to remember that when she wakes the entire household squawking in the middle of the night." Though blind, he wore a cloak of serenity and satisfaction Silas admired.

David's wife, Karen, slipped out of her shoes and tucked her feet up under the hem of her dress on the settee, glancing ruefully at Silas. "You don't mind if I get comfortable? We've been friends long enough for a little informality." She smiled when he shook his head—faint, dark smudges hovered under her eyes. Her hand came up to cover a delicate yawn. "It's been two months since the baby arrived, and I haven't managed a decent night's sleep yet."

Celeste Mackenzie, David and Karen's adopted daughter, sat primly on a footstool beside David. The child wore a spotless pinafore and shiny boots as black as her hair. Her sky-blue eyes, thick lashed and striking, never left the baby's face. Most beautiful of all was her smile.

Only a few weeks ago, Celeste's upper lip had been a ravaged snarl due to a birth defect. Now, after surgery, a thin pink scar showed where repairs had been made. The surgeon had assured her parents the scar should fade in time.

"Are you a big help to your mother?" Silas knew the answer, but he loved to hear Celeste's voice. For so long she'd hidden her mouth behind a scarf and kept her voice to a whisper, speaking only when she had to in a lisp so mangled only those who knew her well could decipher it.

"I try to help her all I can. And Buckford does, too. If I didn't have to go to school, I could help more."

David smiled. "I tried that very argument on mother when Sam was a baby. It didn't work then either. You're going to school, young lady. You're all healed up from surgery, and you start tomorrow."

"I heard you were going to finish out the spring term here in Martin City." Silas gingerly shifted the baby so he could pat Celeste on the shoulder. "You don't need to worry. The teacher is very nice, and you'll have Phin and Tick there to introduce you around. Your cousins like the school well enough. You'll soon find yourself with lots of new friends."

The infant squirmed, squeaked, and shoved her fist into her mouth. Smelling faintly of milk and that special brand-newness that only very young babies have, she snuggled into Silas's arms. An empty place in the corner of his heart swelled a notch. What would it be like to hold his own child?

Jesse strode into the room, his presence filling every corner. "How're my best girls?"

Celeste shot off the footstool and ran to him, hugging his waist hard. Jesse put his arm around her shoulders, grinning.

Silas smothered a smile at how Jesse strangled his normally booming voice into a hoarse whisper so as not to scare his granddaughters. "You'd best be careful Matilda doesn't find out you've demoted her in favor of Celeste and the baby."

Matilda entered the room ahead of the butler with a tray of tea. "It wouldn't be news. He's been besotted since the moment grandchildren came into the family. If he isn't fishing with the boys or teaching them to ride, he's having a tea party with Celeste." Warmth shone from her eyes. Though married for thirty years, the Mackenzies displayed a love and affection that didn't seem to have faded or gone stale.

David rubbed his jaw. "Tell me about it. If he buys one more toy, we won't be able to get into the nursery. I can't tell you the number of times I've gone to get the baby from her nap to find Father there ahead of me cooing and babbling and fussing. I had no idea what a mush lived inside the man."

Jesse grinned, unrepentant.

Matilda poured the tea, placing Silas's cup at his elbow. She poured a splash of tea into Celeste's cup and smothered it with a healthy dose of milk, smiling as she gave it to the little girl.

Silas decided to let the tea sit rather than risk trying to drink while holding the baby. "Thank you for inviting me today. Sharing a fine meal with friends would be enough of an inducement, but couple that with a chance to see this new little sweetheart"—Silas bent his head—"and I was all too eager to accept."

"Mrs. Drabble wasn't pleased you'd escaped her hospitality again." Matilda sipped her tea.

Silas sighed and squelched the first thought that leaped to his tongue, since while truthful, it wasn't edifying in the least. "I'll call on her sometime this week to make amends. I've had conflicts of schedule every time she's extended an invitation lately."

"Lots going on in town this spring. Yesterday I noticed they were putting up some posters in front of the new theater." Karen leaned back into the sofa and closed her eyes. "David, don't forget about the tickets."

"I haven't forgotten." David patted her leg. "Silas, I've acquired a box at the theater for the Friday after next. Not for opening night, I'm afraid, since I have to head to Denver and won't be back in time. Mother and Father and Sam and Ellie will be joining Karen and me, and we hoped you'd be able to come, too."

"I'd like that very much." Pleasure warmed him at being included. Though sometimes he kicked against the demands of his job encroaching on his personal time, he had to admit evenings at home with only the cat to talk to weren't all that stimulating. A chance to spend an evening in good company watching an excellent play...something to anticipate.

"Good." David yawned, apologized, and yawned again.

Dawn squirmed and snuffled, and Jesse leaped out of his chair. "I'll take her upstairs to the nursery. C'mon, Celeste, you can help me." He scooped the baby up and strode toward the staircase, Celeste trotting at his side.

Matilda shook her head. "He's just looking for an excuse to rock her and spoil her some more. I'm going to have a hard time keeping him from invading Denver every week or so to check on her when you go home this summer."

Silas chuckled. Sipping his tea, he glanced at David and Karen on the settee, both with eyes closed. "I think we've lost them to sleep. I'd best be taking my leave, Matilda. Thank you for an excellent meal, and I look forward to the play."

She took his cup and stood. "Do you want me to send around for the carriage to take you home?"

"No, I think I'll walk. Some fresh air and exercise are just what I need."

Striding along the road a short time later, he tried to thrust aside the feelings of discontent and longing nibbling at his heart. Over the past several months, he'd been aware of a growing sense of something missing from his life, of a void wanting to be filled. Being with the Mackenzies both alleviated and accentuated the sensation. It was impossible to be lonely while in their company, and yet the closeness shared by Jesse and Matilda, David and Karen, especially with the addition of that new baby, made him aware of his solitary existence in a new way.

Stripping off his tie, he thrust it into his pocket and shrugged out of his suit coat. Still feeling confined, he unbuttoned his vest and left it open and loosened the top couple of buttons at his collar. When he got home, he'd get out of this starched shirt and into his favorite plaid flannel, a relic from his seminary days when he'd worked on the docks in Sandusky to put himself through school.

An unseasonably warm breeze scudded along the road, kicking up puffs of dust, and to his left, Martin Creek burbled and chuckled, throwing back sparkles and reflections that illuminated the undersides of the trees hanging over the water. The beauty of God's creation moved him to a prayer he often uttered.

Lord, thank You for the people of my flock. Please help me to lead them to know You better and to seek Your will. Give me wisdom to minister to them and to be a good pastor.

Would he be a better pastor if he were married? Did he owe it to his congregation to find himself a wife and start a family? Would it matter to his performance review? The denomination preferred married ministers, but they didn't require it.

He shrugged and shifted his jacket to his other arm. There were several nice young ladies in his congregation who had let him know, through means subtle and overt, they wouldn't be averse to his calling upon them as a suitor, and yet not a one of them evoked a response in him beyond that of their pastor.

He'd always believed he'd know the minute he spotted her—the woman who would make his life complete, the woman who would balance out his shortcomings, bolster his strengths, complement him in every way. There would be a connection between them that neither could deny, a sense of rightness, of inevitability. Was he being stubborn and fanciful waiting for an ideal that wouldn't materialize, or was he right in not settling for something less?

The idea of sharing the intimacies of marriage—not just the physical intimacies, but the spiritual, emotional, mental intimacies—with someone without feeling that spark of attraction and exhilaration was unthinkable.

Renewed resolve to wait—not to be pushed into marriage by Mrs. Drabble, or the denomination, or even his own loneliness and disquiet— flowed through him. He wouldn't settle for second best. He would wait until God brought the right girl into his life.

With his mind at peace, he turned off the road and wended his way toward the creek bed. The sun still had some distance to travel before the mountains to the west obscured it and cast long dusky shadows. Time for a little rock hunting.

Reaching the water, he kept his eyes on the stones under the purling eddies. When an interesting color or shape caught his eye, he plunged his hand into the icy water to retrieve it. The best went into his handkerchief; the rest went back into the stream. He'd almost reached the outskirts of Martin City when movement upstream drew his attention.

A young woman sat on a flat rock at the edge of the stream, her knees tucked up and her head tipped back to soak in the sunshine. She spread her arms in a graceful arc, lifting her hands overhead. Her loose sleeves fell away to her elbows, revealing slender white arms. In a lithe movement, she rose and balanced on the rock, executing a pirouette, a musical laugh flowing out over the sound of the water. Her light skirts belled with her circling, and her hair, her beautiful hair, fell in glossy brown ripples around her shoulders.

Silas stilled, captivated. Such freedom and abandon, such joy in her surroundings—he instinctively smiled. When had he last met someone so carefree?

She began to sing—light, gentle, and dreamy—her voice a perfect match to her fluid movements.

> *"It was many and many a year ago,*
> *In a kingdom by the sea,*
> *That a maiden there lived whom you may know*
> *By the name of Annabel Lee;*
> *And this maiden she lived with no other thought*
> *Than to love and be loved by me."*

As if he had no control over his tongue, his voice rose and blended with hers on the lines of the popular poem-turned-song.

She dropped her arms and stopped mid-pirouette, and his gaze collided with the most incredible pair of gray eyes he'd ever seen.

⁂

The shock of finding she wasn't alone nearly propelled Willow off the rock and into the water. She stumbled, caught herself for a moment, and overbalanced again. A small shriek shot from her lips as she pinwheeled her arms, flailing the air to keep her footing.

Just when she knew she was headed into the icy creek, iron bands closed around her waist and hauled her landward. In a flurry of arms and legs, she and her rescuer tumbled to the grassy verge and landed with a thud. The stranger broke her fall, and the air whooshed out of his lungs.

She lay for a moment imprisoned in his arms, panting and stunned at this turn of events. Her cheek rested against his chest, and the solid thrum of his heartbeats reassured her that she hadn't killed him. Realization flooded her. She was lying in the arms of a strange man!

Scrambling up and away, she managed to elbow him in the stomach and squash his arm before righting herself. "I'm so sorry." A hank of hair slid over her forehead and obscured him from view. She scooped it aside, bunched her curls at the base of her neck, and tugged it all to lie in an untidy pile on her shoulder. "Are you hurt?"

The man propped himself on his elbows and grinned. The most perfect, symmetrical smile with white, even teeth. Warmth flooded his brown eyes, and his rumpled hair fell onto his forehead. She couldn't stop staring at so much handsomeness.

"I think I'll survive. I'm sorry I startled you. Good thing we found a soft place to land. Another yard to the right or left and we'd have landed on boulders." His deep, mellow voice rolled over her like the warmth from a stove on a cold day. He sat up and brushed at the dirt and twigs clinging to his shoulders and sleeves. A healthy grass stain decorated one of his cuffs. "Hmm, Estelle isn't going to like that."

His mutter jarred her. Estelle? Willow edged backward. She shouldn't be noticing how handsome he was, or how strong, or how gallant his rescue of her was when he was a married man. The heat that had rushed into her cheeks when she first realized she wasn't alone intensified until she thought she might burst into flames.

"I'm so sorry. Will your wife be angry?" Her lips felt stiff and uncooperative, and she grasped for her professional demeanor. The cloak of protection that usually came to her aid in tense situations proved uncooperative as well.

His eyebrows arched. "My wife?"

"Estelle? Who won't like that you've stained your clothes?"

He laughed, and her heart tripped at the deep rumbly velvety sound. "Estelle isn't my wife. She's my housekeeper, and she is always after me to keep my Sunday shirts clean."

Relief all out of proportion made Willow weak, and she joined in his laughter. "You really *are* in trouble then. I am sorry."

"No worry, and anyway, I should be apologizing to you. I'm the one who scared you, belting out those lyrics like that." He cast about him as if looking for something. "Be right back."

With a fluid twist he leaped to his feet and jogged downstream.

How had he managed to cover so much ground to rescue her in time?

She took stock of her appearance. A dead leaf curled into her hair, and she'd ripped the lace edging on one of her sleeves. Lovely.

Francine would have a conniption if she heard about this. Imagine one of Isabelle Starr's daughters caught so disheveled in public. *"Your image, my dear. It's all an actress has."*

Her rescuer returned with a suit jacket over his shoulder. The white edges of a handkerchief poked from his other hand. "I was sure I'd lost these when I dropped everything. It all happened so quickly. I thought you were going to get an icy bath for sure. This water comes down from up there." He pointed with his thumb up to the peaks to the north where each rugged edifice bore a shawl of snow. "This creek never gets what you could call warm, but right now, it's dangerously frigid."

She shivered, grateful not to have had a dunking. "I shouldn't have been acting so silly, twirling out there on that rock. I might've gone in with or without being startled."

Opening his handkerchief for a moment, she caught a peek at a handful of rocks before he shoved everything into his pants pocket. *Rocks?*

"Actually, it was refreshing to see someone so carefree. Quite the most charming thing I've encountered since coming to Colorado." His smile and the light in his brown eyes set off a fluttering under her ribs. "I'm only sorry I butted in and scared you."

She wasn't. She'd be quite content to be affected like this every day of her life. When she realized she was staring again, she let her lashes fall. He must think her a simple-minded idiot. And he wouldn't be far wrong, considering how he'd come across her.

"As much as I have enjoyed meeting you"—he glanced at the sky and grimaced—"time's marching on, and I have an appointment soon I can't break. I'd be happy to walk you home on my way."

Willow stiffened and sucked in a gasp. How had it gotten so late? Francine would have plenty to say if she was late for the read-through; and if she showed up in her current disordered state, she'd never hear the end of it. "I'm sorry, I have to go as well. Thank you for rescuing me."

She lifted her hem and scrambled up the bank toward the road, realizing as she fled that she hadn't asked his name.

Chapter 3

W hat's the matter with you, Willow? Get your head out of the clouds." Francine snapped shut her powder compact and set it down with some force on the dressing table. "You might be enamored of being the star of this play, but let me tell you, you're not ready, and I doubt you ever will be. *I* should be playing Jane." Picking up her hairbrush, she primped the heavy auburn ringlets lying on her shoulder. "If Clement had an ounce of directorial sense left in his head, he would see you haven't developed enough as an actress to give a convincing performance."

Willow stifled a sigh and went back to studying her script. Her sister had a tendency to get stuck on a conversational waterwheel, turning and turning and pouring out the same cold, damp accusations. Protesting wouldn't stop the flow.

"You're not listening to me." The brush collided with the tabletop, and Francine's imperious eyes met hers in the three mirror panes—each from a slightly different angle and each pair of black-lashed daggers summing Willow up and finding her wanting.

"I'm trying to learn these lines so I'll be ready for rehearsal." She checked the enamel clock on the shelf. "It's almost time."

"See, this is exactly what I'm talking about. An actress"—Francine drew in a deep breath and spread one arm wide, jangling the bracelets on her wrist—"doesn't 'learn lines.' She *becomes* the character."

How many times had their mother said the same thing?

Francine rouged her lips. "You haven't the faintest clue how to play Jane Eyre. Mother saw to it we had the best acting classes, diction and singing lessons; and anyone with an ounce of sense knows that I'm the better actress. Clement is just being difficult, giving you the lead."

Willow held her tongue.

A knock interrupted the tirade. "Rehearsal."

Willow thankfully closed the notebook containing her script and rose, letting her heavy silk skirt settle around her and making sure her posture couldn't be caviled at. "Are you ready?"

"Of course." Francine stood, checked her appearance once more, and swept out ahead of Willow.

Scooping up Francine's notebook, Willow propped it on her hip with her own and headed to the stage. All the warning signs of a major storm were brewing, and she didn't look forward to a rehearsal with Francine in this mood.

Though she was only a few moments behind everyone else in arriving, she could still feel the half-triumphant, half-accusatory glare Francine shot her way. Clement stood at his lectern marking up his script while several actors waited. Francine swept across the stage and seated herself in the most comfortable chair.

Philip Moncrieff sidled up to Willow. "You look lovely, my dear." His oleaginous voice slid over her. "Clement seems to be of the opinion you and I need some more rehearsing in order to be fully prepared for opening night." Turning his back to the director, he rubbed his hand down Willow's arm. "I'd be happy to rehearse with you whenever you'd like. Especially our more tender scenes."

Willow snatched her arm from his grasp and edged around him.

Clement tapped his pencil to get everyone's attention. "I want to work first on act 2, scene 3. Philip, if you could watch your pacing here. You're rushing a bit, and Francine, though you have a major part in this scene, it won't do for you to obscure the leads. I need you to stay near the settee. You're such a commanding presence and so lovely, you'll draw too much attention away from Willow and Philip if you walk clear across the stage."

Willow had to admire how Clement handled her sister. Through flattery and cajoling, he got her to do his bidding while making her think it was her idea the whole time.

The next three hours taxed Willow's patience to the limit. Nothing she did satisfied Francine, though Clement encouraged her efforts and interpretation and praised her at every turn.

True to form, Francine hadn't bothered to work on her lines much yet, relying heavily on the poor young girl who had the woeful job of being "on-book" for rehearsals, shouting out "Line!" at frequent intervals, and snapping her fingers until the girl supplied the next line.

Oddly enough, on the two occasions when Willow stumbled over a line, Francine supplied it perfectly without waiting for the prompt from the wings.

Still, things were coming together, and Francine Starr was too proud to go onstage for a performance without knowing her own part well. There would be crazed cramming, bouts of tears, and histrionics in the run-up to opening night, but she would appear serene and in command once the footlights were lit.

Clement finally called an end to rehearsal, and Willow sagged into a chair. Acting left her exhilarated and exhausted, a confusing combination that required solitude to sort out. While the rest of the cast and crew filed out of the auditorium, Willow let the ensuing quiet bathe her soul.

Her mind drifted to the place it wanted to be, back beside the stream talking to the extraordinary man who was never far from her thoughts these days. Though she'd returned to the creek twice in the last week, she hadn't caught sight of him. Every time she walked through the hotel lobby or down the main street of Martin City, she searched for his face, but so far they'd not crossed paths again. She couldn't get him out of her head, and the more she remembered his face, his voice, his laugh, and the way it had felt to be held in his arms, the more she longed to see him again, if only to confirm he was as truly wonderful as she'd made him out to be.

Footsteps sounded behind her, and before she could turn, a hand came down on her shoulder, clamping and kneading the base of her neck. "I thought I'd find you here. You're tense. Let me help you."

She shot out of her chair like she'd been snake bit, her script crashing to the floorboards and pages fanning and flapping. "Don't, Philip. I don't like you touching me."

He laughed, and the predatory look on his face was such a contrast to the image she had in her mind of her gallant rescuer of a few days ago, she flinched.

"That's because you're such an innocent. Don't you know that touch-me-not air you wear drives all men mad? It begs a real man to break down those icy walls and touch the fire he knows burns there."

Ignoring his customary flair for the dramatic, she sought to cut him down once and for all. "You wouldn't know a real man if he walked up and shook your hand. If you don't leave me alone, I'm going to complain to Clement." This direst of threats didn't even make him pause.

"If you do, he'll assume we won't be able to carry off our parts on stage as passionate and star-crossed lovers. He's likely to bounce you right out of your role and put Francine in your place." He spoke with such assurance, Willow wondered if he'd already broached the subject with the director. "I've worked with Clement a long time. He won't remove me as Mr. Rochester, because"—Philip held up one finger—"I'm perfect for the role, and there isn't anyone else in the troupe who can play the role, especially not three days from opening night. You, on the other hand, could be ousted like that." He snapped is fingers. "Francine has your lines down perfectly. She's practically salivating."

Frustrated with the undercurrents, the petty squabbles and jealousy, and Philip's slimy manipulation, Willow stooped and gathered her papers. "If you don't leave me alone, she'll get her wish. I'll walk out of this production so fast your head will spin. And then where will you be? What do you think the critics will say, and the public?"

He flinched. The posters around town promised Willow as Jane Eyre, and there were two Denver critics already in town awaiting Friday night. A change in the lead role at this late date would spell disaster, and he had to know it.

Without a word, he turned on his heel and stalked away, leaving Willow alone in the vast auditorium. As she tidied her papers and studied the chandeliers, the rows of seats, and the ornate balcony boxes, she realized she could walk away from all of this without a backward glance. If only she had some place to go.

⁊

Silas pinched the bridge of his nose and tried once more to get the meeting back on track. Committees were one of the most difficult parts of his job. While he knew the need for counsel and getting people involved in the decision making and running of the church, committees leeched time and energy, often created rifts where none would've existed, and taxed his patience.

His board of elders—both of them—and the deacons and deaconesses sat in the front two rows of pews, while he sat in a straight-backed chair before them. His Bible and the meeting itinerary lay on a small writing table at his elbow, and his watch lay open beside them, the hands creeping toward the top of the hour.

"Jesse, could you give us the financial report?" Money and the church. The combination made his stomach tighten. No wonder Jesus addressed money so often in His parables and teaching. No subject got believers worked up quite as quickly as cash. . .unless it was the lack of it.

Jesse Mackenzie shuffled a few pieces of paper and cleared his throat before launching into a detailing of expenses set against the tithes and offerings that had come in the last month. Silas fought to keep his mind on business as various ideas were put forth regarding acquiring an organ and whether to increase the giving to the China Inland Mission.

Inevitably, they reached the line item MARTIN CITY ORPHANAGE. Dissention abounded on this issue, and as he had feared, the center aisle divided the yeas from the nays.

"We're not debating whether or not to help the new orphanage, but rather in what capacity. Mr. Mackenzie has the floor right now. There will be opportunity for discussion as soon as he presents his findings." He gave this gentle reminder when Larry Horton and Beatrice Drabble scowled, and Beatrice looked set to start another diatribe on the orphanage. She set her mouth, reminding Silas of a mule his father had once owned, and crossed her arms, waiting her turn.

The discussion continued, and Silas listened with only half an ear. The rest of his attention drifted to the one thing he couldn't seem to get off his mind.

The girl.

Once more he gave himself a mental kick for not at least getting her name. His search for her had proven fruitless over the past week. Not that he'd had a lot of time to devote to looking. Church business, sermon preparation, teaching his midweek boys' class, visitation, an unexpected trip to a neighboring town—his duties filled his time, and until now he'd embraced them with eagerness.

But that was before he'd rescued an adorable sprite with lively gray eyes and a nose that tilted up at the tip just enough to save her from other-worldly perfection. Her grace and clear soprano voice, her laughter and the delightful way the color rose in her cheeks—he remembered every second of their encounter.

Not to mention the feel of her in his arms, and how his heart had raced with her head pillowed against his chest.

He dragged his mind away. A man had no right to let his thoughts dwell on a woman that way when they weren't even courting.

Courting. He swallowed, and the hunger to know more about her, to find out if she was even free to be courted, tugged at him.

"I don't see why you're all so eager for one ministry to drain the resources of the church in this manner." Mrs. Drabble's voice cut across his thoughts and brought him back to the meeting at hand.

Jesse Mackenzie leaned forward and planted his elbow on the pew ahead of him, resting his cheek on his fist. "Mrs. Drabble, the board of elders brought this motion before the congregation months ago. You voted for it yourself. It's our obligation as Christians to take care of widows and orphans."

"I agree, but I voted yes assuming our contribution would be merely financial. Adding the orphanage to our missions giving is one thing. Expecting me to oversee volunteers, fund-raisers, and I don't know what else. . ." She dabbed her neck with her lacy handkerchief. "It's the windows all over again. People rush to say they want something done, and the work of bringing it about falls upon my shoulders."

Mr. Meeker, who served alongside Jesse as a church elder, cleared his throat and offered as meekly as his name implied, "Mrs. Drabble, if I remember correctly, you declared if the church was going to be headstrong and insist upon having stained-glass windows, you were the only one of the congregation qualified to see the task done. You took over the entire project. We wanted to help you, but you said you didn't need help."

Her lips puckered, and her nostrils flared. "I was the only one who had experience with ordering materials from abroad. Of course I saw it as my duty to shoulder the burden once the board had rushed into the decision."

Silas rapped the tabletop lightly. "Everyone, please, can we stay on the topic at hand? Mrs. Drabble, the windows are beautiful. You chose well, and we all rested more easily knowing the project was in your capable hands." He shot Jesse a warning glance. Mrs. Drabble might be at times a chore, but she was one of the most capable and organized women he'd ever met. When she took on a task, it got done, and heaven help anyone who stood in her way. "That's why we feel you are just the person to be in charge of the orphanage outreach. No one here could see to the needs of these poor unfortunates as well as you."

A flush came to her cheeks. The wrinkles beside her eyes deepened, and she dabbed at her neck once again.

Her husband, a languid, quiet man, nodded and patted her hand. The Drabbles owned the largest mercantile in Martin City, supplying everything from canned goods to chandeliers.

"Beatrice." Heads turned to Matilda Mackenzie, seated beside her husband. "If it will be of help to you, I'd be happy to assist. I'm in rather a unique position as both a board member of the orphanage and a deaconess of this church. Together I'm sure we can find a balance that benefits the orphanage and doesn't tax the church's resources, financial or physical, too much."

Silas called down mental blessings on Matilda for being willing to serve with Beatrice. Then he noticed the tightness around Matilda's mouth. She would bear with Beatrice if it meant bettering the lot of the orphans who had just taken up residence in the new Martin City Children's Home, but she was well aware it would be an uphill battle.

"There is one last thing on the agenda." Silas tapped together a folder of papers. "These questionnaires arrived from the home office this week. Each of the elders and deacons—not the deaconesses, I'm afraid—are asked to fill them out, seal them in the envelopes provided, and drop them in the mail by the end of the month. This is the first step in my performance review."

He handed the folder over the railing to Jesse, who took a set of clipped pages and passed the folder back. "I won't ever see these questionnaires, so you can feel free to be honest. In about six weeks, the district supervisor will arrive to interview the board and me and to sit in on at least one church service." Silas's heart beat faster. "I would appreciate your prayers for myself and for each other in this matter."

The meeting finally adjourned, and he motioned for the Mackenzies to stay behind for a moment so he could thank them privately. But before he could, there was the Drabble gauntlet to run.

She pressed her fingers into his palm. "I'll make sure Walter gets that paperwork filled out and sent in promptly. He has a tendency to let things like that wait until the last minute if I don't prod him along. I have to say, you're looking much too thin these days, Reverend Hamilton. You're not ill, are you? You're working too hard and not getting enough home cooking. I insist you share our evening meal tomorrow night. It won't do for our pastor to be looking gaunt and overtired when the district supervisor visits."

"I'd be delighted, Mrs. Drabble." He accepted, glad for her sake his schedule was open. "Nothing is better than an excellent meal in congenial company. It's nice of you to be concerned about my health."

She beamed. "Actually, it was Alicia who brought it up. She's so caring that way, always looking out for everyone else. Such a giving, compassionate girl. She'll make a man a wonderful helpmeet, don't you think?"

Pitfalls yawned everywhere around this woman. "A daughter to be proud of."

More beaming, and a proprietary gleam in her eye that made his throat go dry. "Tomorrow at six. Don't be late now."

Jesse waited until she was out of earshot then chuckled. "You better be careful, or you'll wake up one day and find you've Beatrice Drabble for a mother-in-law."

Silas gave a shaky grin. "Perish the thought." He held out his hand to Matilda. "Thank you for jumping in when you did. You'll be rewarded in heaven."

Jesse's laugh boomed out. "It will have to be in heaven, because I doubt working with Beatrice here on earth will be rewarding."

Though he echoed Jesse's sentiment, his conscience knocked on his heart. "When I'm tempted to complain about awkward parishioners, God always reminds me He loves them as much as He loves me, and I have more than a few shortcomings of my own that need attention."

"You're right." Jesse gave him a sheepish smile. "We've all got our faults. Although as far as Beatrice is concerned, though you might have some minor issues that need your attention, so far you've only one major flaw."

"Being single?" He rubbed his palm on the back of his neck.

"There's a quick way to fix the situation. If you get married, she won't have anything to complain about."

"Jesse"—Matilda tugged on his arm—"Silas shouldn't get married just to stifle critics. When he meets the right girl, I'm sure he'll be only too eager to wed. Until then, it's his business. Sometimes you barge in where angels wouldn't tiptoe." An indulgent smile took the sting out of her chiding.

"Maybe, but the truth remains. If he wants to get Beatrice off his back, all he's got to do is get married."

Chapter 4

By the third curtain call, with the audience appearing to have lost little steam, Willow knew they had a hit on their hands. The entire cast bowed again to uproarious applause, and though Francine would probably later remark on the behavior as vulgar, the men filling the cheaper seats stomped and whistled.

Philip gripped her hand so tightly her fingers tingled. She had to give him credit. He played his role as the masterful, brooding, mercurial Mr. Rochester with skill and flair. The consummate professional on stage. Too bad that professionalism disintegrated the moment he stepped into the wings.

The house lights brightened, bringing the audience into view for the first time. Though she had told herself not to be silly, she couldn't help searching the sea of gas-lit faces for the one that had occupied her thoughts and even her dreams this week. Curtsying, waving, acknowledging their appreciation over and over, she looked for him. Her chest squeezed when she didn't find him.

Stop it, Willow. Be patient. There's such a crush in here, you probably couldn't find your own sister in the crowd.

This thought did make her smile, since Francine considered it her duty to make sure *everyone* saw her.

Clement leaped onto the stage carrying an armful of red roses. She kept her smile in place, familiar with this opening night ritual, but he didn't stop in front of Francine, as was his custom. This time he breezed past and stopped before her. When he laid the flowers in her arms, the audience erupted again. "Congratulations, my dear. You are a sensation."

Pleased, bemused, and surprised, she cradled the fragrant blossoms. She hoped her makeup hid the blush she knew colored her cheeks. "Thank you, Clement."

He placed his hands on her shoulders and kissed her brow to more raucous applause. "You deserve every rose, every laud, every praise. I have never seen a more gifted performance." He patted her hand. "Now, go get out of your costume and into a party dress. The reception will begin as soon as you arrive."

The opening night gala. A ballroom festooned with streamers and hothouse flowers, a laden buffet table, and hundreds of guests. As she threaded her way back to the dressing room, weariness seeped through her and a faint pounding began behind her eyes. If tonight's party followed the familiar pattern, it would be approaching dawn before she could be alone and sift through all the thoughts tumbling in her head.

"Help me with my dress." Francine, always the last to leave the stage, marched into the dressing room. "Hurry up. We're expected."

Foolish of her to hope for some small word of praise or approbation for a good performance, and yet, the armor she'd grown around her heart where her sister was concerned proved to have a few vulnerable spots still. Francine had taken up where their mother had left off, and Willow saw no end to the criticisms and petty jealousies in sight.

"I must say, I enjoyed my role as Mrs. Fairfax more than I thought I would." Francine dampened a cloth and removed the stage makeup from her face in wide swipes.

Willow said nothing. She unhooked the back of Francine's costume and stepped away to see to changing her own clothes.

"Of course Clement had to present you with the flowers. He had no choice, since you were billed as the lead, but really, you're going to have to work on your role. Wooden doesn't begin to describe you. You could've been reading a menu rather than responding to the love of your life. Philip positively carried you through the proposal scene."

Francine continued her sideways picking all through redressing her hair and reapplying her makeup. Willow could find it in her to pity her sister, so concerned with the outside shell and, nearing thirty, forever in pitched battle against her archenemy, time.

"Hurry up. We don't want to keep people waiting. Help me with my gown." Francine held her arms up so Willow could slip the silvery silk and lace evening gown over her head. The gaslight winked on the crystals sewn into the bodice.

"You look beautiful." Willow straightened a few stray wisps of hair. "Are you going to wear the diamonds?"

"Of course." Francine checked her reflection. "I wouldn't be caught dead on opening night without my jewelry." She opened her case and withdrew the necklace their mother had bequeathed to her. Securing it behind her neck, she dipped in again for several rings, bracelets, and a pair of teardrop earrings that caught the light.

Willow fastened her sister's gown up the back and turned so Francine could help her with the removal of her own costume. Stepping into a white evening gown of chiffon over satin, she held her breath while Francine jerked at the buttons.

Please don't tear the fabric.

273

She finished, and Willow pulled the pins from her hair, letting the brown mass tumble out of the severe style necessary for her role as Jane. Brushing so quickly her hair crackled, she then pinned it up loosely on her head, encouraging a few ringlets to fall over one shoulder and pinning an ostrich feather and crystal clip to the back of her head. She lifted her single strand of pearls, also a bequest from her mother, and clasped them about her throat.

"You aren't even done with your makeup." Francine dabbed on perfume and checked her reflection once again.

"It won't take me long. You could go ahead."

A snort. "You'd like that, wouldn't you? Arriving all alone and stealing the limelight?"

"I only didn't want to hold you up." She wiped off the makeup she'd worn on stage. Though it looked ghastly in the candlelight of the dressing room, the heavy paint was necessary in the lighting of the theater to make her look natural. Without the eye rouge, base, and powder, she would appear so pale and undefined as to be almost faceless.

But a ballroom full of theater guests was a different audience, and she could dispense with the heavy makeup. She took only a moment to powder her face and smooth her eyebrows before taking up her beaded evening purse and cloak, squaring her shoulders to brave the crowd. She swirled the black velvet cloak over her shoulders and tied the strings at her throat.

Her heart thumped against her ribs as she followed Francine from the theater to the hotel next door and into the ballroom reserved for the party. Perhaps *he* would be there, and she would have a name to match the handsome face.

Music and light poured from the ballroom, and people laughed and talked, helping themselves to the buffet and reliving the performance.

Clement met them at the door. "My dears, your public awaits. I've already spoken to several critics, and they're all in raptures." His hands never stopped moving, fluttering over his hair, tugging at his tie, ducking into his pockets, only to be withdrawn immediately. "Let me take you in."

Francine took his arm. "Philip will bring Willow." She raised her chin and flicked a glance at Philip over Clement's shoulder.

Willow hid her grimace and stood back from the doorway to allow Francine to enter alone. A smattering of applause filled the air.

"She's choked with envy." Philip tugged on his white gloves. "And no small wonder. You did play your part beautifully." He offered his elbow. "Come, my darling Jane Eyre. As your beloved Rochester, I shall see you into the party."

She rebelled inwardly at being called *his* anything but untied the strings on her cloak and let it fall from her shoulders.

A hotel servant took the garment, and Philip let out a low whistle. "I say, that dress is striking. You'll upstage every woman in the room." Again he held out his arm.

Laying her fingertips lightly on his sleeve, she put on a calm, pleasant expression and prepared to act the part of the ingenue Clement wanted her to be.

The moment she stepped over the threshold, the room erupted into applause. Bodies pressed close, shaking her hand, showering her with compliments, and each encounter sapped a little more of her energy. Philip and Francine imprisoned her between them.

Several people called her Jane, a testament to her acting skill that they actually thought of her in terms of the character, but it left her hollow—as if she weren't a real person, as if they didn't see the real her.

Francine accepted every plaudit as if it belonged to her, and Willow was more than happy to let her have the attention. When she could finally escape the reception line, she found a quiet corner to sip a cup of punch in and study the crowd.

He wasn't here. She really shouldn't have expected him, and yet though her mind told her heart over and over he shouldn't be this special to her—not after one chance encounter—her heart refused to be sensible.

"My dear, that dress becomes you delightfully," Clement said as he approached.

"Thank you. It's one Francine ordered, but when it came, she thought it made her look pale."

"Well, on you it is enchanting. You look like an angel." His knowing, pale eyes roved her face. "I'm not blind, Willow, nor is the rest of the cast and crew. They see how Francine treats you."

She swallowed, touched by his concern. "It isn't that bad. She just cares so much. Being the center of attention means everything to her. It's all she has, all she knows."

"The theater is all any of us knows. None of us could walk away unscathed."

His words struck her. Was the theater all she had? Could she walk away unscathed?

❧

Silas rested his fishing pole on his shoulder and dangled his tackle box from his fingertips. Shutting the door on the parsonage and his sermon notes for next Sunday, he couldn't help the tickle of anticipation at playing the truant for an afternoon by the creek.

A warm spring breeze, so welcome after the bitter winter just past, brushed across his face. He breathed deeply, hitched the strap on the bag holding his lunch higher onto his shoulder, and set out for Martin Creek.

With each step, he shed the responsibilities and cares of his flock and allowed himself to relax and embrace the beautiful day. Following the burbling stream, he descended the hillside toward the rock-strewn oxbow where rainbow trout darted in the crystal water.

Would she be there?

He chided himself for allowing his thoughts to return once more to the young woman. His attempts at concentration since meeting her had been paltry at best. The fact that he'd been unable to locate her since then had driven him to distraction. If he could only see her once more, convince himself his memory had played him false, that she wasn't as perfectly beautiful as he remembered, then perhaps he could get her out of his mind and focus on his job as a pastor.

And that was the only reason his steps quickened as he reached the place where he'd last seen her.

She was there.

He had to blink to make sure his mind wasn't tricking him.

She sat on the flat rock, her arms wrapped around her up-drawn knees. A wide-brimmed hat shaded her face, and she had her brown hair tucked up, revealing her slender neck and the delicate line of her jaw.

His foot loosened a pebble that skipped and bounced down to the water, and the sound caused her to turn toward him. Even from a dozen paces her gray eyes sucked his breath away.

His memory hadn't played him false.

"Good after—" His voice rumbled in his chest, sounding rusty and hoarse. Silas cleared his throat and tried again. "Good afternoon."

Her welcoming smile made his chest feel like the sun had risen just under his heart. Satisfaction, as if he'd finally found something he'd been looking for all his life, washed over him.

"Good afternoon. I see you came prepared to fish me out if I fell in today." She pointed to his gear.

Laughing all out of proportion to her small joke, he approached her and set his equipment on the bank. "I'm playing the truant from work this afternoon. It's much too nice to stay inside."

"I agree. I escaped for a while myself. Sometimes I just need to get away from everyone."

"Am I intruding? I'll go if you like." *Please say no. Please ask me to stay.* The plea rose up so strongly he almost voiced the words aloud.

"I'd be glad of your company." A blush pinked her cheeks, and her lashes fell. "I'm sorry I had to rush away before. I was late, and my. . .employers won't tolerate lateness."

She lifted a pine branch from the rock beside her and trailed it in the water. Resin from the broken tip created a rainbow pattern on top of the water, and sunshine threw brilliant reflections up under her hat brim and lighted her face with ever-changing dapples.

The burning desire to know everything about this woman surged through him, but he sensed her reserve and cautioned himself to go slowly. "I wasn't offended. Your devotion to your employers is admirable." Seating himself a respectable distance away on another sun-warmed rock, he studied her profile. "It's nice we're both able to take an afternoon off every once in a while. I know I was getting weary battling the books. The boys I was preparing a lesson for would much rather be out climbing trees and playing ducks and drakes."

"Ducks and drakes?" Her tip-tilted nose wrinkled. "I've not heard of that."

"It's another name for skipping stones." He cast about his feet and located a flat stone the size of a silver dollar. He brushed it off and tossed it in his palm, testing the weight. "This is a perfect skipping stone. Watch." Silas stood and hurled the stone, watching in satisfaction when it bounced across the water half a dozen times before disappearing beneath the surface.

Her delighted laughter rippled through him.

She tossed her stick into the stream, rose, and dusted her hands. "I've never skipped a stone in my life. Show me again."

He found another rock, flicked it at the stream, and winced when it ricocheted off a boulder with a *clack*. "Hmm, not so good." He grimaced. "You try it. Find a good flat rock. Those work the best."

She found a stone and tossed it into the stream. *Plop.* "Well, that was unspectacular. What did I do wrong?" A tiny crease appeared above the bridge of her nose.

He found another flat stone. This time his toss netted him eight skips.

She tried twice more with poor results, and each time the concentration on her face deepened and her determination to master the skill became more pronounced.

"You need to throw more from the side. Make the rock fly parallel to the water for as long as possible." He flipped a stone across the surface of the creek. "And don't forget, I've had a lot of practice at this."

Another of her attempts ended in failure and a splash that wet the hem of her dress. "I'm never going to get this." She blew out a breath and went to searching for another stone.

"Here, let me help you." Silas stepped up onto the rock beside her and reached behind her to take her right hand in his. This close to her, he couldn't help but notice the porcelain quality of her skin and the bird-delicate bones of her hands and wrists. Giving her plenty of time to stop him, he eased his left hand around her waist to steady her. "Draw the stone back like this"— he suited action to words—"and throw it like this." He pantomimed, slowly propelling her hand forward on a flat plane. "One, two, three." On three, the stone sailed through the air, skimmed the water, flipped, skipped, bounced, and after a half-dozen hops, plopped into the water.

"We did it!" She turned in his arms, gave a little hop, and hugged him, the light of triumph gleaming in her eyes.

He returned her exuberant embrace, thrilling at the feel of her in his arms.

"Thank you." She leaned back and seemed to realize what she'd done. She let her hands drop from his shoulders and stepped back. Pink surged into her cheeks to replace the glow of accomplishment.

"Careful." He kept hold of her elbows, lest she tumble into the stream in her haste to put some distance between them.

"I'm sorry. I overstepped." She gripped her fingers together at her waist and gave him a good view of the top of her hat.

Reluctantly, he let go of her. "You did nothing of the sort." He put his finger under her chin and raised her face until she had to look at him.

Confusion clouded those gray depths, and an awareness—the same awareness he'd felt from the moment he'd first seen her—that he was a man, she was a woman, and something strong drew them to one another.

He smiled, trying to coax a response from her. "I'm hungry. Will you share my lunch with me?"

She grasped at this as if he'd thrown her a lifeline in the midst of her storm of uncertainty. "I'd be happy to."

He took her hand to help her to the bank but let it go right away. He didn't want to scare her, and the power of his feelings, so fresh and new, surprised him. "I have sandwiches and apples." Digging in his rucksack, he produced the napkin-wrapped bundles. He shrugged out of his coat and spread it on a patch of grass for her. "There. Don't want your dress to get muddy."

"I suppose I should've had a care for that before I sat out there on that rock, but the water seemed to be calling to me, and I just had to get closer to those ripples."

Silas handed her a sandwich. "I'll say grace."

She stilled for a moment and nodded, bowing her head.

"Lord, thank You for Your beautiful creation, for sending spring after winter to remind us of how You are faithful to keep Your promises. Bless this food to our nourishment. Amen."

"Amen," she whispered.

He bit into the thick bread and sliced ham. Bless Estelle for baking a ham for him this week. He swallowed carefully. "I had hoped to see you in church this past Sunday. Martin City only has one house of worship, so I was sure you'd be there." He winced, hoping his eagerness didn't come across as an accusation. For all he knew, she'd been indisposed, or her employer had required her presence on Sunday morning.

She shrugged. "Oh, I almost never go to church."

Cold shock poured over him so he had to check to make sure he hadn't slipped into the water, and he realized how far along the path of his future his thoughts had already raced. The *one* command God required of His children when it came to choosing people to commit to for life, the *only* requirement He stipulated was they be not unequally yoked, believer to unbeliever. It had never entered his mind that this beautiful girl who had stolen his imagination and was on the verge of stealing his heart wouldn't know Jesus as her Savior. His potential bride had suddenly become his mission field.

She appeared unaware of the blow she'd dealt him, taking a delicate bite of her apple and dabbing at her lips with the corner of her napkin. The similarity between the temptation of Eve and his own temptation now yawning before him didn't pass him by without notice.

"Of course, that doesn't mean I'm a total heathen." She scanned the aspens on the far bank. "My father was a man of deep faith, and he passed that on to me. Why, if it wasn't for my faith in God's saving grace, I think I would lose all hope in this life and certainly my hope for the next."

The muscles in his stomach loosened a fraction. "So you know Jesus as your Savior, but you don't go to church?"

"Oh, I'd like to, but my schedule rarely allows it." She tucked her bottom lip behind her teeth, and her eyes clouded. He sensed her backing away from his questions. Glancing at the sky, she wrapped her half-eaten lunch back into the napkin. "I'm sorry, but I have to go."

"Wait." He shot to his feet, tumbling his sandwich to the ground. His apple bounced right into the stream and bobbed away. Before she could escape, he grabbed her wrist. "Please, there's one more thing I have to know about you."

"I really do need to be getting along before I'm missed."

"I can't possibly let you go without telling you my name and asking for yours. My name is Silas Hamilton." He let go of her wrist and held out his hand, praying she would take it.

She hesitated and shook her head as if to chase away a thought. Slipping her fingers into his palm, she clasped his hand and solemnly studied his face. "My name is Willow. Willow Starr." Without another word, she took her leave, slipping through the white aspen trunks and disappearing over the brow of the hill.

He stood on the bank staring after her. Willow Starr. Where had he heard that name before?

Chapter 5

Silas, his hair still damp from his hasty bath, walked along Center Street toward the brightly lit theater, but his mind was still on his encounter with Willow Starr at the stream that afternoon. Her name was perfect, unique, descriptive, fitting. Anticipation lengthened his stride. An evening in the company of the Mackenzies never failed to stimulate and cheer him, and there was always the faint chance he might run into Miss Starr tonight. Martin City had precious few entertainments suitable for a young lady, so it was highly likely she would attend the performance at least once.

There was an idea. He grinned. The next time he saw Miss Starr he would invite her to the theater. First he needed to find the Mackenzies.

Quite a crowd gathered around the doors to the theater, and more people descended from carriages, wagons, and buggies. Being tall, Silas had an advantage, and soon he spotted Jesse Mackenzie's thick head of white hair. "Glad you found us. Quite a crush." Jesse shook Silas's hand. "If David hadn't reserved a box for us a couple weeks ago, I doubt we'd have gotten tickets for tonight."

David smiled and shrugged. Karen tucked her hand into his elbow and sighed.

"Aren't you looking forward to this evening?" Silas studied her.

Before she could answer, David laughed and patted her hand. "She's just worried about the baby. First evening out since Dawn was born." He slipped his arm around her waist. "Now Karen, you promised you would try to have a good time. You know Buckford's more than capable of tending her. He practically pushed us out the front door; he was so anxious to get to rock her all he wanted without you fretting that she would be spoiled. Celeste will help with the baby's bath, and everything will be just fine."

Karen blushed but fought back. "And who was it who went upstairs to check on the girls three times before we left? *And* made sure everyone would know where we would be? *And* made sure someone would be on hand to run for the doctor and the theater if anyone so much as sneezed?"

"All right, all right." David hugged her close to his side. "We're both anxious parents, but we're going to try to have a pleasant time this evening and not talk about the kids the entire night. Although Mother and Dad might not mind, we don't want to bore Silas."

A fist pummeled Silas's shoulder, and he turned to see Sam and Ellie Mackenzie. David's younger brother grinned. "Hey there, Padre. Glad you could come tonight."

Silas shook Sam's hand and then Ellie's. He'd been pleased to officiate at their wedding this past Christmas, and if anything, they appeared to be even more in love than they were just a few months ago. "Are Phin and Tick all set for Sunday afternoon?"

Ellie nodded. "They've spoken of little else since they got your invitation. You'll have your hands full taking all the church boys on a picnic. Are you sure you don't want some of us to come along and help corral them? I know from experience how exhausting they can be."

The doors opened, and people began entering the theater. Jesse handed over the tickets and ushered everyone to the reserved box.

Silas barely had time to assure Ellie he could handle things before he was directed to a chair. "They've done this place up properly." He took in the chandeliers, the velvet draperies, and the gilded woodwork.

A small orchestra played from the pit in front of the stage, and a swarm of conversation buzzed as people found their seats.

Jesse took the chair next to Silas. "I'm glad you could come tonight. I worry about you."

Silas started and drew his attention away from the decor. "Me? Whatever for?"

Jesse's bushy white eyebrows lowered. "I think you're working too hard. You already pile a lot of the load on yourself, and on top of that, we've got this visit from the district office coming up."

The coils that wrapped around his windpipe every time he thought about the performance review tightened, and Silas had to force himself to relax. "I'm the pastor. That goes along with the job. If I don't do it, nobody else will."

"You see, that's where you're wrong." Jesse leaned to the side as Matilda, on the other side of him, shifted in her chair to speak to Sam and Ellie behind her. "You've got to delegate more. You're preaching, teaching Sunday school, not to mention taking the church boys on outings, doing repairs around the church, and last week, didn't I catch you with a mop and a bucket sluicing down the front steps?"

"Well yes, but—"

"No buts. Add that to your visitation, leading the singing, directing board meetings, and lending a hand wherever you see a fellow in need, and you're doing too much. You'll get stretched so thin you'll wear through." Solicitude laced his words and colored his eyes.

"Jesse, I do appreciate the concern, but all those things need doing. I can't just tell the sick folks I won't come see them, and I can't expect anyone else to stand up in the pulpit for me." He spread his hands.

Jesse grunted and crossed his arms. "Maybe not, but there are a lot of things you do that someone else could do for you. You have elders and deacons. You need to delegate."

"I do. Bernice and Matilda are overseeing the orphanage project."

"And how much oversight will you have? You'll be following up after them to make sure things are going smoothly and getting done, which is just as much work as doing it yourself. It's time you let go and let others have the joy of serving. You delegate, but then you wind up spending as much time or energy—or even more—on checking up after folks than if you'd done the task yourself."

Matilda leaned forward. "Jesse, is this really the time to chastise Silas? I thought we invited him out to get him away from work."

Sheepishly Jesse patted her hand. "Of course, dear. Silas, she's right. We brought you here so you could relax, and what do I do but bend your ear with shoptalk?"

Karen tapped Silas on the shoulder and handed him a playbill. "*Jane Eyre* is one of my favorite novels. I'm so glad we get to see a performance, though I can't imagine how they can fit it all in. The book is so big it would make a great doorstop. I hear the actress playing Jane is fabulous."

Silas took the playbill, but his thoughts tumbled over what Jesse had said. Was he failing to delegate? Did his elders think he didn't trust them to do their jobs? As always, his analytical mind picked up advice or criticism and turned it over and over, studying, weighing, evaluating. Would any of these things surface in the reports to the home office?

Flipping the program face up, his heart somersaulted. Willow's beautiful gray eyes looked at him, and her name blazed an inch-high just under the name of the play. Willow Starr as Jane Eyre. Of course! That's where he'd heard of her.

He read every word of the playbill, even the advertisements, then carefully folded the program so her picture wouldn't be creased and tucked the pages into his suit coat just over his heart. He tried to remind himself he was a grown man and should have better control of his faculties, but his pulse leaped and his mind raced at the thought of seeing her on the stage tonight. All thoughts of church and responsibilities and delegating fled.

Thankfully the Mackenzies weren't given to chatting during the play, because Silas wouldn't have been able to concentrate on anything they were saying. From the moment Willow stepped into the glow from the footlights, he was completely captivated. She was nothing short of magnificent. Graceful, appealing, gentle, and yet powerful; she mesmerized him.

Only one thing jarred him throughout the performance, and heat swirled through his ears, and his chest got prickly tight when he realized it. Jane Eyre was in love with Edward Rochester. And Willow played the part perfectly. When the actor portraying Rochester took Willow into his arms, it was all Silas could do not to leap over the balcony onto the stage and rip the man's hands away. He shifted in his seat, tried to relax the grip he had on his knees, and told himself he was being foolish in the extreme.

When the curtain came down on the last act, Silas found himself standing, clapping until his hands stung. The house lights went up as the actors came onto the stage to receive their applause from an appreciative audience. Men in the cheaper seats whistled and stomped. Some threw their hats into the air.

Silas had eyes only for Willow. The footlights picked out the pretty flush on her cheeks and shone in her eyes. He braced his thighs on the half wall in front of him and clapped and clapped.

She looked up, went still, and put out her hand to shade herself from the bright footlights. Her eyes met his and locked. One of the lines from the play came back to him, about an invisible cord strung between two hearts. A week ago he would've scoffed at such an idea. Too fanciful for a grown man. And yet it was as if a warm, golden, vibrating strand connected them. Everything around him disappeared, and there was only Willow. She seemed to feel it, too, for she stood perfectly still, staring up at him.

Jesse clapped him on the shoulder, breaking the spell. "That was something. And there's more. We've been invited to meet the cast at a little reception at the hotel next door."

Silas couldn't stop grinning. And he couldn't wait to tell Willow how amazing he thought she was.

⁂

"You were rather uninspiring tonight." Francine Starr wiped the heavy color from her lips. "I can't think what got into you. Clement must be out of his mind to keep you in the lead role. I'm only glad Mother isn't here to see what's become of all those acting lessons she paid for." She sighed and dipped her fingers into a rouge pot.

Willow, pinning up her heavy brown hair, met Francine's eyes in her mirror and gave in to the rebellion flickering in her middle. "You should never be glad Mother isn't here. Anyway, the audience seemed to like my performance well enough." One in particular. Just the memory of the pleasure and pride on Silas's face was enough to make her breath hitch and cause her to feel reckless. Though she was glad she hadn't known he was in the audience during the play or it might've made her too nervous to remember her lines.

"This ignorant audience doesn't know sic 'em from come 'ere about acting. They'd applaud if you walked on stage and recited the state capitals." Yanking on her gloves and shoving her rings onto her fingers, Francine glared. "What else can you expect from a backwater place like Martin City? Unschooled laborers and artistic cretins. I should be in New York or San Francisco, not stuck here playing bit parts in a nowhere town."

The spark of rebellion against her sister's tirades fanned into a candle flame. "Have you spoken to Clement about this? Perhaps he'd let you out of your contract."

"You'd like that, wouldn't you? Me clearing out and leaving the way open for you to take all the starring roles?" Francine pushed herself up from the dressing table and loomed over Willow. "I intend to regain my leading lady status, and I'll do it with *this* company. Clement Nielson will see reason, or he might find himself without a job. He has risen to his current position on the Starr family's shoulders. First Mother, then me. Without that cache, he wouldn't be able to get a directing job in a two-bit minstrel show. Everyone in this cast knows I should be playing the lead, and if I so much as snap my fingers, there will be a revolt." Her eyes bored into Willow. "I could shut down this show in a trice."

What she said was true. Most of the performers knew Francine's good side was the safest place to be, and she'd been the leading female since Mother died so suddenly almost five years ago. If Francine wanted to make things difficult, she could, and most of the cast would side with her out of a sense of self-preservation.

And if Francine sailed into the party in her current temper, more heads would roll than during the French Revolution, but before Willow could pour some oil on the water of her sister's wrath, Francine swept out of the room, slamming the door in her wake. "Don't be late!" This parting shot came through the flimsy door, followed by the angry tapping of footsteps heading down the hall.

Willow checked her appearance one last time, twisting the curl lying on her shoulder and straightening her necklace. Guilt rose up and snarled with the feeling that she was trapped in a situation she could never change. Francine would *never* change.

Lord, forgive me for baiting her. Please help me to be patient, not to return her sharp words. And Lord, I'd really love it if he *was at the reception tonight.*

Was it wrong to pray that Silas would come to the reception? She didn't know but hoped God didn't think so.

Silas had been in the best box in the house, so he must have some money or influence in this town. Surely he'd been invited to tonight's reception.

A light rap sounded on the door. "Willow, are you ready?" Clement.

She opened the door and smiled. "All set. Is there going to be a big crowd tonight?"

"Not too big. Nothing like it was opening night." He tucked her hand into his arm. "Before we go in, I've gathered the cast together for a special announcement." Leading her toward the stage, his eyes picked up the light from the wall lamps and magnified it. His step was jaunty, and a smile played under his precise mustache. They reached the stage where the actors and actresses clustered.

"Really, Clement." Francine's voice pierced the conversations around her and brought them to a halt. "Is now the best time for this? We've got people waiting at the hotel."

"I won't take long, and I think you'll all want to hear this." He removed Willow's hand from his elbow but kept hold of her fingers. "I've received word of a wonderful opportunity. A tremendous offer has been made to this troupe to appear at the Union Station Theater in New York City for the summer production of *Romeo and Juliet*." He swung Willow's hand and rocked onto the balls of his feet, beaming. "A twelve-week run in New York City."

A jolt went through the crowd, and eyes lit up. Smiles abounded, and everyone spoke at once. Francine stood front and center, biting her bottom lip, her eyes sparkling more than the diamonds at her throat. "*Romeo and Juliet*? New York City. Oh Clement, that's wonderful. I can't wait. I wish we were already finished here so we could leave right now." She spread her arms wide and twirled in a circle. "And at the Union Station Theater."

It was moments like these Willow treasured, when Francine forgot to be haughty or petty and let her natural love of life burst through. Her large green eyes shone, and her porcelain skin glowed with life and excitement. This was the sister Willow remembered best from her childhood, before Mother died, before Francine became consumed with taking her place in the acting troupe. Before the ten-year age gap between them began to dwindle in significance.

"I'm going to be a wonderful Juliet." Francine clasped her hands under her chin and fluttered her lashes. "'O Romeo, Romeo, wherefore art thou, Romeo?'"

Clement cleared his throat. "Actually, Francine, the offer stipulates that Willow be cast as Juliet. They've read the early reviews, and one of the theater representatives was in Denver last month to see the final performance we had there. They were very taken with Willow and want her in New York as soon as possible."

A fountain of warm pleasure bubbled up in Willow's chest. "Really?" Her mind whirled with the possibilities. To play Juliet in New York City.

It didn't get any better than that for an actress.

"What?" Francine's incredulous voice silenced conversation and sucked the warmth out of Willow. "You're jesting, aren't you?"

"I'm not." Clement's voice held a bit of steel. "The offer is very specific. They want Willow in the lead role. Without her consent, the offer is void. Everything hinges on her."

Willow blinked. "They want me? For Juliet?"

A calculating expression flitted across Francine's face before she assumed a smile. "Willow, what an honor. I'm so happy for you." She came forward, gripped Willow's upper arms, and kissed the air beside her cheek. Willow held in a wince at the fierceness of Francine's hold and tried not to shiver at the brittleness in her eyes. They would talk about this later for sure.

Clement continued. "Let's get over to the reception before our guests wonder what's become of us. And for the moment, I would suggest we keep all this under wraps until the contracts are signed." He motioned toward the front doors but held Willow back when she lifted her hem to go. Francine threw a look back over her shoulder, but Clement waved her on. When they were alone, he rubbed his chin. "You need to consider getting an agent or manager to see to your career."

"Francine manages my career."

"That's been fine up until now, but you're destined for bigger things than Francine can deal with. You have no idea your own potential, Willow. Francine will never let your light shine brighter than her own, and hers is waning with each new season. You're on the cusp of an amazing career, bigger than hers, bigger than anything you ever imagined. You'll be famous, and your name will be on everyone's lips. You'll have more money and prestige than you can imagine. It's all there waiting for you. And you'll need someone to guide you, someone to manage things, especially the money you'll be earning. And if you will consider it, I'd like to present my services. I know this business, and I would have your best interests at heart. Would you consider it, making me your manager?"

The life he described—the fame, the fortune—while exciting, didn't seem real, as if he were speaking of another person. While she was flattered and pleased at the offer, her heart didn't skip the way she thought it should. Any rational mind would leap at this chance, right?

He laughed. "I can see I've taken your breath away. But Willow, your mother was a good friend to me, and she asked me to look after you girls."

"This has been a surprise." Her cautious nature exerted itself. "Do they need an answer right away? I'd like a little time to think about it, to sit down with you and go over some of the details, perhaps read the contract myself before I make up my mind."

Tucking her hand into his elbow, he led her into the hotel. "We have some time. A few weeks even, but I'm sure you'll find everything straight-forward. You think about it. It's all there waiting for you, and I'll help you any way I can."

Moments later, stepping into the reception room, Willow searched for Silas. She finally found him beyond the punch table.

And he wasn't alone. Her spine stiffened. Half a dozen young women surrounded him, eyelashes flicking faster than their painted fans. His white smile flashed as he bent his head to hear what one of them had to say.

Before she was ready, his glance met hers across the room. The same swooping, tingling feeling that had assaulted her when she first saw him in the balcony swept over her again obliterating Clement's news and the possibilities it offered. She took several breaths, but each seemed to clog in her throat. Someone at her side spoke to her, but she heard nothing but the beating of her heart.

Silas excused himself and threaded his way through the crowd until he stood before her. "I had no idea you were an actress. You were exquisite. Really amazing." His rich, velvety voice flowed over her.

A warm glow at his praise fizzed up and filled her cheeks. "Thank you. You really liked it?"

As if it were the most natural thing in the world, he took her hand, threading his fingers through hers and squeezing. "I was enthralled from the first scene."

Francine appeared at Willow's shoulder, her brow as serene as it had been stormy before. "Willow, darling, you made it at last." She appeared to notice Silas for the first time, and her lashes fluttered while her lips pursed into a small pout. "Hello." She held out her be-ringed hand. "I'm Francine Starr, and you are?"

Disquiet tiptoed up Willow's spine. She'd not told anyone about meeting Silas on the riverbank, not wanting to share for fear of rubbing some of the bloom off.

Francine had a predatory gleam and was putting herself out to be charm-ing. Would Silas, like so many others, be drawn to her great beauty?

Silas bowed and took Francine's offered hand. "Silas Hamilton. A plea-sure, Miss Starr. I enjoyed your performance very much this evening."

"My, my, Mr. Hamilton, you have a wonderful voice, so deep and full. Have you ever considered the stage?" Francine kept hold of Silas's hand, and Willow forced herself not to react.

He smiled, and deep creases formed on his cheeks. Not quite dimples, but almost. "I guess you could say I've done my share of public speaking, but I'm no actor. I'll leave that to professionals such as Willow and yourself.

Your performances were so compelling, I lost all track of time and place tonight. Of course that happens every time I'm in Willow's company." Though he spoke to Francine, his warm gaze locked with Willow's.

Francine arched one carefully sculpted eyebrow. "That is, of course, the goal of any actress, to captivate her audience to the exclusion of all else." Her glance went from Willow to Silas and back again, and Willow could almost hear the wheels turning.

A large, white-haired man clapped Silas on the shoulder. "Fine performance tonight."

Silas introduced him as Mr. Mackenzie and went on to make introductions for the rest of his party.

Willow smiled and talked and played her part, but in the back of her mind the uneasiness lingered, fostered by the appraising gleam in her sister's eyes.

Chapter 6

The evening after seeing the play, Silas fought to concentrate on his sermon notes. Every time he relaxed for an instant, his mind wandered to Willow. Because he found this a pleasant pursuit, he found his mind relaxing all too frequently.

She was exquisite. Everything about her appealed to him. And to find she was as talented as she was sweet and beautiful. . .

His chest swelled, and his mouth stretched into the ridiculous grin he'd spied on his face every time he looked in the mirror lately. Only the knowledge he had a sermon to prepare for the morning kept him from attending the theater again tonight.

His black-and-white tomcat hopped up onto the desk, crinkling papers and scattering notes. He sniffed the sermon notes and flopped down across Silas's open Bible, yawning and showing a lot of sharp white teeth and pink tongue.

"Come on. The sermon can't be that boring, Sherman." Silas cupped the furry head, smiling at the rumbling purr deep in the cat's chest.

The cat regarded him with green eyes before falling to licking his snowy paws. Silas propped his elbows on the desk and planted his chin on his fists. "I know. I should be working, but it's hard to concentrate."

A knock sounded on the side door. Grateful for the interruption, Silas went to open it.

"Kenneth, hello. What brings you out tonight?"

The young man stood on the stoop, his hat brim crushed in his fists. "Evening, Pastor. I saw your light on. Hope you don't mind me dropping in like this." He shifted his weight from foot to foot.

Silas stood back. "Of course not. My door is always open. I'm happy to see you. Though Sherman is a good listener, he isn't much of a conversationalist." He waved to where the cat lolled on the desk. "Come in."

Kenneth Hayes shuffled in, shoulders drooping.

Silas ran through what he knew about the young man and couldn't come up with a ready reason for his distress, but even his short time in the pastorate had taught him to be prepared for anything. What he saw with parishioners wasn't necessarily what he got.

"Have a seat." He directed the young man to the chairs before the cold fireplace. Kenneth was so ill at ease, having Silas sit behind his desk might scare him off altogether. Even now as he lowered himself onto the chair he looked about ready to bolt. "Would you like some coffee? I can brew up a pot in a jiffy."

"No, I'm fine." He tried to smooth out the creases in his hat, then rubbed his palms down his thighs one at a time. He swallowed hard.

Silas sat across from him. Leaning back, he relaxed hoping Kenneth could do the same.

Sherman dropped off the desk and came over to investigate the visitor. When Kenneth leaned down to scratch the cat's ears, Sherman ducked and moved away to sit on the cold hearth. He wrapped his tail around his feet and went still as a statue.

"Don't mind him. He's a bit antisocial. You'd think a cat living in the parsonage would learn some hospitality, but I haven't managed to teach him yet." Silas changed the subject. "I heard you got promoted over at the Mackenzie mine. Congratulations. Shift manager, isn't it?"

"That's right. Pay increase and day shift." Kenneth couldn't seem to find anywhere to look for long, and he avoided Silas's gaze completely.

Silas decided to jump right in. "What's bothering you? You'll probably feel better if you get it off your chest."

The young man's eyes widened, and his look collided with Silas's for an instant before dropping to the floor between his boots. "I guess you could say I have some girl trouble."

Silas nodded. "Girls do have a way of tying a fellow up in knots."

"This girl could give lessons." He fisted his hands and tapped on the arm of the chair. "I've never been so snarled up. She loves me. I know she does."

"And I take it you feel the same?"

Kenneth nodded, his shoulders slumping. "More than I can say. I can't stop thinking about her. I want to spend every minute with her, and I want to tell the world she's mine."

Silas blinked. Kenneth had summed up rather neatly the way Silas was beginning to feel about Willow. "What's holding you back?"

"She is. It's like she's ashamed of me or something. I want to go to her father and ask permission to court her, but she won't let me. Says she knows her folks won't say yes."

"What objection would they have?" Silas frowned. Kenneth was a fine, upstanding young man with good prospects. He had a good job, came to church regularly, and Silas had never heard of him getting into any kind of trouble.

"I'm not good enough, I guess. I thought getting promoted at the mine might change her mind, but she's standing firm." He sighed.

"Maybe I could help persuade her parents if you told me who she was."

Kenneth shook his head. "Naw, there's nothing you can do. She wouldn't like it if she knew I was here talking to you about it, but I'm going crazy. I had to talk to someone."

"If you aren't calling on the girl socially, where do you see her?"

A flush mottled his face, and he cleared his throat.

"I take it you've been together when her parents don't know?" Silas kept his voice as neutral as possible, wanting Kenneth to see the wrong without having to be bashed over the head with it.

"I know. It's gotten to the point where she's lying to get out of the house."

Silas pursed his lips, considering. "I can appreciate how you feel, being in love, wanting to be with someone. But you have to realize that a relationship based on lies and sneaking around is on rocky ground. She's put you in a bad position by not letting you declare your intentions, and you've put her in a bad place by encouraging her to be untruthful."

Kenneth rubbed the back of his neck and nodded. "I know."

"And you know you have one of two choices to make this right?" Silas leaned forward and put his elbows on his thighs, clasping his hands loosely. "You either have to go to her father and declare your intentions, or you have to stop seeing this girl. Nothing good will come from your continuing to meet in secret. You've already compromised this young girl's reputation by seeing her without her parents' permission."

"There's one other choice." Kenneth mumbled the words.

"Oh?"

"We could elope, just run off and get married. Her folks couldn't say no to me if the deal was already done." A defiant light sparked in Kenneth's eyes. His chin came up, and he gripped his knees.

Silas took a moment to marshal his thoughts and select his words. "That's pretty rash. I know you feel desperate right now, but I would caution you to think this through. If this girl still lives at home, then she's under her father's protection. It is her obligation to honor him. You don't even know if your suit would be denied. Before you do something as drastic and permanent as getting married in secret, it would be best if you talked to her father man-to-man. How would you feel if it were your daughter? Would you want her to run off and get married, or would you want to sit down and talk things out?"

The starch drained out of Kenneth, and he sagged into the chair. "You're right. You're not telling me anything I haven't told myself a hundred times. I guess I just needed to hear it from someone else. If someone ran off with my daughter, I'd hunt him down and fill him full of buckshot."

"Maybe you two are worried about nothing. Maybe her folks will like you just fine."

"I think they're aiming higher for their daughter than a simple shift manager."

"Who's to say you'll stop at shift manager? You've got great potential. The Mackenzies already see it, promoting you so quickly. I have a feeling, if you put your mind to it, you could own and operate your own mine before too long. Don't sell yourself short."

Kenneth shrugged and rose. "I've taken up enough of your time. Thanks for listening."

"Before you go, can we pray about this?" Silas invited Kenneth to sit once more. "I think we'll both feel better if we take it to the Lord."

At Kenneth's nod, Silas bowed his head. "Dear Lord, You know what's on Kenneth's heart. You know how much he loves this girl and wants to be with her, but You also know he wants to do what is right, what You want him to do. I pray You would give him courage to talk to this girl's father, and that if it is Your will, her father would consent to Kenneth courting his daughter. In all of this, we want to glorify You, and we ask for wisdom and for Your will to be made plain. Amen."

"Amen."

When Silas closed the door and returned to his sermon notes, he had to move Sherman off his Bible once more. The cat sat on the corner of the desk, staring at him unblinkingly.

Silas picked up his pencil and bent over his papers, but the cat's unnerving stare made the hair on the back of his neck itch. Finally he threw down his writing utensil. "Fine, you don't have to say it. I know."

Sherman gave one, slow blink.

"I know I need to ask permission to court Willow. It's hypocritical to tell Kenneth what he needs to do to make things right when I've been lax myself. I'll tend to it Monday morning."

❧

Willow kept her head lowered, hoping to slip into the church without being recognized. She stifled a yawn, wishing she could've skipped the reception last night. Falling into bed exhausted at three in the morning was no way to prepare for Sunday worship.

Organ music filled the room, and great blocks of colorful light fell across the congregation from the beautiful windows.

Willow found a seat near the back and placed her Bible in her lap. Worshipping with other believers after such a long absence felt like a favorite shawl wrapping around her. *I'm sorry I've neglected coming to church for so long, Lord. Please forgive me.*

She raised her head just a bit and watched her fellow worshippers from under the edge of her swooping hat brim. Silas must be here somewhere.

He'd mentioned church on more than one occasion. She studied the backs of the men in front of her and took surreptitious peeks at those on either side. The place was full. Perhaps he was up near the front. She spied the Mackenzie family, Silas's friends who had brought him to the theater. Perhaps he was sitting with them. Craning her neck slightly, she tried to see, but too many people blocked her way. Short of standing up and making a fool of herself, she had little hope of finding him. She'd have to wait for the service to conclude.

Focus on worship. That's why you're here, not to gawk after Silas.

A side door on the platform opened, and a tall man slipped in. Willow's breath caught in her throat. Though he had his back turned to her to shut the door, she knew in an instant it was Silas. He must be a deacon or something. Perhaps he was reading scripture before the pastor took the pulpit. Pleasure that he would be such an active member of the church warmed her insides. No wonder he was curious as to her church background.

"Please rise and open your hymnals to song fifty-four." His deep voice filled the room. He seemed so comfortable up front; he must help out with the services often. She could hardly wait to hear his singing voice, remembering how rich and mellow it was.

Fabric swished and pages rustled as the congregation found the right song. And when Silas began to sing, Willow wasn't disappointed. His voice reached her over everyone else's, and she wanted to close her eyes and savor the sound. Guilt at her distraction flew in on swift wings, and she found her place in the hymnal.

After the singing Silas invited them to join him in prayer. He spoke from the heart, his words sincere as he asked God's blessing on the congregation and their time of worship and on the reading of God's Word.

"Today, I'd like to begin a series of sermons on living a godly life. I'd like to open the Word with you and see what God has to say about our hearts and how they affect our actions. The text for today comes from Romans, chapter seven."

Realization swept over Willow, bringing numbness. Silas wasn't just helping with the service. He was the preacher. Her mind hop-skipped, trying to sort the ramifications of his occupation. Though she hadn't pegged him as a preacher, it certainly fit with his demeanor, the caring look in his eyes. But did it fit with the thoughts she'd had about him, the stirrings of romantic notions that had colored her world since she first met him?

Onionskin pages whispered, and Silas paused so everyone could find the passage. He read the chapter with conviction and feeling, and Willow's skin tingled. Such authority in his voice, such power.

"Isn't this just like us? Don't we often suffer the same affliction as the apostle Paul?" Silas scanned the crowd. "The good deeds we want to do we don't do, and the bad deeds we don't want to do are exactly what we find ourselves doing."

Drawn in by the power of his sermon, she forgot where she was, focusing on the truths revealed, immersing herself in once again sharing the fellowship of a church. His description of the struggle against sin mesmerized her. She tucked her lower lip in and pondered his words.

"We forget that as believers we are dead to sin, that sin no longer has the power to control us. We don't *have* to sin, even though we often behave as if we do."

The sermon ended all too quickly for Willow. Why hadn't she seen it before? The power and conviction behind Silas's preaching showed he was born to this calling. He couldn't be anything but a preacher. She was so proud of him that she wanted to stand and applaud.

As everyone rose for the closing hymn, his eyes locked with hers. That familiar and yet strange sensation of being deeply connected to one another made her skin tingle. She responded to his broad smile with one of her own, suddenly eager for the service to be over so she could tell him how wonderful his preaching was.

And yet, when the service ended, Willow hung back, trying to remain inconspicuous until the majority of the parishioners had greeted Silas and exited the church. Several people nodded and said hello to her. The Mackenzies greeted her on their way out. Silas glanced at her several times, smiling, asking her with his eyes to wait.

At last the crowd thinned to an expectant group of boys near the door. Silas came toward her, hands outstretched. "You came."

She returned the pressure of his fingers, unable to quell the joy bubbling through her. "It was a wonderful service."

"Are we going to go now?" The plaintive cry came from a small, tow-headed boy with rosy cheeks and pale blue eyes. "You said we could go right after church."

"Just a minute, Tick." Silas turned back to Willow.

"You have to go?" She tried to hide her disappointment and feared she failed.

His hands tightened on hers. "The boys and I are having a picnic and doing some fishing this afternoon. It's a reward for all their hard work in Sunday school. Every last one of them has memorized three different Psalms and the Ten Commandments this winter." He didn't sound as enthused as the boys, and she hoped it was because he didn't want to leave her any more than she wanted him to go.

But duty called, and he must answer. She nodded. "Sounds like fun. I hope you all have a good time."

"Say, why don't you come with us? The theater is closed on Sundays, isn't it? You can spend the afternoon with me and the boys and show off your newfound rock-skipping skills."

She glanced at the children. The younger ones didn't seem to mind, but the oldest one—tall, thin, and with a hank of black hair hanging over his forehead—rolled his eyes, shoved his hands in his pockets, and sighed.

"Phin, do you have any objections?" Silas asked the boy.

For a moment he looked as if he wanted to protest, but in the end he shrugged as if he didn't care one way or the other and herded the rest of the boys out the door.

She tucked her hand into Silas's offered arm. "I'd be delighted."

Chapter 7

Silas's blood hummed in his veins, and he knew he was wearing that ridiculous grin again, but he couldn't seem to help it and, truth be told, didn't really want to. Sunshine bathed the world in a yellow glow, and at the center of that world was Willow. The speed with which she'd captured his heart still amazed him, and yet it seemed inevitable, too.

The boys scampered ahead, their high voices piping skyward through the trees. Phin carried fishing poles, while Tick carried the bait bucket. The other three boys, the Hebig brothers, tussled, threw sticks and rocks, and chased one another like puppies.

"Estelle packed enough food for an army." Silas lifted the basket he carried in his left hand. Willow held his right arm, and he could feel every one of her fingers through his shirtsleeve, though she touched him lightly.

She clasped the picnic blanket to her middle. "Thank you for inviting me. I've never been on a picnic before."

"Never?"

"No. Theater life means a lot of moving and schedules and performance halls, not sunshine and fresh air and blue skies."

The wistfulness in her voice caught at Silas. "Then I'm glad you get to experience your first picnic with me. I'm an expert."

"Really? How did you become an expert?"

"I grew up in Sandusky, Ohio, on the shores of Lake Erie. My mother loved to go down to the shore and picnic, and we went dozens of times each summer."

She tilted her head as if trying to picture him as a boy, scampering along the shoreline with wind-tousled hair and rolled-up pants.

He could almost smell the lake and hear the scrape and shush of the water as it rolled in and broke on the shore. And he could hear his mother's laughter, which, like the warmer temperatures, always came out in the spring and disappeared in the fall.

"How about here?" Phin popped up at Silas's elbow. "Is this a sunny enough spot?"

"Here is perfect."

The boys fell to work spreading the plaid wool blanket and opening the hamper. Apples, rolls, fried chicken, cookies. In an incredibly short amount of time, they devoured their share and took off for the stream.

Willow, only halfway through her meal, blinked after their retreating backs. "They'd give a hoard of locusts a run for their money."

"They're boys. You wait. They'll be back before long looking for something to eat."

"They can't possibly. After all that food?"

"It's true. Estelle knows boys." He lifted a towel from the basket and revealed a pan of turnovers. "After they've run around for a while, climbed a few trees, and fought a few imaginary battles, they'll be back and ravenous."

"They seem like nice boys. I have to admit, I can't find any resemblance between Phin and Tick. Where did he get such an unusual name, anyway?"

Silas smiled. "You won't find a resemblance because Phin and Tick are adopted. Tick got his nickname because he always sticks so close to Phin. Though now that he's got a stable family, he seems to be gaining confidence and branching out a little on his own. He's also much stronger now that he's got steady medication. Tick's got a heart ailment, and before his adoption it nearly did him in a few times."

"That poor boy. I'm so glad he's found a family and a place to belong."

Again the wistfulness in her voice tugged at Silas. He had the urge to put his arm around her. "I met your sister the other night. Is it just you two, or are your parents traveling with you?"

She shook her head and lowered her chin until her hat brim shielded her face. "My parents are both gone now, my father when I was ten and my mother more recently."

"I'm so sorry. I know how that feels. My mother passed away when I was twelve."

When she raised her beautiful gray eyes, they were clear and untroubled. She busied herself folding napkins and stowing things in the basket. "So it's just Francine and me. But the acting troupe is like a family. My parents were both actors, and Francine and I have followed in their footsteps."

"So you've never known another life but the theater?"

"No. It's been my whole life up to now."

Her profile did all sorts of strange things to his concentration. When she turned to look at him, he found himself staring at her pink lips and had to tear his gaze away to focus on what she was saying.

"What do you remember best about your mother?"

"Rocks."

"Rocks?"

"She loved to collect rocks. We'd walk for miles along the lakeshore, and she would pick up rocks. Interesting shapes or colors. We'd take them home and polish them. Sometimes we'd find an agate and break it open.

Mother always said collecting rocks reminded her of how temporary we are and how big and powerful God is. Those rocks had been around since creation in one form or another, and here they were on the shore just waiting for us to come along and polish them up. And she could spot the potential, the beauty inside the rock that just needed to be let out. She said rocks were like people. If we let God polish us, He can reveal His good work in us until we can be things of beauty to glorify Him."

"I wondered why you had a handkerchief full of rocks the first time we met."

He grinned. "I still collect rocks, fossils, petrified wood, anything that catches my eye really. You should hear my housekeeper complain about dusting them. They are a nuisance, I suppose, but I like them. Though Sherman knocks them on the floor from time to time when he's put out with me."

"Sherman?"

"My cat. He came with the house. I named him Sherman because he's as relentless and bossy as a general."

"I'd love to meet him sometime."

"I have a feeling you will. Let's go see what the boys are up to." He took her hand and helped her to her feet.

When they got to the shore, the boys were ready to fish. Willow grimaced as they baited their hooks, and Phin swaggered a bit when he told her it was all right, he'd bait her hook for her since she was a girl.

"What do I do if I actually manage to snag a fish?"

"Holler and we'll come help you." Phin swung her hook over the water and handed her the pole. He scampered away to join the boys upstream.

Once he was out of earshot, she laughed. "He's quite the gallant young man under all that bravado."

"That's Phin. He wants everyone to think he's tough, but there's a heart of butter in there. Watch how he manages the younger boys. They think the world of him. Natural leadership there. I have a feeling he would make a great pastor someday."

"Speaking of pastors, I had no idea until today you were a minister. It's clear you're in the right profession. I've never listened to a more gifted preacher."

Pleasure shot through him at her praise. He shrugged, but he knew he'd pull out her words to treasure again later.

"Did you always want to be a minister?"

"I come from a long line of ministers, and I never really considered doing anything else. I can't imagine not being a pastor."

"Your father must be so proud of you."

He shook his head, his chest pinching. "I hope someday he will be. He's not too pleased at the moment. His plans for me never included a small congregation in Colorado. My father is Dr. Clyburn Hamilton, and he serves as the head of our denomination. According to him, I'm supposed to be teaching in the seminary where he is currently the president, writing theology books, and pastoring a large church in Philadelphia where he would be able to better oversee my advancement within the ranks."

"Why aren't you?"

"That might be right for some pastors, and I know a lot who would jump at the chance, but my calling is to preach and serve in a smaller congregation. My father didn't mind my getting a few years of experience in a church in Kansas City, but he's never approved of my taking this position. In fact, he's sending someone out to review my performance soon, and I have a suspicion if there is the tiniest blemish on that report, he'll see that I'm recalled to Philadelphia before the summer is over."

"He can do that?"

"He's the head of the denomination, and he's determined to bring me to my senses."

Her eyebrows drew together. "It's hard to live up to other people's expectations. Sometimes it's impossible. Opportunities arise, and you realize you have to take them, even if someone else is let down because of them."

"You sound like you speak from experience."

She shrugged. "I have a couple of decisions facing me at the moment."

"Anything I can help with?" He chuckled and covered her hand with his, thrilling at the jolt of pleasure that shot up his arm at the contact. "I'm a pretty good listener."

At that moment the cork float on her line jerked under the water. "What do I do?" She sprang to grab the rod before it landed in the stream.

The boys dropped their poles on the bank and pelted toward them.

Phin reached for her rod, but Silas stopped him. "No, let her do it. Everyone should bring in their first fish by themselves."

"Silas, please." She cast him a pleading glance. "Help me. What do I do?"

"Keep the line tight. Don't let it go slack, or he'll get a run and maybe break it. Keep the tip of the pole up."

The boys all shouted encouragement and advice.

Willow tucked her lower lip in, set her jaw, and braced against the tug of the fish and the current. In no time at all, she'd landed the trout.

"That's a beaut." Phin bent over the fish flopping on the grass. "Biggest trout I've seen."

"Is it?"

"What a whopper. Wait till Dad hears about this." Tick shoved his hair out of his eyes.

The Hebig boys whistled and crowed.

Willow seemed to take this for the applause it was. "What do we do with it now?"

"Take the hook out, put it on the stringer, and peg the line to the bank. Fish for supper."

"Oh no, don't do that." Willow knelt on the grass beside the fish. "The poor thing. I want to let it go."

"What?" Phin jammed his hands on his hips. "After all that work you ain't even gonna eat it?"

Willow cast Silas a pleading glance.

It hurt him to let the fish go—after all, people caught fish to eat them. But he said, "It's her fish. She can do what she wants with it." He lifted the trout and removed the hook. "But you have to let it go yourself. The fisherman in me can't do it."

With a squeamish grimace, she took the slippery animal and leaned over the bank. "There you go, you poor thing. I'm sorry for hauling you out of your home like that."

With a flip and a flicker, the trophy fish disappeared under the rippling water. She rinsed her hands in the stream and wiped them with her handkerchief. "I'm afraid I'll never make a fisherman."

"Just like a girl." Phin grabbed a rock and flicked it at the water where it bounced four times and sank.

"I'll tell you something I am good at though." She picked up another rock and sent it winging over the water. "Seven. Beat that."

The battle was on. They laughed and threw rocks and challenged one another to impossible feats until finally the boys declared they were starving. Willow brought out the turnovers. They ate, licking their fingers and dabbing at the crumbs, not wanting to waste a bite.

Silas leaned back on his palms and stretched his legs out. "You boys can play for another half hour or so. Then we need to head back."

As they bounded away, Willow shook her head. "You're very good with them."

"I was just thinking the same about you." And more. All afternoon he'd been captivated by her. Everything about her pleased him, and he could see her as the mistress of his home and his helpmeet in the church. He could envision her directing the Christmas play and organizing a children's choir. Better yet, he could see her opening his home to hospitality and welcoming him in after a long day at the church.

Silas leaned closer to her and lowered his head. His heart knocked against his ribs, and his palms sweat. He had a feeling his future happiness rested squarely on her answer to his question. "Willow, is there someone I should speak to about courting you? Someone I should ask?"

Her mouth opened, but nothing came out.

He wasn't worried though. The light that had come into her eyes—a look of wonder, hope, expectancy—was answer enough. He threaded his fingers through hers and pressed their palms together.

She found her voice. "There's no one you have to ask but me." She swallowed, pink coming to tinge her cheeks.

"And?"

"I'd like nothing more."

&

When they returned to the church, Silas introduced Willow to a waiting Sam Mackenzie, a handsome, easygoing man who put his arms around each of his sons while he thanked Silas for taking them for the afternoon. Mr. Hebig shook Silas's hand and gave Willow a quizzical look and bustled his boys into the wagon for the ride home.

"Let me drop this stuff off at the house. Then I'll walk you home." Silas lifted the bundle of fishing poles and the bait bucket.

"I'll take the basket and the blanket."

They rounded the church to the parsonage. "Just through here. Estelle doesn't work on Sundays, so there's no one here but Sherman." He set the poles on the porch and reached for her burdens. "I'd love to invite you in, but. . ."

"I understand." How nice to have someone so concerned with her reputation.

The minute Silas opened the door, an enormous cat stepped out, wound around his legs for a moment, and regarded her with brilliant green eyes. "This is Sherman. Now you be nice, cat, or you'll be sleeping outside tonight." He ducked into the house to put away the picnic paraphernalia.

Willow sank to the stairs. "Hello, Sherman. My, but you're a handsome fellow in your evening dress."

The animal tilted his head, listening to her, before approaching with his tail held high. She rubbed his cheek, and he butted his head against her hand and let loose a deep purr. Without fear, he climbed into her lap, lay down, and turned over, exposing his white belly for her to rub.

"I've never seen him do that before." Silas leaned against the doorframe and crossed his arms. "What a mush." He'd donned his suit coat and tie and smoothed his hair.

"He's just a big baby, aren't you?" She stroked his soft fur, and he wriggled with pleasure. "I've never had a pet before. We moved around too much. One of the actors in the troupe had a parrot once, but it bit and said naughty words, so my mother made me keep away from it. Sherman seems like a friendly fellow."

"He's usually content to rub against someone's leg, but he never lets a stranger pet him like that. I guess he's got good taste." Silas bent and rubbed Sherman under the chin. "Come on, you silly cat. I've got to get her home."

Walking to the hotel on Silas's arm felt so right, Willow didn't want the trip to end, but her stomach tightened as they approached the theater. What had she done agreeing to Silas's courting her? The offer from New York and all that hung upon her acceptance of it dragged at her like a ball and chain. The company was counting on her to get them to New York City, so much so that they were already making plans, assuming she'd said yes. Only Clement knew she'd asked for time to consider. "You don't have to walk me in. My sister will be waiting for me. She was going to run lines with Philip late this afternoon, and I was supposed to join them."

"Nonsense. I'd like to see where you work, and I'd like to meet your sister again."

Apprehension feathered across Willow's skin as she let them in through the side stage door. Though she knew Francine would eventually need to know about Silas, Willow was loathe to reveal their relationship so soon. What she felt for Silas—feelings that were growing every day—was private. And his desire to court her was so new and fresh that she feared laying herself open to her sister's criticism or judgment would somehow tarnish it. "We can peek in and see if they're here. If not, she'll be at the hotel." They walked down the narrow hallway full of doors. "This is my dressing room. Well, Francine's and mine. We share."

Passing into the wings, Francine's voice came to them, and Willow's heart sank. "Where has Willow been all day? When she left, she said she was going to church of all places. I don't know where she gets these odd notions."

Footsteps tapped on the stage floor, and heat rushed up Willow's cheeks. She called out before Francine could say anything else to embarrass both of them. "Is anyone here?"

"You're certainly late enough. Do you have someone with you?"

"I'm sorry for being late, though there was no set time for this rehearsal," Willow gently reminded Francine. "And yes, I've brought someone with me." Half the lanterns along the footboards had been lit, casting odd shadows on the painted backdrop depicting Ferndean Manor. "This is Silas Hamilton. You met him earlier this week. Silas, my sister, Francine Starr, and this is Philip Moncrieff."

Francine's eyes glittered. "So that's where you've been disappearing to. I might've known it. Meeting a man on the sly."

Philip rubbed his chin and leered. "Hmm, you've got some unsuspected depths, my dear."

Willow's back stiffened. "This is the *Reverend* Silas Hamilton. He pastors a church here in Martin City."

The transformation from petulant to flirtatious happened in an instant. Francine's eyelashes fluttered, her mouth went into a pout, and she held out her hand. "My, my, Reverend Hamilton. It is a pleasure to see you again. Willow tends to wander off at every opportunity, and I do worry about her. I had no idea she was in your company."

Silas took her hand briefly. "Miss Starr, Willow was kind enough to help me this afternoon. I had five small charges eager for a picnic. She accompanied me, helping me keep them entertained."

"You must call me Francine." She folded her hands at her waist and raked her gaze over Willow. "An afternoon shepherding children at a picnic explains Willow's windblown and disheveled appearance."

Instinctively, Willow's hands started up to smooth her hair, but she forced herself to lower her arms and stand still. It wouldn't matter anyway. The damage had been done. How many times had first her mother then Francine drilled it into her that she must appear professional at all times in public? It was her duty as an actress to preserve the illusion of perfection, lest the patrons of the theater decide she was a mere mortal, breaking the spell and thus the desire to believe in the performance.

"Willow always looks charming." Silas sent her a smile, his eyes seeming to drink in her face.

Philip strolled over to Willow's other side, standing way too close, nearly gagging her with the cloying scent of hair oil and cloves.

Silas squeezed Willow's elbow and guided her closer to his side. "Miss Starr—Francine—I'd like to invite you and Willow to dinner at the hotel tonight. I would enjoy getting to know you better." He turned to Philip. "You're invited as well, of course."

"Oh, he hasn't the time, since he's supposed to be blocking a scene with Clement in just a little while, but I'd be delighted to take supper with you." Francine edged between Willow and Silas, taking his arm and not bothering to look at Willow. "Thank you for looking after my little sister this afternoon. I'm sure she and the boys had a nice time on that picnic. It's so rare she gets to spend time with children her own age." She led him away, and Silas cast a helpless glance over his shoulder to Willow.

Willow ground her teeth. Just like Francine to put her in her place, relegating her to the rank of child who needed to be watched. She followed them, and Philip fell into step with her.

Philip's laugh slid over her like axle grease, thick and black, and he lowered his voice. "I thought there was something different about you lately. You've got even more of a dreamy-eyed look than usual. I suspect yonder swain is the cause? A preacher? How quaint. But don't expect Francine to take it lying down."

Willow said nothing and kept walking.

He leaned closer. "I always suspected your still waters ran deep." He reached for her hand, and she flinched. "A little seasoning will be the making of you, get you ready for New York." He laughed again and turned in at his dressing room.

"Willow? Are you all right?" Silas turned at the stage door to wait for her.

She straightened. "Of course."

Silas frowned. "Was that man pestering you?"

"Philip was just being Philip. It's nothing to worry about."

"Come along, Willow." Francine crossed her arms. "Stop dawdling with Philip. You've still got to clean up and change. I'm not going to be seen in public with you looking like that. While you're doing that, I'll freshen up as well."

Willow kept her chin high and refused to let her hurt or embarrassment show. One would think she would be used to the constant criticism, but somehow having it happen in front of Silas made it so much worse.

Chapter 8

Willow battled the diving swallows in her middle as she made her way downstairs to the hotel foyer, smoothing the skirts of her pale pink dress and fingering her single strand of pearls.

Francine came behind her, wearing the diamonds and an elaborate evening gown that showed off her tiny waist and curving bosom.

Silas met them at the foot of the stairs and led them to the dining room. The restaurant, lavishly appointed with chandeliers, crystal, china, and pristine linens, buzzed with conversation. Discrete waiters threaded through tables with laden trays.

"You look beautiful. That's a very becoming dress." Silas's look was appreciative and just a hint possessive, sending a thrill through her. He bent to whisper in her ear as he held her chair. "And I'm not just saying that. You take my breath away." He hadn't even looked at Francine.

"Men, aren't they funny?" Francine smoothed her bodice and opened her fan. "Of course you wouldn't know that dress is not exactly the latest fashion, but Willow insisted on wearing it tonight. I try my best, but. . ." She spread her hands as if she couldn't possibly be blamed for any of Willow's shortcomings.

The confidence his compliment had given her drained from Willow like an audience leaving a theater.

A waiter handed them each an enormous handwritten menu in a leather cover.

"Hmm." Francine sniffed, though she'd eaten in this same dining room daily and knew every dish on the menu. "I suppose this establishment isn't terrible, but when I think of some of the fine restaurants I've dined in. . . Have you ever been to New York, Reverend Hamilton?"

"Please, call me Silas, and yes, I've been to New York several times."

"Really? I'm quite impressed. So far, I haven't found a really well-traveled male in Martin City. Are you perhaps from somewhere back East?"

"Ohio originally. On Lake Erie. More recently my family hails from Philadelphia."

Silas smiled at Willow, sharing a private moment of remembrance. He didn't seem inclined to open up to Francine about his father the way he had to Willow, and she cherished his trust in her.

Francine spent the meal being charming and carefully edging Willow out of the conversation. Silas proved adept at including her, and when his hand came under the tablecloth to clasp hers, she wanted to laugh. He had caught on quickly to Francine's ways and didn't seem inclined to be blinded by her charm.

The waiter poured their after-dinner coffee. Would Silas tell Francine he was now courting Willow, or did he think Willow should be the one to share that information?

"Why, hello, Reverend Hamilton. I didn't expect to see you here tonight." A matronly woman Willow recognized from church that morning—she'd taken considerable time greeting Silas after the service—stopped by their table. A man and younger woman—a daughter?—stood behind her.

Silas rose, placing his napkin on the table. Though he smiled at the new-comer, Willow had the feeling it was forced. "Mrs. Drabble, good evening. Have you met the Starrs?"

The woman's eyebrows rose until they nearly collided with her hairline. "I haven't had the pleasure." An edge to her voice caused Willow to doubt any pleasure the woman might be claiming.

Silas let his hand rest on Willow's shoulder in a possessive gesture. "Have you had a chance to attend the theater? Willow is truly amazing as Jane Eyre, and Francine will delight you in her role as well. Willow, Francine, this is Mr. and Mrs. Drabble and their daughter, Alicia."

Mrs. Drabble's upper lip twitched like she'd just smelled sour milk. "Of course I haven't been to the theater. A young man asked only a few days ago if he could take Alicia to the theater. He left with no doubt as to my feelings on the subject of such idle entertainment. I'm shocked you admit to attending."

Willow knew that look and that tone. There were some who felt female entertainers were synonymous with fallen women, that they did more than sing, dance, or act for a living. Her cheeks reddened, but she held her composure.

Francine rolled her eyes and seemed to be sizing up the other woman. If it came to a war of words or worse, Willow's money was on Francine to win.

A bemused smile took hold of Silas. "Why should it surprise you that I would enjoy an evening's entertainment and culture? I enjoy a good thes-pian endeavor as much as the next man, minister or not. I'm expecting to attend several more times before this play has finished its run here in Martin City."

Mrs. Drabble gaped, not unlike the trout Willow had landed earlier that day. The resemblance caused a giggle to shoot out of her, and she tried to disguise it as a cough. From the stormy look the woman shot at her,

Willow had to assume she'd failed.

Her eye caught that of the young blond woman beside Mrs. Drabble, and she nearly giggled again at the mischievous light there. Something about Alicia Drabble appealed to Willow, and she thought they could easily be friends.

Mr. Drabble checked his watch. "I think it's time to go, dear."

When he had led his wife away, Willow relaxed.

Francine sipped from her cup. "A member of your congregation, I take it?"

"Yes, he serves as a deacon and she as a deaconess."

Willow swallowed. Silas didn't seem at all worried about how his courting her might affect his church, and he knew them better than she did, but she couldn't help the uneasy feelings coursing through her.

Francine placed her napkin on the table. "Thank you for a nice evening, Mr. Hamilton, but Willow and I should be going. We need our beauty sleep after all."

Silas pulled out her chair then Willow's and walked them to the base of the stairs. He held on to Willow's arm, letting Francine go up first. "I hope you have pleasant dreams. I'll call on you soon." His fingers squeezed her arm, and he took his leave.

Once in the hotel room, Francine eyed Willow. "You surprise me. Playing paddy fingers with the local preacher? Still, I guess you've found a way to amuse yourself for the next few weeks before we go to New York."

Willow unclasped her necklace and laid the pearls in their velvet box. She moistened her lips and swallowed, staring into the mirror on the dressing table.

"You are just amusing yourself, right?" Francine marched over and grabbed Willow's shoulder, turning her around. "Dally all you want, but don't let it go to your head. The entire company is counting on you. You heard Clement. Without you, there will be no New York City. If I thought for a minute you were serious about Silas Hamilton. . ." She searched Willow's face, then tipped her head back and laughed. "Of course you aren't. Nobody would turn down New York for a backwater preacher, no matter how handsome he is."

⁂

A week after his dinner at the hotel, Silas drew his chair up to the Drabble table. Time for pouring a little oil on the water.

"I'm so glad you could make time to visit. You've been so busy. Why, I even stopped by the parsonage twice in the evening this week only to find it dark." Mrs. Drabble set the last serving dish on the table and took her place across from Silas.

Walter Drabble bowed his head, mumbled a few words of prayer, and grabbed the soup tureen.

Alicia sat next to her mother, as pretty as always, but she reminded Silas of a porcelain doll, closed off and aloof. He knew it wasn't fair to compare her to the vibrant, glowing Willow, but he couldn't seem to help himself. Where Willow experienced life around her, Alicia seemed merely to observe. And yet, he chided himself. Perhaps Alicia was only unresponsive to him, as he was to her. Perhaps if she truly came to care for someone, she would come alive to that man, and he would see her as Silas saw Willow.

You're getting fanciful. You're seeing the world all rainbows and music. And all because of Willow.

"Aren't you hungry, Reverend Hamilton?" Beatrice held out the plate of roast beef, inviting him to take a portion.

"Oh yes. I'm sorry. It smells wonderful."

"Alicia made it." Beatrice beamed. "She's such a good cook, and she took such pains when she knew she was preparing dinner for you."

Alicia closed her eyes for a moment and took a slow breath. She picked at her food, rolling the creamed peas and onions on her plate with the tines of her fork.

Mrs. Drabble smoothed her hair toward the coil on the back of her neck—hair so black it must surely owe its jetty tones to artifice? "You didn't say where you were during the evenings this past week. Has someone fallen ill? Are you visiting parishioners?"

Silas finished chewing the tender roast and swallowed. "The members of the church seem to be in remarkably good health. I haven't had much visitation, and I've accomplished much of that during the day. I find evening visitation of the sick to be too disruptive to the household."

"I see. But if you weren't visiting, where have you gotten to at night?" Beatrice fixed him with a stare that said she wasn't going to give up until she knew his whereabouts.

"Actually, I've been enjoying the theater this week." Willow had left tickets for him at the office for any night he could come, and both times he could make it, he'd taken Willow out afterward to the hotel restaurant for coffee and long talks. He was already plotting when he could free his schedule up to see her again. If it wasn't for Mrs. Drabble's insistence and his twinges of guilt at avoiding her, he would be in the front row of the theater right now.

Mrs. Drabble sniffed. "Reverend Hamilton, you're young, so I'm sure you will appreciate the guidance of those with a bit more experience of life than you. I think, as someone who feels, well, a certain motherly regard toward you"—she cast a fond glance at Alicia then back to Silas—"I think I must caution you against your current actions. The theater isn't the best place for a pastor to be seen. As to socializing with those actors and actresses. . ." She stopped, shook her head as if any imbecile should know the dangers, and continued. "It casts a rather bad light on the church. You know as a pastor you are called upon to represent the church in the community. To have you frequenting that establishment and fraternizing with those people besmirches our reputation."

Silas held on to his temper. "Mrs. Drabble, I assure you there is nothing objectionable in the play, and the cast members are fine, upstanding people. Perhaps if you came to see the performance and spent some time with the actors, you'd see there's no harm in it. Several of the congregation have attended the play."

"You're leading them astray with such an attitude. They are partaking in questionable entertainment only because of your example." Her mouth puckered like she'd bitten into a green apple. "You act as if there is nothing wrong with such entertainment or the people who purvey it."

"That's because I do believe there is nothing wrong with it or the people. I would encourage the members of the church to see the play. It will edify and enrich, broaden their perspectives, challenge their minds, and give them much enjoyment, not to mention the interaction with others in the community." His voice had risen, and he strove to modulate his tone.

Walter ignored the conversation, shoveling food into his mouth and keeping his eyes on his plate. Alicia's eyes flicked to the clock on the wall behind Silas every few seconds as if willing the evening to be over soon.

"As to the people, I find them delightful." *Especially Willow.*

Mrs. Drabble put on her most patient face.

Silas gritted his teeth and took a firm hold on his tongue. Mrs. Drabble being annoying and opinionated was hard to deal with, but Mrs. Drabble being patient and instructive was worse. Much worse.

"I only caution you because I care. I understand what it is like to be young and to have your head turned by someone unsuitable." Here her glance shifted to take in Alicia, and she frowned. "It's hard to be objective when feelings become entangled. One might get the wrong idea if you were to keep company with one of those actresses I saw you dining with."

"Mrs. Drabble, thank you for your concern, but—"

"Now, hear me out. One must be so careful when one is in a position of leadership. If you were to become. . .entangled with an actress, even only in rumor, it would damage your reputation. Someone might get the idea you were actually courting one of those girls with the idea of marrying her. The person you marry must be suitable not only to your personality but to your position. After all, Caesar's wife must be above reproach, and bright is the light that shines upon the throne. . .or in this case, the pulpit."

He inhaled deeply and set his fork on his plate. "Mrs. Drabble—"

"Now, I know it's hard, but if you'll just listen to reason, there are plenty of nice girls in the church. As you know, I've cherished the notion that you might find Alicia more than pleasing. She would make a lovely minister's wife. She has a spotless reputation—I've seen to that. She can cook and clean and sew, and she's excellent with children and organization. And I'm sure you would agree she's more than passably pretty."

Silas pushed his chair back.

Alicia stepped in before he could say something. "Mother, that is enough." She rounded on Silas. "Why don't you tell her to keep her nose out of your business? Mother, I have no intention of marrying Silas Hamilton or anyone else you might try to push me at. Silas must be weary of it, and I know I certainly am."

Beatrice reacted as if she'd sat on a branding iron. She jumped up, threw her napkin on the table, and plunked her fists on her hips. "Young lady, don't you take that tone with me, especially not in front of a guest. You don't know what's best for you. I do. Now apologize to the reverend and sit down."

Alicia returned to her seat, but her eyes glittered with rebellion. "I do apologize to the reverend. Silas, I'm sorry for the way my mother tries to manipulate you. I'm sorry she's plotted our marriage when it's plain we are unsuited for one another. You've been patient and gallant. Too patient perhaps. I could tell the moment I saw you with Willow Starr you had great feelings for her. I only hope she returns those feelings for you. You deserve to be happy."

Mrs. Drabble sank to her chair, her mouth slack.

Silas was sure her daughter had never spoken so boldly against her mother. He admired her grit. Not too many folks had the fortitude to take on such a determined woman.

"Is it true? You have feelings for an actress?"

"That's right, Mrs. Drabble. I'm courting Willow Starr."

The shock vanished from her face, replaced by anger. "The board is going to hear about this. Can you imagine what the district supervisor will say when he hears? Not to mention what your father will say."

The threat in her voice tightened Silas's neck muscles. What would his father say about Willow? He folded his napkin. "I think it is time for me to go. I'm sorry you feel Willow Starr isn't right for me, but I am a grown man and able to make my own choice. I'm sure that when you get to know her, you'll recognize what a special young woman she is. I do hope you'll do your best to welcome her into the congregation."

As he walked up the hill to the church, he couldn't help but feel proud of

Alicia for finally standing up to her mother. At least that was one problem off his plate. No more trying to find a tactful way of evading Mrs. Drabble's matchmaking plans. And probably no more escaping her invitations to dinner. He doubted he'd be invited back anytime soon.

As to what his father would say. . . He sighed. It had been such a long time since he'd pleased his father in any way. Their communications tended to be formal, stilted, and on his father's side at least, loaded with long-suffering patience as he waited for his son to get his ridiculous notions out of his system and return to the life mapped out for him since birth. Silas was sure Willow Starr factored nowhere in his father's plans.

But clearing the air with Mrs. Drabble had assured Silas of one thing. He knew without a doubt his heart belonged to Willow. He was in love, and he couldn't wait to find just the right way to tell her.

Chapter 9

A busy week followed his dinner at the Drabbles, and he found himself unable to spend much time with Willow after all. Mrs. Drabble sent word she would be unable to help with the orphanage. He knew he should go see her and try to smooth out the rift between them, but he kept putting it off.

Sunday morning, Mrs. Drabble was absent from church, though Alicia and Mr. Drabble attended. He tried to speak to Walter Drabble before they left but got waylaid by the Mackenzies and an invitation to lunch. Mr. Drabble slipped out, taking Alicia with him.

Willow came to church, edging into the back at the last minute, and at the Mackenzies' insistence was included in the lunch invitation. The meal and the company were excellent and encouraged Silas. Willow was especially taken with the baby, and something about seeing her holding an infant, so enraptured, made Silas's insides turn to porridge.

Monday evening, Silas found himself yawning right after supper. "Sherman, if I didn't have these church records to catch up on, I'd fall right into bed."

Sherman seemed unconcerned, continuing to wash his snowy paws.

Another yawn overtook Silas, and he scrubbed his hair, stretching and trying to wake up. He hadn't been sleeping too well. Thoughts of Willow kept him awake. And the issue of the ill feelings between himself and the Drabbles. He was also worried about Kenneth Hayes. Since their talk, Kenneth had missed several Sundays in a row at church. "Tomorrow I need to go see him."

If Kenneth had made his intentions known to the girl's father and been rejected, it might explain his absence, but if he'd put off asking permission and didn't want to face Silas, that might also prompt him to avoid church. And there might be another reason altogether. No matter. It deserved investigation.

A knock sounded on the door, and Silas levered himself up from his desk. He hoped whoever it was wouldn't want to stay long, and he squashed that inhospitable thought before it could take root. If someone needed him, he was there to serve.

Jesse Mackenzie stood on the porch, his face like a thundercloud.

"Evening, Jesse. What's wrong? Is it Matilda? Or one of the grandkids?"

"No, no, nothing like that. The board has called a special meeting over at the church." He shoved his hands into his pockets and rocked on his heels.

Silas blinked and reached for the doorjamb. "A special meeting? Tonight? What for?"

"Mrs. Drabble called it. Well, I suppose officially Walter Drabble called it, but she's pulling the strings, same as always. Says he's got something important that needs to be discussed."

Silas reached for his suit coat and tried to tamp down his ruffled hair. "Is everyone there?"

"Yep, the whole board, elders and deacons and the two deaconesses. Mrs. Drabble seems to have made a good recovery from whatever kept her away from church yesterday." Jesse paced the porch. "She won't say why she called the meeting, just insisted everyone attend, especially you."

A knot formed between Silas's shoulder blades as he shrugged into his coat, but he cautioned himself against giving in to dread and despair. If only he hadn't put off going to see her. These kinds of problems never got solved by ignoring them. "Maybe something to do with the orphanage again. The open house is set for next week." A weak hope, but something to grasp on to.

Jesse shrugged and continued to pace the porch floor while Silas doused the lamps and closed the door.

Lights blazed from the church windows, and Silas paused on the top step to appreciate what a pretty picture the white-steepled building made with all the colored glass windows.

When they entered the building, the tension in the room bombarded him. Five people stared back at him, six if you included Jesse. Two elders, two deacons, and two deaconesses. Matilda wore a worried look but smiled encouragingly, while the Drabbles looked grim. Mrs. Drabble in particular looked as if she were sharpening her verbal knives. The other two, Larry Horton, a deacon, and Ned Meeker, an elder, had separated into their usual seats. Larry sat with the Drabbles, and Meeker just behind Matilda. Jesse strode up the aisle and took a seat next to his wife.

"Good evening." Silas walked up the aisle and turned to face them. "I'm afraid you have me at a disadvantage. I don't know why this meeting has been called. Does it have something to do with the orphanage?" He searched Matilda Mackenzie's face, but she shook her head and gave a slight shrug. Clearly she'd been kept in the dark as well.

Mrs. Drabble poked her husband in the ribs. "Go ahead."

Walter took his time unfolding himself from his seat. "Silas—"

"Reverend!" Mrs. Drabble hissed the word, poking him again.

Walter began again. "Reverend, it has come to the attention of the board that you may be. . .socializing with an undesirable element. Some of the board members feel you shouldn't do this." He sat down again and folded his arms across his chest.

"An undesirable element?" Silas's heart began to thud, and his ribs squeezed tight.

Mrs. Drabble leaned forward and grasped the back of the pew in front of her. "Don't pretend you don't know. You told me with your own mouth you were courting an *actress*." Her eyes glowed like coals, and hectic color stained her cheeks. "It's unseemly, and it's got to stop."

Silas braced his palms on the railing that divided the platform from the pews. "You called a board meeting to discuss my private business?" He kept his voice even, but his fingers bit into the banister.

Her chin went up. "You have no one to blame but yourself. I tried to follow the biblical procedure. I tried to talk to you about this privately in my home, but you wouldn't listen. Now I have no choice but to bring it before the board."

Jesse leaned forward. "Is this about Willow?"

"Exactly." Mrs. Drabble snapped off the word like a breaking a twig. "And what kind of outlandish name is Willow anyway? It's probably not her real name at all. All these actor-types use fake names. It's like lying."

Every time she spoke, Larry Horton nodded, and Silas had the feeling she'd been over it all with him already. He seemed firmly in her camp.

Larry squinted. "I can't believe this even needs to be brought up. Everybody knows women entertainers are of low character. You might's well have paraded up Main Street with one of the working girls from the Lead Pig Saloon on your arm as bring that actress to church."

Silas's head snapped back. "That is a scurrilous remark if I ever heard one. You're making generalities and assumptions that could have serious consequences. Rumors like that do a lot of damage, and I take exception to you speaking that way about the woman I'm courting."

Jesse nodded. "Have you even met this girl, Larry? Do you know her? I have. She's been a guest in my home. She's as lovely and charming and as good as your own daughters. I'd stake my silver mine on it." His mighty fist slammed down on the rail before him. "She's an actress, and a very good one, I might add, and nothing in her behavior indicated she had anything in common with a saloon girl. As far as I'm concerned, she's welcome in my home and in this church."

Larry's neck grew mottled with red splotches. "We're not talking about your home, and she's certainly welcome to attend church and change her ways. What we are talking about is Silas keeping company with a woman of poor reputation and compromising the work of the church and the very Gospel he proclaims."

Matilda cleared her throat. "Larry, those are some very strong words. As Jesse has said, we've attended the play being performed, and we've had Willow in our home, not to mention meeting her at a reception in the hotel where her manners and behavior were exemplary. She's done nothing and said nothing to indicate she is of low moral character. In fact, it is just the opposite. She speaks of her faith naturally and openly. You mentioned her reputation, but reputation is something manufactured by others. Reputation has nothing to do with character, and everything I've witnessed tells me her character is very good."

Ned Meeker raised his hand. His pale eyes looked out of a face as wrinkled as crumpled paper. He had years of wisdom, experience, and leadership to draw on, and Silas had always found him a good advisor. "Folks, how many of us here have met the young lady in question?"

The Mackenzies raised their hands.

Mrs. Drabble did as well. "I met her at the hotel restaurant where our pastor was dining with her and her sister. Bold as anything."

Ned pursed his lips. "Have you spoken to her beyond saying hello?"

Silas cast back to that evening and realized Beatrice hadn't even acknowledged the Starrs beyond a scowl or two.

"Well no, not to say spoken to. But I'm no fool. I know what I know."

Ned eased himself to his feet, his knees cracking. "Folks, this whole meeting leaves a rather bad taste in my mouth." His gnarled hands grasped the pew ahead of him, and his breath wheezed, testament to years spent in mine shafts and rock dust. "Pastor Hamilton has never given us cause to doubt his judgment. If he says Miss Starr is a fitting companion, then that's good enough for me. There's them that talks about being good and aren't, and them that are good and find themselves talked about." His gaze rested heavily on each one there before he eased back down onto the pew and rested his hands in his lap.

Matilda turned and patted his hand.

Silas decided it was time for him to step in. "I thank you, Ned, for your support, and you, too, Jesse and Matilda. I think the crux of the matter here is that there have been opinions formed without knowing the facts. Perhaps if you were to get to know Willow, you'd all come to see what I've seen." He looked sternly at the Drabble contingent. "All I'm asking is that you give Willow a chance. Get to know her and the other folks at the theater. I'm not saying they're all saints, but Willow is a fine young woman, and I intend to marry her."

Mrs. Drabble sucked in a gasp and coughed. "Marriage?"

Silas frowned. "Mrs. Drabble, surely you didn't think I would court a woman if I didn't think she was suitable for marriage?"

She fanned herself with her handkerchief. "You mean you would refuse my daughter and all the other nice church girls in favor of an *actress*?"

"Mrs. Drabble, I don't think a church board meeting is the place to discuss this. Alicia and I have made our feelings clear to you on this matter. She has no more interest in marrying me than I have in marrying her."

Larry stood and creased the crown of his hat, his jaw set like granite and a flinty look in his eye. "Looks to me that even if we was to vote, we'd be split, just like usual, and the pastor would break the tie in favor of himself. But I warn you, if you bring that woman into the parsonage, you'll find more than a few families in this church unhappy about it. Not to mention the denomination. I haven't turned in my questionnaire yet, and neither have a few others. If you insist on cramming this woman down our throats, you might find yourself on the outside of this church looking in."

He jammed his hat onto his head and stalked out. Mr. and Mrs. Drabble followed after him, leaving Ned and the Mackenzies.

Silas sank onto the front pew and put his face into his hands. He'd been blithely following his heart while a chasm opened between his feet and split the church board right down the middle. He had underestimated Mrs. Drabble's vitriol. Larry's words both surprised him and hurt him, since he'd never borne any ill will toward the man and had assumed they were not only friends but had a mutual respect for one another.

Jesse squeezed Silas's shoulder. "I'm sorry, Silas. I had no idea this was coming, or I'd have tried to head them off somehow."

He raised his head to look at Jesse, Ned, and Matilda. "What should I do about this?"

Ned pursed his lips and rubbed his hand down his cheek. "For now, nothing. Best to let us try to talk to them. They're so worked up, I have a feeling anything you tried to do would be taken wrong."

Matilda threaded her reticule over her wrist. "What about the supervisor's visit? We really should try to get this resolved before his arrival. A church board with daggers drawn wouldn't be the best endorsement for our pastor's leadership abilities."

Silas shuddered, imagining what his father would say. *"I told you not to take that church. You've failed. Failed me. Failed the denomination. Failed God."*

"Now Matilda, don't tease like that. You've made Silas go white as a winter moon." Jesse whacked him on the shoulder. "I'm sure we can get this thing turned around before it comes to that. You're a fine pastor, and you're not doing anything wrong. The church will see that, and Beatrice will, too, once she gets over her peeve at you not marrying Alicia."

"I hope you're right. I just know if people will give Willow a chance, they'll come to love her like I do."

"Leave it to us. We'll see what we can do." Jesse helped Matilda to her feet.

❧

Early Tuesday afternoon Willow slipped from the theater in search of solitude and a place to think. Philip had been particularly obnoxious today, standing too close, whispering crass comments and suggestions until she wanted to slap his face. He'd gotten worse ever since he'd learned Willow was seeing Silas, as if her being in a relationship with a man meant she was open to much more.

The early morning showers had given way, and the world reminded her of a freshly scrubbed child, rosy and warm. She lifted her face to the sunshine, letting it warm her through, trying to forget for a moment the expectations and responsibilities of the theater, especially those of Philip and Francine. And yet no amount of fresh air and sunshine could lift that weight.

What was she going to do? Clement was pushing for her to sign the contract, Francine had already started planning her new wardrobe for a New York fall season, and more than one of the cast and crew had congratulated Willow on her success and commented on how they were looking forward to the big city.

And every moment she spent with Silas, every long walk, every time he held her hand, every time he caressed her face, bound her more and more to him and his future here. How could she choose? How could she follow her heart and stay when her head said she had to go?

Downstream the trees grew closer to the water, and Willow had to duck under their branches. The game path she followed beckoned her to continue, and she wended her way along Martin Creek farther than she'd ventured on previous rambles.

Around a bend, the trees opened on a little glade with a cabin in the center. As she stood undecided whether to go on or turn back, a movement caught her eye.

The door opened, and a man and woman emerged. The woman threw herself into the man's arms, and he kissed her.

Willow realized she was intruding on a private moment, and she turned to hurry away. Her foot landed on a twig, snapping it like a rifle shot. The couple broke apart, and Willow froze.

She knew them. Or the girl, at least. Though she was disheveled, Willow recognized the girl she'd seen in the hotel restaurant with Mrs. Drabble. This had to be Alicia. Silas had mentioned in passing that Mrs. Drabble recently had hopes of his marrying her daughter, but that they weren't at all suited. And here she was alone with a man in an isolated cabin. Tears streamed down the girl's cheeks, and her shoulders shook.

"Are you all right? Do you need help?" She didn't want to intrude, but neither did she want to leave the girl if she truly was distressed. Willow took the measure of the man still standing in the doorway holding Alicia's hand, but he seemed to pose no threat to her or Alicia.

Regardless, they shouldn't be here alone together, and the guilty looks on their faces said they knew it.

Alicia held out her hand. "Please, don't go."

The man frowned. "What are you doing?"

"We can't go on like this. I have to talk to someone—" She broke off on a sob.

The man shoved his hands in his pockets and stared at the ground.

Willow walked up the slope slowly. "You're Mrs. Drabble's daughter, right? Alicia?"

"Yes." The girl hung her head.

Knowing she must choose her words carefully, Willow clasped her hands at her waist. "Are you in some kind of trouble?" Stepping close to Alicia, she lowered her voice. "Does your mother know where you are?"

"No, and she can't know." Alicia grabbed Willow's arm. "Please, promise me you won't tell her, and please, please, don't tell Silas." Tears flowed down the girl's cheeks, and she bit her lower lip. Dropping her clasp on Willow's wrist, she turned and threw herself into the man's arms, sobbing on his shoulder.

He held her tenderly, his face a mask of misery and tenderness. "You're that actress, Willow Starr, aren't you?" He spoke across the top of Alicia's head.

"Yes, I'm Willow Star." She eyed the young man and leaned a bit to the side to see into the cabin. A table and two rough chairs, a cold fireplace, and a bed in the corner with the blanket hanging half off comprised the furnishings.

"My name's Kenneth Hayes. All I did was kiss her, I promise. Nothing else happened."

Willow pressed her fingertips to her brow and squeezed her eyes shut, trying to think. Alicia's sobs made it difficult. She wanted to believe them. What should she say? What should she do? What would Silas do in this situation?

Opening her eyes, she decided to take charge. Clearly neither of these two was capable at the moment. "Alicia, stop crying and come down to the stream with me. We'll wash your face, and you can try to get a hold of yourself." She motioned for Kenneth to stay behind. "We'll be back."

Alicia sniffed and nodded, following Willow like a child.

When they reached the stream, Willow handed her a handkerchief. "Wash, and we'll talk."

"You won't tell my mother, will you? Or Silas?"

"I won't make a promise I can't keep, Alicia, and I won't lie. You know meeting a man alone like this is wrong. If anyone came to find out, you'd be ruined. Who is Kenneth Hayes anyway?"

"He's the man I love more than anything in the world. And he loves me." She dabbed at her red-rimmed eyes and blotchy, damp cheeks. "I've loved him since the moment I first met him."

Willow kept her voice neutral. "You realize you're compromising your reputation by meeting him here? And you're putting yourself in a situation where things could quickly get out of hand and overwhelm you. You might find yourself, in the heat of the moment, doing something you'd later regret."

Alicia wadded the handkerchief into her fist. "I know, but what can we do? I knew my mother would never let me marry Kenneth, and he even went to Silas for advice. Silas said it was Kenneth's duty to ask permission to call on me, that sneaking around was wrong." A hiccup jarred her. "So he did. He asked permission, and they refused. Mother wouldn't hear tell of my marrying a mere miner. And Father does whatever Mother says. She threatened to lock me in my room or send me away to my aunt's. And she forbad me ever to see Kenneth again."

"I'm sorry, Alicia, but is sneaking around the best choice here?"

"It's the *only* choice. What would you do if you couldn't be with the man you love?" Her chin lifted, challenging Willow to walk in her shoes for a while.

Her heart broke for the couple. What an untenable position. If she had to stop seeing Silas, it would break her. She couldn't imagine her life without him. The power of her love for him overwhelmed her, changed how she saw the world, how she saw herself. In that moment, indecision fell away, and her future crystallized. She was willing and ready to give up her career and everything it offered the minute he asked her to. Her future was here, with Silas.

"I don't know what to tell you, but I do know you have to stop seeing each other in secret. Meeting together like this, away from everyone, with your feelings so strong, eventually your emotions are going to get the better of you, and you'll cross a line you can't get back over ever again. Please, go to Silas together and ask him what you should do. He'll help you. He can talk to your parents."

"He can't. My mother is so angry with him right now I don't know what she would do if he showed up at her house. After his last dinner at our place, she wouldn't take a diamond-studded suggestion from him. I've never seen her so angry. Then there was the board meeting. If she was angry before, she was white-hot afterward."

"What happened?"

"When Silas came over for dinner, we both made it clear to Mother that marriage to each other was out of the question. Mother already knew I was in love with Kenneth, and Silas all but declared his love for you. She really let him have it, about how you weren't a suitable candidate for a pastor's wife and how he owed it to his congregation to choose someone who was above reproach. She's very class conscious, and she thinks actresses are the lowest form of society."

A cannonball took up residence in Willow's chest. Poor Silas. She closed her eyes for a moment against the pain of prejudice. Why hadn't he told her any of this?

Alicia sniffed. "I don't feel that way, and I don't think the majority of the congregation would feel that way. It's just Mother has these odd ideas, and once she sets her mind on something, it's hard to get her to change it." She shook Willow's arm. "I think you're perfect for Silas. He's so nice, and he deserves to be happy. And he is so happy now that he's met you. He'll be a better minister, and the church will be better for his marrying you."

Willow savored the words for a moment, allowing them to soothe the hurt of Mrs. Drabble's dislike, but there was still the issue at hand to deal with. "Thank you. I hope what you say is true. Now that you've calmed down a bit, we should talk with Kenneth. He's worn a path in front of the cabin."

As they walked up the bank, Kenneth stopped pacing and shoved his hands into his pockets. "Are you going to go to her parents or the preacher?"

"No, but you should. Both of you." *Lord, help me be bold to speak the truth, but in a way that they will hear and respond to. Give me the words.* "Kenneth, it's plain to me you love Alicia dearly, and she clearly feels the same for you."

He nodded and put his arm around Alicia. "I'd do anything for her."

"If you truly love her, then you want to protect her from any harm. You're endangering her reputation and both of your characters by meeting like this." She swallowed and looked from one to the other. "If you continue, no good will come from it."

Kenneth rested his chin on Alicia's head. "How is it you know so much? You can't be any older than Alicia."

Willow sighed. "I'm right out of my depth here, but I'd hate to see you two ruin your lives. I've come to the conclusion that if God puts a fence around something, He means it to be there."

She glanced at the sun. "Alicia, it's getting late. We should go."

Kenneth's arm tightened around Alicia. His face twisted in anguish as he brushed a kiss across her temple and bent for a moment to rest his forehead on hers, as if afraid he might never be with her again.

As Alicia slipped from his arms, Willow offered one last plea. "Please, go see Silas again and explain everything. I'm sure he can help you both."

Walking along the stream bank, conscious of the need to hurry, Willow contemplated the young couple's situation. Had she helped the situation or only made it worse?

Chapter 10

And you're sure it's not a problem? Not with the board or with the church?" Willow smoothed her skirts, swaying to the rocking of the buggy. Worry over what his church thought had her tossing and turning most nights and fretting during the day until she couldn't wait any longer to broach the subject.

"Don't worry about it. Jesse and Matilda and Ned told me not to worry, and I'm telling you. Mrs. Drabble is a bit upset, but she'll get over it." Silas flicked the reins. "Jesse is proud of his mining operation. The minute I told him you'd never been in a silver mine, he insisted I bring you to his."

Willow let the matter rest, not wanting to mar their happiness with talk of unpleasant things. This afternoon was a gift, precious time with Silas, and she intended to make the most of it.

They pulled to a stop at the top of a steep grade. Silas hopped from the buggy and came around to help her alight. "I'm glad Jesse provided the transportation, too. Since I live alone, I usually go everywhere I need to on foot or on horseback." He smiled. "Looks like I might need to see about getting another conveyance in the near future."

Willow bit her lower lip to control her smile. The warmth in his eyes spread through her clear to her toes. "I'm a little nervous. The thought of being so far underground with all that rock over my head. . ."

He squeezed her hand. "You don't have to go down if you don't want to."

"No, I do. And I wouldn't want to disappoint Mr. Mackenzie after he's been so generous. I'll be fine as long as you're with me."

Jesse stepped out onto the porch of a wooden building, spied them, and jumped down without bothering to use the steps. "You made it. Great. We just finished the shift change, so the bucket's free."

They followed him to an open-sided shed. Willow whispered to Silas. "The bucket?"

He winked. "They lower us into the mine via a big bucket. That's how they get the ore up, too. Then they load it into carts, and it travels on these tracks over to the stamp mill." He pointed to the rails and ties leading away toward a tall building built into the side of the mountain from which pounding, grinding, crushing sounds rumbled and rolled. "They crush the rock there and use chemicals to extract the silver and lead and whatever other metals or minerals they are looking for."

Jesse motioned to a worker who pulled a lever, starting a clanking donkey engine and bringing an enormous metal container to the surface. "Here you go." He held out a hand to help Willow over the side.

Her heart lodged in her throat, and her mouth went paper dry. She tried not to think of all the empty space beneath her feet nor the darkness. What had come over her to say yes to this venture?

Silas swung his long legs over the rim of the bucket, setting it to swaying and making her stomach lurch. Jesse joined them, bringing a lantern along, and they began their descent. Yellow light bounced off jagged rock, and the chain rattled as it unwrapped from the winch overhead. Several pipes ran down the shaft.

Jesse pointed. "For pumping in clean air and pumping out water. Always a problem trying to keep a mine dry. There's talk of building a communal tunnel through the mountain someday to drain the mines above it."

Down, down, down. The farther they descended, the higher her heart rose in her throat.

Silas found her hand and slipped his arm around her waist. "You're freezing. Are you all right?"

She nodded. "It's rather. . .thrilling, isn't it?"

Jesse raised the lantern. "We'll go down about six hundred feet today. This shaft goes deeper, but we'll stop there and head into a side stope. My son David is the mine engineer, and he's got a nose for silver that puts every other engineer in the Rockies to shame. This stope is the richest we've ever brought in."

The bucket lurched to a stop beside a tunnel on Willow's right.

Jesse clambered out, holding the lantern high and reaching to help her. "Here we go. Watch your head, Silas."

Rock gritted under her shoes, and the whole place smelled like damp earth and dust. A trickle of water ran down the wall toward the vertical shaft and disappeared over the edge. At periodic intervals in the tunnel they walked, iron rings had been driven into the side walls at about head-high and held tallow candles that dripped onto the rocks below. The clink of metal on metal came to them, the sound magnified by ricocheting off the walls.

"Here we are." Jesse stopped beside two miners with pickaxes and metal hats. "We've cleared this tunnel after the last blast, and these men are drilling new holes for more explosives."

The miners straightened, their faces gleaming with sweat and streaked with dirt. They removed their gloves, and the taller one took a kerchief from his pocket and swiped his face. "Boss." He nodded. "It's pretty slow going through here, but we're making progress. Should be ready to blast tomorrow if everything goes well."

"Sounds good." Jesse blew out one of the candles, removed it from the holder, and hung the lantern in its place. "Boys, you know Pastor Hamilton? And this is Miss Starr. You might've heard of her, too. She's one of the actresses putting on the play at the new theater."

"Preacher." They nodded, but they didn't look at Silas. Their eyes were on her. Dirty, hardworking, smelling of earth and sweat and smoke. Hard-rock miners. "Miss, it's a pleasure to meet you." The spokesman of the pair removed his hat to reveal a balding head, and the one who had yet to speak nearly tripped over his feet to shake her hand.

Francine would have a fit if she knew Willow was socializing with common laborers, but Willow didn't care. These men were the salt of the earth, as good as anybody and better than many of the people Francine sought approval from. She took his grimy hand, smiling. "I'm pleased to meet you. You've very brave working so far underground like this. Please, tell me what it is you're doing here. I've never been in a mine before, and I'm eager to learn."

ॐ

Silas hid his smile, but he couldn't quell the satisfaction and pride he had in Willow. Her kind reception of a class of men she'd most likely not come into contact with before pleased him greatly. There she stood between two rough miners, listening avidly, accepting them for who they were and not worrying if she got her dress dirty.

The miners responded to her friendliness, telling her everything they could about what it was like to dig for precious metals in the bowels of the earth.

"The engineer tells us how deep to make the holes and in what pattern. When we've got it just right, the powder man sets the charges." The taller miner pointed and made twisting motions with his hands as if connecting fuses. "Then we clear the mine, and"—he made a plunging motion with his hands—"kaboom!"

The shorter miner, not to be outdone, elbowed closer. "After the dust settles, we come back in and start clearing the rock. Out it goes to the shaft and up to the stamp mill, and there you go. In the end, they have lovely silver pigs."

"Pigs?"

He rubbed his nose with the back of his hand. "Yep, when they're done extracting the metal at the stamp mill, they pour it into bars called pigs. Then they ship them out by rail to places where they refine it and turn it into teaspoons and sugar tongs and the like."

Jesse tugged on Silas's sleeve and pulled him aside. "She's great with them. I wondered how she'd take to the workers, but you'd think she'd been with them all her life."

"She's interested in people. Just like she was with the Sunday school boys. Treats everyone the same."

"She'll make you a fine little wife if you can get Mrs. Drabble off your back. She hasn't let up about you courting an actress. I've tried, and Matilda has tried to get her to see reason, even to go to the play and see for herself there's nothing objectionable in it, but she won't budge. She truly believes the theater is wicked and so is everyone associated with it."

Silas loosened his jaw muscles. "Thanks for trying. I'll confess I'm at a loss to know how to continue. I've tried to apologize and let her know I have no ill feelings toward her, but she is adamant that she is right, and nothing short of total capitulation on my part will satisfy her."

"That kind of narrow thinking tends to sow discord in a congregation. I've seen things like this cause such a rift between folks that a church fractures. I don't want that sort of thing to happen in this church. They're a fine group of folks, but having Mrs. Drabble dripping her unhappiness into everyone's ears is bound to have an effect."

"What do you think we should do about it? I can't give up Willow just to make Mrs. Drabble happy, but what if the church comes apart? What if the district supervisor is of the same mind as Mrs. Drabble and forces me to choose between Willow and the church?" The very thought had kept him awake for hours each night, praying, searching his heart and the scriptures.

Jesse leaned his shoulder against the wall and crossed his arms, the lantern light flickering across his face and making shadows. "I'd hate to have to make this a matter of church discipline, but the truth is she's gossiping and spreading ill feelings, and she's not respecting the authority of the pastor. If I thought for a moment she had a real issue, if you were doing something contrary to scripture or detrimental to the church, I'd be the first to come to you with it. But you're not doing anything wrong by courting Willow. She's a believer, right?"

"Yes. I made sure before I asked to call on her."

"And she's a good girl—anyone who has spent five minutes with her can see that. She's kind and generous and sweet. A woman a man could be proud to call his wife. Matilda likes her, and I'd back my wife's judgment anytime. Mrs. Drabble needs to stop what she's doing and leave you two alone, or there's going to be real trouble."

As they rode the bucket back to the surface, Silas tried to ignore the heavy, churning feeling in his gut. Real trouble in his church. How could he avoid it and keep Willow? He was sure she was the one God wanted him to marry, but how could he if it meant dividing his church? He'd been called to be a pastor. He couldn't fail his parishioners, not even Mrs. Drabble.

When they stood in the bright sunshine again, Willow breathed deeply, turning her face to the warm rays. "I'm so glad to be out of there. I could never work in a mine. I'd suffocate."

"I wouldn't have guessed, the way you were talking to those miners. Thank you for being so nice to them. They'll be talking about it for a long time."

Jesse blew out the lantern and returned it to a shelf in the shed. "Before I forget, I wanted to thank you for the tickets for the men."

"Tickets?" Silas's eyebrows rose.

"Yep, she's giving tickets to all the Mackenzie miners over the next week or so." Jesse grinned. "A block of ten front-row seats every night this week."

Silas reached for her hand. "That's very generous of you."

Her cheeks went a little pink, and she shrugged. "I wanted to show my appreciation to Jesse and to the workers for letting me tour the mine. Jesse, they can call for the tickets at the window. I'll let them know in the office."

"And I'll deliver the tickets to Mrs. Drabble like you want, but don't get your hopes up."

Silas took Willow's hand. "What's this?"

She shrugged. "I thought if only she would come to the theater and see for herself what the play was like, and maybe come to the reception afterward, she could see we're not evil people bent on dragging God-fearing folks to destruction. It's worth a try, anyway."

Chapter 11

Willow took Silas's helping hand and climbed out of the buggy behind the rear stage door. She smiled at the guard posted there and stepped into the familiar area of the theater away from the stage, breathing in the scents of fabric, dust, makeup, and kerosene lamps. Everything known and familiar.

Silas closed the side door behind them and put his hand to the small of her back to guide her through the hallway. "We aren't late, are we?"

Willow edged around an open trunk frothing with costumes and props and stepped over a rolled-up canvas backdrop. "Someone needs to organize these things better. We're constantly tripping over equipment. And no, we're not late." Glancing through the open door of her dressing room, she spied Clement and Francine deep in conversation.

Not wanting to intrude, she tugged Silas's hand, drawing him toward the wings of stage left. The indigo velvet drapes surrounded them. "I used to watch my mother every night from the wings when I was a little girl. The feel of velvet always brings back those memories." In the low light of the performance theater, she studied his face.

"I wish I had known you as a little girl. You must've been adorable, all big eyes and ringlets. Did you always want to act? Did you dream of taking the stage?" He took her hands and drew her toward him.

"No, not really, but it was all I knew. For Francine it is a burning passion, and one she and my mother shared. I think Mother never really knew what to do with me. Francine says I was a homely child, awkward and clumsy. Francine was ten when I was born, and I guess I was a bit of a surprise to my parents. They thought they were done having children. Then my father passed away, and my mother had two girls to support with her acting. When she died, it was just Francine and me. Francine lives for the stage and the fame and the starring roles. And I. . ." She swallowed. "I feel like I have just been existing, putting in time, until now."

He brushed the hair away from her temple, his touch as soft as mist. "So you might be happy away from the stage? You could be content in another way of life?"

"It would depend on what that other way of life was, but yes, I could be very happy away from the stage." Willow breathed deeply, inhaling his scent—soap and sunshine and Silas.

"Hmmm." His voice rumbled deep in his throat, and he eased his arms around her waist. "What if that life was with me?"

Her hands went up his lapels and twined around his neck. "Then I think I could be very happy indeed."

He bent his head, brushing her lips with his, sending a shock through her. Her eyelids fluttered closed, and his embrace tightened. Again his lips caressed hers, and then more forcefully as if he wanted to consume her. She poured all the love in her heart into that kiss where it met his love like the crashing of a wave on a rocky shore.

Never had she expected to find something like this, so powerful, so precious, so perfect.

When the kiss ended, he continued to hold her close, his breath harsh against her cheek.

"Willow Starr, I love you as I've never loved anyone. Please say you'll marry me. Say you love me and you'll share my life forever."

Her hands came up to cup his cheeks, and she looked deeply into his dark brown eyes, as velvety as his voice. She swallowed, trying to absorb all the wonderful sensations coursing through her, wanting to remember everything. The feeling that together they could conquer anything, that they could tackle any problem and come out the victors, swept over her. Worries about his church and her acting company slipped away, drowned by the love in his eyes and her heart. "Yes, Silas, yes. I love you, and I will marry you." She could've stayed there in his arms all evening, but a clatter of footsteps and the sound of voices forced them apart.

Silas, as if reluctant to break contact with her, raised her fingers to his lips, planting a kiss across her knuckles before turning her hand over to place a kiss in her palm. He closed her fingers and squeezed, winking at her. "I'll be watching the performance tonight. You'd best get changed and ready before someone comes looking." He turned her around to head her in the right direction. "I'm going to nip home and change, but I'll be back."

Her mind still spinning and her heart full to bursting, she nodded and made her way to her dressing room. Clement and Francine had vanished, which was just as well. She couldn't have borne it if her sister made some condescending or trite comment that rubbed the bloom off the moment.

She stepped into her costume for the first act and fumbled with the buttons, her hands shaking. An uncontrollable urge to dance, to laugh, to sing, to somehow let the entire world know of her happiness kept breaking over her. And when she sat at her dressing table to arrange her hair and put on her makeup, the stars in her eyes dazzled her. She wore the unmistakable look of love.

❧

Silas couldn't stop grinning. He hurried to the parsonage, grateful to still have the loan of Jesse's horse and buggy, though the time he saved in travel was eaten up by having to unhitch and turn the horse out into the glebe. A hasty wash, fresh shirt, and carefully knotted tie, and he was on his way back to the theater on foot.

Following Willow's instructions, he bypassed the still-locked front doors and entered at the side of the building under the knowing eyes of a stagehand. "Evening, Parson. You're back quick. Gonna be a good show tonight."

Silas nodded. "Thanks, Bill."

The hallway bustled with cast members and crew as curtain time approached. He navigated the props and scenery stacked along the hallway, flicking a glance at Willow's closed dressing room door as he edged past a man in a frock coat. He recognized the actor as St. John in the play. At least it wasn't that rather oily fellow who played Rochester. Something about him raised Silas's hackles. He chuckled. Unreasonable, really. Projecting his jealousy of Willow onto the circumstances of the play. He paused to allow two stagehands carrying a desk between them to pass.

"Excuse me, are you Willow's friend? The preacher?"

Silas swiveled to locate the voice. A slender, pale man in a tan checked suit leaned back in a chair in a side room.

"Yes. I'm Pastor Hamilton."

"Come in. I was hoping I'd get a chance to speak with you soon." The man rose and held out his hand. "Clement Nielson. Director."

Silas shook his hand. "Willow speaks very highly of you."

"I'm glad. I think quite a bit of her myself, which is what I wanted to talk to you about." He motioned to an empty chair and resumed his own. "Has she told you about the offer she's received to play Juliet this fall in New York? A starring role in one of the biggest theaters in the country. It's the opportunity of a lifetime."

Silas sat up and leaned forward a bit. "This fall? New York...as in city?"

"That's right. You can't imagine the prestige that comes along with a role like this, especially if the actress can deliver the goods. And Willow can. She's the most gifted, natural actress it has been my privilege to work with, and she will be the darling of the New York theater crowd. Money, fame, the best of everything. It's all waiting for her."

Silas struggled to grasp the significance of the director's words. New York, this fall? But what did that mean for him? Willow had only an hour before agreed to be his wife. "Has she accepted?"

"No, and that's what I want to talk to you about. I've put it to Willow, and she's been silent on the subject ever since. An added pressure is that without Willow's consent, none of us are going to New York. I told her to take her time and really consider the options, but our time's running out. I have to know her answer, and I'm afraid of what it will be."

Silas gripped his knees, his mind reeling. "She hasn't mentioned any of this to me."

"You'll be wondering what my stake is in all this." Clement picked up a letter opener from the desk and toyed with it. "When I first told Willow of the offer, I suggested she needed a manager, and I proposed myself for the job. She would need someone who truly had her best interests at heart to look out for her in the big city." He quirked his eyebrow. "As you can imagine, Francine is far from being that person. I proposed myself for a couple of reasons. First, I truly do care about Willow. She's a wonderful young woman who hasn't had the easiest job being Francine's sister. And second, Willow's father was my best friend, and I promised him I would look out after his girls."

A stagehand knocked on the half-open door. "Five minutes to curtain."

"Thank you, Mel. Now"—Clement continued as if he hadn't been interrupted—"you're probably thinking that I would push Willow to accept the role, go to New York, and make us all famous, but you'd be wrong. I've watched Willow the past few weeks since she met you, and I can say without reservation, I've never seen her happier. It's like she's all lit up inside. I think she wants a home and a family more than she wants anything, and I think you're just the man to provide her with those things. She's not cut out for the big city and all the demands she would meet there. I want her to be happy, and I think she's happy with you."

Silas sat back, stunned by this turn of events. "That's very big of you."

The director shrugged and pushed himself up. "I just wanted to warn you. Francine won't take this lightly. I'll do what I can to protect Willow, and you need to do the same. It might be best if you eloped before Francine could do anything about it."

Though the idea strongly appealed to Silas, he shook his head. "No, I won't marry Willow on the sly, as if we were doing something wrong. I have a ministry and a congregation to consider. We'll be married in the church and in the presence of our friends. She agreed just today to be my wife."

"I guess that means I'll have to tell New York and this acting company that Willow is retiring from the stage." Clement shoved his hands into his pockets. "On the one hand, it's too bad. The theater is losing a great actress, but on the other, I'm very happy for you. Congratulations. But watch out for Francine. She's not a woman who enjoys being thwarted, and she was counting on New York."

Silas made his way to the balcony box seat Willow had reserved for him, his mind in turmoil. He was grateful and flattered that Willow had chosen him over such a fantastic opportunity, because it meant she must truly love him, and he was glad he hadn't known about the offer before he'd proposed.

The sweet memory of her kiss, of her arms around his neck and her fingers tangling in his hair, of holding her close swept over him. And just as sweet, her declaration of love and promise to be his wife. He needed to make plans to tell his congregation soon.

Which meant informing Mrs. Drabble. He scanned the boxes and seats, hoping Mrs. Drabble had accepted Willow's peace offering and attended the play, but he couldn't see her anywhere. A knot squirmed in his stomach.

The curtain went up, and the play began. True to her word, Willow had reserved seats on the front row, and a group of miners and their wives sat together, faces rapt. She was so generous and sweet, surely once the congregation took the time to get to know her all reservations would be dropped and they would embrace her and accept her as his bride.

Once more her performance took his breath away, and she played the part of a young woman in love so well he had to quell his jealousy of Mr. Rochester again. At the conclusion, the audience surged to its feet. The miners were especially enthusiastic, stomping and whistling, bringing the cast back again and again for curtain calls, though it was Willow's name they shouted the loudest.

Her eyes met his. A flush decorated her cheeks, and her eyes shone. She waved to him, and with refreshing spontaneity, she blew him a kiss, which set the audience into another uproar. He couldn't wait to be with her again. They had so much to talk about, and if he could manage it, he planned to get at least one more kiss before saying good night.

He made his way down the stairs. When he reached the foyer, he was surrounded by the men he'd met at the Mackenzie mine earlier that day. They pumped his hand, grinning, introducing their wives and girlfriends, thanking him and asking him to be sure to pass their thanks along to Willow for the tickets. Best time they'd ever had, and wasn't she something?

Silas wholeheartedly agreed. It was all he could do not to announce to every person he saw that Willow was his fiancée. A steam engine of anticipation surged away in his chest. He couldn't wait to see her again. Though he wanted to bolt around to the back of the building and wait for her at the stage door, he couldn't be rude to these men. Anyway, it would take her some time to change. Telling himself to be patient didn't make the wait any easier.

One of the miners shoved his hands into his back pockets and lowered his voice to speak just to Silas. "Reverend, I haven't made much of a point of going to church in the past few years, but after meeting you and Miss

Starr, you can count on me being in the front row come Sunday morning. And I know a lot of the other fellows feel the same. Most high-quality folks like Miss Starr wouldn't bother to spit on hard-rock miners if they was on fire, but she was kindness itself. If she wasn't so sweet on you, and I wasn't old enough to be her pappy, I'd go after her myself. You're a lucky man." He grinned, deepening the lines on his face.

"Blessed. I'm a blessed man." Silas nodded. Here was proof positive for the congregation that Willow would be an asset to his ministry. Come Sunday morning, everyone would see what a perfect pastor's wife she would make.

Chapter 12

The applause, especially from her guests in the front row, thundered through the performance hall and made the lamplight flicker. It was hard not to respond to such wholehearted approval. Her cheeks hurt from smiling. Philip held her hand on one side and Francine on the other as they bowed, answering yet another curtain call. With each trip back onto the stage, her sister's grip tightened until Willow's fingers stung. She finally extricated herself from them both to wave and accept the flowers the miners offered from the edge of the stage. Her eyes sought Silas's in the balcony, and the warm pride and love in his expression echoed louder in her heart than the applause of the crowd.

The minute she stepped out of view of the audience after the last round of cheering, she blew out a big sigh. How she'd managed to remember her lines and hit her marks, she didn't know, since all she could think about all evening was Silas and his proposal. And his kiss.

She was getting married. Squealing and hopping around probably wasn't the best way to express her happiness, but she was very tempted. A giggle erupted as she tried to imagine what Francine would say at such a display. Willow decided to save the squealing and hopping until she could be alone.

Cast and crew thronged the wings, their conversations washing around her like a tide. She caught sight of Francine disappearing into Clement's office. Good, she'd have the dressing room all to herself.

Though her blood sang in her veins and she had a feeling she could fly right up to the catwalk with happiness, the draining of strength that always followed a performance had begun. A quick glance at the clock as she entered the room told her she should hurry, or Silas would be kept waiting. She laid aside the flowers and stepped behind the screen in the corner to rid herself of her costume.

Once into her own clothes, it was a matter of minutes to remove hairpins, brush out the severe style, and pin it up in her natural, loose knot. Clasping her string of pearls around her neck, she ran her fingers over the cool beads. A little ache pinched her heart. She wished her father were here. He would've loved Silas.

Glancing at the clock, she reached for her handbag. He must be at the stage door by now.

A knock sounded. Silas. Grinning, she ran to open it. "I'm sorry to keep you wait—" She stopped, deflated.

Philip.

"What do you want?"

"What kind of greeting is that?"

"Francine isn't here. I think she's in Clement's office."

"I didn't come to see Francine."

"Well, I hope you didn't come to see me, because I've got to go. I'm meeting someone." She held on to the edge of the door, waiting for him to step back.

"That goody-goody preacher? I don't understand what you see in him, and I never would've expected a pastor to enjoy a little springtime dalliance. I bet you thought no one saw you throwing yourself at him in the wings before tonight's performance. I have to say, you surprised me with your. . .ardor?"

Her cheeks flamed, and her throat tightened. He'd seen? Who else? Her hand went to her throat and tangled in her necklace.

A sneer smeared Philip's mouth. "Still, you live and learn. I hope you don't break his heart when this play is done and we move on to New York."

"For your information, when *Jane Eyre* finishes its run, I'm not going to New York. I'll be staying with that 'goody-goody preacher' who has asked me to marry him. And his name is Silas Hamilton. You may call him Reverend Hamilton."

Fire shot into Philip's eyes, and he put his hand flat on the door, pushing his way inside the dressing room and forcing her back. He closed the door behind him. "What are you talking about? You can't possibly mean to stay in this backwater with that no-account pulpit pounder. What about New York? What about me?"

Anger sizzled in her veins at his maligning of Silas. "You don't enter into this at all. And Silas isn't a no-account. He's worth a dozen of you with change left over, you arrogant toad. Now get out of here. You shouldn't be in a lady's dressing room." She pointed to the door.

His scowl deepened, and she moistened her dry lips. Fury emanated from him in waves, and she backed up another step.

"Arrogant toad?" In two strides he crossed the small open space and grabbed her wrist. "So, you'll share your favors with the preacher, but not with me? Well, if you won't share, I'll just take what I want."

"Let me go, Philip. You're going to regre—"

She understood his intent a fraction of a second before his lips came down on hers. His hand clamped on her jaw, and he pushed her up against the wall. Pummeling his shoulder with her free fist, she struggled to break the kiss, but he paid no heed to the blows, and she was pinned so effectively she couldn't get a good swing. His lips squished against hers, and his hands maintained their iron grip. His solid body blocked any escape attempt, pressing against her.

Why didn't someone come? Where was Francine?

Silas. Where are you, Silas?

Tears stung her eyes. Keeping her lips rigid, she let herself go limp, hoping to catch Philip off guard. He raised his head and stroked the hair at her temple. "That's it, my sweet. I knew you'd give in to me if you just gave yourself the chance."

Gathering all her strength, she shoved against his chest, forcing him backward using the wall for leverage. "I'll never give in to you. If you ever lay a hand on me again, I'll scream." She bolted for the door, but her feet tangled in her hem, slowing her down.

Philip grabbed her around the waist and flung her down on the chaise Francine used for preperformance naps. She bounced and scrambled, trying to evade his clutching hands. When his face loomed over hers, she slapped it as hard as she could.

"Why, you little—" He caught her wrist, and she let out a shriek.

The door flew open and hit the wall like a rifle shot. "Willow?"

"Silas!"

In an instant, concern, comprehension, and anger crossed his face. He was on Philip in a single leap, tearing the actor away from Willow.

Philip swung his fist, connected with Silas's left eye, and sent him reeling. Turning back to Willow, who had frozen at the sight of her beloved storming to her rescue, Philip reached for her again. "I'll show you, you little minx."

She scrambled off the chaise, clutching for something, anything to ward him off. Her fingers closed around the vase standing ready for flowers.

Before she could swing it around, Silas's arms came around Philip's shoulders, dragging him away from her. Staggering, they crashed into the wall. The impact loosened Silas's grip, and Philip swung around on him.

Silas was ready. His fist smacked into Philip's jaw, dropping him into a heap on the floor. His chest heaved, and his eyes sought Willow's.

People crowded into the doorway, headed by Francine. "What on earth is going on here?" Her imperious voice cut the air.

Willow let the vase slip from her hands, and it met disaster, shattering near Philip's head and bathing him in china bits and cold water.

He groaned, roused by the dousing.

Willow ignored him and flew to Silas.

His arms opened, and he gathered her close. "Are you all right? He didn't hurt you?" He whispered the words against her hair, and she raised her hands to cover her face, shaking and shivering in spite of his embrace. His heart thundered under her ear, and his breathing rasped.

"Willow, please, tell me if you're hurt." He raised her face and peeled her hands away.

Looking into his eyes, she bit her lip and shook her head. Feather light, she touched his eyebrow and the swelling already starting there. "I'm not hurt. But your eye." By tomorrow he'd have a purple shiner.

Movement behind her made her turn her head. She placed her palms on Silas's chest to steady herself. Philip groaned again and lurched to his feet, assisted by one of the stagehands.

Clement elbowed into the room. "What is all this?" He looked from Silas to Philip and back. "Moncrieff, what have you done?"

"Why are you blaming Philip?" Francine asked, her cheeks red and eyes snapping. "He's the injured party here. That man knocked him right out."

Clement put his hands on his hips, very much the boss and commander. "Well?"

Philip put on a martyred air and touched his jaw, wincing. "It was just a little misunderstanding."

Silas gathered himself to protest, and Willow tugged on his lapels. "Don't," she whispered. "Just get me out of here, please?"

His arms tightened, and his eyebrows came down—well, one came down, the other was too swollen. "You're sure?"

She nodded and moved to his side. He kept his arm around her waist.

Clement studied them for a moment and turned to the faces in the doorway. "All right, get moving, folks. The excitement's over."

Reluctantly, the doorway emptied. Philip cast Willow a black look and made for the hall.

Clement stopped him. "I'd like a word with you in my office, Moncrieff. I'll be there shortly."

Philip's footsteps could be heard all the way down the hall, and a door slammed.

Willow relaxed, sagging into Silas's side.

"Willow, what is the meaning of this? Two men brawling in our dressing room? Look at this mess." Francine waved toward the broken glass, the water puddle, and the costume rack now toppled onto the floor. "And what did you do to my chaise?" The lounge had been knocked askew and all the pillows scattered in the melee.

"Francine, perhaps now isn't the best time." Clement put his hand under her elbow. "I'll send someone to clean this up. For now, perhaps you'd like a cup of tea? I know these little upsets can be stressful for such a high-strung, creative talent as yours."

At his placating, solicitous tone, Francine lost a bit of her imperiousness. "Yes, I could use a cup of tea." She took his arm and allowed herself to be led away.

At the last minute she looked back over her shoulder. "Willow, we will discuss this later." And her expression boded ill for Willow's already fragile peace of mind.

৯

Silas let Willow push him into a chair, though he should have been the one comforting her.

She went to the pitcher on the stand in the corner, wet a cloth, and brought it back. "Your poor eye. Does it hurt?"

"No, I'm fine." He took the cloth and held it against the sting. "I'm more concerned about you. What happened?"

She blew out a breath and crossed her arms at her waist.

A shudder shook her, and he reached for her hand, drawing her down until he held her on his lap like a little girl. Smoothing her disheveled hair away from her face, he asked again, "What happened? You can tell me."

"We were. . .arguing, I guess. He saw us before the play—when you proposed." A delicate flush pinked her cheeks, and she swallowed. "I guess it made him angry. He's made advances before, and I've always put him off."

His arm tightened around her waist. Advances? He wanted to punch the scoundrel again. Though not a man of violence—Silas couldn't remember ever punching anyone before—the strength of his protective fury surprised him. He didn't regret knocking Philip Moncrieff out one bit.

She tucked her head onto his shoulder. "I told him I was going to marry you, and I called him—" She broke off, embarrassment coloring her words. "I called him," she whispered, her breath brushing against his neck, "an arrogant toad."

He wanted to laugh. His gentle, sweet Willow a spitfire? Keeping his voice even so she wouldn't think he was laughing at her, he said, "And that made him mad."

"Very. He said if I wouldn't share my kisses with him, he'd just take what he wanted." She sat up, her gray eyes inches from his. "I really think he only wanted a kiss, but I fought him, and he seemed to lose control. Things got out of hand so fast. I'm glad you came through that door when you did."

"I am, too." Silas wanted to drop a kiss on her adorable nose, but he forced himself to refrain. "What happens now? Will Philip be fired?"

She studied her hands in her lap. "I don't know. It will depend on what Philip tells Clement. There isn't anyone in the cast who can take over

Philip's role as Mr. Rochester. Though I wish there was someone. I can't stand pretending to be in love with him in the play. It was bad before. It will be nauseating now."

"You can't think to continue after what happened tonight?"

"I have to. I have a contract with the company, and no matter what happens behind the scenes, I have to honor it. The show is the most important thing, and over the next three weeks, I *am* Jane Eyre. I won't let Philip prevent me from doing my job."

Determination stared out of her eyes, and while he admired her grit, the thought of her enduring the presence of that cad for twenty-one more days twisted his innards. He planned then and there to have a talk with both Clement and Bill, the guard at the back door, about seeing that nobody, especially Philip, bothered Willow again. And as much as he was able, he'd be at every performance to see she got to the hotel safely. "What about Francine? What will you tell her?"

"I'll tell her the truth about what happened, but I don't expect her to take it well."

"Have you told her about our engagement?" Just saying it aloud pleased him. Made it more official. She took the wet cloth from his hand and dabbed at his eye. Her fussing pleased him, too. It was nice to have someone care about him.

She caught sight of the back of his hand and gave a little squeak. "Oh, your knuckles."

He glanced at the split skin, bruised knuckles, and swelling. Philip's jaw had felt like punching an anvil. He flexed his fingers, trying not to wince.

She dabbed at the cut, her lower lip tucked behind her front teeth. The soft crooning sounds she made sounded sympathetic and contrite at the same time.

He caught her hand to still her ministrations. "My hand will be fine. Did you tell Francine about our engagement?"

"I haven't told her yet. There wasn't time before the show, and you'll think I'm silly, but I wanted to. . .I don't know, savor it for a while before I let anyone else know." She folded and refolded the damp cloth.

"I don't think that's silly at all, though I admit I had just the opposite reaction. I wanted to shout it from the housetops. I wanted to yell it from the balcony the minute the play ended." Eyeing the open door, he stole a quick kiss. "Clement told me about the job offer from New York. Honey, I want you to be sure, really sure you would rather marry me than accept that role." Though it raked his heart to say it, he knew he had to. "I don't want you to have any regrets."

Her eyes widened. "He told you?"

"It's a big decision, affecting not just your future but the entire company. You know I want you to stay here and marry me, but I can't ask that of you unless you're very sure. Especially since not everyone will be happy if you turn it down."

She twined her arms around his neck and rested her head on his shoulder. "Silas, I'm sure. I've never been so sure. New York has nothing I need. Everything I want is right here." She pressed her hand to his chest just over his heart.

His throat lurched, and he tightened his hold. "I'd better get you to the hotel before it gets too late. Considering everything that's happened, I think the sooner we announce our engagement the better. Sunday morning—two days from now—after the morning service, I'll let the church know." Ignoring the thrust of worry at what some of the church members might say, he hugged her. "Let's get you home."

The desire to protect her nearly overwhelmed him, and it was getting harder and harder to drop her off at the hotel each night. They needed to decide on a wedding date, and whenever it would be looked a long way off to him.

Chapter 13

I won't have it. You're going to get this nonsense out of your head and accept that offer, and that's that." Francine sat propped up against the head of the bed, her hair in twin plaits on her shoulders and her face a mask of white cream. She rubbed goose grease into her hands from a small pot on her lap. "And causing a row with Philip? Whatever did you say to lead him on that way?"

Willow put the brush on the dressing table and met her sister's eyes in the mirror. "I did nothing to lead him on. Philip didn't need any encouragement from me. He's been pestering me for some time, and he finally got what he deserved."

"You must've done something. Philip wouldn't have given you so much as a nod otherwise. It's just like you to try to steal him from me."

"Steal him?" Willow turned on the bench. "I didn't realize he belonged to you. I don't want him. You can have him gift-wrapped for all I care, though you'd be foolish. He's a cad and a rogue, and I can't wait to be away from him."

"You're not fooling me. Playing one man against another. Did you feel triumphant when they fought over you?"

"I was appalled and grateful to Silas for coming to my aid. Philip deserved to be trounced, and he was. If you'd heard what he said to me, what he tried to do to me, you wouldn't be so eager to defend him."

"You're being melodramatic, as usual. I'm sure the situation could've been resolved with a few words instead of fists. Philip will be furious. And he has every right to be. I'm so angry with you I could scream. You're just being selfish not taking the job in New York. How can you be so stupid?"

"It's not stupid to fall in love. I love Silas, he loves me, and we're getting married."

"But what about me? What about the company?"

"The company got along just fine before I came along, and it will do just fine without me. New York isn't the only place Clement got offers from, and he'll book you somewhere for the fall. I thought you'd be happy I was leaving. You've done nothing but gripe about me getting the lead in *Jane Eyre*. With me staying here, you'll have top billing again."

"Don't do me any favors." Francine tugged gloves over her greasy hands and slammed the pot of goose grease onto the bedside table. The crystals hanging from the lamp swayed as she swung her feet out of bed. "Clement will sign us up for some other mining town or cow camp, and I'll never get to New York."

"There's no saying you have to stay with this company. You could try New York on your own."

"A lot you know. If you'd take this offer, we'd all arrive there with jobs and lodgings and a bit of security. I can't just pack a bag and head off not knowing what might happen. This company is all I have, all I've known, and I can't leave it on the off chance I might find work somewhere else." Desperation colored Francine's voice, and guilt pinched Willow's chest. "You're ruining my dreams." A sob caught in her throat.

Willow sent up a quick prayer for help but backed it up with a prayer for strength of purpose. "Francine, I'm sorry. I really am, but I have to follow my dreams. I can't go against what I know is right for me, what I feel God calling me to do."

Francine jerked and clutched the bedclothes on either side of her. "Don't play that God card. You're doing this because it's what you want, not because of any God thing. You'd stay here just to spite me, whether Silas was a preacher or a street sweeper. But this isn't over. The whole company will know by now you've turned down the role and denied them their chance to make it big."

The thought of facing everyone tomorrow, knowing they'd be disappointed, made Willow quail, but she stiffened her resolve. She was doing the right thing. It wasn't fair of the producers in New York to put such responsibility on her, and Clement should've come to her with the offer in private before he told everyone else. Though at the time, she supposed he never would've thought she'd say no. Still, she had to do what she thought was right.

Francine glared, sliding back under the covers, jerking the quilt around. She didn't wait for Willow to get into bed before she turned out the light. "You're going to be sorry."

Willow barely caught her sister's mutter, and a shiver went up her spine.

❧

Silas, too keyed up to sleep after leaving Willow at the hotel, went to the church instead of the parsonage. He could always find something that needed doing there. His eye stung, and the lid was so swollen it obscured his vision, but he didn't have a shred of regret he'd defended Willow's honor with his fists.

Lighting the wall sconces, he circled the perimeter of the room, delighting in the comfortable, familiar feel of the sanctuary. A peace he could only find here invaded his soul.

Lord, thank You for bringing me to this place, for all the hurdles and moun-tains I had to climb over to get here. Thank You for the people of this church who challenge and enrich and encourage me. Help me to be the pastor You want me to be and the pastor they need me to be to help them grow and glorify You.

The oft-repeated prayer ran through his head. The burden of being the spiritual leader to this diverse group of believers weighed on him, but it was a pleasant weight most of the time. He knew he wasn't up to the task alone, but with God's help, he would do the best he could. And not only God's help, but soon Willow's, too. No more coming home to an empty house, no more being unable to offer hospitality, no more discussing church issues with the cat.

He grabbed a dustcloth and began on the left side of the church wiping down the pews. His congregants were creatures of habit, and each family usually sat in the same place week after week. As he progressed down the row, he prayed for the members as he came to their customary seats.

When he got to the Drabble pew, right side, second row, he knelt and put his elbows on the seat. This prayer was going to take more time than could be accomplished in a quick wipe-down.

"Lord, thank You for bringing the Drabbles to this church. Thank You for the acts of service they perform that edify the church and help us share Your Gospel with this community." He swallowed. Easy part done.

"Father, I ask You to help me to heal the rift between Mrs. Drabble and myself. These hard feelings have broken our fellowship and are detrimen-tal to the church and Your name. Help me to forgive her, and humble me to ask her forgiveness. We need Your healing here to kill our pride and help us to submit and serve one another in love."

The front door scraped on the floor, reminding him he needed to re-move it from the hinges and plane the bottom. Breaking off his prayer with a hasty "Amen," Silas lifted his head to look over the back of the pew.

"Pastor Hamilton? Are you in here?" Kenneth Hayes.

"Over here." He stood, dusting his knees.

Kenneth let out a breath. "Oh, good. I sorta panicked when the parson-age was dark. What happened to your eye?"

Touching the swelling, Silas winced at the pain. "It's nothing. A little difference of opinion."

Kenneth stared as if fascinated. "What's the other guy look like?"

Worse than me, I imagine. "What can I do for you? I've missed you in church the past couple of weeks." The less said about his altercation at the theater, the better. All sorts of rumors might start flying around, and he didn't want things to get blown out of proportion.

Dusky red crept around Kenneth's collar, and he ducked his head. "Well,

I'm sorry, but I came here to do something about that." He returned to the front door and held out his hand. "He's here. C'mon in."

He drew a woman into the room, and Silas's eyes went wide. Alicia Drabble. A few puzzle pieces clicked together in his brain. Kenneth's certainty his ladylove's parents wouldn't relent, and Alicia's going toe-to-toe with her mother over dinner and being set down. Alicia kept her eyes lowered.

"It's awfully late for you two to be out together, isn't it?" Silas stepped into the aisle. Mrs. Drabble would have a conniption. "Alicia, your folks will be worried."

Kenneth squared his shoulders. "They don't need to worry about her any longer. Alicia and I are eloping, and we want you to perform the ceremony."

"Eloping?" Silas dropped his dustcloth.

Kenneth wrapped his arm around Alicia and hugged her to his side. "Don't try to stop us. If you won't do the honors, we'll ride over to the next town, and the next, and the next, until we find a preacher to marry us."

"Let's sit down and at least talk about this."

"No, our minds are made up. It has to be tonight." Kenneth's jaw set, and his eyes narrowed a bit.

"Alicia?"

"Please, Silas." She still didn't look at him. "I'm not going back to my parents' house without a wedding ring and marriage certificate. I can't." Desperation smothered her voice, and she turned her face into Kenneth's shoulder.

"It's really important we get married tonight. We *need* to get married." Kenneth's expression begged Silas to understand.

Alicia choked on a sob.

Silas's mind circled the implications and ramifications as he motioned for them to sit in one of the pews. His heart sat like a cold rock in his chest. Marriage should be a joyous time of celebration with friends and family, not a covert, desperate matter conducted in the middle of the night.

When they were seated he took the pew in front of them, turning sideways and laying his arm across the back. "Now, explain to me so there are no misunderstandings just why you have to get married tonight without the blessing of Alicia's parents."

They both stared at the floor. Kenneth reached over and clasped Alicia's clenched hands in her lap. "I did like you said and went to her folks again, but they refused to let me see Alicia. So we arranged to sneak out so we could be together."

"I see."

Alicia raised her chin. Her eyes swam with tears. "But you knew, didn't you? Didn't Willow tell you? She saw us together not long ago. I was sure she'd tell you all about it."

"She didn't say a word." Silas rubbed his jaw.

"Don't be mad at her. She said she wouldn't lie to you, and that you would have to know, but she wanted us to be the ones to tell you. I'm sure she wasn't going to keep it from you forever. Willow told us we'd get in trouble if we didn't stop meeting like that." Alicia blinked, sending the tears down her cheeks. "And she was right. We should've listened. She told us to come to you for help. And yesterday. . ."

Kenneth took a deep breath and looked Silas right in the eye. "Yesterday our feelings got the better of us. We stumbled. It was my fault. Please don't blame Alicia. We're both sorry, and we're here to make it right. We need to get married as soon as possible."

Silas grimaced and sent up a prayer for wisdom. "That certainly puts a new light on things. Would you be willing to wait until morning, and we could all three go to Alicia's parents and talk this out?"

"No. They'll contrive some way to keep us from getting married. They'll send Alicia away." Kenneth leaned forward, gripping the pew in front of him. "If you won't do it, we'll find someone else. She's not going back. We're both adults. We can make up our own minds. We'd like to have her parents' blessing, but we don't need their permission."

Silas rubbed his forehead, forgetting his black eye until he touched it. Mrs. Drabble was going to explode. And yet, what Kenneth said was true. They were old enough to choose for themselves, and they had excellent and expedient reasons for marrying in haste. "If you're sure about this, I would rather perform the ceremony myself than send you to someone else. But I have a few things to say first."

Kenneth nodded. "We figured you would."

"You both understand you've chosen a hard road. By giving in to temptation, you're starting out your marriage under a cloud. And"—Silas swallowed and took a deep breath—"there could be other consequences."

"We've talked about that. That's one of the reasons we want to get married as soon as possible."

"There's also the matter of Alicia's parents. You are both old enough to marry without their permission, but Alicia is their daughter, and you will need to do everything you can to make amends and restore fellowship there. Though you will be man and wife, living on your own, you are still tied to the Drabbles as their daughter and son-in-law, and eventually you'll have children who will be their grandchildren. You're burning a very big bridge here, and it will take time and effort to rebuild it."

"We'll deal with that later."

"Then we'll need a witness to make things legal. I'll perform the ceremony, and I'll mail the registration papers to the courthouse over at the county seat first thing Monday morning." Silas pushed himself upright. "I'll go knock on Ned Meeker's door. He and his wife can stand up with you."

Having one of the elders there might deflect some of the coming Drabble wrath. But then again, it might just draw Ned into her crosshairs. Still, Ned lived closest to the church. And he could be counted on not to run straight to the Drabble house and sound the alarm.

Ned and Trudy came, roused from their bed and hastily dressed. Ned glanced at Silas's eye but asked no questions. After hearing why the pastor had knocked on their door so late, they agreed to serve as witnesses, though Trudy's brow wrinkled, and she asked Alicia twice if this was what she really wanted.

The ceremony was simple, unadorned, and quick. His heart broke for the young couple. This couldn't have been the wedding Alicia had envisioned. They would have some rough days ahead. The path was always more complicated and full of pitfalls when things weren't done God's way. They were so in love, so desperate to be together, they'd compromised what was best about love and marriage.

It was a sobering lesson not to sacrifice the future on the altar of the immediate.

Chapter 14

Silas arose early in spite of not getting to bed the night before until well after midnight. His reflection told him the few hours of sleep had reduced some of the swelling around his eye, but the color had come up in a purplish-blue splotch. No way to disguise or diminish the angry-looking mark.

He spent time in prayer, asking for God's wisdom to help him deal with the rift in the church. His Bible reading brought him to Proverbs four, verse eighteen.

"But the path of the just is as the shining light, that shineth more and more unto the perfect day."

"Lord, this is what I want, and what I need. Please make me a good example to my church and to those in the community who are watching. Help me to humble myself and ask for forgiveness where I need it and to extend forgiveness where it is due. Help me to take instruction from fellow believers, but help me also to follow Your will first and foremost. Help Your light to shine through me in all my dealings with Willow, Mrs. Drabble, and the congregation. And I ask that Your will be done regarding the district supervisor's visit."

Finally feeling equipped to face the day ahead, he shrugged his way into his suit coat and tried to loosen the squirming ball of nerves in his stomach. First on the agenda, a visit to the Drabble household to begin healing the breach between them. Though he had a feeling that when he told them about Alicia and Kenneth, any hope of reconciliation would disappear.

Clouds hid the sun, and a fine spring rain pattered on the grass and made puddles on the road. Silas ducked his neck into his overcoat and hurried. Gaining the steps to the Drabble house, he shook the water from his sleeves and hat brim before knocking on the ornate oak door. Gingerbread trim dripped, and gusts of wind spattered the porch boards with droplets.

A figure moved behind the etched-glass oval in the door, and the knob rattled.

"Good morning, Hannah. I need to speak to Mr. and Mrs. Drabble. Are they home?" Silas stepped into the foyer as the young woman in the mobcap and black dress held the door.

"Good morning, Pastor Silas. It seems all I'm getting done today is answering the door. We're not used to so many early morning visitors." She smiled and shrugged, as if she realized she might've been a bit ungracious. "Please wait here. I'll go see."

When Hannah returned, she motioned for him to follow her. "They're in the breakfast room."

The smell of fried ham and hot potatoes greeted him, reminding him he'd had nothing but a slice of bread and butter—all he could force into his stomach this morning—for breakfast.

Walter Drabble looked up from his plate for an instant, grunted, and tucked back into his food. Lightning flashed, followed by a low rumble of thunder that rolled from peak to peak.

Mrs. Drabble's stare sent a tremor up Silas's spine. Her glare lingered on his black eye, and he waited for her to ask.

Instead, she creased her napkin into precise folds, laid it alongside her plate, and placed her hands in her lap. "Good morning, Reverend Hamilton. After our first visitor of the day, I thought you might come by." Her voice was so knife-edged, he wondered why she didn't choke.

A pang hit his heart. Here was his sister in Christ, a deaconess in his church, a member of his congregation, and his very presence raised her hackles to the point she could barely be civil.

"Mrs. Drabble, I've come to speak with you, to ask your forgiveness and hopefully make a start on restoring fellowship between us. It saddens me to be at odds with anyone in my church, and I hope we can get everything out into the open and come to a place of peace."

A satisfied smile stretched her lips, and she sat back in her chair. "At last." She sighed and softened, letting her shoulders and spine relax. "I knew you'd come to your senses, though I'm sorry it had to come to a head like this. I'm glad we have a chance to put all this behind us before any permanent damage was done. Please, sit down. I'm sure we can resolve everything nicely."

Silas blinked at this turnabout. He pulled out an empty chair and eased onto it, accepting the olive-branch gesture. "Mrs. Drabble, before we discuss anything else, I need to talk to you first about your daughter."

Her smile widened. "You're showing good sense at last. After everything I was told this morning, I'm not at all surprised you've come to talk about Alicia. It's only natural you'd change your mind once you had all the facts, and I assure you, I'm not one to hold a past folly against a man. I'm only sorry I sent those telegrams, but no matter now."

"Telegrams?" Mystified, Silas swallowed his apprehension and clenched his hands on his thighs.

"Yes, well, never mind. I'll take care of that later." She unfolded her napkin and motioned to Hannah. "Set a place for Reverend Hamilton. You will join us for breakfast, won't you?" Her tone took it as a matter of course. "There's so much to plan and discuss. You won't want a long engagement, will you? I think June will be best, but that only gives us about five weeks or so. Good thing I've got most of the wedding planned already."

"The wedding?"

"Yours and Alicia's, of course. That is why you came this morning, isn't it? To formalize the engagement now that you're finished with that. . . actress person?"

Silas seriously considered knocking his fist against his forehead. "Mrs. Drabble, stop. I've come to tell you that Alicia is married. She got married last night. I performed the ceremony myself."

Mr. Drabble stopped shoveling scrambled eggs into his mouth, and his wife gasped.

"That's ridiculous. Alicia is upstairs in her room asleep."

"I'm sorry, Mrs. Drabble, but she isn't. She and Kenneth Hayes came to me last night at the church, and I performed the marriage ceremony and blessed their union." Silas braced himself for the wrath to come.

Mrs. Drabble's face got redder and redder until Silas feared she might do herself harm.

"How dare you? You married them? Kenneth Hayes?" With each question her voice rose and so did her body. By the time she screeched Kenneth's name, she was on her feet leaning over the table, bracing her palms on the tablecloth.

Lightning flickered through the lace curtains, followed by a booming crash that vibrated through Silas. "Please, let me explain."

"Hannah!" Mrs. Drabble turned and shouted in the direction of the kitchen. "Go upstairs and fetch Alicia. I don't care if she's still asleep, just get her down here."

Silas gripped his knees and sought wisdom. Though he was not unused to family crises, the one looming now was by far the worst he'd dealt with. And though he'd anticipated some high emotion, he had a feeling Mrs. Drabble's response was just getting rolling.

Hannah scuttled into the room, her hands wrapped in her apron. "I'm sorry, ma'am, but she's not there. Her bed hasn't been slept in, and her personal items are missing from her dressing table." The girl's eyes rounded, and creases marred her usually serene brow.

Walter Drabble stopped munching his toast, swallowed, and shook his head. "She really did it?" He scratched the side of his head. "She threatened it, but I never thought she'd go through with it."

Mrs. Drabble subsided into her chair, her jaw open and her arms lax. The enormity of the catastrophe seemed to hit her, and she jammed her napkin to her lips, stifling a sob.

Silas swallowed. "Please, Beatrice, calm yourself. This isn't the tragedy you seem to think it is."

She stopped sobbing, and her eyes blazed. "Don't tell me to be calm. This is your fault. You should've hauled Alicia right back here the minute she showed up at the church. It was your Christian duty. If you would've done as I wanted and married her yourself, this never would've happened." This last bit came out a wail. "How am I ever going to show my face in this town again? This is all your fault. Yours and that actress. You allowed your head to be turned by a common trollop. And Alicia is the one who will pay for it."

"Mrs. Drabble, Alicia is a grown woman and capable of making up her own mind whom to marry. Kenneth and Alicia are very much in love. Though it pained Alicia to go against your wishes, she has the right of it. She needed to leave her father and mother and cleave to her husband. If I hadn't agreed to perform the ceremony, they were prepared to travel to Leadville or Idaho Springs or Denver until they found someone who would. Instead of worrying about your image and reputation in town, you should be proud your daughter chose a young man with a heart for serving God, who loves her and will spend his life trying to make her happy."

She stood trembling and glared at Silas. "If you thought to come here to resolve our differences, you have another think coming. You've helped my daughter defy me, and you'll rue the day. The whole world is going to come crashing down on you, mark my words." She stalked out of the room, her shoulders squared and her back poker straight.

Silas dragged his hand down his face, forgetting his eye and wincing when he touched it. "I'm sorry, Walter. I hate discord in the church, and I fear this situation is getting out of control. I had hoped to be able to talk things out calmly and reach some sort of an accord."

"Bea isn't one to get over things too quickly." Walter sighed and pushed his plate back. He dug in his vest pocket. "Forgot to tell you, telegram came. District supervisor will be in church tomorrow."

❧

Willow slipped from the hotel and headed to the theater, dodging raindrops and clutching her shawl around her shoulders to ward off the chill. Too bad about the rain. She would've liked to enjoy the solace of the stream this morning, but her dressing room would have to do. Lightning played around the mountaintops, and thunder blanketed the town, drowning out even the persistent noise of the smelters and stamp mills that never ceased.

Francine's bed had been empty when Willow awoke. Odd, since Francine loved to sleep late. Still, considering their sharp words of the previous night, perhaps it was better this way. Give them both time to cool down.

Bill let her in the back door of the theater. "Morning, Miss Willow. You're not the first one here today."

"Oh? Francine came in early? I thought she'd be at breakfast still."

"Miss Francine came in a while ago, all dripping wet like she'd been out walking in the rain. Don't usually see her in such a state. But I wanted to warn you. Mr. Moncrieff's here. In his dressing room." The watchman crossed his arms. "After last night's shenanigans, you can bet I'm keeping my eye on him. If he bothers you, you just holler. I'll come running."

"Thank you, Bill." She patted his forearm. "You're a good friend."

"What he did wasn't right, and I aim to see he doesn't try it again."

"I'm sure he won't, especially not with you looking out for me."

She passed Philip's dressing room on the way to hers. A creepy feeling squirmed up her spine, and she hurried down the hall. The matinee would require all her acting abilities in full force to get through the scenes with Philip.

The deeper she went into the building, the more the rain receded. By the time she got to her dressing room at the end of the hall, even the thunder failed to make much of an impression. She unwound her shawl and brushed at the raindrops on her hair and face before opening the door.

She braced herself for a confrontation with her sister, but the room was empty. And clean. Clement had kept his word and sent someone in to straighten up the disorder from last night.

Draping her shawl over the back of a chair to dry out, she moved to light a few lamps. With everything in its proper place, the only evidence of the altercation was a small crack in the corner of one of the dressing table mirrors. Francine would complain about that for sure. Willow eased down onto the chaise, putting Philip and her sister out of her mind, letting her thoughts wander to Silas and his brave defense of her. And his kisses. She touched her lips.

Engaged. It seemed so unreal to her. That she would be staying in Martin City. In her entire life she'd never lived more than six months in any location, and she'd never had a home, always living in hotels or in the theaters themselves if necessary. She didn't know how to keep house or do laundry, and as for cooking, she'd never even boiled water, much less prepared meals for a man.

Would Silas care? Perhaps the woman he currently engaged as a house-keeper would be willing to give her a few pointers. Or the Mackenzies. They'd all been so nice, especially the women. Surely Matilda, Karen, and

Ellie would have good advice for her.

Footsteps sounded in the hall.

Please, pass by. Go on. Leave me alone.

The door opened, and Willow sat up.

Francine breezed in. She was halfway across the room before she seemed to notice Willow. Her footsteps slowed, and her expression hardened. "Oh, I thought you'd be with your precious Silas."

Willow sucked in a deep breath. "Francine, please, I don't want to be at odds with you."

An unladylike snort erupted from Francine, and she swung away toward the costume rack against the far wall. The clothes hangers clacked and scraped on the metal rod, and she flipped through the dresses so quickly, she couldn't possibly have examined any of them.

Willow noted Francine's wet hair and dress. "Where did you get to this morning?"

"I can't see how it's any of your concern what I do or where I go." She selected a dress and ducked behind the screen. "You're obviously going to do what you want without thinking about me anyway."

"Francine, please. I don't want to rehash everything we said last night. You're my sister and my only family. I'd like you to be happy about my coming marriage."

"Happy! I'd have been happy in New York. I spoke with Clement this morning. He told me he's sent your regrets. Regrets?" Several thumps came from behind the screen. "You're going to regret it, that I can assure you. Whatever happens is your own fault."

"My only regret in this entire situation is that you can't seem to get over the fact I've found my calling in life, and it doesn't line up with what you want." Willow rose and lifted her own costume for the first act from the rack. "And I'm sorry about that, but you throwing a fit isn't going to change my mind. I'm in love with Silas, and I'm going to marry him."

Francine emerged and propped her hands on her hips. "We'll see about that." She threw her damp dress into the corner. "I've heard his church isn't exactly happy with his choice of a bride. And if he doesn't go through with the wedding, where will you be?"

The fierceness in her eyes brought Willow up short, and uneasiness hitched up her spine. "What have you heard about his church?"

A triumphant smirk crossed Francine's features. "I know more than you think, and you'll find out soon enough." She sat down at the dressing table and turned her back. "You wouldn't listen to me, so you'll have to learn the hard way."

"Francine, please."

Her sister refused to speak, concentrating on applying her makeup.

Willow went behind the screen to change. Francine had always been moody, petulant, and more than a little selfish, but she'd never been truly vicious. Surely she was only speaking out of a place of hurt, not meaning what she said.

The clock reminded Willow they had a performance soon, and she would need to pretend not to be repulsed by Philip, not to be at odds with her sister, not to be wishing she were anywhere but in the theater. And the minute she was free, she needed to see Silas. He would make everything in her world right again. Being with him calmed her fears, assured her of his love, and made her feel like there was nothing they couldn't conquer together.

She buttoned up her costume, her fingers chilly. That was it. All her fears would be allayed if she could just see Silas. If only they didn't have two performances and a reception. And Silas would be busy with his sermon preparations. Tomorrow after church they would sort everything out.

&

"Is Mr. Mackenzie at home?" Silas removed his hat and stepped into the foyer of the Mackenzie home.

"Good evening, Pastor Hamilton." Buckford took his dripping coat and hat. "The family is in the parlor. I'm sure they will be glad to see you." In keeping with all Silas knew about the manservant, Buckford gave no indication he had even seen Silas's black eye, and he certainly didn't ask about it.

"Actually, I'd like to talk to Jesse privately." Though Silas loved the Mackenzie family, he needed wise counsel from one of his elders rather than an evening of fellowship.

"I see. Would you like to wait in the study while I fetch Mr. Mackenzie?" He motioned to the door on his left.

"That would be perfect. Thank you, Buckford." Silas entered the study and plucked a match from the holder on the desk to light the lamps. Red globes bathed the room in rosy-yellow light. Removing the fire screen, he poked the bed of coals glowing in the grate and added a couple of logs. Rain continued to pelt the windows.

A glance at the clock on the desk told him Willow would be in the middle of act 3 of the evening performance. With Philip. His hands fisted. Bill, the theater guard, had assured Silas that Willow would be safe, that he would watch out for her tonight. Though Silas wasn't in the habit of attending the theater on Saturdays, reserving that day for sermon preparation and prayer for the coming Sunday, it had required all his self-discipline not to show up and watch over Willow himself.

"Silas?" Jesse strode into the room, his presence as always charging the air with a feeling that nothing was impossible or as bad as it seemed. A more capable, stalwart man Silas had never known.

"Evening, Jesse. I'm sorry to drop in on you like this."

"Nonsense. You know you're always welcome. Anyway, your being here saves me a trip. I was just heading into town to see you." He shook Silas's hand. "That's some shiner. Did you walk into a door?"

"Not exactly. I ran into a fist."

"Oh?"

As succinctly as possible, Silas recounted the events. "The eye will heal. What's important is Willow wasn't harmed, and Philip Moncrieff will think twice before he bothers her again."

"Good for you. I'm not a man of violence, but there are times when it is the most effective and reasonable response."

Silas nodded. "Why were you coming to see me?"

Jesse grimaced. "There's trouble brewing. Ned Meeker stopped by this afternoon and told me that Larry Horton and Mrs. Drabble had their heads together over at Drabble's Store, and when they saw him, they hushed up right quick, but not before he heard your name and Willow's."

Silas rubbed his hand down his face. "I've never dealt with anything like this before. It seems no matter how much I try to placate Mrs. Drabble, things just get worse and worse. That's what I wanted to talk to you about. I visited the Drabble home this morning with the unpopular news that Alicia is now married."

Jesse's eyebrows rose, and he bent to poke the fire. "Who did she marry, and how did you find out about it?"

"She married Kenneth Hayes, one of your shift foremen, and I found out about it because I was the one who performed the ceremony."

"Hmm. Kenneth came to me yesterday morning and asked for a week off to take care of a family matter. Didn't know he meant to get married. Well, that's a poke in the eye for old Beatrice, isn't it? How'd she take the news?"

"About like you'd expect. I tried to reason with her, but she's blaming me for not dragging Alicia home and running Kenneth off."

"Why didn't you?"

"I had some very good reasons for going ahead with the wedding, but I can't go into them with you. You'll have to trust me when I say their getting married was the right thing to do."

"I see."

"But I'm afraid Mrs. Drabble will never forgive me. And Alicia's marriage is only part of the reason for her antagonism. Jesse, I'm worried.

Mrs. Drabble's unhappiness with me is just the sort of canker to spread right through a church. It's already divided the board, and it's only a matter of time before it divides the church."

Jesse eased onto the settee and motioned for Silas to sit in a chair opposite him. "Sadly, I'm afraid it already has. More than one person has asked me about your relationship with Willow. I've told them all I support you, and if they have a problem they should talk to you personally. I've seen this kind of thing happen before, and I'd do about anything to head it off. If it continues, pretty soon folks are deciding which side of the church aisle they'll sit on, and little things that shouldn't be a problem become a shooting war. And the major casualty is the church. Gives the congregation a black eye worse than yours."

Silas dragged his hand across the nape of his neck. "How did we get here, Jesse? All I want is to be a good pastor. I went against my father's express wishes when I took this church. I turned my back on everything he'd planned for me. And it wasn't a decision I made lightly. I prayed and prayed about coming to Martin City, and I was sure God had brought me here."

"What makes you think He didn't?"

"How can a church in turmoil be God's will? If I hadn't come here—if a married man with a family had taken the position—Mrs. Drabble wouldn't have been obsessed with Alicia marrying the minister. She wouldn't have become dead set against Willow. And the ministry here wouldn't be in jeopardy."

"What does Willow say about all of this?"

"She doesn't know. I haven't seen her today. Saturdays are extra busy for her with two performances, and I try to focus on the preparations for Sunday services. Willow knows some people have skewed ideas about actresses and such, but she doesn't know of Beatrice's animosity. I thought if the church folks just got to know Willow, they'd see what a wonderful person she is and what a great pastor's wife she would make."

"She is a wonderful person, and folks will come around if they only give her a chance."

"But will they give her that chance before the district supervisor visits and finds the church in an uproar?" Silas pulled the telegram from his pocket. "Walter Drabble gave this to me this morning. The Reverend Archibald Sash will arrive on the midnight train and be attending church tomorrow morning. The Drabbles are meeting his train and taking him home with them tonight. I can only imagine what they will say to him. After the services, there is a board meeting, followed by a one-on-one interview for me. When is the church supposed to have time to change their minds about Willow?"

Jesse grimaced, showing a fair number of teeth. "What rotten timing." He rubbed his chin. "I don't want you to take this the wrong way or assume I'm anywhere but squarely behind you on this, but is there any chance you can maybe back off things with Willow to let people get used to the idea? Just to lessen the tension and give folks time to come to their senses?"

Only the sincerity and warmth in Jesse's expression kept Silas from giving in to the despair rising in his chest. "I can't. I've asked Willow to marry me, and she's agreed. I can't back away, and I wouldn't even if I could. Giving in to Mrs. Drabble's tyranny isn't the way to heal the church. I'd only be prolonging the trouble."

"You're right. It wouldn't be fair to Willow, and it wouldn't change anything for tomorrow. It's like we're sitting on a powder keg, and there's a fuse burning."

Silas nodded, his heart sinking. "I don't know how we got here so quickly. Everything was fine, or so I thought, and within the space of a few weeks, the church is coming apart at the seams. I feel as if God is asking me to choose between my church and the woman I love. I was sure I was supposed to pastor the Martin City Church, and I was sure I was supposed to marry Willow, and now I'm not sure of anything."

"I'm not saying you're right about God wanting you to choose, but if you had to, would you walk away from this ministry to be with Willow? Or would you walk away from Willow for the Martin City Church?"

Silas tunneled his fingers through his hair. "I don't know. Right now I feel as if either would rip my heart out. How can I turn my back on my ministry, on my flock? And yet, how can I let Willow go?" He pounded his fists on his thighs. "I can't. There has to be another way."

Chapter 15

Silas arose from a troubled sleep to a world washed new and blanketed in sunshine. It was out of balance with the sense of foreboding in his chest. The vigor that usually surged through him on a Sunday morning eluded him. As he dressed in his starched shirt and freshly pressed suit, he felt as if he were donning armor, one piece at a time.

He glanced out the window across the lawn to the church. How odd that the storm clouds had cleared from the sky yet still seemed to hang over the cupola.

Lord, I don't believe You want to force me to choose between the church and Willow, and I pray that You would go before me, that You would work in the hearts of the congregation so that a choice isn't necessary.

Sherman regarded him with solemn eyes from the bedroom doorway. That cat was like another conscience with his penetrating stares.

And Lord, if I'm misreading everything, then please open my eyes. Show me what to do, and give me the strength to do it. Make me willing to sacrifice my desires to Your will.

Unable to face the idea of breakfast, he strode across the wet grass to open up the church and prepare for the service.

≈

Willow ignored the tea tray on the dressing table. "Francine, I want to know what you're up to. Where are you going on a Sunday morning all dressed up?"

"I can't see how that's any of your affair." The squashing reply came in an airy voice.

Willow picked up her Bible and purse. "I'm going to church. Will you be here when I get back?"

Francine shrugged and skewered her cartwheel hat to her hair with a couple of wicked-looking hatpins. "I don't know. Depends on what happens this morning."

The tickle of unease that had flitted through Willow's chest when Francine rose early that morning developed into a nubby-fingered fist prodding her innards. "What are you up to?" she asked again.

"I would think, rather than poking your nose into my affairs, you would be wise to look out for your own. Why don't you give some thought to the dismal performance you put on yesterday? I've never seen anything so hideous as you standing poker stiff in Philip's arms. You were supposed to be declaring Jane's love for Mr. Rochester, but you sounded more like you were reciting the times tables. I was so embarrassed I could hardly keep watching you from the wings." Francine rolled her eyes and touched her nose with a powder puff. "Even Clement commented on your wretched performance. It wouldn't surprise me a bit if he didn't replace you as Jane, since it's obvious you can't work with Philip any longer."

Willow's throat lurched. Yesterday had been awful, but she hadn't been able to help it. Every time Philip stepped onto the stage, her flesh crawled, and she wanted to run away.

"It isn't as if he didn't apologize to you," Francine said. "And very nicely, too, in front of the entire cast and crew. You're the one who won't forgive, for all your pious talk. And you engaged to a minister." Her thrust went deeply, as she must've known it would. A triumphant little smile played around Francine's lips, and she straightened from the mirror with a supercilious arch to her brow. "You're going to be late to church if you don't hurry."

Willow glanced at the clock, picked up her hat, and left. But Francine's accusations followed her every step of the way to the church, as did the sense of foreboding she'd awakened with.

❧

Silas tried to quell his rioting nerves as he left the anteroom to his office and stepped into the sanctuary. He placed his Bible and notes on the pulpit and took his seat as parishioners arrived and got settled. The church pianist played the prelude, and he scanned the congregation. Tension painted the air, pulling on his thoughts, stealing the peace he usually encountered before a Sunday service.

Congregants continued to file in. The Mackenzies entered, Jesse and Matilda, David and Karen with Celeste and the baby, Sam and Ellie with Phin and Tick. They came all the way to the front and filled an entire pew. Jesse wore a foreboding expression, and David and Sam only a little less so. While it warmed Silas's heart to know they were ready to fight for him, he grieved that such a stand was necessary.

Behind the Mackenzies sat a row of miners. When he met their eyes, they nodded and smiled. Ned and Mrs. Meeker sat with them.

The Drabbles arrived, and between husband and wife strode the portly figure of Reverend Archibald Sash. Mrs. Drabble's mouth wore a pinched, rhubarb smile, and Reverend Sash looked sternly out over his gray whiskers.

Proper etiquette dictated that Silas should rise and greet the district supervisor, but halfway out of his seat, he froze, staring at the doors.

Willow was as fresh and beautiful as always. She stood in the doorway, scanning the crowd.

Jesse, with an agility that belied his years, left his seat and went to Willow's side. Tucking her hand into the crook of his elbow, he led her to the front row to sit with the Mackenzies in their already-full pew.

Silas could almost see the daggers flying from the Drabble pew across the aisle. Willow, sweetly bewildered, sat between Jesse and Matilda, smoothed her skirts, and sought Silas's face. Her smile, tremulous at first then more confident, warmed him through. Just seeing her settled his nerves and made him think there was nothing they couldn't conquer together. They would get through today and have all their tomorrows waiting.

He broke eye contact with Willow, gathered his thoughts, and remembered he was supposed to greet Reverend Sash. Halfway down the steps to the Drabble pew, he halted once more, his attention drawn by a commotion in the foyer.

Laughing, talking, and jostling, a dozen people entered the sanctuary and filed into the last rows. Francine Starr and Philip Moncrieff led the group, the first time any of the actors besides Willow had come to the church. Even from this distance, Philip's bruises stood out, much as Silas's had when he'd checked his eye in the mirror this morning.

His glance went to Willow, who had turned to look at the noise. Her mouth opened, and she gripped the back of the pew. Clearly, she hadn't known they were coming. What did they want? Clement Nielson brought up the rear, his hands shoved into his pockets and his tie askew.

Quickly entering behind the actors, Kenneth and Alicia Hayes slipped in, both beaming and self-conscious, their hands linked. They slipped into the back pew opposite Francine and company. Hardly an empty seat remained in the church.

The pianist finished the song, and silence descended. Silas, suddenly aware that he stood halfway between the platform and the rail, shook his head and retreated. He'd greet Reverend Sash after the service. He couldn't take any more shocks before his sermon.

When he reached the pulpit, he forced a smile and laid his hands on the cover of his Bible already waiting there for him. "Good morning." With all the turmoil in his mind, his voice sounded far away. He cleared his throat. "I'd like to welcome you all to church this morning, especially our guests. The Reverend Archibald Sash is with us this morning, as well as several other visitors."

The back door opened, and Silas found himself staring into the eyes of the last person he'd expected—the Reverend Doctor Clyburn Hamilton.

Silas couldn't say how he got through the sermon, not with his father's eyes boring into him from the back where he'd slid into the pew alongside Kenneth and Alicia. Mrs. Drabble continued to glare at him from the front row, and Francine and Moncrieff laughed and whispered constantly. He could hardly find a safe place to rest his gaze and had to settle for staring at the back wall for much of the service. With the tension mounting in the congregation, he doubted they were listening anyway.

At last they finished the final hymn. Silas closed his hymnal, but not a soul moved toward the exit. Something was afoot, and Silas's breath shortened as Jesse Mackenzie rose and turned to address the congregation.

"Friends, it has come to my attention this morning that we have a matter to discuss as a church body. I know we have a lot of visitors, some of them quite distinguished." He nodded to Reverend Sash, who inclined his head. "If any of you visitors don't want to stay for an impromptu congregation meeting, now's the time to skedaddle."

No one moved. Silas stayed in the pulpit, not knowing what to do. Jesse hadn't told him anything about a congregational meeting. What could've occurred between last night and this morning? What must his father and Reverend Sash be thinking?

"This morning one of our board members came to my house early with an accusation against someone in this church. If these rumors are true, the person they are against must be dealt with. If they are not true, then the person who has started the rumor and those who have carried it on must be dealt with."

Silas's knees trembled. Jesse's voice commanded attention and brooked no argument. He continued. "First, Pastor Hamilton knows nothing of these rumors. I thought it best not to disturb his sermon preparations this morning by telling him something that would undoubtedly upset him and is probably not true in the first place."

Mrs. Drabble sputtered and jerked. "Not true? I have it on good authority."

"That remains to be seen, and you'll stay quiet until you're called upon." He pointed to Mr. Drabble. "Walter, keep her quiet, or you'll both wait outside."

His sharp tone set Mrs. Drabble back into her seat.

Silas cleared his throat. "I don't know what this is all about, but I'm sensing whatever it is has the potential to cause some heated debate. I would suggest we open with prayer, and then, all of us need to take it upon ourselves to remain calm and to weigh our words carefully."

"Good idea." Jesse resumed his seat.

Silas swallowed, trying to moisten his dry mouth. "Lord, we ask Your guidance on this meeting. We ask that whatever is said and done here would glorify You and unify this church rather than divide it. Amen."

Before Jesse could take over again, Silas stepped around from behind the pulpit and descended the steps to stand in the aisle. "I'm glad we're having this meeting, because there are a few things I need to address. Jesse?"

"Go right ahead."

Silas turned to his congregation, trying to ignore the runaway train feeling coursing through his body. "As you are all aware of by now, I have been courting Miss Willow Starr for the past few weeks." He flicked a glance at her pale face and lustrous eyes. "I realize some of you have a misconception about the work Miss Starr does. These misconceptions have taken hold in your minds and caused some of you to form opinions based upon lies, not facts."

Aware of both Sash and his father, Silas took a deep breath and forged on. "Miss Starr is an actress. She is a talented thespian who has studied her craft and worked hard to achieve her success. She is also a fellow believer. A sister in Christ, and a woman of high moral character. She is not, as some have claimed, a loose woman, a charlatan, or deceiver. I happen to love Willow Starr, and I've asked her to be my wife."

A ripple went through the crowd. Silas ignored them and held out his hand to Willow. She appeared dazed, but rose and edged past Jesse. When their fingers locked, Silas's heart surged. He turned Willow to face the church and put his arm around her waist. "She has graciously consented to marry me, and I'm thrilled. She will be an excellent helpmeet for me and a wonderful addition to our church."

Mrs. Drabble jolted to her feet. "Never. Never while I live and breathe will a woman of her type live in the manse. You have been duped, Reverend Hamilton. I have it on good authority she has had more than one illicit affair in her lifetime and has, even since arriving in our fair city, been seen cavorting with a man in a cabin south of town."

Chapter 16

Willow sucked in a breath, and black dots appeared at the edge of her vision. The thrill she'd experienced when Silas vowed his love for her before his congregation fled in the face of such a bold-faced lie.

"I never!"

"Don't lie to me or this church any longer." Mrs. Drabble's face reddened. "You should be ashamed of yourself, waltzing in here and turning our pastor's head with your flirtatious ways. You've done enough damage here, and I intend to see it goes no further. Not only are you unfit to be a pastor's wife, you've dragged him down with you. Look at his face. He's been brawling with other men over your affections."

Silas's arm tightened around Willow's waist. He gently put her behind him. "Mrs. Drabble, you're making serious accusations you had best be able to substantiate." He turned to Jesse. "Is this what you were starting to say?"

"Yes, son, it is. I'm as sorry as I can be that it spilled out like this, but maybe it's better to deal with it and get it done."

Willow edged around Silas to face her accuser. "Who told you such a thing?"

"Your own sister. Yesterday morning. Came right to my house to tell me, since you'd let her know you were going to marry our pastor. She said she couldn't rest easy unless the church knew what kind of woman you were." Mrs. Drabble crossed her arms and thrust her chin in the air. "And I guess we know now, don't we?"

The shock of betrayal went clear through Willow as if she'd been impaled. So many pieces fell into place. Francine's vow that Willow would be sorry for turning down the job in New York, her absence from the room early yesterday morning, her desire to be here today to see the destruction she had caused. Betrayal gave way to anger, which gave way to a strength-sapping sadness that her sister could be so cruel.

She searched for Francine, who set her jaw, crossed her arms, and glared back. Completely unrepentant and unashamed.

"It isn't true." The words limped out, wounded and lame. Willow's hands trembled and she gripped the end of a pew to keep her balance.

"Do you think I'm a fool? I didn't just take your sister's word for it. I went to the cabin she described, and I found this." Beatrice dug in her handbag and pulled out a handkerchief. "Are those not your initials?"

Her monogram, in palest green, screamed at her from the linen square. The handkerchief Willow had given to Alicia to mop her tears when Willow had come across Kenneth and Alicia in a cabin in the woods.

A gasp from the back of the room drew Willow's attention. Alicia had her hand over her mouth.

To say how the handkerchief came to be at the cabin would be to betray the young couple. She couldn't do that, not in front of the entire church. "Yes, that's my handkerchief."

"I knew it."

Willow turned to Silas. "I'm so sorry. I never meant for any of this to happen."

His dark eyes burned with questions, and her heart ripped in two. "It isn't true. I won't believe it."

"Silas, I can't marry you. Mrs. Drabble's right. I've done terrible damage here today." She'd come between Silas and his church, caused nothing but strife, dragged her sister's vindictive wickedness into their midst, and shamed Silas in front of his friends and a visiting reverend. Snatching the handkerchief from Mrs. Drabble's hand, Willow ran up the aisle and outside before the sobs wrenching her throat could come out.

❧

Silas stood rooted to the spot for a moment before heading after her. Jesse's hand restrained him, and it was all Silas could do not to shove the older man away.

"Son, we need to deal with this first, and then you can deal with that." Jesse waved to Willow's retreating form.

Silas quivered, whether from shock, anger, or both, he didn't know. The force of his feelings startled him. He hadn't felt so primitive since slugging Philip Moncrieff.

Francine gathered herself to leave, and this time Silas did shake off Jesse's hand. He sprinted up the aisle and closed the doors. "Nobody leaves, especially not you, Francine."

She slunk back to her seat.

"You should be ashamed of yourself, lying like that about your own sister."

Clamping her lips shut, Francine stared back at him from under insolent lashes.

Mrs. Drabble propped her fists on her hips. "What more proof do you need that she didn't lie? That handkerchief proves Willow was in that cabin, and you heard her yourself. She confessed."

Silas's father rose from the back pew. In all the uproar, Silas had forgotten his father's presence. "Son, I'll guard the doors. I believe your place is up front."

Though his father's eyes couldn't exactly be called kindly, there was a fair bit of staunch support gleaming there. Silas nodded and strode to the front of the church praying with every step God would give him the right words to say. And that He would watch over Willow until Silas could get to her.

"Mrs. Drabble, please take your seat." Silas leaned against the rail and crossed his arms. "As your pastor, it breaks my heart to see the manner in which this—I suppose it amounts to a disciplinary hearing—has been conducted. Rather than you, Mrs. Drabble, going to Willow to ask if these accusations were true, or even taking one or two other believers with you to ask, you've chosen a public venue, hoping to shame Willow in front of as many people as possible."

He glanced from face to face. "Do you know the purpose of church discipline? It's provided to us as a means of reconciling a brother or sister, not as a weapon to wield against those we don't like. Whatever your accusations against Willow, choosing to expose them here was wrong of you. You weren't seeking a reconciliation or restoration to fellowship. Your motives weren't nearly as pure as that. What was it? Revenge for my not marrying Alicia? Pride in the power you wield over your husband and those you tyrannize? Or just frustration that you couldn't manipulate me the way you wanted?"

Mrs. Drabble gaped and blinked.

"Whatever your motivations, it stops now. You say you have proof Willow was meeting a man in the woods? Because you have her handkerchief?" He shook his head. "Paltry proof at best. Maybe she dropped it on one of her rambles along the stream. Maybe someone else took it and put it there." He stared hard at Francine. "However it got there, I know for certain Willow didn't leave it behind after dallying with a man in that cabin."

"How do you know?" Larry Horton, who had been silent until now, stood up behind Beatrice Drabble.

"Because I know Willow. I know her character."

"That's not good enough."

Alicia rose from her place beside Kenneth. "Stop it. All of you."

"Alicia!" Beatrice choked on her daughter's name. "What are you doing here?"

"I'm stopping this terrible farce from continuing. Willow wasn't meeting a lover in that cabin."

"Alicia," Silas said, "you don't have to do this."

Kenneth stood and took her hand. "Yes, we both do. We can't let Willow be attacked like this and not try to help her." He squared his shoulders and faced the congregation and his mother-in-law. "Mrs. Drabble, it wasn't

Willow. It was Alicia meeting me. Because you forbid me to court her, we met in the woods at a cabin. Willow found us there. She told us we had to come clean, but we were afraid you'd send Alicia away."

Alicia bit her lip and blinked rapidly, but she kept her chin up.

Kenneth slipped his arm around her waist. "We owe the congregation an apology, and we ask for your forgiveness. It was wrong of us to sneak off together, and we've done everything we can to make it right. Pastor Hamilton married us Friday evening."

Beatrice Drabble crumpled and covered her face with her hands. "How could you do this to me?"

Silas nodded to Kenneth, who sat, drawing Alicia down with him. Every eye in the room focused on Silas. His father stood with his shoulders against the doors and his arms crossed.

Silas took a fortifying breath. "Folks, it's plain some of you have been given some wrong information about my fiancée, Willow. I'm asking you to please get to know her before you make up your minds about what kind of a woman she is. I'm also asking you to trust my judgment in this matter. I would never court a woman I thought wouldn't be an asset to me, because God has placed His calling on my life to be a pastor. The truth is I don't know how much longer I will be your minister here." He indicated the front row. "The Reverend Sash is here to evaluate my performance as your shepherd, and I fear after today, he might feel the church would be better off with another leader."

A murmur went through the congregation, but Silas ignored it. "The truth is I'm far from perfect. I've made mistakes, but Willow isn't one of them. Oh, and while I have your attention, and because I don't want any more rumors running rampant, I should explain my black eye. I got it defending Willow from the unwanted attentions of another man." He flexed his sore fist and smiled ruefully. "Though I don't advocate violence, there are times when it is the only means available."

Philip Moncrieff shifted in his seat as several of his cast members leaned forward to gauge his reaction.

"Now, I'm going to leave you all in the capable hands of the board. Jesse and Ned and Larry and Walter will be meeting with Reverend Sash, and I imagine my father, Dr. Hamilton"—Silas indicated his father in the back—"who is in attendance today. But before I go, I want you to know I bear no malice toward anyone here. I ask that you move forward in a way that would make reconciliation possible with restoration as your goal. I ask that you accept apologies that are given and extend forgiveness to one another. And if you, as a church, or as a board, or as the denomination officers, decide this church would be better off with another pastor, I submit to that decision. But you all need to know that if you want me as your pastor, you will accept, welcome, and honor Willow as my wife."

Jesse rose and held out his hand, shaking Silas's firmly. "Go after her. We'll take care of things here, and I'll come and find you when we're done."

Silas headed out of the church. Jesse's voice followed him, excusing the visitors.

His father clapped him on the shoulder as he hurried by. "We'll talk later, son."

Not stopping, he flicked his hand to let his father know he'd heard him. He had one destination in mind, and he found her exactly where he expected.

❧

Willow huddled on the rock by the stream, hugging her shins and resting her forehead on her knees. She'd ruined everything. In the space of a single spring, she'd started an earthquake in a church, fractured the acting company, thrown away her future—not once, but twice—and managed to disgrace the man she loved more than anything in the world in front of his congregation.

Her sister's betrayal and the accusations and rumors Mrs. Drabble had flung at Willow in front of the congregation shamed her to the core. How did one combat such lies? She had no defense that wouldn't betray Kenneth and Alicia. The rancor in the church proved she would never be accepted here, that she'd done irreparable damage to Silas.

Too distraught to cry, she could only rock, hugging the ache to herself, sending out wordless prayers, begging God to understand what she was too wounded to say.

Footfalls dislodged pebbles on the path behind her, and she lifted her face. If only whoever it was would pass by and leave her alone.

"I knew I'd find you here."

Silas. She spun around, almost losing her balance and scrabbling to stand.

"Easy there. Seems I'm always about knocking you into the drink." He hopped down the last bit of bank and grasped her elbows.

Standing on the rock with him on the dirt, their eyes were level. "What are you doing here?"

"I came to find my fiancée. She left the church in a hurry."

"I didn't know what else to do. Between Francine and Mrs. Drabble. . . They lied, but I couldn't refute the lie without betraying someone else."

"I know they lied, sweetheart. And I'm sorry. I wish I'd known what they were up to so I could've spared you that."

Her chin dropped. "I'm the one who is sorry, Silas. And I understand, I really do. Breaking the engagement is the only logical choice. I won't make any more trouble. I promise." Her heart shattered like a cracker under a boot heel.

Silas tugged her off the rock and into his arms. He forced her head against his chest and rested his chin on her hair, squeezing her tight. "I imagine you're going to cause me all kinds of trouble, but I'll have you know I'm asking nothing more of life from this day onward."

She tried to ease back to look at his face, but he hugged her tighter. "Don't say anything until I tell you a few things."

The comfort of his embrace, the steady beat of his heart against her cheek, and the peace of the stream and forest glade wrapped around her. How she was going to miss this.

"First, I know all about Kenneth and Alicia, and now so does the entire church. They stood up in front of everyone and confessed their sin and announced their marriage. They cleared you of any suspicion."

"They're married?" She pulled back to look into his eyes, and he allowed it for a moment before tucking her head back under his chin.

"Yes. I performed the ceremony night before last and told Mrs. Drabble about it yesterday morning."

"She must've been furious with you. As angry as Francine was with me about refusing to take her to New York."

He brushed a kiss across the top of her head. "And together they concocted a story to rip us apart."

"And it worked. Silas, we have to break the engagement. Even though the lie has been exposed, the church is still fractured. I can't come between you and your church, between you and your calling." Willow edged out of his arms and stepped back.

"I'm not letting you go, Willow. Whether we stay here or go to another church is in the hands of God and the congregation, but wherever I go, you're going with me as my wife." His dark eyes had a flinty look.

"But you love this church. I don't want to be the cause of you having to leave."

"I do love these people, but if I leave, it won't be because of you. It will be because they no longer trust me to be their leader."

"They'd be foolish to let you go."

"And I'd be foolish to let you go." He gathered her close again. "And I promise, go or stay, I'll have no regrets."

Someone cleared his throat behind them, and they sprang apart. Jesse stood on the road above the creek bank. "I hate to break this up, but I figured you'd want to know the verdict." He smiled, the creases beside his mouth deepening. "It was unanimous. Every single member voted for you to stay on, and everyone is in favor of your marrying Willow as soon as possible."

Silas swooped Willow into his arms and swung her around. Joy burst over her as she clung to him. "Thank You, Lord. Thank You, Lord."

When he set her down, Jesse stood beside them. "After you left, Mrs. Drabble broke right down and cried, asking everyone to forgive her, and she seems to be willing to accept Kenneth as her son-in-law. That director fellow, Nielson, caught me outside the church and said for you, Willow, not to worry about the rest of your contract. He'll have your sister fill the lead role for the last week or two, and then they'll move on to their next engagement."

Willow nodded. It was for the best. She and Francine would both be better off apart.

"Oh," Jesse snapped his fingers. "I near forgot. You are both invited to our place for an engagement party tonight. Matilda invited the whole church, including your father."

"Your father?" Willow squeezed Silas's hand. "He's here?"

Silas shrugged. "I'm as surprised as you are. He strolled into the church this morning just before the sermon."

"Seems Mrs. Drabble wired him," Jesse said, "when she wired Reverend Sash about you courting Willow. He hopped on a train the same day." He stepped back. "Well, I'll let you get back to what you were doing." He winked. "Don't forget. Our place at six o'clock."

Silas opened his arms, and Willow went into them like she was coming home. His kiss sent her head spinning. He eased back in increments, with small kisses and whispers. Cupping her face in his hands, he planted a kiss on her nose.

Her eyelids fluttered open, and she was grateful for his steadying hands.

His voice rumbled in his chest, sending a shiver across her skin. "I love you, Willow. You're my God-given gift, the woman I've been waiting for all my life. And you were definitely worth the wait."